Call of Chaos

Book One: Chaos Reigns Saga

Carol Hightshoe

I0546019

WolfSinger Publications ⚜ Security, Colorado

2nd Edition

Originally Published by Double Dragon Publishing 2008

Cover art copyright © 2014 by Lee Kuruganti

ISBN 978-1-936099-61-0

Printed and bound in the United States of America

Chapter One

Kyrianna slipped out the window and dropped to the ground. Her soft leather boots made a slight thud and she froze for a moment, crouching in the shadows as she surveyed the area. She released a silent breath and watched as the moisture condensed in front of her. The moon was a few days past the first quarter, waxing toward full and provided enough illumination for her eyes to pick out the shimmering frost on the rocks, bushes and statuary scattered between her location and the back wall of the estate. She continued to study the area, searching out the best route through the clutter.

This was a small estate and she judged it only a couple dozen paces from where she was to the wall, but there had to be over fifty items of statuary and bushes in her path.

"Ibacia, master of shadows and patron of thieves, guide my steps," she whispered as she made her way through the clutter. She half danced as she avoided the clutching branches of the bushes that threatened to capture her. Rocks and broken pieces of marble bit at her feet, but her training had taught her to move with a light step— even at a quick pace. However, as her right foot slid over an icy piece of stone, she was glad she had an even softer step than most.

"Chaos, where is it?" she muttered as she searched for the message tube her guild mentor, Silvis, had told her to find. Most of the noble estates in Nydith, like this one, had several in various locations on the grounds so messages could be passed if there was something preventing normal communications. If not for those instructions, she would have slipped back out the small gate near the stables where she had entered.

After what seemed like an eternity, though the moon had not moved from its watchful position, she located the message tube in the northeast corner of the back wall. The opening was overgrown with flowers and grass; and it was only the slight sparkle of the silver and gold marker crystals that allowed her to find it. Kyrianna released the breath she hadn't realized she was holding then pulled the small packet of papers from under her tunic, rolled it tight and slid it into the tube.

Before moving away, she took a few seconds to straighten the flowers and smooth the dirt. *There, it would take someone with the proper training to see the area has been disturbed*, she thought.

Still moving cautiously, she made her way to the other corner of the wall where the small statue of a unicorn stood. As soon as her hand touched the white marble, she jerked it back. She had felt warmth and the slight tremor of flesh, but this was just a statue. How could it be alive?

Kyrianna stared at the statue, holding her breath, for several heartbeats. She reached back out and placed her hand on the unicorn's smooth neck. As the cold, ebony eyes watched her; she rubbed the hard surface of stone. For the briefest moment, there was a sparkle in the unicorn's eyes that should not have been there. She blinked and looked again—it was gone.

"My apologies," she whispered as she used the statue to climb to the top of the wall.

Kyrianna froze on top of the wall as footsteps echoed in the small alley. What little light the moon had been providing was now hidden behind the morning clouds and she forced herself as flat as she could as she waited.

The footsteps continued, regular and even in their stride. *Three or four, walking together*, she thought, *must be the Watch. However, it's too early for the morning patrol, why are they here?* Knowing the odds were already against her if this was a special patrol; she mouthed a silent prayer her brother wouldn't be with them.

Kyrianna shifted her head, to see the patrol and frowned at the flash of gold on the shoulder of one of the group. *Chaos take it, Erudus is with them.*

She breathed a small sigh of relief when she saw her brother's attention seemed to be focused on the walls opposite her position. As long as his attention was elsewhere, she was safe; human eyes wouldn't see her in this darkness.

However, even that slight sound was enough to betray her. Erudus jerked his head up and turned to scan the wall where she was. His eyes widened as he tapped the shoulder of the guard next to him and pointed in her direction. "The informant was correct," he whispered.

"By Ibacia," Kyrianna muttered as she jumped from the wall and ran to the front gates. *If luck is with me, I will be able to get out before they can begin their search.* She sprinted around the corner of the house, stealth forgotten in her haste. Loud footfalls approached the gate. Her elven born reflexes prevented her feet from sliding on the pebbles of the courtyard as she stopped. There was no decent place to hide and no time to get over the gate. Her hand went to one of the daggers on her belt then stopped. She listened to the sounds again. There were at least two groups of guards on the street; she would have no chance against them. An echoing creak told her someone was opening the gate near the stables and a muttered curse floated from the back of the estate, followed by the splintering sound of stone breaking.

She had no way out of the estate. It was almost as if they had been waiting for her. She knew she couldn't risk being caught in the house. At this point, all they had were suspicions. There was no evidence of anything except her trespass on Lord Ravel's estate. Still it would be better to not be caught at all. With a heavy sigh, she stepped back against the wall of the house, crouched down behind a large shrub in the shadows and hoped for the best.

"Kyrianna?"

She swallowed silently and refused to answer the familar voice calling her name.

"Kyrianna?" The voice was a bit more insistent this time.

She again held silent refusing to answer. Still holding her position, she listened to the footsteps of the guards as they moved around the area. Several people walked by the shrub she was hiding behind. Finally, one of the searchers stopped in front of the large bush.

"Kyrianna, I know it is you, do not make this any harder than it already is." The shrub rustled, and Kyrianna inhaled sharply as Erudus' sword stopped less than an inch from her face.

She took a slow, deep breath and closed her eyes to calm herself, then stood; her hands held well away from her weapons.

Erudus only stared at her as he sheathed his sword, the sound of the sliding metal loud in the silence of the night. Kyrianna flinched, but otherwise didn't move.

"Why?" Erudus stared at her for several seconds then nodded toward her weapons and held his hand out.

She only shrugged in answer as she removed the daggers she was wearing and placed them in her brother's hand. The weapons handed over, Kyrianna held her hands out, waiting for him to bind them.

Erudus glanced down at the symbol engraved in the hilt of the daggers. With a frown, he jerked his head toward the gates. "Let's go."

"Commander." The guard saluted as he and an older gentleman approached. "This is Lord…"

"Lord Ravel." The older man glared at the guards as he looked around. "What is going on? The guardsman said someone was caught trespassing."

Kyrianna's eyes widened as she studied the gray haired, portly man standing there wrapped in a brilliant green cloak over his nightclothes. She had never met Lord Ravel, but she still knew this person. *Silvis!* She felt her breath catch in her throat. *Was this a test or a set-up?*

Lord Ravel, Silvis, looked at her and smiled. She shuddered at the malice she saw in his expression and moved several steps closer to her brother.

Erudus bowed slightly. "My Lord, this person was observed on the back wall of your estate. We have not yet ascertained whether she was entering or leaving the grounds."

"I have checked; there is nothing missing or disturbed within the house. I would surmise you were able to apprehend her as she was entering. I leave this matter in your hands. Please inform Lord Brygan I will expect his personal report regarding this matter."

Kyrianna's head snapped up at the mention of her father and she frowned at the look Silvis was directing toward her. *Chaos take it, this was a set-up.*

"I will relay your request, My Lord," Erudus whispered.

For a moment, Kyrianna wondered if he had been hoping to hide the incident from their father.

"Very good." Silvis turned and walked back toward the house.

Kyrianna glanced back over her shoulder as her escorts walked her through the gates and saw Silvis standing at the door smiling at her. He moved his hands in a series of quick movements. "Thank you for your service to the guild," his hands said.

She moved her hands behind her back and signed back. "Chaos take you."

Erudus dismissed all but two members of the guard and motioned for her to walk beside him with the two guards behind them. The streets of Nydith were deserted as the four of them made their way back to the guard barracks for this district.

Kyrianna clenched her hands and fought the shiver that slid up and down her spine as they approached the building. One of the guards opened and held the door as Erudus motioned her through. They walked in silence to one of the offices. Kyrianna held her head down, not looking at the familiar weapons hung on the walls or the plaques honoring those recognized as heroes by the Lords of Nydith. Several of those weapons and plaques belonged to Lord Brygan of House Dalynne, her father.

"Ryia, fetch Lord Brygan and the Magistrate. Vailken, remain here. Admit no one until one of them arrives," Erudus said when they reached the interview room.

Both of the guards saluted then left the room.

"Sit down," he ordered as the door shut behind them.

Kyrianna walked around the small desk and pulled out the chair facing the door. She looked at her brother, who had positioned himself in the corner to her right. He was ignoring her, so she sat down, crossed her arms on the table and put her head down to wait until her father arrived.

A soft, feminine voice whispered in her ear, calling her name and Kyrianna looked up. There was still no one else in the room other than her and her brother. She put her head back down and the voice was there again, stronger.

"Kyrianna, you don't belong in this place," the woman's voice said. "You are too independent to be tied to the rules or prejudices of Nydith. You know in your heart you will be sent away. Remember when they reject you, you can call on me. I welcome you as one of my daughters."

"Who are you?" Kyrianna mouthed the question, although she knew it was her thoughts the woman would hear more than any verbal expressions she might make.

"You will know; when it is time." The voice and the presence attached to it faded.

~ * ~

Kyrianna, you have really done it this time, she thought when she raised her head. She had no idea how long she had been there, but was getting anxious to get this ordeal over. She glanced at her brother, still standing in the corner, then slowly stood and stretched. Careful, so as to not appear threatening, she lifted her arms over her head and reached toward the ceiling. Despite her height, her finger-tips did not make contact with the smooth wood of the ceiling. Relaxing from the stretch, she lowered her arms and crossed them behind her back then began twisting her upper body from side to side. With slow, deliberate movements, she bent at the waist and pressed her forehead against her legs. That got a response from her brother, who cleared his throat and frowned at her. Kyrianna followed the direction of his gaze to the small bulge in her right boot.

So, you know the daggers are there; yet, you didn't remove them when you searched me. She nodded her understanding and kept her hands away from the boots as she straightened and again took her seat. She glanced around and frowned at the lack of windows in this room, a security feature, but it also prevented anyone in the room from having any idea what the time might be.

"Where is she?" Kyrianna flinched at the anger in her father's voice as he yelled from down the corridor. Instead of looking up as the door slammed open, accompanied by the sound of wood cracking and splintering against the wall, she kept her gaze locked on the table.

"Kyrianna?" The voice was different; she looked up, then immediately dropped her gaze back to the table. Behind her father stood an elf with long silver hair and gray eyes flecked with silver and blue, Lady Arielle—her mother.

This is even worse than facing Father. He brought Mother with him, she thought hearing the sadness and disappointment in her mother's voice.

Arielle reached out to lift her chin so she would have to look at her. Kyrianna jerked away.

"What is this?" Brygan dropped one the daggers Erudus had taken off Kyrianna onto the table. Engraved on the hilt was the mark of Ibacia, the patron God of Thieves. "Where did you get it?"

Kyrianna looked at her father. Despite the anger in his eyes, she saw something else; a slight quiver at the corner of his mouth. Though she had seen him angry many times, never had she seen any sign of weakness in his stance or demeanor—until now. *He is hurting almost as much as Mother is. Good,* she thought as she remembered all the arguments they had had over the years. Him wanting to make her into something she did not want to be. Pushing, always pushing her to be other than she was. Kyrianna immediately regretted the thought; much of her father's attitude came because of her appearance. Elves were not well thought of in Nydith or in any of the human controlled areas. Lord Brygan had had to deal with that prejudice since the day he married Arielle.

Even though her father was no longer the commander of the city troops; having retired as a minor noble, title and estates granted him by the Lords of Nydith, he was still a highly respected man and still served as the senior arms master to the guard. He also worked closely with the current commander of the guard. That he, as a human, had had the indecency to marry an elf was something overlooked by the much of the nobility. That his son had inherited his human appearance and had never adopted any obvious elven habits or traits was something he was complimented on in private. That the only features his daughter had inherited from him were his golden brown hair with the copper highlights and his height was something never talked about.

"What do you think it is and where do you think I got it!" Kyrianna jumped up and slapped her hands on the small table where the dagger was laying. She was careful to keep them well away from the weapon. There were now guards in the room other than her brother; and she knew she would not live long if they thought she was threatening their arms master. Erudus placed his hand on her shoulder and pulled her back from the table. He was taking no chances her actions might be misinterpreted either. Kyrianna sighed and shook her head; her temper was something else she had inherited from her father.

Lord Brygan looked up at his son and his scowl deepened. Kyrianna saw the frown and realized her brother was in almost as much trouble as she was. *Father will be proud he did his job properly, not allowing the fact I am family to stop him from arresting me, but he will be angry at the same time. Because of the damage it will cause his reputation, Father would have preferred something like this be handled within the family. Of course, that was not the intention of the Guild.*

"Arms master?" One of the guards cracked opened the door and looked in. "The Magistrate wishes a word with you and your lady."

Brygan looked at her and shook his head as he turned to leave the room. Arielle followed him.

"How long have you been a member of the Thieves' Guild?" Erudus asked after they left.

"Two years." She turned to look at him, arms crossed over her chest as she studied him. He was so much like their father in appearance, except for the eyes. True he had Brygan's dark brown eyes, but there was a softness in Erudus' she had never seen in their father's. *Perhaps when he has lived as long and seen as much as Father has, he will lose that as well. I hope not.* The two were a close match in size and build, Erudus while not quite as burly as his father—a product of his elven heritage was still a large, well-muscled man. His dark brown hair had never been as unruly as their fathers or hers and flowed smoothly to his shoulders.

Erudus swallowed hard as he looked at his sister. "Kyri." He used the old nickname then looked away. "I did not know it was you at first and when I realized it, it was too late as the alarm had already been sounded."

"You didn't know it was me! Who are you kidding? Just how many elves or half-elves live in this city?"

He still refused to look at her.

"The only ones I know of are you, me and Mother," she said after a few minutes of silence. "You looked right at me before you alerted the rest of your patrol; so don't tell me you didn't know who I was. I knew who you were immediately and you should have known me."

"You are correct." He straightened his back and looked her square in the eyes. "I did know it was you, but I had a job to do. You should never have put me in that position."

Kyrianna took a breath as she realized she had pushed her brother into a corner he had been hoping to avoid then smiled as she looked at him. "You've never been good at lying to me, you shouldn't have tried. I understand it was your job and I know I made the mistake. You caught me, don't apologize for it." She reached out and took hold of his hands, squeezing them lightly. "Just don't let Father find a way to blame you for my actions. You made the correct decision tonight."

Erudus looked at her the trace of a smile on his lips. Unlike her, Erudus was indistinguishable from humans. He had none of the light-heartedness of his elven kin and his appearance was that of a human. However, when he did smile, rare as it was, his eyes would light up in way Kyrianna had only seen in their mother's. That light was there as he looked at her.

"I think the Magistrate will release you to Father's custody," he said.

"I would rather take my chances with the council than with Father." She gave him a crooked grin.

"Kyrianna, don't say that." He pulled his hands from hers and grabbed her shoulders. "You know the penalty for attacking one of the nobles is death. That you are obviously half-elven will only make that sentence more likely." He looked away again.

"And yet, you were the one who spotted me and raised the alarm—knowing what the possible penalty would be." She took a step back and stared at her brother. "Wait a minute? Attacking? I never attacked Ravel. You have no evidence of that or of anything other than trespass as there was nothing taken or found on me."

"We had been informed of a possible plot by the Thieves' and Assassins' Guilds to have Lord Ravel killed. Both Ryia and Vailken had heard through their own informants you were the one assigned the task. A member of the council requested I be part of that patrol tonight—I do not know which one." He took a deep breath. "If I had not alerted them, and something had happened to Lord Ravel, I would have been implicated as well. Father possibly also, as he and Ravel have had public disagreements recently." He took another breath. "Kyri, Ryia had already spotted where you were and would have attacked if I hadn't intervened."

"Erudus, there's something more going on here...." The door behind her opened, and she turned to see her mother entering the room.

"Kyrianna," Arielle said softly.

As she looked at her mother, Kyrianna took a step back. She had not noticed earlier, but Arielle was wearing her sword and her left hand gripped the hilt. She wasn't holding the weapon to draw it, but seemed to be using it almost like a touchstone.

"Your father has convinced the Magistrate and Lord Ravel to drop the charges and release you into your family's custody. Your brother and I are to escort you home."

Kyrianna took a deep breath and nodded. *This is not going to be pleasant*, she thought as she followed her mother out of the room.

Chapter Two

Kyrianna paused as she stepped out of the building with her brother. Their father was standing by the horses, not looking in their direction as he attached a lead rein to the bridle of a tall gray gelding.

"Come on, Kyri," Erudus whispered behind her.

She held her head high as she approached the horses and ignored the guardsman who offered to help her mount. She swung up into the saddle with ease then placed her hands in her lap and stared at the twitching ears in front of her.

The guardsman, still waiting by her foot, cleared his throat. Kyrianna glanced down, her eyes wide when she saw the length of cord he held.

"I'm sorry, Kyrianna," he whispered "Your father's orders."

She jerked her hands back and shook her head. "You are having my horse led." Her gaze moved from the guard back to her father. "I will not submit to being bound as well."

"You are my daughter and you will do as you are told." Brygan reached up and grabbed her hands.

A shrill neigh pierced the still dawn as her horse half reared and turned to bite the person attacking his rider. Brygan reached out to slap at the horse's muzzle and Kyrianna grabbed his hair. "You hit Smokemist in that manner and I will forget you are my father," she whispered. One of the small boot daggers her brother had ignored in his search was now in her other hand and held across her knee.

"I have no daughter." Lord Brygan jerked away from her, strode over to his horse, mounted and left.

Kyrianna stared at the quickly fading figure, her mouth open. She flinched as Erudus took the small dagger from her hand then removed the other one from her boot.

"Leave!" Erudus glared at the guard until he complied with the order. He grabbed the lead rein and snapped it off. "Prove you actually care about this family," he said, slapping Smokemist on the back.

Kyrianna tightened her grip on the horse's mane and leaned forward as he sprang out of the barrack's courtyard. They quickly caught up to her father. Without a word, Kyrianna passed him the reins and sat quietly as he led her through the awakening streets of Nydith.

~ * ~

The hooves of the two horses rang with a bell-like tone when they arrived back at the small estate. There were no other sounds and Kyrianna flinched as the hoof beats seemed to echo forever. One of the stable hands came out and took the reins of the horses.

Her father paused as two more horses came into the court-yard. He nodded then held the door open for Arielle as she entered the house, Kyrianna following her.

Kyrianna watched as her father passed her and moved quick-ly down the hallway. His normally straight stance was hunched slightly. Not enough it would be noticeable to anyone, except his closest friends and family, but it was there. She knew he wanted to get away from her and compose himself before he formally banished her. His statement to her back at the barracks continued to echo in her ears as she walked through the familiar hallways.

'I have no daughter,' he had said. She had told Erudus she would have preferred taking her chances with the council than being released to their father's custody and this was why. Facing a possible death sentence for something she didn't do would have been far less severe than what she was facing now. Never one to think about the consequences of her actions in the past, she was finally realizing the price of that folly. It was a price that was too high; it was a mistake she never wanted to make again.

The walk to her father's office seemed to take forever as Kyrianna followed her mother. She glanced at her mother's back; her long silver hair shimmering in the flickering torchlight created the illusion of a glowing aura around her. Arielle's steps hesitated as she walked past a coiled whip that hung dusty on the walls. The whip began glowing as Kyrianna approached it; in the center was a swirling cloud of color: no discernible shapes or pictures, only a chaotic mixture.

Arielle gasped then swallowed hard. A barely audible whisper escaped her lips as she turned her back on the whip. "Not her. Please not her."

Kyrianna glanced back at the whip several times before they reached her father's office. Of the various weapons and trophies on the walls, this was the only one her parents had never explained the story behind. It was the only one never taken down or cleaned.

Kyrianna entered her father's office and stood quietly facing the large desk that dominated the room. Along the walls were shelves of books and maps. *Something I have always admired about Father, he does not fit the stereotypical mold of a soldier*, she thought. *He is well educated and reads books on many subjects other than tactics and warfare. He also knows much about the region and its inhabitants. If I am lucky, he will impart some of that knowledge to me before he exiles me. Even if it was only said in anger, I know* Lord Brygan *will never retract the statement he made about not having a daughter.*

"Brygan," Arielle whispered, touching him on the shoulder.

"Arielle, I have made my decision." He crossed his arms over his chest and looked at his daughter. "She is no longer welcome in my home. This is not the first time Kyrianna has deliberately chosen to ignore my wishes. However, it will be the last."

Kyrianna bowed her head at his statement. *He is correct of course. I guess the main problem was—I was not willing to be what he wanted me to be. He wanted me to wear my hair so it would hide my ears, and I've always pulled it back. He wanted me to follow the path of order as Erudus has done and I prefer to follow the whims of the moment.*

Arielle nodded then gestured to the far corner of the room. "There is still something we need to discuss, before you do this," she whispered.

Kyrianna slowed her breathing and listened closely as her ears strained to pick out the whispered words.

"The Lady is stirring again." Arielle gripped the hilt of her sword tightly. "When we passed the whip, it woke up. I'm worried about what it might mean. We could be doing just what She wants."

Brygan glanced at his daughter who looked away quickly. "She is not ready for this. However, my decision is already known. It was part of the agreement reached with the Magistrate. She cannot remain in Nydith." He placed his hand over Arielle's then took a deep breath. "I leave it to you then. Tell her as much or as little as you deem fit."

As he walked past her, Brygan reached out and placed his hand on Kyrianna's shoulder. He stared at her for a moment then squeezed her shoulder gently before leaving the room.

Kyrianna turned her attention back to her mother standing there watching her. Arielle's head was cocked to one side and her hand still rested on the sword.

"He will not formally disown you; however you are aware of his feelings. You will be banished: Not only from here, but also from Nydith." She paused and her grip on the sword tightened. "You will be allowed to remain here long enough to gather your things before leaving." She paused again. "You may take your weapons and equipment as well as Smokemist and his gear. If you are able to prove yourself something other than a common thief, there may come a time when you are welcome back in this house."

Arielle walked past her daughter, toward the door, her step heavy as she left Kyrianna standing there—alone.

Kyrianna stood there looking around the room. She and her father had had numerous discussions and arguments in this room. Standing there she found only one that seemed to stand out more than any of the others. It was the time a wandering mage had come to the estate. She had been ten years old and the mage had tried to convince her father to allow her to apprentice to her. While the woman had had a kind face despite her depthless black eyes, Kyrianna understood, even at that age, how most people felt about magic and those that tried to wield its power.

She remembered how she had forced herself to remain polite as she told the woman she had no interest in pursuing magic. The woman had continued pushing the issue saying Kyrianna had high potential. Lord Brygan had finally had to intervene and ordered the woman out of the house. Before she left though, the mage knelt down and took Kyrianna's hands in hers. "There will come a time, little one," she said, "when you will be forced to find your own path. As long as you are true to your soul, you will find your way to the place you belong. Do not be afraid and always follow your own path, not the paths others would lay out for you."

Standing there, Kyrianna realized just how much influence that woman had had over her. She had grown up with a rebellious streak, never wanting to follow any path but her own. She had found ways to fight what her father wanted her to do, even when she didn't necessarily disagree with it. *However, something within me told me not to let him dictate my path and I refused to listen to anything he said to me. I eventually rebelled to the point of joining the Thieves Guild.*

Now, look at where that has led me. I allowed the Guild to embarrass Father. Even though it has not been mentioned, Silvis will have demanded Father stop his investigation. Moreover, because of all this, Father has disowned me, maybe not formally but in every way that matters. In addition, he has also banished me from my home. She walked over to the bookshelves and ran her fingers across the leather bindings. *Despite our problems, I will miss him.* She turned back to the desk and opened one of the drawers. Inside were several leather bound books, the crossed sword and bow emblem of House Dalynne embossed on the cover. She picked up the top book and flipped it open. The pages were blank. *I doubt he'll mind too much,* she thought as she took another of the journals out of the drawer.

Kyrianna jumped as the door behind her opened. She turned to see her uncle Dysiren standing there, a dagger held in his hand.

"Here!" He thrust the dagger toward her, hilt first. Kyrianna stepped forward, her head cocked to the side as she looked at him. Uncle Dysiren, even if he was her father's brother, had always been one of her supporters in their conflicts.

"You should never let a blade of this quality go to waste," he said with a smile.

Kyrianna nodded as she took the weapon. Her head jerked up to look at her uncle as she felt the heat still lingering in the hilt of the dagger.

"It took a bit of work," he said. "However, the symbol has been changed."

Her eyes widened as she looked at the hilt. The complicated symbol of Ibacia had been replaced with the rearing unicorn of Frayrith. Kyrianna turned the blade over; there was no evidence the original symbol had ever been there and the acid etched unicorn appeared to have been part of the original forging. She placed the dagger into her boot sheath, threw her arms around her uncle, and hugged him tightly. He returned the hug then stroked her hair for several minutes.

"No matter how flawed we may think a weapon is, there is always something special about it. There is always something that makes it worth trying to salvage and redeem. You remember that, Kyrianna. Keep it close in your heart," he said softly. "And, remember too, you will always have friends and allies in this house." He gave her a light kiss on the forehead then left the room. "Walk your own path, niece; not the path others would lay out for you," he said as he walked down the hall. He paused for a moment and looked back over his shoulder at her. "Just be careful which path you choose," he said then left.

She watched him for several moments before smiling and heading for her own rooms.

~ * ~

Kyrianna stood at the window and watched as the city started to come to life. People moved through the streets, several guardsmen arrived at the estate for training. A couple of weapon merchants were talking to Dysiren as he showed them a collection of short swords. Life was continuing both in Nydith and on the Dalynne estate as if nothing has happened. *Perhaps it is for the best*, she thought.

After several minutes, she turned away from the window. She opened the wardrobe and removed one of the gowns hanging there. Dark blue, almost as dark as the night sky with silver trim, the fine elven silk was light and seemed to shimmer with an inner light. She looked at the battered pack on the bed and at the gown again. She shook her head then hung the gown back with the others. She pushed the gowns to the side and began pulling out her hunting clothes. She changed into one the older sets then glanced at the polished steel mirror. *Was Uncle Dysiren trying to tell me something with his gift?* Frayrith was the patron deity of those who walked the forest paths. Looking at her reflection in the mirror, she definitely looked more like she belonged on the paths of Kilenter than the streets of Nydith. *Perhaps it would be an appropriate calling. After all, Mother walked those paths as one of Frayrith's Chosen. She has taught me much of wilderness lore and the ways of the forest.*

The decision made, she finished gathering her gear. She put the journals in last then grabbed her packs and started to head to the stables. She stopped and stared at Erudus standing in the doorway.

"What did you mean about there being more to this situation?" He closed the door.

Kyrianna took breath before speaking. "Lord Ravel is also known as Silvis within the Guild. He was my mentor and the one who assigned me to steal some papers from Ravel's office."

"What papers?"

"I don't know. I didn't read them. I doubt they were really anything. What he wanted was for me to get caught by you so they could pressure Father into stopping his investigation. Don't let him do that." She set the pack back on her bed and held out her hand. "Promise me you won't let him do that."

Erudus touched her fingers with his and nodded. "The pact

is sealed. I will do what I can to prevent him from abandoning his investigation."

"Good." Kyrianna picked the pack and took a step forward. She stopped when Erudus didn't move. "I have to go," she whispered.

"Father will come back around, if you can stay out of trouble," he said placing a hand on her cheek.

"I'll try."

Erudus gathered her into a tight hug and Kyrianna felt her eyes starting to burn. "Be careful and send me messages occasionally. You know most of the guard; you know which ones will make sure I get them."

She nodded as she stepped back. "I will. I expect you to be Commander of the Guard in a few years. Maybe I'll be able to attend the ceremony."

"Of course you will. Come on, I'll walk with you to the stables." He held the door open for her.

She paused at the door and turned to look at the room one last time. The large canopied bed with all the stuffed animal toys she had had growing up was the dominant feature, followed by the still open wardrobe. A flash of silver drew her back and she removed the blue gown again and held it up against her face, letting the soft material caress her cheek. Erudus grinned, but didn't say anything as she folded the dress, wrapped a blanket around it then placed it into her pack.

Her mother was waiting for her, Smokemist's reins held in her hands. Throwing the packs she had brought with her over the saddle, Kyrianna paused as she glanced at the bulging saddlebags already on the gelding.

"I would not send you unequipped into the wilderness," Arielle said. "Even the best blade requires a sheath to protect it." She took both of her daughter's hands in hers, lifted them to her lips and kissed them gently. "May you find your true path, my daughter. Frayrith's Blessings on you."

Without another word, Arielle turned and walked back to the house, Erudus following her. Kyrianna mounted the horse and with a loud war cry, thundered out of the courtyard and away from the house.

Chapter Three

Kyrianna didn't bother trying to rein the racing horse in as he galloped through the streets. She smiled and waved at a group of clerics, who yelled curses after they dodged out of her way to avoid being run over. The laws of Nydith didn't allow horses to be ridden faster than a trot, except by the guard, but she didn't care anymore. After all, she wasn't ever going to be able to come back.

It didn't take her long to reach the northern gates of the city. Both of the guards at the gate also had to jump to the side as Smokemist charged between them. However, they managed to maintain their balance, draw swords and take up defensive positions, while several of the clerics had had to pick themselves up out of the mud.

Several yards from the gate, Kyrianna reined her horse in and turned in the saddle to take a last look at the city that had been her home.

The walls were black in many areas; evidence of the attacks Nydith had faced in her history. Yet, despite the surface damage, nowhere was there any sign of major repair to those walls, a testament to their strength and to those who defended them. The guards looked at her, shook their heads then sheathed their weapons. They both waved to her and she waved back. She knew these two; both were men her father and uncle had trained. The taller of the two was Tynal. Fair-haired with a sleepy appearance, he had been a frequent sparring partner when her uncle had trained her. She remembered Dysiren swearing the young man had to have elven blood in his background due to the speed and grace he demonstrated in the training ring.

Rieger, the other one, was loud, boisterous and her father claimed he was one of the best riders he had ever trained. Two men she was glad to have as friends at one time. She frowned as a runner came up to the gate and handed Rieger a note. The guard looked at it then thrust it towards Tynal. They both nodded to the runner acknowledging receipt of the message then turned to look at her.

Tynal cocked his head to the side and she knew he wanted to

ask the question, but didn't know how. She shook her head then raised her hand to wave again before turning back to the road. Both of the guards offered her a formal salute then turned their attention back to the gate. *They both know about the problems father and I have had over years. Instead of thinking me a criminal, I would be willing to bet, they are guessing we had another argument and Father is responsible for my being banished,* she thought. Still, she knew they would perform their duty and follow the order barring her from entering the city. For a moment, she thought about riding back to the gate and verifying they did receive that order from the runner then decided against it. It wasn't worth having to explain the situation or putting them into a position where they would have to tell her to leave. Instead, she tapped Smokemist with her knees and he trotted down the trail into the forest.

~ * ~

Kyrianna took a deep breath as the road entered the forest of Kilenter. Smokemist tossed his head several times, arguing with the pull on the reins, but otherwise stood patiently as she looked around. Kilenter was an old forest, the trees tall and heavy as they cast twilight shadows on the ground. Here and there, beams of sunlight passed through the dancing leaves, creating a glowing aura in the canopy overhead.

The main road branched off into a couple of different paths as well as continuing its own winding path until it emerged two weeks later near the town of Bretinia.

Bretinia, Kyrianna thought scanning the road. *I don't want to go there; they have even less use for those with elven blood than do the people of Nydith. At least in Nydith, I was relatively protected because of Father's status. In Bretinia, I would be in serious trouble.*

A small trail faded into the underbrush to the north. Overgrown with a lack of use, this path led to the Dragon Flame Mountains. The mountains guarded the valleys where dragons still dwelled. It was extremely dangerous territory to travel into, without an invitation, and sometimes even with one. Several centuries ago, the dragons had agreed to leave the lands south of the mountains to the humans and elves and they were to be left alone as well. Rumors persisted of humans living in some of the lands north of the mountains, but that was all they were considered to be—rumors.

Another path, not as overgrown, as the one to the north,

turned south toward the elven lands. There were many small communities of elves scattered throughout Kilenter, but their primary home was now far to the south, across the Sea of Dreams. While there were three main races of elves known to the humans of Rhysia, the majority of their contact was with the Rynial, Midnight Elves as the humans called them and the Taladilith or Twilight Elves. The Alowien or Dawn Elves had withdrawn from these lands just as the conflicts with the humans had started.

At one time the forest of Kilenter had been heart home to the elves. Then humans had come to Rhysia and began building their cities. They wanted to control the resources of the forest and tried to drive the elves out. The Alowien had quietly retreated to the south, while the Taladilith had tried to reach an agreement with the humans. In the midst of the negotiations, the Rynial started a war with the humans. Somehow, they had even convinced the dragons to join them.

Kyrianna sat on Smokemist, still staring at the southern path, her mind mulling over the history her mother had taught her as she considered her options. *Perhaps I will go there. Being half-elven, I do not know what kind of welcome I will receive from my mother's people, but at least it is an option.* She paused and shook her head. No, it wasn't as option, she was half human and the memories and life spans of true elves were long. Just as many humans condemned her for being an elf, elves who remembered the wars would condemn her for being human. There were also the Rynial to consider. They controlled many of the southern passages and after the Taladilith had worked to help the humans in their battles against them and the dragons, the two races were now bitter enemies. It had been Clyniellian, the speaker for the Taladilith, who had managed to get the dragons to agree to end their attacks in return for the human's promise to leave their lands alone.

Kyrianna sighed and shook her head. The elven lands to the south were also closed to her. Taking another deep breath she flipped the reins lightly and Smokemist started down the road.

About an hour later, Kyrianna spotted a game trial crossing the main road and continuing to the south. Smokemist snorted a protest as she turned him off the road and onto the narrow track. The trail opened up a few minutes later into a clearing with a small pond to one side.

Dropping Smokemist's reins over his head, she slid out of

the saddle. The horse immediately turned his attention to the grass and began pulling up mouthfuls. Kyrianna laughed and patted the horse's neck then walked over to the small pond. Several different tracks surrounded the water and she studied each one of them. The training her mother had given her came in handy as she identified them, all small animals; no large predators other than a couple of weasels and foxes. More interesting though were the delicate cloven-hoofed prints of a unicorn. This would be a good place to rest for the night.

She removed the gear and packs from Smokemist then gave him a quick rub down with a rough cloth. "What do you think?" She asked when she finished. The horse snorted then pushed his muzzle against her chest. "You think you deserve a treat, that's what you think." She rubbed his nose for a moment, then moved to the pile of gear and opened one of the packs.

Smokemist snorted again, his breath warm on her neck as he reached out and nipped at her hair pulling it. "Impatient aren't you." Kyrianna laughed and tapped his nose as she turned around. The horse bobbed his head twice then reached for the carrots she was holding.

She stood there for several minutes, listening to the sound of the horse chewing on the carrots and staring into the depths of the forest surrounding her. Her eyes were burning as she glanced back at the trail she had followed. "Chaos take it!" Several birds took off from the trees at the shouted curse and she dropped to the ground as she finally stopped fighting the emotions that were overwhelming her.

There is nothing I can do about what has happened; it is time to figure out what I am going to do for the future, she thought as she stood up and shook her head to clear it. She glanced up at the now darkening sky. "Frayrith guide me," she whispered as she began to set up camp.

~ * ~

"I told you, you would get us lost. Why didn't you stay on the main road?" A female voice said in the morning stillness.

Kyrianna sat up, her hand on her sword as four people pushed through the trees into the clearing. "Well met on the journey," she said.

"If we weren't lost, it would be," the woman whose voice had awakened her said. Despite the sarcastic nature of her words, her manner wasn't angry.

"Perhaps I can help." Kyrianna stood up and smiled at the group. "I'm familiar with this area. Where are you going?" She had made the decision to follow the path of Frayrith and had asked the Lady of the Forests to guide her. Frayrith was seen as the protector of all life not just that of the forest. Kyrianna knew if she were to follow the goddess, She would expect her to help those who needed help. Perhaps Frayrith had even caused this group to become lost and wander into her camp as a test.

The woman looked at the others in her group: two men and another woman. The second woman shook her head slightly, but the two men nodded silent assent. "We are on a pilgrimage to the shrine of Ghainaess in the Dragon Flame Mountains."

"The Dragon Flames are dangerous for humans to enter." The woman who shook her head started to say something and Kyrianna spoke quickly before she could interrupt. "However, I do know the paths that lead to the shrine and can guide you there if you wish."

"If you will guide us to the foot of the mountains and see we are on the correct path, that will be enough," the younger of the two men said.

"Very well. I believe it will take five or six days to reach the point you have specified. Allow me to gather my gear together and we can get started." She saddled Smokemist, placed the gear and packs on him, then gathered her weapons.

"I am called Lash," the woman leading the group said as they left the clearing. "The others are Prelari, Cering and Fraedian." The other members of the group nodded as they were introduced.

"Frayrith's Blessing on you all. I am called Kyrianna." She studied the four of them for a few minutes. Their features were hidden by the cowls of their traveling cloaks, but they all appeared to have lean, strong builds under the multi-colored cloaks. The colors of the cloaks all seemed to swirl together in no discernible pattern and shimmered with a light silvery sheen. Kyrianna could see no evidence of swords under their cloaks, but did note that all of them carried themselves with the confidence and balance of trained fighters. She had no doubts they were able to defend themselves if necessary.

The four of them traveled well together as Kyrianna led them back to the main road through the forest. From here, she took them west until they came to a rough path. "This way has not been traveled much in many decades," Kyrianna said leading Smokemist on foot along the rocky terrain. "Since the agreements were reached with the dragons, most humans avoid the Dragon Flames."

"We understand," Lash said.

~ * ~

It was approaching dusk on the fifth day when the group reached the foot of the mountains. "The path to the shrine is only a short distance away. We can camp here for the night and I can show you the path in the morning, or we can continue. I leave the choice to you," Kyrianna said.

"You are of elven heritage, are you not?" Lash looked at her.

"I am half-elven, yes." She felt herself tense waiting for the inventible condemnation of her heritage she had come to expect from most, however, Lash only nodded.

"Then you can still see well enough to travel," she said. "As can we. We would prefer to continue."

"As you wish."

With the fading light, it took the five of them almost an hour to reach the spot where the path entered the mountains. The ground was covered with various dragon scales of differing colors and sizes. Scattered among the scales were numerous bones as well; the bones of creatures not welcomed by those who guarded the mountain paths. It was a clear warning to anyone without an invitation to stay out of the area.

"From here we must travel alone. We thank you for your assistance. May the Great Mother spread her wings over you."

~ * ~

Kyrianna returned to the small clearing where she had set up her camp and looked around. *From here, I can travel the forest. It is off the main path, so I will not get many visitors, but I will know about travelers.* As she sat down, her back to one of the trees, she pulled her dagger from her belt, her fingers brushing across the unicorn etched in the hilt. Smokemist snorted and she looked up to see a silver-white unicorn enter the clearing.

She felt her breath catch as she watched the graceful creature pick its way across the clearing and over to her. Bright amethyst eyes looked at her, judging her as she was drawn into their liquid depths.

She finally forced herself to close her eyes and bow her head.

She jerked her head up and opened her eyes as the dagger in her hand heated suddenly. The tip of the unicorn's horn now rested on the blade of the weapon. Heat radiated through the blade into the hilt and the acid etching Dysiren had placed there was now a beautifully inlayed design of silver and gold.

"Lady Frayrith," Kyrianna whispered. "I pledge myself to thee and to those under your care and protection." She placed the dagger on the ground, her hands held out to her sides in supplication.

The unicorn exhaled gently across the back of her neck, the breath warm and moist, and Kyrianna looked up. Again, she looked into eyes that were judging her, but this time she did not look away. The unicorn nodded her head once then touched her right wrist with her horn.

A silver tattoo of a rearing unicorn appeared on the inside of Kyrianna's forearm. It was a tattoo like the one her mother wore; a tattoo Arielle had told her marked her as one of Frayrith's Chosen. The unicorn reared, her forelegs held tucked in close to her body as she neighed. She spun on her hind legs then bounded out of the clearing.

Kyrianna placed her left hand over the silver mark and stared after the vanishing unicorn. *My pledge to the Lady of the Forests has been accepted. But, why would she give me—an exile and thief, this honor?*

Kyrianna reached down to pick up the dagger and looked up as Smokemist whinnied. A large black, silver-tipped wolf was entering the clearing at the same spot the unicorn had left. He ignored Kyrianna for a moment to approach the horse. Smokemist lowered his nose and the two creatures greeted each other as if they were old friends. The wolf then padded over to her and touched the silver tattoo with his nose.

Kyrianna gasped as the cold, wet nose of the wolf created a sharp contrast to the warmth still in her arm from the unicorn's touch. His golden-brown eyes met hers and for a moment, she felt a connection to his mind. *I am called Shadow Seeker*, she heard a voice say in her mind before the connection vanished.

"Shadow," she said as she reached out to ruffle the wolf's ears.

He growled playfully and bobbed his head in agreement.

Frayrith has sent me a companion, Kyrianna thought as she continued to rub the wolf's ears. *Is he a gift from the Goddess or her way of ensuring I honor my pledge to her?*

For a moment, she remembered the voice that had called to her in the guard barracks. There had been something in that voice; something that spoke of shadows and chaos, something she didn't want to embrace. The woman had said she could call on her when the others had rejected her. But, they had not all rejected her. Her uncle had reminded her she had supporters, her brother had told her to stay in contact and her mother, while supporting her father's decision had made sure she was properly provisioned. And, now, Frayrith had accepted her as well. With Her to guide, she knew she would finally find the proper path for her life and would be able to avoid the shadows and chaos that had tried to call to her.

Chapter Four

Kyrianna slapped at the cold, wet nose that pressed against her ear. Her hand encountered the wolf's muzzle and she felt him snap gently at her fingers. She ignored Shadow Seeker and pulled her blanket tighter around her body. "Ugh, dog breath," Kyrianna said as she sat up and pushed him away. The wolf sat there, his tongue still hanging out of his mouth and his head cocked to the side as he waited.

"Okay, okay," she said getting up. "I suppose you want to go hunting or have something I need to do." She rolled her blankets up and dropped them with the rest of her gear. With a quick glance around the clearing she picked up her belt, buckled it on, and reached for the bow resting on her pack.

A low growl echoed in the silence of the morning and Kyrianna looked up to see Shadow Seeker backing away from a dark mist rolling into the small grove. A shrill neigh pierced the air and Smokemist began backing away also.

"Chaos take it!" Kyrianna grabbed her pack and reached for the horse's bridle as something cold and wet wrapped itself around her ankles. She was frozen to the spot and cried out as Smokemist jerked his head from her grasp, the leather of the bridle cutting her hand.

The mist continued to wrap itself around her and she found herself surrounded by swirling colors and a cacophony of sounds filled her ears blocking all other noise. As the mist continued to enfold her like a wet shroud, Kyrianna felt herself falling as the ground evaporated from under her feet.

It was not truly falling, as if down a pit; instead it was more like settling into a thick pillow with the mist supporting her weight. Time became meaningless to her, as she could no longer hear anything other than the ever-changing noises of the fog—not even her own heartbeat or breathing. The din that filled her senses faded slightly and Kyrianna now heard a familiar female voice whispering in her mind.

You see I was correct in what I told you would happen. Your family has rejected you. Your brother could have protected you from detection, yet he chose to expose you; even knowing you might face a death sentence. When you are ready, I will welcome you as one of my own.

"Who are you?" Kyrianna shouted into the swirling chaos.

You will learn that soon enough; once you are ready to take your proper place. Your path and your training start here. The voice faded and Kyrianna found herself kneeling on a stone floor in a place of total darkness.

"My path will be determined by me and not you, whoever you are," Kyrianna said. "You may have brought me here, but you will not control me." She waited as her voice echoed in the darkness.

Despite the normally keen eyesight of her elven heritage, Kyrianna was unable to see anything in the blackness that surrounded her. She reached out slowly, her hands sliding on the smooth stone under her, searching for anything that might have been brought here with her. Her fingers found her buckler and bow then her pack. She could find nothing else. Still, she had her weapons, armor, some gold and other supplies. Hopefully, she would have enough to survive until she could find out where she was and how to get back.

Without thinking, she gathered and secured the loose items; thankful for the training her uncle had given her in arming in total darkness. She started to slip her sword from its sheath then paused and reached into a belt pouch and removed the flint and steel. By feel, she removed a sheet of parchment from the map case and knelt back down. The parchment held under her boot, she struck the flint and steel together, sparks glowing like miniature stars in the darkness. It took several tries but finally, the paper caught and a soft glow burned in the room for a moment before the dried paper was left in ashes.

Despite the briefness of the light, it was enough to show she was indeed in a structure of some sort. The sword made a loud hiss in the stillness of the room as she drew it from the sheath and stood up.

Her guild training took over, as she listened for any sounds. There were none. Her sword held in a defensive position, she held her other hand in front of her and inched her way to a wall. She turned to the left and kept her free hand on the wall, as she crept silently in the darkness. After what felt like hours, sounds of movement—metal armor clinking and boots scuffling against the stone, echoed in the passageway.

She paused and listened carefully before turning to the left, an apparent cross passage to the one she was now in. Her free hand still trailed along the cold stone as she moved down the hallway.

Kyrianna kept her footsteps light as she walked. In the darkness, a light appeared. It appeared to be the light from a torch, but it was only lighting the corridor for about twenty feet around it. She froze and studied the small group in front of her.

A girl with long blonde hair in worn leathers stood next to a tall, burly man in ring mail holding a broadsword. Another woman, holding a long sword, dressed in a chain shirt was a few paces in front of the others. Two more men in robes stood behind the man and woman.

The girl pointed toward Kyrianna and the woman in the chain shirt raised her sword in front of her. "Who are you?"

Kyrianna paused at the musical quality of the woman's voice, it was almost elven, but her appearance was human. She stepped out from the wall, her sword held low in a non-threatening posture. "My name is Kyrianna. Who are you and what is this place?"

The woman lowered her sword slightly and nodded. "I and my companions were brought here by unknown magics. I am Myrith, a knight of Geladas."

"My apologies, but I do not know the name Geladas," Kyrianna said. "I follow Frayrith."

"On my world, Geladas is considered a God of Justice whose followers are charged with protecting others," Myrith said. "And Frayrith?"

"She is known as the Lady of the Forests."

"Then she would generally be counted with those gods that are considered to be good by most mortals," Myrith said.

"She is. And your Geladas?"

Myrith took a step back, shock on her face as she looked at Kyrianna. "I believe I have already answered that."

Kyrianna bit her lip and nodded.

The rest of the group stepped up around the woman. Myrith held the torch out toward each one as she introduced them. "This is Etewyn," she said nodding toward the large man in the ring mail. "Next to him is Hendandra." The girl with the long blonde hair nodded and elbowed her companion who also nodded. "Falden and Bukon. These four are from a place called Shokar. I am from a place is called Taladar." She paused and seemed to be studying Kyrianna for a moment.

"Well met on the journey," Kyrianna said holding out her hand.

Myrith hesitated for a moment, her eyes darting to the tips of Kyrianna's ears. She shifted the long sword she carried to her other hand and grasped Kyrianna's in the traditional warrior's clasp. Her grip was strong for one so slightly built.

"As this does not appear to be the place any of us are from, it might be in our best interests to work together to find our way back to our homes," Myrith said.

"I agree," Kyrianna said.

"We welcome your sword," Myrith said.

Kyrianna nodded and withdrew her hand.

"My companions and I have been here for only a few days. There are a few others here also—members of a group called the Moon Swords. They claim they have come here to cleanse this temple of the evil that is holding it and to retrieve an ancient artifact. The one leading them, Timber, has also told us there is a device here that can be used to open portals through the planes and perhaps it can be used to send us home."

"Then why are you still here?" Kyrianna asked.

"Until the Artifact of Order and Chaos is found and protected, we will not open the portals," a voice said from behind her.

Kyrianna spun around at the new voice. An elf of average height and build stood behind her. His gold eyes sparkled in the torchlight and his gold hair was streaked with red. He was dressed in simple leathers. "The Artifact of Order and Chaos?"

"That is what it is called. It is an ancient artifact; one that contains the spark of Order that is a part of all things, even Chaos itself," he said.

Kyrianna shuddered as the elf's gold eyes locked on hers for a moment.

"What does this artifact look like?" Bukon asked.

"No one knows for sure," the elf said. "In keeping with its nature, its appearance is said to be mutable, though it is most often depicted as a crystal orb filed with gold and silver mists." He bowed his head slightly as he glanced at Bukon before turning his attention back to Kyrianna. "Once the artifact and the temple are secure we will be glad to help you return to your homes. However, even without the portals, the power here is growing." He paused and glanced from her to Myrith. "And now it appears that power may have begun bringing others here. For what purpose?" He shrugged his shoulders. "We do not know."

"So we're stuck here until it's safe to risk going home." Kyrianna took a step back, her hand resting on her sword hilt.

"That is true. Perhaps you will consent to help us until that time."

"Our purposes seem to run together. I will lend my sword to your cause," she said, bowing her head slightly.

"I am called Timber and I offer you my thanks. If you will all follow me, I will show you to an area where you may rest."

He led the group through several narrow passageways to a large hall. There were a few other groups scattered throughout the hall, some resting and others looking like they were making plans to leave the area. Timber led them to a quiet corner. "Rest well, tonight. If you are still willing, you can join us in our search for the artifact in the morning. If you need anything else, let one of the others know and they will help you if they are able." He nodded to Myrith then turned and left.

"How did you come here," Bukon said looking at Kyrianna.

She looked around at the group then took a deep breath. "I really don't know. I had just awakened when this strange mist surrounded me. It was filled with swirling colors and sounds. No patterns to any of it; only a chaotic blending. It seemed to act like a portal and I found myself here. And, the rest of you."

"Hendandra, Etewyn, Falden and I had recovered some items taken from the temple of Rhyra by a group from the local temple of Ballan," Bukon said. "The High Priestess of the witch goddess had apparently cursed the items and after we delivered them to the temple of Rhyra, we were surrounded by a fog similar to what you described and found ourselves here."

"That's not entirely correct," Hendandra said. "They were the ones to deliver the items to the temple of Rhyra. I had parted company with them. Before that, Falden had given me a ring, which I believe was to help him locate me if he wanted to hire me again."

"Hire you?" Kyrianna interrupted.

"I have some skill in acquiring things," Hendandra said.

Kyrianna frowned, but didn't say anything further.

"Now, as I was saying," Hendandra said. "He had given me a

ring. I dropped the ring after they left, but it apparently had other ideas. I was sitting at home and found the ring in one of my pouches when a thick mist surrounded me. When it faded I found myself here with these guys." She turned and looked up at Falden. "When we get out of this, I am holding you responsible if any part of the fee I collected from that last job is missing as I didn't have time to properly secure it before you brought me here."

"I did not cast the magics that brought you here. If you wish to place blame for your abduction, I suggest you talk to the Dark Lady."

"The mist came from the ring and you gave me the ring. You or your goddess is the one responsible." She turned and walked away from Falden.

"Interesting, but I have no idea why a goddess from another world would be interested in me," Kyrianna said looking at Bukon. "And, it would appear the same power was involved in my being brought here as you, based on your description."

"Perhaps Ballan has a counterpart in your world. Many of the gods and goddesses found throughout the worlds are only aspects of each other," Bukon said. "On Shokar, Ballan would be the goddess of magic in its darkest forms."

Kyrianna frowned slightly. "On Rhysia, we have Nynia, the goddess of magic. However, while Nynia is not generally counted among the *good* deities, neither is she counted among the *evil*. I do not believe an act of this nature would not be in keeping for the Mistress of Magic," she said.

"And what of you, Myrith?" Kyrianna asked.

"I was sent here, by Geladas. He told me I was to fight a great evil. I assumed at first he meant the tyrant who ruled our land. Perhaps he meant the evil that is seeking to control this place. I do not know for sure. However, I will do my best to follow my Lord Geladas' wishes and fight the evil in this place. Hopefully, he will find me worthy and return me to my home to further serve him."

Kyrianna turned her head to hide the grin on her face and she saw Hendandra roll her eyes behind Myrith.

"Hey wait a minute," Hendandra said. "How is it we understand you two." She looked from Kyrianna to Myrith. "After all, four of us are from the same land, but you two are from different places." She turned and looked at Falden. "Did you cast some sort of magic on us without telling us?"

"No, little one, I did not," Falden looked up from the book he was reading. "While there are magics, both arcane and divine that will allow those with different tongues to be understood, I did not cast them." He paused and looked around at the others. "Perhaps we were brought together for a purpose and some other power has seen to it we are able to communicate."

"That would only make sense for Myrith and Kyrianna," Bukon said. "It is more likely that there is a connection between our lands so our languages are related enough we are able to understand each other without difficulty. After all, there are many who believe the deities of other lands are nothing more than aspects of each other, perhaps the same is true of the worlds as well?"

"Perhaps," Myrith said.

"It is definitely better than the idea something brought us here for a reason," Hendandra said. "Even if the circumstances make it look like that in certain cases."

"Whatever the reasons, we should be glad we are able to communicate and continue working to find a way to get back to our homes," Falden said.

The others nodded their agreement. Kyrianna took a deep breath and shook her head. She had been brought here by magic unknown to her and had heard a voice speaking to her. The explanation had to be more complicated than what Bukon was suggesting, however, she wasn't sure she wanted to know the real reasons.

Kyrianna glanced around at the group; Etewyn sat by the fire with several pieces of raw meat sitting above it on arrows laid across steel spear shafts. She regarded the man and his dinner. The others had salted or dried meat.

She looked over at Hendandra who sat nearby with her own dried meat and water. "What is he cooking?"

"You know, I have been afraid to ask," Hendandra said. "That man has a stomach as thick as his head," she added after a moment.

Myrith laughed softly from behind the two of them. "Good sword. Strong arm. Loyal blade. But, not very smart or clean." She sniffed the air and frowned. "His taste in food and drink is questionable at best and absolutely gut wrenching at worst."

"So, what's he cooking?" Kyrianna glanced from Myrith back to Hendandra.

Myrith smiled. "Ask him."

"Okay." She stood and walked over to the fire and sat down as Etewyn carefully rotated the arrows. "What's for dinner?"

He looked over at her and grinned. "Lizard. You hungry?" He pulled one of the arrows from the fire and held it out to her.

Kyrianna took the meat, studied it for a moment then sniffed it. She looked up at Myrith. "Lizard is hardly a first choice, but it is edible."

Laughter echoed around the group and Kyrianna glanced from Etewyn to Myrith and back.

"Lizard? Why don't you ask where he found the lizard?" Myrith smiled again.

Kyrianna turned back to Etewyn who now had brought out a small pouch and was seasoning his dinner. "Where did you get the lizard meat?"

"Let's see, the room with all that muck. It almost ate the little one."

"Actually, it had me beneath its feet and was about to tear me apart with its two mouths. I was lucky Myrith's blade found its mark and took it down." Hendandra looked at her darkened armor for a moment. "I just wish she hadn't opened the thing up when it was on top of me. The smell of that thing's blood was absolutely horrible." She shuddered. "Entirely too close." She looked up. "I don't want the lead position anymore." She sniffed at her sleeve. "The job stinks."

Kyrianna frowned. "Comes with the job description. However, I am acquainted with the tasks of a scout. I am willing."

Hendandra smiled at her and Kyrianna looked away.

Myrith looked from Hendandra to Kyrianna. "How are you at picking locks and finding traps?"

"My skills are probably not as good as those more practiced in the *art* of thievery." She glanced at Hendandra again. "But, I have received some training."

"Hendandra, she has relieved you at point. Keep in mind you may still be needed at any doors we must open."

"But, that is where the thing tried to eat me."

"It is okay, little one," Etewyn said pausing in sprinkling the seasoning over his food. "I will take the doors with you. After all, if we lose you who will carry all the valuables?"

Several of the group smiled and smirked at the small woman who blushed in the firelight and looked quickly at the ground.

Kyrianna frowned as she considered the meat on the arrow she was still holding. Etewyn was now sprinkling some of his seasoning on it. "Two heads? The lizard had two heads?" She looked at Etewyn. "No lizard has two heads."

"Scales, claws, teeth, walked on four legs, well at least four legs. Lizard." He pulled one of the arrows off the fire and took a bite, then motioned for Kyrianna to taste hers.

Kyrianna sniffed the meat again then looked up at the rest of her companions. "That description could fit almost anything including a dragon."

"Of course a dragon is a lizard. Really big one though," Etewyn said. "Wonder how it would taste."

"I think it would do the tasting," Bukon said with a laugh.

"Maybe that is our secret weapon," Hendandra said. "Something eats Etewyn and dies from all the *food* he has eaten." She rolled over laughing as Bukon grinned at Kyrianna. Falden sat in his corner shaking his head. Etewyn ignored the laughter and continued with his meal.

"So what is the seasoning?" Kyrianna asked taking a tiny bite.

"Death Knight Pepper."

Kyrianna sputtered and dropped the meat into the fire as she spat out the bite. "Death Knight…" A hand dropped over her mouth.

"I think we would all eat better if that question had not been asked," Myrith said.

Kyrianna looked at Etewyn and saw the amusement in his eyes as he watched her and Myrith. The rest of the group burst out in laughter as they opened their bedrolls and began settling down to sleep.

Myrith shook her head then looked at Kyrianna. "Will you stand first watch with Etewyn?"

"I will."

"Wake me and Hendandra in three hours."

Kyrianna nodded. "Frayrith, Lady of the Forests, please watch over Smoke and Shadow until I return." She whispered the prayer as she drew her blade and took up a watch position with Etewyn while the others slept.

Chapter Five

Kyrianna watched as Myrith and Timber talked for several minutes the next morning. After Timber walked away, Myrith returned to the group. "Timber has asked us to go into the western corridors in search of this artifact," she said.

"Any ideas where it might be?" Bukon asked.

"No. He will be putting other groups together to take the other corridors," Myrith said.

"Let's get to it." Etewyn drew his sword and headed toward the doorway.

The rest of the group glanced at the fighter then back at Myrith. She shook her head, laughed softly then drew her own blade and followed Etewyn. Kyrianna readied her bow and glanced once at Hendandra as the girl hurried to the front of the group. It would seem she had changed her mind about being the scout.

Kyrianna stayed in the back of the group and concentrated on watching the areas behind them. The light from the magical torches did little to penetrate the darkness for any distance and they stayed close as they moved through the corridors.

"Myrith, open door on our left," Hendandra's voice called back softly.

Myrith motioned to Kyrianna to move up and cover the doorway as she and Etewyn stepped past Hendandra. The room was dimly lit and Falden and Bukon's torches cast shadows from where they stood on the sides of the doorway.

"I hear water splashing," Hendandra said.

"A fountain possibly," Kyrianna said as she positioned herself just to the side of the door. It gave her a slight amount of cover while allowing her to see inside the room. Her bow was up and ready as she watched Etewyn and Myrith enter the room.

"Clear," Myrith called after a couple of minutes.

Kyrianna followed Falden and Bukon into the room.

In the center of the room sat a large fountain carved from white stone. A spray of water rose from the center and splashed noisily as it cascaded back down. Hendandra moved slowly around the base. After two circuits, she looked up and shook her head. "No traps or hidden mechanisms that I can locate." She took the torch from Bukon and held it down next to the surface. "There are no inscriptions of any kind either."

Falden handed his torch to Bukon and moved his hands through a short pattern while muttering. "There is an aura of magic on the liquid," he said when he was done.

"Perhaps, one of us should try it," Falden said.

Etewyn nodded and moved toward the fountain.

Hendandra grabbed the man's arm with both hands and shook her head. "Not a good idea," she said.

"Considering the nature of this place, I doubt tasting the liquid would be wise," Bukon said.

"Uh, Myrith," Hendandra said pointing toward the fountain.

A pair of eyes appeared in the water as it rose from the bubbling pool and blinked several times.

"Well met," Myrith said stepping up to the fountain.

The eyes only continued to watch the group. No other features were noticeable in the water. After a moment, the eyes moved slightly and stared at each person in turn, pausing twice as long as they rested on Kyrianna than any other member of the group. When they reached Hendandra, one of the eyes winked playfully then they vanished.

"Either it is not willing to talk to us, or it doesn't understand us," Bukon said. "We should move on."

Myrith paused and glanced around. "We move on then," she said.

~ * ~

They wandered through the twisting passage for almost two hours before it finally opened into a large chamber, which had been partially flooded. Bukon and Falden held their torches up as they approached the water. At the very far edge of the light was another wall.

"It appears the wall ends, just above the water," Kyrianna said. "Perhaps the passage continues on the other side."

"However, we have no idea how thick that wall is or what might be in the water. Perhaps it would be better to return to the main area and see if there is another route to the other side," Bukon said.

The clang of steel on the ground caught their attention and Kyrianna turned to see Myrith holding her sword, dressed only in her long tunic as she dove into the water.

"I guess that settles that," Bukon said grinning.

The group waited; swords out and ready.

"How long do we wait before someone goes looking for her?" Etewyn looked around at the others.

"Good question, but I believe it is no longer valid," Bukon said as Myrith's head appeared from under the wall.

Bukon held a hand out to assist Myrith out of the water, but she ignored it. "It is a standard wall," she said as she got out. "The swim on the other side is about the same as on this side. Another corridor leads out from that side. Anyone here not know how to swim?" She glanced around. "Good. I believe Etewyn and I are the strongest, so we will carry anything that needs to be carried for the others."

Kyrianna glanced at Myrith and frowned. "You will be carrying the most, just carrying your own gear. And you have already made the swim once. It is obvious the water is cold. That will have sapped some of your strength." She glanced at the woman's bare arms, which were very pale in color. "I am fairly strong myself. Etewyn and I can carry the extra items." She reached down and picked up Myrith's crossbow, shield, and backpack. She looked at the pile of armor, but a glare from the woman stopped her from touching it or her sword.

Hendandra and Falden handed their packs to Etewyn, while Bukon held onto his.

As soon as Myrith had her armor in a bag and secured, she jumped back into the water and headed across. The rest followed her.

Kyrianna outdistanced the others and reached the other side first. She was out of the water quickly, her sword in her hand as she took a guard position and waited for the others.

Myrith glared at her as she pulled herself out of the water. "If you were such a good swimmer, why didn't you come across first?" She opened the bag and started removing her armor.

"You didn't ask." Kyrianna sheathed her sword and dropped Myrith's backpack.

"You could have volunteered."

Kyrianna stepped back, her hands on her hips as she returned Myrith's disapproving glare with one of her own. "As I recall we were still discussing options. You didn't give anyone else an opportunity to volunteer. You stripped off your armor without saying anything and dove in. Perhaps if you left the *better than you attitude* back where you originally came from, you would be willing to ask for help when it's needed. You might even realize other people are capable of doing things and you are not the only one who can handle a situation." Kyrianna spun around so her long hair whipped past the older woman's face.

Kyrianna readied her bow and went to stand with the others. "Whenever you're ready, *your holiness*," she said glancing at Myrith. "You can lead us on," she said offering the woman a half-bow.

Once Myrith was dressed and her gear back together, she picked up her sword and headed for the corridor, waiting only long enough for Hendandra to again take the lead. She didn't even glance at Kyrianna as she again took a guard position in the back of the group.

~ * ~

"This is getting ridiculous," Myrith said looking at the dark water and the wall that divided another partially flooded chamber. "I noted no change in the level of the floor. Rangerette?"

Kyrianna shook her head.

"I'll take a look," Bukon said dropping his pack. "Be right back."

Kyrianna frowned as she watched Myrith pace back and forth along the edge of the water.

"Even in Order there is Chaos," a voice whispered in her ear.

Kyrianna jerked her head up and spun around, dropping her bow as she drew her sword.

"What is it?" Myrith stood next to her, her own sword at the ready.

"Thought I heard something," Kyrianna said.

"Hendandra?" Myrith asked.

"I didn't hear anything," Hendandra said shaking her head.

"I must have been mistaken." Kyrianna slowly sheathed her sword and retrieved her bow.

"At least you were paying attention, which is more than I can say for others."

Kyrianna followed Myrith's gaze to where Falden sat, a book

held in his hands, as his eyes appeared to be following words on the pages.

"He's been gone too long," Myrith said after several more minutes had passed.

"I'll go look for him," Kyrianna said watching Myrith as she again started pacing beside the water.

"Hold on," Myrith said pointing to movement in the water.

Bukon surfaced at the edge of the pool. "Sorry. I found a small room down there," he said climbing out of the water. "Not much in there, except for this." He pulled a scabbard from his belt. "I don't use weapons." He handed the sword to Kyrianna.

Kyrianna pulled the sword from the scabbard and examined the blade. "Very light," she said moving it in a defensive pattern before sheathing and attaching it to her belt.

"The metal is interesting," Bukon said. "I wonder what it is."

Kyrianna drew the blade again and held it up as it shimmered with a pale green color. "The shimmer is part of the steel itself." She said.

"Anything else down there beside the blade?" Myrith asked.

"Nothing. I found no ways out of this area," Bukon said shaking his head.

"Looks like we may have missed a corridor somewhere," Myrith said. "We can work our way back to find it, or we can camp here."

"I say we go on," Bukon said looking around at the others. There were several nods of agreement.

"What about you, Rangerette?"

Kyrianna didn't answer as she drew her long sword and began working it and the new blade through several defensive patterns. She grinned at the look of surprise on Myrith's face as she sheathed the blades.

"I agree. Let's move on." Kyrianna readied her bow and frowned as she noticed Bukon watching her closely.

~ * ~

"Finally," Hendandra muttered after an hour of examining the walls of the corridor. She took a deep breath as she studied the area of the wall, where the door had been hidden. "Okay, no traps." She glanced back at Etewyn as the large man hovered over her. "Excuse me, a little room to work here." She pushed on his legs.

Kyrianna laughed as she watched Etewyn take a half step back, his sword held in position to be swung over Hendandra's head if necessary.

Hendandra reached into a pocket of her pack, pulled out a pair of lock picks and set to work on the well-disguised lock. "Leikor's cursed luck," she muttered as the picks broke in the lock.

"My turn, little one." Etewyn stepped forward, placed a hand on her shoulder and guided her behind him as he swung his broadsword. The wood splintered and he swung again, widening the opening.

The corridor ended in a set of stairs descending into darkness. Myrith looked at the stairs then at the group. "We should rest before continuing," she said.

"First watch," Bukon and Falden said together.

"The Rangerette and I will take the second. Hendandra and Etewyn can take third," Myrith said.

Chapter Six

Etewyn looked from where he was cooking breakfast. "Care to try it?" He held several strips of meat out.

Kyrianna took the meat and nibbled at it.

"Remember the lizard and the seasoning, Rangerette," Myrith whispered as she walked past Kyrianna.

"Thanks," Kyrianna said as she coughed and sputtered. She shook her head as Hendandra burst out laughing.

"As soon as everyone is ready, we need to move on. While I suspect the odor of *breakfast* might have been enough to drive away the vermin and smaller creatures, I wouldn't make any bets on whatever else is down here being so affected," Myrith said.

Once the rest were ready, Myrith drew her sword and led the way down the stairs, Kyrianna again stayed in the back. The stairs descended for quite a distance, the light from the torches sending ghostly shadows flickering on the walls beside the group. The passage narrowed and Myrith paused at the archway to the next chamber.

Hendandra moved up next to Myrith and began an examination of the archway. "Nothing here," she said.

Myrith nodded and motioned Hendandra back as Etewyn stepped up next to her. They both stepped through the archway together. Bukon frowned as he glanced around. "An embalming chamber perhaps," he said.

Kyrianna shuddered as she stepped into the room. Along the walls were several oblong tables with a roughly human-shaped depression in them and a long groove around the edge that led to a drain hole at the feet. Brown-red stains covered many of the tables along with cracked, yellowed pieces of bone.

"It could also have been used as a torture chamber," Bukon said. He held up a rack of dusty glass vials. "There are many drugs that can only be obtained through the torture or death of a living creature."

"Myrith, look at these," Hendandra called pointing to a small cache of clay jars under one of the tables.

Myrith pulled out one of the jars and carefully lifted the lid. She pushed the jar away from her and it fell over spilling its contents on the floor. "Torture chamber." Her voice was harsh as she stared at the collection of bones and teeth that now lay on the floor.

Hendandra reached under the table and removed another jar. This one was untouched by the dust covering the rest of the room and the linen cloth that sealed the mouth was still soft and pliable. She started to peel the cloth back and was stopped by Bukon, who reached down and plucked the jar from her hands.

"Sorry little one, but I think this would be better handled by one with more religious training than you," he said.

She nodded.

Bukon peeled the cloth back and gagged as the stench wafted out. "Blood. Congealed, but still sticky," he said replacing the cloth and returning the jar to its previous location.

"We should move on," Myrith said moving to the other doorway.

Myrith spun around as a loud screech echoed in the chamber. Kyrianna stood beside her, her bow at the ready as she watched the archway.

"Hold!" Falden said as a small, winged shaped glided into the room. "It is only Talon; my new familiar." The hawk landed on the mage's shoulder and he reached up to stroke the bird's neck.

"You spent the time you were on watch involved in the rituals of calling a familiar?" Kyrianna stared at Falden for a moment before turning toward Myrith. "No concern for anything beyond his own power—typical behavior for a mage. Did you know about this?"

Myrith frowned at Falden and the hawk, which was watching them with bright blue eyes. "I did not. If the only reason you volunteered to stand a watch was to perform some magic ritual, you could have told us and another would have taken the watch while you were occupied."

Falden rolled his eyes and smirked. "You think you know so much. However, you understand so little. I did nothing that compromised the safety of this group and the magics I cast before beginning the ritual created barriers across the door and over the stairs. Nothing would have been able to approach without alerting Bukon or myself."

Myrith spun around. "You knew what he was doing? Why

didn't you wake one of us to stand watch with you?"

Bukon straightened as he glared at Myrith. "I did not know what the specific ritual was, but I knew about the protective nature of the spells. There was no need for another to join me at that time. Besides it is not like we've been attacked by anything since heading in this direction." He turned and walked away from Myrith.

"That is not the point. Falden, you volunteered to stand a watch and that is what was expected of you. While your magic may have provided better protection than if you had remained alert and awake, there is also a chance someone or something could have dispelled it. If that happened, Bukon would have been alone and could possibly have been caught by surprise. You will not stand watch again." Myrith turned and headed toward the doorway.

~ * ~

Myrith paused as she stepped out of the hallway onto a long bridge. The bridge was about ten feet wide and stretched into the distance; the far end lost in darkness. "Kyrianna?"

"This appears to be a large cavern, but there is an artificial feel to it." She glanced around. "The darkness is too deep for me to make any estimates on size. I suggest Hendandra and I both lead, about fifteen feet in front of the rest. Those with bows should have them readied."

"I believe I have a better solution," Falden said.

Myrith nodded. "And that would be?"

"Talon can fly ahead of us as a scout and I can sense what he sees and hears. He is fast and small and should be able to get himself out of harm's way if necessary."

Kyrianna frowned as she glanced at Talon, then back at Falden. "I don't know anything about the bond between familiars and their masters; however hawks do have exceptional eyesight and good hearing. They are predators and can defend themselves against many creatures—if he can't get away from it that is. However, I doubt he can fly well enough to move as slowly as we walk and I doubt he will be willing to fly into the darkness. If we are moving fast enough to keep up with a hawk in flight, we will be defeating the purpose of having a scout."

Falden turned his head slightly and looked at the bird on his shoulder. His eyes seemed to lose focus for a moment then the hawk glided off his shoulder and walked to the edge of the light cast by the group's torches.

Bobbing his head, the hawk looked back at them and gave a soft squawk.

"I believe he is trying to prove his worth to you," Kyrianna said. "It would appear he is willing to serve as the scout and move at an appropriate pace."

Myrith looked from her to Falden, then at the bird pacing at the edge of the light, studying the bridge. "Okay, let's go."

Myrith and Kyrianna flanked Falden as he turned his attention back to the link he had with his hawk. They moved slowly, torches held high as the bird moved at the edge of the light examining the stone.

"Wait," Falden said.

Myrith stopped and held up her hand to signal the others. "What?" She turned to look at the mage.

Falden closed his eyes and his brow wrinkled in concentration. "Scratches," he whispered. "Scratches in the ground."

"I'll check it," Hendandra moved forward to where the bird was staring at something. Etewyn followed behind her.

Hendandra knelt down and slowly slid her hand on the walkway. "It appears to be a line cut around the middle of the bridge. It could be a box of some kind," she called back. She stood and moved to the right side of the bridge then back to the left. "There is room on the sides to pass by without crossing the line." She paused for a moment. "There are also two large statues here."

"Wait there," Myrith called.

The hawk glided back to land on Falden's shoulder as Myrith and Kyrianna led the group forward.

Hendandra looked up from the statue she was studying. "There's writing here, it looks like it could be a form of elvish, but I can't read it." She looked at Kyrianna.

Kyrianna she knelt down to look at the flowing script on the base of the statue; Myrith stood behind her watching. She traced one of the runes with her fingers, *Thynitic*, she thought. *First, the chaos portal and now this. What is going on here?* She shook her head a couple of times before she finally stood up.

"It appears to be a form of the language of the Midnight Elves, but I can't make it out," she said. "It could be an ancient dialect of the language. The only symbol I recognize is this one." She pointed to the one she had touched. "It is the symbol they use for

Thynitic's name."

"Thynitic?" Myrith looked at her. "You said you followed a goddess called Frayrith. Who is this Thynitic?"

Kyrianna took a deep breath. "She is also called the Lady of Chaos and is considered to be one of the darkest deities in all of the planes. She is a primordial goddess born from the chaos that first formed the planes and worlds. She takes pleasure in chaos and in the pain and torment chaos can bring. She is the goddess of Chaos, Pain, Retribution and Mercy." She glanced back into the darkness toward the last room. "If this was once a temple of Thynitic then that last room was indeed a torture chamber. Many of her priestesses would have used it to practice various types of torture techniques on different subjects as well as each other."

"Mercy?" Myrith placed a hand on Kyrianna's shoulder. "She is also considered a goddess of mercy?"

"Yes, mercy is one of those areas where she has power. Her doctrine teaches that pain and suffering become worse when unexpected mercy and kindness are shown to the victim. And, it is also in keeping with her chaotic nature." Kyrianna's voice dropped to a whisper.

Myrith nodded as she looked up. Kyrianna followed her gaze. The statue was of a tall human male dressed in simple leathers and holding a sword upraised in a gesture of defiance.

"Was he a follower of this Thynitic," Myrith said softly, "or an enemy?"

"No way to be certain," Kyrianna said as she looked at the writing again. "However the lack of any of her symbols on his person seems to indicate he wasn't one of her more devout followers. And, while humans do sometimes follow the Lady of Chaos, it is rare. She is an elven deity."

"The writing on the other one seems to be different," Hendandra called.

Kyrianna took a deep breath as she tried to read the writing. It was different, but the style seemed to shift as she studied it. The only thing she was certain of was that Thynitic's name did not appear in it.

Kyrianna looked up. It was the same person, again dressed in simple leathers, but holding a staff in a defensive position in front of his body.

"Any traps?" Myrith asked.

Kyrianna looked away to see Hendandra brushing dust from her pants.

"Not that I can locate, but as I said there is room on either side for us to pass without crossing. I would recommend that route," Hendandra said.

Myrith tightened the grip on her sword and nodded. "Kyrianna, you take rear guard as we cross," she said.

She readied her bow as her answer and waited.

~ * ~

Myrith paused as she passed a third statue. "Kyrianna." She pointed to the writing.

"Again, it is an ancient form of the language of the Midnight Elves." Kyrianna paused and studied the writing. "The symbol for Thynitic." She touched one of the runes. Her hand then moved from that one to another and then a third. "This is one of the symbols for Frayrith and this is a symbol for Galolith. They are the three elven gods of my world. However, there appears to have been a fourth symbol here," she said touching a damaged area of the writing. "I don't know what it may have represented as there are only three gods in the elven pantheon of my world. The Midnight Elves revere Thynitic, while the Twilight Elves honor Frayrith and the Dawn Elves honor Galolith."

She glanced up at the figure, the same person as the other two, but holding a bow this time, before she moved to the last statue. Here the figure was holding a large mace in both hands. She cocked her head to the side as she studied the writing on the pedestal. "Enemy of Chaos," she said slowly as she looked at the runes. The form is newer than the others, but still very old." She looked back at Myrith. "This passage here." She pointed to the last line of writing. "I believe it reads: Enemy of Chaos. The problem is the rune is damaged." She rested her fingers on the pedestal. "It could also mean Consort of Chaos."

"Enemy of Chaos or Consort of Chaos?" Myrith looked up at the statue. "Two very different things. Was he considered an enemy of chaos or did he fight against this enemy of chaos as the consort of this Thynitic?"

"The fact he is depicted as holding different weapons suggests a certain chaotic nature on his part," Bukon said.

"True, but if he were a follower of Thynitic; particularly one who was deserving of honor, I would expect to see evidence of him carrying her favored weapon—a whip or scourge. I would expect that even more if he was recognized as her consort." Kyrianna paused for a moment and looked away from the two of them.

"Consort of Chaos," Kyrianna whispered as she looked up at the statue.

Neysinal was his name, the voice whispered in her head. Kyrianna stepped back and shook her head.

"Rangerette?" Myrith placed a hand on her shoulder. "Are you alright?"

She nodded a couple of times, then forced a smile. "Sorry, thought I missed something in my memory, but it was nothing." She walked to the side of the bridge and stared out into the darkness that surrounded them.

And Chaos grows, the voice whispered again.

Kyrianna swallowed and closed her eyes. *Thynitic*, she thought.

There was no answer, but she thought she could sense a feeling of satisfaction as the presence faded.

"Myrith."

Kyrianna turned at the panic she heard in Hendandra's voice. The girl was kneeling on the bridge, examining a cut in the stone.

"Yes?"

"The area was trapped. Either it is only on this end, or I missed it on the other side. It is rigged to drop if anything weighing more than seventy-five pounds crosses this line. It is too complicated for me to disarm."

"Then your caution in advising us not to cross was warranted."

"Yes, but what if I hadn't been suspicious and had assumed it was safe?"

"Don't second guess yourself, Hendandra. If you start doing that, you will make mistakes. Just continue to be suspicious and check things as best you can." Myrith paused and glanced around. "We've spent enough time standing around, let's get going," she said.

Kyrianna turned back toward the darkness. The presence was gone, but she was still worried. She took a deep breath. "Frayrith guide me," she whispered.

"Kyrianna, we need to get going," Myrith said again.

"I heard you the first time," she said as she turned and readied her bow.

Chapter Seven

"I find no traps," Hendandra said after she finished checking the archway at the end of the bridge.

Myrith immediately stepped past the girl into the room. Kyrianna knew Hendandra would still be worried about not finding the previous trap until they were past it. Myrith was showing her she still trusted her skills.

As they entered the room, a soft light began to radiate from the ceiling. On the far wall was a large door. On the floor, directly in front of the door an octagon was inlayed in silver. At each of the corners was a small depression, as if something were meant to be placed in them. Kyrianna glanced at the sidewalls and saw four alcoves to her right and another four to her left.

Hendandra moved to the far door and began examining it. "No traps, but it is sealed magically. I can't open it." She looked down at the silver octagon in the floor. "I would wager this has something to do with how the door is opened."

"I agree; but what?" Myrith asked as she looked around.

"These probably need to be placed in the depressions in some specific order," Bukon said holding up a small ceramic jar. "There is one of these in each of the alcoves and they seem to represent the four elements: fire, air, earth and water. Falden what do you have on your side?"

Falden stepped out of the last alcove on the right. "The four on this side are hard to make out, the images are faded. However, I believe they represent a person or persons engaged in different activities; at least three of them that is. The last holds only the picture of a sword."

Other than the door, the small alcoves, the octagon and the depressions, there was nothing else in the room. No clues to the actual function of the symbol inlayed in the floor or of the ceramics jars.

"Well, what do we want to try?" Bukon held two of the elemental jars and Etewyn the other two.

Myrith shook her head. "I agree it looks like the jars are supposed to be placed within the depressions, but what is the order? There is nothing here to give any kind of clue."

"I would recommend we place the elements on the cardinal points, but again we are left with the question of where to start," Falden said.

"They should probably be placed so their opposites are aligned across from each other," Kyrianna said. She walked slowly around the octagon. "This is north," she said stopping at the point in front of the sealed door.

"Fire to the north?" Bukon asked.

"It's a place to start," Myrith said.

Nothing happened as the jars with the elemental symbols were placed into the depressions. Falden and Bukon moved forward with the four other jars. "We think we should try these based on the order they were in the alcoves," Falden said. "At this angle, this corner seems to point to the first jar..." His voice trailed off as he placed the first jar then the second. Bukon moved to other side of the design and carefully placed the last two jars into the remaining holes.

As the last jar settled into place, the area inside the octagon began to fill with smoke and several large creatures stepped out laughing.

"Chaos demons!" Kyrianna dropped her bow and drew her swords.

"Guess that wasn't the order," Etewyn said drawing his sword and moving to stand in front of Hendandra.

"Hold position," Myrith called. "The symbol may contain them if we don't violate the boundaries."

"You violated the boundaries by placing the jars," one of the demons said as they stepped over the silver lines.

The fight was over quickly, each of the demons vanishing as they fell. The smoke and demons gone, the jars vanished from the holes in the floor and were back in their alcoves.

"So which ones did we get wrong and how do we know?" Myrith asked as she walked around the symbol. "There is nothing here to give us any kind of clue."

She seeks to impose Order on Chaos. Kyrianna shook her head slightly to clear it.

"Perhaps there is no actual pattern. If this place was dedicated to Thynitic the order may be random to honor the chaos she creates," she said.

"The statues may have held the clues," Bukon said looking at Kyrianna. "Too bad no one can read them properly."

Kyrianna took a deep breath then took a slow step toward Bukon. "Are you implying something?"

"It just seems odd you recognize certain runes on the statues, but cannot read them."

"Midnight Elves revere the Lady of Chaos and in keeping with her nature and their own; their language is chaotic and changes form on occasion. There are some runes and symbols they have never changed and those are the ones they use for Thynitic, Frayrith and Galolith." Kyrianna stared at Bukon.

"You two stop it!" Myrith stepped between them. "We cannot afford to start fighting among ourselves."

Kyrianna dropped her head for a moment. "My apologies. In my land humans hate and distrust elves because of a war centuries ago. However, the elves who were responsible for that war are also enemies of my mother's people and I do not appreciate being compared to them."

Bukon nodded. "I apologize also. It was not my intent to insult you. I know nothing of the people of your land and without the information you have just given me it did seem odd you could read portions of the writing, but not all of it." He bowed his head to Kyrianna.

"Good. Now, that you two are not about to attack each other, can we get back to the problem at hand?" Hendandra started to giggle, but a stern glance from Myrith quieted her.

"Unless we are willing to return to the upper level and look for other passages, this appears to be the only route through this area," Hendandra said after composing herself. "Personally, I have no problems with going back."

"Let's put the elemental jars back in the positions we had them in the first time," Myrith said looking at Bukon and Etewyn.

"What about the others," Falden asked.

"Let's try starting with the one in the furthest niche in the northeast slot and work counter clockwise," Hendandra said.

"Any particular reason," Myrith asked.

"None, other than it's different than what we did last time. Anyone else have an idea?" She glanced at the rest of the group.

"Might as well give it a try. Right now any idea is as good as another," Bukon said.

As the last jar was put into position, the area again filled with smoke and this time, half again the number of demons as the first time stepped out to face the group.

As the last of the demons fell, Kyrianna looked around at the rest of the group. They were all breathing hard and looked pale. Bukon was bandaging a cut on Myrith's arm while Hendandra took care of a gash on Etewyn's shoulder. "This time there were more of them and they seemed stronger," she said as she sheathed her swords.

"We cannot keep guessing and hoping we get this right. There has to be another way to figure this out," Myrith said.

Bukon glanced at Kyrianna before he spoke. "I still think there may be something about the statues that we missed. Although the figures are hard to make out, on three of the jars there appears to be a person engaged in some sort of activity. The fourth jar only holds the picture of a sword. Maybe the placement of the statues and the weapons they are holding correspond to the required placement of the jars."

"That could indeed be it," Falden said. He lifted one of the jars from its shelf and seemed lost in thought as he studied the picture on it. "It is still hard to discern any details, but in this picture the figure appears to be in a library or study. This could be representative of a mage. Didn't one of the statues hold a staff?"

"It did," Hendandra said. "I believe there was also a sword, a mace and a bow."

"I can go back and check the placement of the statues as well as look for anything else we might have missed the first time," Bukon said.

"No." Myrith's voice was sharp and echoed in the room. "We stay together. There is too much we don't know and too much chaos in this place for us to risk being split up."

~ * ~

Kyrianna pulled a page out of her journal and sketched which weapon each of the first two statues was holding. She folded the paper and placed it in her belt as she knelt down and stared at the runes on the pedestal of the mace-wielding figure. After a few minutes, she shook her head and stood up. "Sorry, I can't decipher anything, other than what I already have. Let's go check the others."

Kyrianna led the way to the other two statues and marked the weapons they held on her paper. As they returned to the chamber, she paused in front of the figure with the bow. She reached out and placed her fingers on the symbol that represented Frayrith's name and looked up. She had pledged herself to the Lady of the Forests and that pledge had been accepted. However, the only voice she heard speaking to her since was one she believed belonged to Thynitic. "Frayrith, guide me," she whispered. "Please."

She will abandon you, Thynitic's voice said, *just as she did another before you.*

Myrith placed a hand on Kyrianna's shoulder. "Come on Rangerette, let's go," she said.

~ * ~

"We'll put the elemental jars in the original locations and try positioning the others the same as the four statues," Myrith said when they entered the chamber.

"This is interesting," Bukon said holding up one of the ceramic jars. "The picture is much clearer now."

"As I suspected, a mage," Falden said looking at the jar.

The same figure represented by the statues was seated in a room reading a book. He then stood and moved his hands in a complex gesture.

Kyrianna looked at her sketch then pointed to the southwest corner of the diagram.

The next jar showed the same man facing a group of skeletons; a glowing mace held in his hands. The next only had a glowing sword on its surface and the last showed the man with a bow raised, the arrow pointed at a target that would be above and in front of the jar.

When Falden placed the last jar, there was a click and the four jars representing the four statues vanished from the depressions. The four elemental jars remained and the center of the diagram again filled with smoke and ten large demons stepped out of it.

"Here we go again," Hendandra said as she drew her rapier.

Kyrianna found herself standing back to back with Myrith as she drew both of her blades. "Chaos take it!" She danced away from the demon grabbing for her. The creature grabbed again and she swung her sword down hard cutting into its arm.

"Hendandra!" Etewyn's voice echoed in the room.

Kyrianna swung both swords in an x-pattern across the throat of the demon she had injured. Black blood spurted from the cut across her face, blinding her. She screamed as something sharp hit her in the abdomen and tore her skin. She stumbled and fell to the floor as someone pushed past her.

"Here," Myrith's voice said. "Let's wash that out of your eyes."

Cold water splashed on Kyrianna's face and she blinked several times, trying to clear her vision. "Hendandra?" she asked.

"Will she be alright?" Myrith asked glancing from Kyrianna to Bukon, who was working on the girl.

"Yes." He helped the girl into a sitting position as he held out a vial of blue liquid. "She will need some time to rest."

Etewyn walked over and handed Kyrianna a vial of a blue liquid. "Bukon tends to the little one; you must tend to your wounds as well."

Kyrianna took the vial and nodded. "My thanks," she whispered. She looked down at the rip in her armor and shook her head. The demon's claws had only scratched her, but the poison on them had burned deeply. She looked at the vial in her hand, then up at Myrith.

"It is a healing potion," Myrith said. "Drink it, it will stop the poison and greatly speed the healing of the injury."

"The statue jars have vanished," Falden said. "They are no longer in the depressions, nor are they back in the alcove."

"Then maybe we got those correct," Myrith said turning back to the group. "What about the others?"

"Still here."

"I still think the opposition elements should be placed across from each other," Bukon said. "But that gives us three more possible tries before we might get it right. Personally, I don't think we're up to facing these things three more times with their numbers and power increasing the way they are."

"I agree," Myrith said. "Anyone have any suggestions."

Kyrianna studied the diagram for a moment. "Move fire to the east and air to the north," she said after a few minutes.

"Your reasoning?" Bukon glanced at her.

"The sun is also representative of fire and it rises in the east; air to the north because of its association with cold. It's only a suggestion." She shrugged and looked at Myrith.

"Let's give it a try."

"Wait," Etewyn said. "The little one is not up to a fight, if you get it wrong."

Hendandra forced herself to her feet and slowly drew her rapier. "I can handle myself. Let's get this over with."

Kyrianna stood up and sheathed her blades as she retrieved the elemental jars and placed them in her suggested locations. As the last jar was set in its depression, a loud click echoed in the room.

The large door slowly opened into another corridor.

Chapter Eight

Kyrianna glanced around as she stepped through the doorway. Statues lined the passage, which appeared to go on for several hundred yards.

"Look at this one," Hendandra said stopping at one of the statues about halfway down the corridor. "It's the same guy as the others."

Myrith paused and glanced up at one of the statues. The features were indeed the same person who had been represented on the bridge and on the jars. "An elf?" she whispered as she stared at the ears. All of the other statues had depicted the man's hair covering his ears; this one had the hair pushed back, revealing the pointed ears.

"An elf?" Myrith said behind her.

"That may explain the reference to the elven pantheon," Kyrianna said.

"Okay, but why? Why are we here? Other than you, none of us have any ties to these gods. Moreover, you are the only obvious elf in the group. None of this makes any sense." Myrith turned and walked away.

"No, it doesn't," Kyrianna said. "When when one deals with the Lady of Chaos, things do not make sense until she wants them to."

Myrith stopped and turned back to stare at her. "For one who claims to not follow this Lady of Chaos—you seem to know quite a bit about her."

"The Midnight Elves are the racial enemies of my mother's people. It is only good sense to much as you can about your enemies. As one trained in the arts of war, you should understand that."

Myrith took a step back then resumed her path down the hall. Kyrianna waited a few heartbeats before following.

She paused as she reached Myrith, knelt by the archway and peered in. Four figures in black robes knelt before an altar. They appeared to be focused on their prayers and unaware they were being observed. She held up four fingers behind her then pointed into the room.

Chaos! She jumped up and readied her bow as Myrith's armor hit the wall and the four figures stood.

"Kyrianna, hold!" Myrith grabbed her arm as she released her arrow. The shot went wide and hit the altar where the four robed figures had been kneeling.

"Why do you invade this place?" One of the figures stepped forward and pushed the cowl of her robe back to reveal an elven face with dark black eyes and black hair.

"Myrith, these are Midnight Elves, followers of Thynitic, be careful what you say to them," Kyrianna whispered.

Myrith nodded. "We are here at the request of the Moon Swords," she said. "We seek to remove the evil that has taken residence in this temple."

"We do not follow the paths of Chaos, although they run alongside the paths of Lord Neysinil," the woman said looking at Kyrianna.

"Lord Neysinil?" Myrith whispered.

"The name sounds elven, possibly even of the Twilight Elves, but I am not familiar with it," Kyrianna whispered. "Yet, they know who Thynitic is and associate this Lord Neysinil with her."

Neysinal was his name, Kyrianna thought as she watched the four elves.

"We do not know this Lord Neysinil of whom you speak," Myrith said turning back to the woman.

"He is the Consort of Chaos," she said. "We seek a way to return him to his place alongside Chaos." She raised her hands slightly. "That you do not know of Lord Neysinil tells me you are one of those who would keep him imprisoned," the woman said continuing to watch Kyrianna. "Perhaps it is you who serve Chaos."

"What?" Kyrianna's bow shook as she stared at the woman.

Before she could say anything further, Bukon charged past Myrith followed by Etewyn. His fists hit the woman who had spoken, knocking her back against the altar as Etewyn's blade sliced across the throat of one of the others. Kyrianna jerked her bow up and fired several arrows at the woman Bukon had struck. Bukon and Etewyn turned to the remaining two figures. Both of the women fell before their attacks.

"That's enough. They did nothing to provoke this attack," Myrith said grabbing Kyrianna's bow. She glared at Kyrianna then turned to Bukon. "I want to know why you attacked them without them attacking or threatening us."

"They were lying to us, that much is obvious from Kyrianna's reaction to the name of the deity they claimed to follow. They tried to disassociate themselves from Thynitic by making up another deity. One they claim is the Consort to Chaos. If that were true, then they would know Thynitic and follow her as well."

"What we have seen strongly suggests Thynitic may be the one behind the evil in this place," Kyrianna said. "The demons we just faced resemble what I have learned about the lower castes of chaos demons who serve Her. Then there are the references to chaos on the statues. If the elf they picture is the goddess' consort, then he is her ally and their purposes run together." She gestured toward the bodies of the four women.

Kyrianna took a deep breath. "If these served him, whoever he is or was, then they also served her," she said.

"There is still the fact, they did not attack or threaten us," Myrith said. "You may have been insulted by the one's comment about you serving chaos, but that was hardly enough to warrant attacking her."

"Then the fact she was preparing to cast a spell, should be," Falden said softly. "She raised her hands into a position where she could cast. I could sense magical energies being called."

"Then why did you not also attack or call out a warning." Myrith turned to face Falden.

"Because, I could not determine the type of energies she was channeling," he said. As far as I could tell, she may have been preparing something defensive at the time. But, combine that with the answers she was giving you and I believe Bukon had sufficient cause to believe she was going to attack the party."

Myrith looked around at the others and nodded slowly. "Very well. And, no one here knows anything about this Neysinil who was mentioned?"

Kyrianna shook her head.

"The name is unfamiliar to me as well," Hendandra said as she stood from checking the bodies of the four women. In her hand she held six gold chains with different symbols on them.

Kyrianna found herself staring at one of the pendants. A small oval shaped stone swung on the chain, colors swirled and shifted across its surface. She felt drawn to the pendant and started to reach out for it when she felt someone touch her shoulder.

Bukon took the chain away along with a second one with a red flame on it from Hendandra and dropped them into his pack.

"You okay?" Myrith asked as she looked at Kyrianna.

"Yeah, fine." She started to walk off, but stopped as Hendandra held out another pendant. On the delicate gold chain hung an ivory disk with a rearing unicorn carved into the surface.

"A symbol of your Frayrith?" Hendandra nodded toward Kyrianna's wrist. "Perhaps this would be better suited in your hands."

"Thank you." Kyrianna took the pendant and slipped it over her head.

"And what about the others?" Myrith asked.

Hendandra held up the last three pendants.

The first was a crescent moon with an arrow laid across it as if it were a bow; the second was a small green star and the third was a larger black disk with the other symbols, except the unicorn set into its surface. "The moon bow is the symbol of Galolith," Kyrianna said. "He is considered the father of the elven race and just as Frayrith is the protector of the wilderness and forest; he is the protector of the cities and civilization. The star I do not recognize either."

"So at least three of these symbols belong to the elven gods of your world," Myrith said. "Yet, you claim to know nothing of the other two."

"Are you trying to imply something?" Kyrianna asked.

"No; only looking for clarification."

Hendandra started to tuck the remaining symbols into her pack then paused. She held the chains with the star and the crescent moon on them out to Kyrianna.

"Thank you. As these seemed related to the elven gods of my world, may I also have the ones you are holding Bukon?" Kyrianna asked.

Bukon hesitated for a moment then nodded as he handed her the chain with the flame on it as well as the multi-colored portal of Thynitic.

Kyrianna took the two chains and dropped them into her pack without looking at them.

"May I see the disk?" Bukon asked.

Hendandra handed him the black disk.

Myrith shook her head as she stepped past Bukon and into

the room.

Kyrianna followed her and stopped as she looked around the room. The four symbols that were on the pendants were also engraved on the top of the black altar. On the walls several murals were painted. Two of the murals showed a male and female elf standing together, each wearing one of the four symbols. She recognized the symbol of Thynitic around the neck of one of the female elves. The male next to her was wearing the flame symbol. The others were wearing the star and crescent moon symbols. The deities were on opposite sides of the room while the wall behind the altar showed a swirling portal of color that seemed to erupt into various landscapes. Two unicorns flanked the portal.

"Frayrith and Galolith." Kyrianna's voice was a reverent whisper as she looked at the mural.

"And the other two would be Thynitic and this Neysinil?"

"The woman is Thynitic. The man I do not recognize other than a resemblance to the statues we have already seen. However, it seems reasonable to assume he is." Kyrianna's gaze returned to the portrait of Frayrith. "I don't understand," she whispered. "She's wearing the green star, not the unicorn." She turned to look at the painting of the chaos portal on the wall behind the altar.

The colors swirled and moved—as if alive. She felt her heartbeat and breathing quicken as she took a step toward the altar. "It is from chaos that all life is born and renewed."

"Out!" Myrith took a step toward her, forcing her to step back. "I want you out of this room until we have checked it."

Kyrianna blinked several times then nodded and backed out of the room.

Myrith moved so she was standing in the doorway, blocking her from coming back into the room. "Hendandra there has to be a way out of this area, find it!"

Kyrianna stood a short distance away from the door, her head down as she wrapped her arms around herself. *What is going on here?*

She tried to focus her thoughts on Kilenter and her home in Nydith, but the only thing she could see was the portal that had brought her here.

Daughter of Chaos, she heard a woman's voice whisper in her mind. *It was the First Daughter who sought to destroy Order. It will be the last daughter, who will seek to destroy Chaos, which will restore Order and bring*

Balance. The voice faded.

"What?" Kyrianna's head snapped up and she looked around. The voice had been different than the one that had spoken to her before.

"Rangerette?"

Kyrianna looked up and saw Myrith looking at her.

"Sorry," she said. "It was nothing."

She ignored Myrith and kept her eyes on the ground.

"Hendandra found a passage from the room," Myrith said. "We should get moving."

Kyrianna nodded as she hurried through the room and into the dark corridor.

~ * ~

The corridor ended in a large room, with only a fountain in the center. Kyrianna found herself staring at the fountain. *Do you see the Order in the Chaos?* The same voice she had heard earlier whispered in her mind.

"Did we miss something?" Myrith said.

"I don't think so," Hendandra said as she moved around the fountain. "The same symbols we found in the last room are also inscribed here," she said.

"The upper tier of the fountain resembles the base of the fire symbol," Falden said. "I'm getting a magical aura from the fountain as well as from the corners of the room. It is faint, but it is there. It's possible there is something that needs to be placed in the corners to activate the magic."

"The statues," Bukon whispered. "Perhaps the statues in the hallway should be placed there."

"Why do you say that?" Hendandra looked up from where she was studying the symbols on the fountain.

Bukon glanced at Kyrianna and frowned slightly. "We have reason to suspect Thynitic, the Lady of Chaos, is behind the evil invading this place and we also have reason to believe those statues represent someone who was known as the Consort of Chaos. A person it seems is looked at as a member of the elven pantheon from your home. However, something happened that caused this god or demigod to be forgotten by almost all those who might have once known of him. It is logical to assume one of the unknown symbols is his and since the other statues held the clue for the last area it is also logical to see if they hold the key to this area as well."

"It couldn't hurt to take a look," Hendandra said.

"Very well Bukon, Etewyn and I will go check the statues. The rest of you wait here," Myrith said.

Chaos must balance Order, the voice whispered.

Kyrianna shook her head to clear it then turned toward Myrith. "Excuse me, but you will need me as I am the one most familiar with the gods of *my* world," she said.

"I agree," Bukon said. "She should go with us."

Myrith nodded. "Fine." She turned and headed back into the hallway.

~ * ~

"Nothing," Myrith said looking at the last of the four statues. "There's nothing here."

"Actually, these statues can be moved," Kyrianna said pointing to the floor. "See the scratches here and here."

"Then let's try and move them. You do remember the previous placements, as it will probably be the same as the jars were."

Kyrianna nodded as she shouldered her bow and stood next to one of the statues.

It took all four of them to move each of the statues back to the room. As soon as they wrestled the last of the statues into place, the fountain erupted into a kaleidoscope of color. Fires sprang up from the four tiers. The first layer shifted and swirled, the colors changing constantly. The second tier was a brilliant spring green while the third was a shimmering gold. The upper tier was a steady red flame. As the lower three layers of flame faded the fountain slid away from the door revealing a set of stairs descending into darkness.

Myrith moved to one of the statues and motioned for Etewyn to help her as she pushed it out of the corner and the fountain once again covered the stairs. "We will rest here then continue on. I'll take the first watch, Etewyn the second and Bukon the third. Hendandra you and Etewyn go and see if you can find a way to close and secure the door in the altar room from this side."

Hendandra smiled, tapped the large fighter on the arm then hurried back through the corridor.

Kyrianna released the breath she hadn't realized she was holding when she heard the slight click of the door closing. She placed a hand on the second tier of the fountain, the one that had produced the green flames, and closed her eyes as she took several deep breaths. *What is going on here?*

She stepped back from the fountain and looked around. Both Myrith and Bukon were watching her. She ignored them as she moved to one of the corners and began to lay out her bedroll.

Chapter Nine

Kyrianna lay on her bedroll and watched as Myrith sat in the middle of the room where she could observe the door and have time to respond to any threat that might appear. Falden had cast some sort of magic on the fountain so they would be alerted if anything tried to come into the room from that direction. She sighed as Myrith glanced around the room, her eyes resting a bit longer on her than the others. *She doesn't trust me*, Kyrianna thought.

Why was I affected by Thynitic's symbol? It makes no sense. I don't remember anything in Mother's books or the other records regarding this type of thing. Kyrianna closed her eyes and took a deep breath as she tried to recall something; anything that could give her some kind of clue.

She forced herself to relax as she tried to search her memories. She smiled slightly as she heard Myrith shift her position; no doubt the woman figured she was asleep like the rest of the group. She had inherited her mother's ability to get by with little to almost no sleep. As a result, when the majority of the household was asleep, she had found herself, often times in either her father or mother's office reading their journals and books.

It was in her mother's books and scrolls she had learned about Thynitic. Even though, she had been given an introduction to all the gods worshipped on Rhysia, her mother had not allowed her to spend any time learning about the Lady of Chaos. All she had told her was that Thynitic was called the Lady of Chaos, she was the patron deity of the Rynial who were the racial enemies of the Taladilith and she was considered one of the darkest goddesses in all the planes. Beyond that description and a general warning to never seek her or those who followed her dark and twisted paths, she had not received any education regarding the Lady of Chaos. What she learned had come from her visits to her mother's study. Even then, there had been books and journals she couldn't access; tomes that were locked and sealed beyond her ability to open. She had tried a couple of times after she had joined the guild, but eventually gave up. Whatever methods her mother used to protect the secrets she kept in those books; they were able to defeat even a trained thief.

She continued to lie there, trying to focus on the memories of what she had read and learned during that time. After several minutes, she threw her blankets to the side and stood up.

"What's going on?" Myrith was on her feet, her sword in her hand.

"Nothing, I just can't sleep," Kyrianna said. "And two sets of eyes on a watch are better than one."

Myrith nodded then resumed her position in the middle of the room.

Kyrianna moved to sit to the side of the doorway, where she could watch the fountain as well as see if Myrith reacted to anything in the corridor.

"Why do you call me Rangerette?" Kyrianna grinned as she looked at Myrith.

"Because you are so young in comparison to the rest of us."

"Excuse me?"

"I personally have seen twenty-eight springs. Etewyn is only a couple of years younger than I am."

Kyrianna stared at Myrith. *She says she is twenty-eight? She has to have elven blood, as she doesn't look that much older than me*, she thought. "Hendandra is younger than I am," Kyrianna said glancing at the sleeping girl.

Myrith seemed to study her for a moment. "You don't look older."

Kyrianna nodded. "How old do you think I am?"

"I would estimate you at about fifteen or sixteen."

Kyrianna smiled. "I have seen twenty springs. Because of my elven blood, I age slower than a true human."

Myrith paused for moment and Kyrianna saw a slight crease on her brow.

"Hendandra is nineteen winters," Myrith said. "Bukon has never said how old he is, but I would estimate him at around twenty-three years and Falden is closer to thirty, I believe."

"Tell me about Geladas," Kyrianna said after a few minutes of silence between the two.

Myrith stared at her for a second then frowned. "While I know he is considered a god of warriors and of justice, I do not know as much about Geladas whom I follow as you seem to know about this Thynitic whom you claim not to follow. The land I am from is under the rule of a tyrant who brought a foreign goddess with him and prohibited the worship of our own gods."

"Yet, you are a warrior of this Geladas." Kyrianna cocked her head to the side as she studied the older woman.

"A puzzle isn't it?" Myrith looked around the room at their sleeping companions then turned her attention back to the doorway.

Kyrianna smiled softly. Here was someone who didn't like to talk about herself. She debated trying to get more information out of the older woman, but decided it wasn't worth the trouble at this time.

"On Rhysia, the gods take an active interest in the mortal realms. When I offered my pledge to Frayrith, she sent her avatar as a sign she had accepted that pledge." Kyrianna held out her right wrist with the unicorn mark on it. "She marked me as one of her chosen."

Myrith's eyes widened a bit as she looked at the mark.

"What?" Kyrianna pulled her arm back close to her body.

"Nothing, it's just that the Overlord uses a unicorn as his symbol."

"Unicorns are usually associated with those who follow the deities of light; though they are also often used by elves in their personal symbols as well."

"The Overlord is an elf, though many believe his symbol is a variation of the one for the goddess he follows." Myrith kept her eyes on the doorway, not looking at Kyrianna.

"Do you know the name of this goddess?"

"No. Her name has never been revealed. Lord Lavial and those who follow her only refer to her as 'The Lady'."

Kyrianna nodded as she recalled all the entries in her mother's journals that only referred to Thynitic as 'The Lady.' After a few seconds, she looked back at Myrith. "Have you ever seen this Lord Lavial?"

"Very few people have ever seen the Overlord. It is rumored he has hair and eyes as black as the darkest night. Many of those who serve him also have black hair and eyes."

"Midnight Elves have black hair and black eyes," Kyrianna whispered.

"I doubt there's any connection," Myrith said.

"It's just another puzzle, isn't it?" Kyrianna smiled.

Myrith frowned and turned her attention back to the doorway. Kyrianna realized she wasn't going to get any further conversation out of the woman and leaned back against the wall, her sword resting on her lap as she watched Myrith and listened to the sounds of her companions sleeping. She suppressed a laugh as Etewyn started snoring and Hendandra woke, sat up and threw a small rock at him. He rolled over without waking and the girl grinned as she caught Kyrianna's eyes before laying back down.

~ * ~

The group was quiet as they gathered their equipment and prepared to descend further into the depths of the temple. As Myrith and Etewyn slid the statue they moved the night before back into place, Kyrianna nocked an arrow to her bowstring and held it ready as the fountain opened.

The stairs descended into darkness and she found herself straining to listen to any sounds that might come from that darkness. A slight rustling of air was all she heard as she glanced toward Myrith and nodded. "I'll take the rear," Kyrianna said, shouldering her bow and drawing her swords. The older woman raised an eyebrow then nodded once as she unsheathed her sword and headed down the stairs.

They found themselves on a stone stair in what appeared to be a large cavern. The stairs were rough, as if hewn from the rock of the cavern itself. The blackness of the room seemed to absorb the light from their torches as they descended deeper and deeper.

"Hold for a moment," Kyrianna said. She waited as the rest of the group stopped moving.

"What's wrong?" Myrith called.

"Thought I heard something," Kyrianna said.

"Starting to hear things," Hendandra muttered. "That's twice now, not a good sign."

"Hush!" Myrith said.

Kyrianna paused and listened carefully. There was a rustling from the shadows overhead and she frowned as several darker shapes moved in the shadows. Several high-pitched squeaks sounded as more shadows moved and a group of bat-winged imps soared down over the group.

"In the shadows, above us," Kyrianna said. "Chaos imps. Their claws and stingers contain a poison, which causes the person struck to become confused and disoriented. Not a good thing to have happen at any time, but even more of a concern considering where we are." She glanced over the side of the stairs at the seemingly endless blackness that would swallow any who fell into it.

"We should get moving," Myrith said. "Everyone stay alert."

Kyrianna hung back as the others started moving down the stairs putting some distance between her and Hendandra in front of her. She wanted room to fight if the imps attacked them and didn't want to have to worry about hitting the smaller girl. The imps appeared to be ignoring them as they continued. She held her swords ready as she continued to scan the darkness above her.

"Head's up," she yelled as several of the imps screeched and dove at the group. Hendandra ducked as two of the imps flew past her, their claws extended as they flew at Kyrianna.

She brought her blades up and blocked the first attack, swinging her short sword as they passed. Her momentum, combined with the force she put into the swing, caused her to spin around. "Chaos take it," she muttered as she fought to regain her balance. The sword Bukon had given her was about half the weight of a normal blade, and she had put the same power into the swing she would have with a normal blade.

Kyrianna planted her right foot as she started to slide toward the edge, fighting to keep from falling. One of the imps turned sharply and came back at her. As she swung her swords again, it grabbed at the short sword knocking it from her grasp. The glowing green metal rang with a clear bell-like tone as it slid down the stairs. She dropped to the stone as her balance grew even more precarious and grabbed hold of the carved surface to keep from falling.

"Kyrianna?" Bukon's voice echoed in the cavern as the imps returned to the darkness of the ceiling.

"Still here," she said. "Though only barely," she whispered. She sheathed her long sword then unshouldered her bow as she stood and again began scanning the area.

"Good, I have your sword," Bukon said.

"Thank…." Her reply was cut short as two of the imps swooped down on the group. This time toward the front of the line and Kyrianna saw a flash of bright red hair as Myrith dodged the aerial attack. She drew an arrow and fired. Her shot glanced off one of the creatures as it returned to the upper levels of the cavern.

Hendandra turned and held out the short sword, a grin on her face. "Myrith says you need to hang on to this better," she said.

Kyrianna laughed as she took the sword and sheathed it. "Thanks."

~ * ~

"Hey, some of us aren't as long as the rest of you," Hendandra called after the group had resumed moving down the stairs. "Can we slow it just a bit?"

Kyrianna grabbed the girl's shoulder as she stumbled.

"Thanks," Hendandra said.

"I want off these stairs and onto solid ground as quickly as possible," Myrith called. "We don't need to risk losing anyone, the way the Rangerette almost lost her sword."

"And, if I fall because of trying to keep up with you trees, what then?" Hendandra paused for a moment and massaged her right calf.

"If it'll make you feel better, I can tie a rope around you," Kyrianna whispered.

Hendandra glared at her for a moment then hurried to catch up with the others.

It was almost an hour before the darkness of the cavern gave way to a hazy overcast sky. They didn't really seem to emerge from the cavern into an open area; it was more like the scene had changed. Kyrianna took a deep breath as she stepped off the stair and looked around. There were none of the normal scents of the forest or earth and the air was stale and musty.

"What is it?" Myrith looked at her, concern on her face.

"Something's not right here," Kyrianna said.

"You're just now figuring that out," Hendandra said with a laugh.

Kyrianna grinned. "More so than what we've already seen. This place feels artificial—not real. The light doesn't have the warmth or life of a true sun. It's almost as if this place was created to be a twisted reflection of somewhere else." She looked around at the mushroom stalks that surrounded them like the trees of Kilenter forest and shook her head. "I don't like this place; it's an aberration of nature."

"Which way do we go from here?" Falden looked from her to Myrith and back.

"One way seems about the same as the other." Myrith turned back to Kyrianna. "What do you suggest, Rangerette?"

Kyrianna looked around for several minutes, studying the giant mushrooms and the other vegetation. She sighed and shook her head as the glanced around at the group. "Perhaps Talon could give us a brief aerial recon of the area. Otherwise, I have no clue how to read directions in this?" She gestured at the mushroom stalks.

The mage concentrated for a moment, then held out his arm as Talon flew down and landed on it. He stared at the hawk for a moment then raised his arm as Talon took to the air again. The hawk slowly flew in increasingly larger circles before he dove at something on the ground.

Falden shook his head a couple of times then turned his attention to Myrith. "There is a large body of water in that direction." He pointed behind Myrith as the hawk flew back and landed on his shoulder.

"Falden, may I see his prey, please?" Kyrianna held her hand out.

The hawk squawked and dropped the small creature into her hand.

"It appears to be a mouse of some kind, but it has reptilian eyes and scales." She handed the rodent back to the hawk. "Another aberration."

"Let's get going," Myrith said. "What do you think about heading toward this body of water, Rangerette?"

"Works for me." Kyrianna picked up her pack, glanced at Myrith then headed off in the direction Falden had indicated. She took several steps then turned and smiled at Myrith. "If no one has any objections, that is."

Both Myrith and Falden laughed as they gathered their gear. The woman's laugh was light and had a brightness to it that reminded her of her mother's laugh, while Falden's laugh was deep and seemed to echo throughout the area. Kyrianna looked at him and shook her head. With his soft voice, she would never have suspected Falden of having such a laugh. This was the type of laugh she would have expected from Etewyn.

"Lead on." Myrith motioned the others to follow.

Kyrianna drew the glowing, green sword and took a deep breath as she scanned the ground for any signs of a possible trail through the forest of mushroom stalks. She felt her heart start to race as she realized this was her first true assignment since her failure for the guild. And that failure didn't count anymore. *I was set up by that bastard Silvis*, she thought as she finally settled on a path and headed deeper into the shadows.

She wasn't counting the four people she had guided to the Dragon Flame Mountains either. She had grown up in Nydith and Kilenter both, finding a known trail really wasn't the challenge this was. Here she was responsible for finding the way and making sure her companions were safe. It was something she would not fail at.

Chapter Ten

Kyrianna paused and glanced back at the others. Myrith was watching her, the slight scowl, which seemed to be a permanent feature, on her face. Bukon was standing near the older woman and though he turned his attention to the mushroom stalks surrounding them, she had seen he was watching her also. She had no doubts Myrith was concerned about trusting her and she doubted the woman would ever truly trust anyone other than herself. That was an attitude she could recognize and understand, even if she didn't know the reasons for it.

Kyrianna shook her head to clear it then scanned the ground again, looking for any signs of tracks. There were none she could find, so she continued toward the lake.

"Let's find a place to take a break," Myrith called as they entered a small clearing after what felt like several hours.

"This place should work as well as any other," Kyrianna said as she checked the area. "I find no evidence of any large creatures using this area."

"Good," Hendandra said as she dropped to the ground. She opened her pack and began rummaging through it. "Traveler's Biscuits." She broke off a piece of the hard bread and glared at it. "Anyone else have anything actually worth eating?"

"Sorry, but that appears to be all that's left of our rations, little one," Etewyn said as everyone checked their packs.

"Maybe the mushrooms are edible," Falden said with a grin.

Etewyn nodded then drew his knife and sliced a piece off the nearest stalk.

"Etewyn, don't!" Kyrianna darted toward him as he took a bite. She knocked the remainder of the plant from his hand.

"Many types of mushrooms are poisonous, you idiot," Bukon said drawing a potion vial from a pouch. "Here, a potion to neutralize poison, just in case."

"Since he has already swallowed the substance, I believe we should wait and see if there are any adverse effects," Falden said.

"I agree," Etewyn said holding up his hand. "If it's not poisoned, then we can eat it."

"Speak for yourself," Hendandra said. She began nibbling on the hard bread she was holding and frowned. "I'll stick with what I know is safe, even if it is hard enough to use as ammunition for a sling."

"Where's your sense of adventure?" Etewyn asked smiling at Hendandra.

"My sense of adventure is considerably weaker than my sense of self-preservation, thank you. Remember the only reason I am here at all is because I was sent here against my will and I agreed to work with the rest of you in finding a way home. Which, by the way, it really doesn't look like we are making any progress toward. Though once we do, I still expect to be paid for this little adventure." She looked at Falden. "I've broken one set of lock picks and you did agree to replace damaged equipment."

"Ah, but that agreement was for a different contract," Falden said. "We have no such agreement in this place."

Hendandra muttered something under her breath as she turned her attention back to her food.

"The Moon Swords told us they have access to several portals that can probably get us home," Myrith said. "If we are able to assist them in recovering the artifact they are looking for, then they will able to allow us access to those portals."

"I know, I know. It just seems like we are moving blind through this place with no idea where to look for this artifact."

"We all want to return to our homes," Falden said placing a hand on Hendandra's shoulder. "I'm sure it is just a matter of time before we are able to get back."

Kyrianna turned away at Falden's mention of returning home. She wanted to go back, but knew she still wouldn't be able to go home.

"We're all tired," Myrith said after a few minutes. "Perhaps we should find a place to camp for the night."

"I don't think we're more than about thirty minutes from the lake Talon spotted," Kyrianna said turning back to face the others. "We can probably find a place to camp near there."

"Before we decide anything, we need to wait and see if Etewyn is going to be okay," Bukon said. "I still think you should drink this and be thankful it didn't affect you instantly." He held the potion vial back out.

Etewyn looked at Hendandra who nodded. "Okay," he said as he took the vial. "However, I still feel fine." He drank the liquid and handed the now empty vial back.

"When everyone is ready, we can continue," Myrith said.

Kyrianna stood apart from the group, her back to the clearing as she leaned against one of the larger mushroom stalks. The unnatural feel of this place increased as she glanced up at the sky. The hazy light had never changed in intensity nor had the temperature or feel of the air. However, every so often the haze would burst into swirling colors then fade back into the gray overcast. She missed the soft green light that filtered through the overhead canopy of Kilenter along with the normal smells and sounds of the forest.

"You okay?" Myrith spoke softly.

"It's nothing," Kyrianna said.

"Doesn't look like nothing."

"I said it was nothing."

Kyrianna started to walk away, but Myrith grabbed her elbow.

"I consider the safety of everyone here my responsibility," Myrith said. "If you're upset, you might miss things when you're trying to guide us through this place and that puts everyone in danger. That makes your nothing into something. Now, what's going on?"

"I was just feeling homesick, leave me alone!"

"I'm sorry about that; however anything that affects this group and its possible safety, I need to know about. Do I have your word you'll tell me when those conditions are a consideration in how something is affecting you?"

Kyrianna looked up at Myrith and nodded. "You do."

"Good. Now, get yourself together so you don't get lost trying to find this *large* lake."

Kyrianna nodded, drew her sword and headed back into the forest of giant mushrooms.

~ * ~

"Nice estimate on the time," Myrith said as the group stood on the open ground between where the forest ended and the edge of the lake.

"Thanks," Kyrianna said.

Myrith looked up at the sky. "It still hasn't changed."

"Except for those bursts of color," Bukon said. "Have you noticed they are similar to what you and Kyrianna described as the portals that brought you here?"

"Thynitic," Kyrianna whispered.

"Why do you say that?" Myrith looked at her and frowned.

"You saw the symbol and the painting. The chaos portal is Her chosen symbol," Kyrianna said. "The appearances of the colors in the sky indicate She has some sort of connection to this place. Something beyond just having been worshipped here at one time." Kyrianna stared at the sky.

She shook her head then grinned as she glanced out over the water before she turned to Myrith. "Your turn," she said. "Though it may be a little too far to swim." She pointed toward a group of islands near the horizon.

"Was that a challenge?" Myrith grinned at her.

"I suggest we send a couple of people to scout in each direction," Bukon said interrupting. "Take approximately an hour, then return here. Kyrianna and I, and perhaps Hendandra and Etewyn."

Kyrianna started to refuse then took a couple of deep breaths and nodded her agreement.

Hendandra tapped Etewyn on the elbow and nodded her agreement as well. "We'll go that way," she said pointing to the left of the lake. "You guys can take the other direction."

"That's fine," Bukon said. "Let's go."

~ * ~

"If it's not too forward of me to ask, what's the deal between Hendandra and Etewyn?" Kyrianna waited until she and Bukon were out of earshot of the others before speaking.

"Nothing really," Bukon said. "Etewyn is about as bright as a rock, but he's got a good heart. As you saw with the mushroom—if you tell him to do something, he will do it without hesitation. He also has a tendency to jump into things without thinking. Hendandra has appointed herself as his babysitter. She keeps him out of trouble and he protects her." He paused and pointed to a scuffed area on the ground several yards in front of them.

"Several humans or human type creatures," Kyrianna said as she walked slowly around the area. "The area is too disturbed to get a count." She paused and knelt on the ground, her hand brushed some dried vegetation from the tracks. "It looks like they headed off in this direction." She stood up, brushed the dust off her pants and continued following the tracks along the shore of the lake.

She stopped and pointed to a depression in the mud of the bank. "I would say they came ashore there," she said.

"Let's proceed a little further, then we'll go back," Bukon said.

Kyrianna nodded then turned her attention back to the tracks. About fifteen minutes later, they came to another disturbed area.

"Looks like the remains of a camp," Bukon said. "Probably a fishing camp." He pointed to a pile of fish heads and guts.

"I find it interesting that nothing has disturbed the remains," Kyrianna said. She glanced up, scanning the sky and frowned. "No signs of any birds." She walked around the pile. "No signs of any scavengers or predators, either." she continued to walk around the camp.

"Fishing party," Kyrianna said. "Came ashore to clean their catch and rest before returning home." She looked out at the lake and the islands in the distance.

Bukon paused at a large fire pit, knelt down, pulled out a dagger and began sifting through the remains. "This appears to be a regular camp for these people, whoever they are," he said.

"So where did they come from?" Kyrianna asked. "Something doesn't quite make sense; they came ashore back there and moved to camp here. The shoreline here appears no different from where they put in. And, the area there is not significantly different than here."

"You noted nothing had touched the remains of the fish. There may be things we are unaware of. If they fish these waters regularly, they will know about local hazards which we don't."

Kyrianna nodded. "Let's get back," she finally said.

~ * ~

"You're late," Myrith said glaring at Kyrianna as she and Bukon came back.

"We found evidence of civilization," Bukon said. "A fishing camp and it was used recently." He went on to explain about the remains of the fish and fire.

"Anything else?" Myrith asked.

"It was approximately a fifteen minute walk from where they

came ashore to where they camped. I could see no obvious reason for why they would have put that kind of distance between the two areas," Kyrianna said. "What about Hendandra and Etewyn?"

"Nothing," the Myrith said. "We'll go in the direction you tried. At least there you found evidence of possible habitation."

"It's getting late," Hendandra said. "Perhaps we should wait till morning."

"How can you tell what time it is?" Kyrianna looked from Hendandra to the hazy sky and back.

"I'm basing it more on how I feel than any true measure of the actual time," Hendandra said.

"I agree," Myrith said. "We should make camp and get some rest before continuing."

"Also, it is possible night will fall suddenly and I don't relish the idea of trying to move through unknown territory in the dark," Bukon said.

Kyrianna nodded. "In that case we should move away from the water," she said looking around. "We don't know anything about what creatures might inhabit the lake." She walked over to the shoreline and dipped her hand into the water. She sniffed the water then cautiously tasted it. "Fresh not salt. This could be the primary water source for this area, and may draw dangerous creatures in from the forest as a result."

"I'll leave the choice of a camp to you," Myrith said.

Kyrianna studied the ground for a moment then moved from the water to the *tree* line and back several times before starting down a narrow path. She paused at a small clearing then moved slowly around the perimeter. "No signs of anything using this area. No recently used trails in or out. This should work," she finally said.

"Watches will be three hours, two people each," Myrith said. "Kyrianna, Etewyn and I will be the primary on each watch."

"I'll stand with Etewyn," Hendandra said.

"I'll stand with Kyri," Bukon said.

"That leaves you with me," Falden said with a grin.

Chapter Eleven

"Falden," Kyrianna said after the group moved back to the lake. "Can Talon reach those islands and return without problems, or do you think it's too far for him?" She turned to face the mage.

Falden's eyes lost focus for several minutes before the hawk launched himself into the air and started toward the islands.

"Apparently, he thinks he can," Falden said. His eyes followed the path of the hawk closely and several furrows appeared on his brow.

"Hawks aren't stupid," Kyrianna said placing a hand on Falden's shoulder. "He knows what he has the strength to do."

"The islands appear to be closer to the right shoreline," Bukon said. "If we begin moving in that direction, we might be able to save him some distance when he returns.

Myrith glanced toward Falden.

"Okay." Falden's voice was barely audible as he continued to stare out across the water.

"Rangerette, this is the way you and Bukon went yesterday, I believe you two should take the lead," Myrith said.

Kyrianna nodded as she headed off along the shoreline.

~ * ~

"Still hasn't been touched by anything," Kyrianna said poking at the pile of fish heads and guts with her sword. This just isn't right."

"What?" Myrith looked at the pile.

"We have no idea how long this has been here and there is no sign of anything having approached it. There aren't even any of the normal insects that feed on rotting flesh. Something's not right." Kyrianna turned around and looked up at the older woman and frowned.

"I find it hard to believe there are no predators or scavengers in this place," Kyrianna said. "We have seen evidence of prey animals—the rodent Talon caught. If there are no predators to control them, this place would be crawling with the creatures."

"I agree," Myrith said. "There is something unnatural about this place. We should get going." She turned and glanced toward the shoreline. Falden was standing there staring toward the islands. "Falden?" She called.

"He is telling me he needs to rest," Falden said without turning around. "It was longer than he thought."

Myrith placed a hand on Falden's shoulder. "Is he in a safe location?"

"He thinks so."

"Then thank him and tell him to rest."

Falden nodded. "He found humans on the biggest island." He pointed to the island nearest the shore. "There."

"Now, all we need to do is find a way to get there," Myrith said.

"Why?" Hendandra looked around at the others. "We can just rest here until the hawk is ready to come back, then go back to the temple."

"We agreed to help the Moon Swords find the artifact," Myrith said.

"There is no reason to believe the artifact is on that island." Hendandra put her hands on her hips and glared at Myrith. "And, all we're doing is moving further away from where the Moon Swords are based. That doesn't make any sense. I say we head back. They may have even found that so-called artifact and we can go back to our homes *now*, instead of continuing to wander around lost in this place."

"The little one has a point," Etewyn said. "We did agree to work together to find a way out of here."

"And, we are. Do you want to take over leadership of this group?" Myrith looked down at the Hendandra. "Does anyone?" She looked at the others.

"You're right Hendandra," Kyrianna said. "We have no real reason to believe the artifact or any information about it is on the island. However, we also have no reason to believe it is not. We have found nothing to give us any clues to follow. Myrith has led us this far, I will abide by her decision in this."

"As no one wanted to claim leadership of this group, I say we check out the islands," Myrith said. "Now, we need to find a way to get to the island. If there are people there, perhaps they have information on this artifact or even on a way out of here."

"I have seen very little wood here, certainly not enough to make a raft." Kyrianna kicked at a piece of driftwood that crumbled. She looked toward a group of the giant mushrooms. "I wonder if those will float."

Etewyn drew his sword and headed into the forest. "Be right back," he said.

"You idiot," Hendandra said. "Did you forget he takes things so literally? Now, we have to go looking for him."

"Give him a few minutes," Bukon said. "Etewyn is capable of protecting himself, and we have seen nothing to suggest any dangerous predators in this area."

Myrith drew her own sword and started toward the forest after Etewyn. "I don't like the idea of anyone going off on their own. We'll stay together and go find him."

Before the others could join her, the sound of something crashing came from the forest, followed by Etewyn dragging a large mushroom back to the group. "Floats," he said after tossing it into the water.

"I guess that answers that question," Kyrianna said with a laugh. "Now we have to hope they can hold our gear and us. We need to find at least two, maybe three that are large enough to turn into canoe type boats."

"There were several very large ones in the stand there," Etewyn said pointing to the area he had come from.

"You and I can get them," Myrith said. "Kyrianna, you stay here and keep watch."

Kyrianna nodded as she drew her swords.

~ * ~

"Anyone ever make or see one of these made," Kyrianna said as she walked around the mushroom logs Myrith and Etewyn had brought back. Both were reasonably large and she noted one of them had removed the cap to show the top of the stalk was closed.

"You're the one with the wilderness training, not us," Hendandra said.

"Then, I guess I get to do both of them. The rest of you might as well relax; this is going to take some time." She drew her dagger and carefully began digging a shallow depression in the top of one of the logs. She glanced at Myrith, who also had a dagger in her hand, as did Bukon. "The idea is to hollow out the center, leaving the sides and ends along with a solid bottom to support those in the canoe. We need to work slowly as we don't know anything about these things."

"Uh, while you guys are carving, Etewyn and I will go look for something to use as oars."

"Don't go far and stay together," Myrith called.

~ * ~

"Where are those two," Myrith said looking toward the forest. "We've been done for almost an hour."

"Maybe she found her portal home," Falden said.

"Hey, I would come back and tell you if I found the way home," Hendandra said coming up behind the mage. Etewyn stood behind her holding several oars.

"Found back where the boat came ashore," Hendandra said. "They were stored in a hidden room near the largest of the dunes."

"Was there anything else?" Myrith asked.

"Not really. There were some foodstuffs, but I left those as it looked like they were set aside as an emergency store."

"Okay."

Kyrianna looked up from where she was rubbing the inside of one of the canoes with a handful of cloths. "We should still test one of these before we put all of us in them."

"Since I'm probably the heaviest with my gear, I'll do it," Myrith said.

Kyrianna drew her dagger out and put a small hole in one end of the boat, near the top. She gathered up the rope Myrith had used to pull the stalk back with and threaded it through the hole. Once she was satisfied with the knot, she pushed the boat into the water.

Hendandra laughed when Myrith slipped and splashed water into the boat as she waded out. Etewyn stood behind Kyrianna as she held the rope and began playing it out slowly as Myrith began paddling.

Several feet from the shoreline, Myrith placed the oar on the bottom of the boat and stood up. She took a deep breath then jumped several times. The boat rocked in protest, but didn't appear to lose any buoyancy.

"Okay bring it back," Kyrianna called.

"No problems," Myrith said as she stepped out of the canoe.

"It seems to be solid; although paddling will get tiresome. I suggest we divide the weight as evenly as possible between the two boats, with Bukon and I paddling in the first boat; Kyrianna and Etewyn in the second."

"I'm riding in the boat with Etewyn," Hendandra said picking up her pack.

"Falden be in our boat as well, considering the weight of your equipment," Kyrianna said.

Falden nodded, his eyes still focused on the islands.

Kyrianna followed Falden's gaze. "Has he communicated anything else?"

"No."

"He's probably sleeping," Kyrianna said. "Let's get going. You can call him when we get closer to the island."

The two groups stayed close together, as they paddled out into the lake.

After several hours, a shriek pierced the air and Talon swooped down to land on Falden's shoulder.

Falden reached up to stroke the breast feathers of his familiar and smiled as the bird nipped at his ear.

"Rangerette," Myrith called as she pointed to a small wooden pier stretching out from the shore.

Kyrianna nodded her understanding.

The group climbed out of the boats and looked around. Kyrianna took a long deep breath and smiled and she stood on the pier. "This is more natural," she said. She paused and glanced behind Myrith. "We have company," she said.

Myrith turned around, her hand reaching for her sword. She stopped as Kyrianna placed a hand on her shoulder. "This is their home, we are outsiders. Be cautious, but let them make the first move," she whispered.

Myrith nodded as an older man stepped out of the group of men. "Well met," she said.

"Well met," the man said holding his hands out. "Are you here to help us?"

Myrith paused before she spoke. "We are here with a group working to cleanse the temple of the evil that has invaded it. They are also searching for something they call the Artifact of Order and Chaos."

"Then our paths may run together," the man said. "Come

with us and we will see you are fed. Then we will tell you about the evil from the temple as well as the artifact you search for." He gestured to a path leading to a small town.

Chapter Twelve

Kyrianna watched as Myrith kept her hand close to her sword as they were escorted through the small town. The older man stopped in front of a well-kept tavern and opened the door as he waved them into the brightly lit room.

Myrith hesitated in the doorway and Kyrianna frowned slightly as she looked at her. There was anger and something else in her face—fear. Myrith's hand rested on the hilt of her sword and she locked her gaze on the back of the man who was leading them through the crowded tavern.

One of the patrons pinched one of the servers on her rear and the girl slapped his hand away. Kyrianna caught her breath as she realized Myrith had stopped and started to draw her sword, before taking a deep breath and continuing.

Hendandra drifted back to where Kyrianna followed behind Myrith. "Did you catch the name of this place?"

Kyrianna looked at her and smiled. "The Dancing Unicorn," she said. "I'll take it as a good omen." Her fingers rested for a moment on the unicorn symbol she wore.

"Good day Mister Mayor," the young man behind the bar said nodding to their escort. "I will be with you in a few minutes."

"No hurry, Sven. Please have dinner prepared for my guests on the council's tab. We will be in the back room when you get caught up."

"Of course. Gillian, you and Sonja tell the cook to prepare the meals. Have drinks delivered as well."

"One other thing," the mayor said. "Have a runner fetch Ravlian."

"Tomas," Sven called.

A young boy near the door stood up. "On it," he called as he darted out the door.

Kyrianna smiled as the young man looked at them and winked.

"When you get to it, I'll take a Sven Surprise," one of the female patrons called.

"How big do you want it," the barman called back.

Kyrianna turned and glanced again at the young man behind the bar, letting herself appreciate his appearance. He was well built with shoulder length blonde hair and a warm smile that reflected itself in his dark brown eyes. It was the kind of smile that was genuine in its warmth. The type of smile both mother and brother had.

Hendandra took a seat next to Kyrianna at the long table in the room the mayor led them to. Only their group and the mayor remained in the room when the doors closed and Kyrianna noted Myrith sitting where she could watch the mayor and the door. Bukon was also seated where he could observe the door and the rest of the group.

"About the temple and the artifact?" Myrith's voice seemed to echo in the silence of the room.

"Ah, yes, the temple…." The doors opened again and Sven and the two women he had told to see to the dinners entered carrying several platters of food and drink.

One of the servers came around with the drinks. "Two Sven Surprises," she said as she sat glasses in front of Hendandra and Kyrianna.

"Thank you," Kyrianna whispered. She felt her face grow warm as the girl let her lips brush across the tip of her ear. There was a pause and she heard a small, sudden inhalation of breath from the girl before she took a slow step back.

It wasn't until the servers exited the room that the mayor started speaking again. "You said you are here about the evil inhabiting the temple. It is an ancient evil brought here from another land by those who worshipped the one who embodies chaos in its darkest forms. They built the temple to honor their dark goddess, one who takes joy in chaos and pain. Under her influence pockets of chaos moved across the land changing it in unexpected ways. The followers of chaos held sway for many centuries. Then a group called the Moon Swords came to find a secure place for an artifact they called the Artifact of Order and Chaos. They used the powers of this artifact to restore order to this island. And those of us who had been mere slaves under the rule of the others were given what should have been a safe haven. They created a planar shield that was supposed to prevent anyone from being able to enter this realm unless they came through one of the portals guarded by the Moon Swords."

"It would appear the shield has failed," Falden said.

"Anyone who thought the magic of a group of mortals would prevent the minions of a goddess from returning here if they desired was a fool." The mayor spat on the floor. "Now, there is a powerful demon who has managed to breach the shield and is bringing more agents of chaos into this realm. They are also seeking this artifact."

"We have encountered several demons and imps in our travels here," Myrith said.

"Their numbers are growing." The mayor paused as the door opened again. A middle-aged man with a neatly trimmed black beard and a dark blue robe entered the room, followed by the two previous servers with more drinks.

"Ah, here you are, Ravlian. Please take a seat. I was filling our guests in on a bit of the history of the temple."

The new arrival only nodded as he took a seat at the far end of the table. Kyrianna looked away as his gaze seemed to lock on her. She nodded as one of the girls reached over her shoulder to put another cup in front of her. The girl's hand brushed her hair for a moment then she left.

"Ravlian has learned the demon calling and controlling the others has moved from the great temple to one of the smaller ones on the island south and east of us." He paused as the server leaned forward to hand him a drink and whispered something.

The mayor's head jerked up to stare at Kyrianna. Myrith also turned to look in her direction then turned her attention to Ravlian.

"What is this?" The mayor stared at Kyrianna. "You claim to be working with those who say they are seeking a way to prevent the returning chaos, yet you bring one of those who follow chaos with you."

Kyrianna pushed her chair back and stood quickly as Hendandra tried to grab her arm. "I do not follow the Lady of Chaos," she said. "You don't know me; you are making assumptions based on things you have no knowledge of."

"Kyrianna, sit down!" Myrith stood up and took a step toward her.

Hendandra placed a hand on Kyrianna's arm and forced her to turn toward her. "These people are not your enemy," she said. "You yourself have commented on the state this land is in."

Kyrianna stared at Hendandra for a moment then sat back

down. She kept her eyes locked on the table, refusing to look up at Ravlian who was still watching her.

"You ask us to help you then you verbally attack one of our group," Myrith said. "If it were not that our causes seem to follow the same path, we would leave now."

"I will not apologize. If you knew what our people suffered under the whips of those who followed chaos, you would never have brought her here."

"I would be curious to know how it is the elf knows exactly which goddess we have been speaking of," Ravlian said in a harsh gravelly voice. "None here have mentioned her by name, yet your companion knew she was called the Lady of Chaos. I find this most interesting."

Kyrianna felt Hendandra's grip on her arm tighten and she took a breath before speaking. "I am from a land where Thynitic, the Lady of Chaos, is known and worshipped. However, that does not mean I worship her, only that I know of her."

The mayor turned his attention to Myrith. "I will have your bond for her behavior. If she causes any trouble or does anything even remotely related to Thynitic, it will be you who answers for it!"

Myrith glanced at Kyrianna then turned back to the mayor and nodded. "I will be bond for her behavior. There will be no issues, you have my word on it," she said.

Kyrianna offered Myrith a weak smile, then touched the unicorn medallion she wore. "My word on it," she whispered.

Myrith gave her a slight nod to indicate she understood.

"What can you tell us about this artifact?" Bukon looked from the mayor to Ravlian.

"The Artifact of Order and Chaos," Ravlian said. "It is an ancient artifact created in another land. It was brought here to keep it away from those who followed the Lady of Chaos. It is rumored the power of the artifact is what maintains the balance between Order and Chaos and if it is controlled by one side or the other balance will be lost and Chaos will be unleashed."

"Even if the powers of Order controlled it?" Kyrianna stared at Ravlian.

"Even if. Without balance, Chaos will be able to assert itself over the powers of Order...,"

"No!" Myrith interrupted. "It is Order that keeps the balance, Chaos cannot be the more powerful."

Ravlian smiled. "It is not a matter of being more powerful, but the basic nature of Order and Chaos. If the balance is gone, Chaos is unleashed. If that happens Chaos can overcome Order."

"Even in Chaos there is a spark of Order. If balance is lost then that spark is destroyed," Kyrianna said. "At least that is what the Twilight Elves of my home believe."

"Interesting belief for those who very nature tends toward Chaos." Ravlian reached into his robes and pulled a slender silver wand out of an inner pocket. "I am willing to go with you to the temple as there is something there I wish to obtain. If you are willing to assist then I will pay for your assistance with this wand." He held the wand up.

"Anything of value that you find within the temple, other than what Ravlian is seeking, is yours to claim as well," the mayor said.

Myrith looked around the table. "Are there any objections?"

No one said anything.

"As you seem to be willing to travel to the island, I would recommend you get some rest and start fresh in the morning," the mayor said as he stood from the table. "If you need supplies, go to Farrell's. Arrangements have been made with him to charge reasonable supplies to the council." He locked his eyes with Myrith's. "I trust you not to abuse the privilege."

"My honor on it."

"Very good." The mayor headed for the door with Ravlian following him. "Oh, one other thing," he said turning back to face the group. "I suggest the elf not go anywhere alone. In fact it would be best if she stayed out of sight as much as possible and kept her ears completely hidden."

Bukon stood up and turned to face the mayor. "I've had enough of your insults toward our companion," he said.

"This is for her own protection. Many here have heard the stories about how our people were treated by hers all their lives. The hatred is still there and strong." He turned and left the room, closing the door behind him.

"What do you think?" Myrith asked after everyone had sat back down.

"I'm concerned about taking on anything that can break through a spell designed to protect this realm from the power of Thynitic," Kyrianna said.

Myrith nodded. "I understand your feelings; however we have been able to handle the creatures we have faced so far. I think we have a chance at defeating this demon as well. Plus, we will have another mage with us. That should help."

"Still, it will not be easy," Bukon said. "We should get a good rest tonight then see about supplying ourselves in the morning."

"Myrith, what about Ravlian if he starts causing problems for Kyrianna?" Hendandra looked up at Myrith.

"I'll deal with that if it becomes necessary." Myrith turned her attention to Kyrianna. "Just try to not provoke him, okay."

"I will do nothing to intentionally provoke him; however, I will not let his insults pass unchallenged either."

Kyrianna stood and headed for the door. "I'm going to see about getting a room. I swear I won't be out of it the rest of the night."

"I'm coming with you," Hendandra said. "I think we should only get two rooms and stay together tonight."

"Agreed," Myrith said.

Chapter Thirteen

"Are you okay?" Myrith placed a hand on Kyrianna's shoulder as they entered the room.

"I'll be fine. It has been a long time since I had to deal with that kind of outright hatred before. Because of my father's position, the most I usually ever had to deal with were the veiled looks and muttered comments. Granted, I knew how most humans truly felt about elves and half-elves, but I never had that hatred directed at me before—at least not in that manner." Kyrianna's voice was barely above a whisper as she spoke.

"Don't take this the wrong way, but I think you should leave your hair down when we leave tomorrow. Let's try to avoid any additional problems if we can."

Kyrianna nodded slowly then moved to stand at the window, ignoring the other women as they began checking their equipment and deciding what they wanted to get the next day. She continued to stare out the window for several minutes watching the occasional bursts of color that reminded her they might soon be facing a demon who served a powerful goddess. She glanced back at Myrith for a moment. She no longer had any doubts Thynitic had been responsible for bringing her here. And, if the Lady of Chaos wanted her here there was a reason for it. One she knew she would have to discover no matter how much the idea of doing so frightened her. Despite Myrith's lack of discussion regarding the events that brought her here, it seemed she had also been transported by the same magic, and that meant there was a good chance the goddess was interested in her as well.

She believed Hendandra when she claimed her three companions were here as a punishment for stealing from the temple of a goddess of their home and she had been a victim of a spell cast by Falden. But, if only she and Myrith were brought here by Thynitic what did the Lady of Chaos want with them? Why had she brought them here?

You are beginning to ask questions that are more appropriate than making the demands you previously did, the voice she now believed was

Thynitic's whispered in Kyrianna's mind. *Do not make the mistake of believing these people are truly your friends, for they will eventually turn on you just as your family did and just as the guild did. Did they not also act like they were your friends, showing concern and offering help? All they cared about was using you. You were a tool to them; a pawn and that's what you'll be to these people as well.*

You are asking questions and that means your mind is open, but I do not sense you are ready yet, so those questions will not be answered at this time.

Kyrianna shuddered as another brilliant burst of color appeared in the sky and the voice faded from her mind. "Frayrith guide me," she whispered.

"Rangerette," Myrith called. "You need to get some rest. Forget about what happened, it's not worth this much grief."

"You're right," Kyrianna said as she turned around.

"I'm a knight, a holy warrior of Geladas; I'm always right," Myrith said. "Now get some rest."

Kyrianna nodded as she dropped her backpack and bow on the empty bed. She unbuckled her sword belts and laid them on the bed before she sat down and started inventorying her supplies. She felt Myrith's eyes still on her when she finished checking her pack and finally lay back and closed her own eyes. Myrith was concerned, but she wasn't sure if was for her, about her or both.

~ * ~

"Good morning ladies," Falden's voice was followed by a light knock on the door.

Myrith sheathed her sword then opened the door. "Good morning," she said as the three men entered the room.

"If you are ready, we can go down and see about getting some breakfast," Bukon said. "Then we can get this demon hunt started and over with."

Hendandra laughed at his comment, but Kyrianna saw the scowl on Myrith's face deepen.

"This is not a situation to be joking about," Myrith said. "If what Ravlian and the mayor said is even close to true, this demon is a powerful minion of a goddess. This is no mere demon hunt." She turned and stormed out of the room.

"Someone needs to lighten up," Hendandra said as she grabbed her pack and followed Myrith out of the room.

"It is only that she considers the safety of everyone her responsibility," Kyrianna said as she buckled on her swords. "My father and brother are the same way when they're in charge of something. It is irritating but I would rather see her focused like this instead of seeing one us on the ground bleeding because we weren't serious about something."

"Maybe you should relax a little as well," Bukon said. "And, why are you hiding who you are?" He reached to push her hair away from her ears.

Kyrianna jerked her head away from his hand. "Myrith asked me to keep my ears hidden and I agreed," she said.

"So you give in to the prejudices of these idiots. You let them win. I would have thought you were the type to walk your own path, Kyrianna; not the path others laid out for you."

She stared at Bukon. He had no way of knowing about the mage she had met a decade ago; yet, his words echoed hers. "I walk my own path. However, that does not mean I will foolishly ignore the requests of others when they have reason to make them. I agreed to accept Myrith's leadership, as did you. It would only risk causing serious problems for all of us if I decided to flaunt my heritage. That's a risk I am not willing to take." She grabbed her bow and headed for the door.

Kyrianna paused when she saw Myrith standing on the landing waiting for them. The woman only looked at her as she walked past her.

She heard me, Kyrianna thought as she headed down the stairs. *And, she doesn't understand why I stood up for her like that. I wonder if anyone has ever taken her side before.*

One of the serving girls from the previous night pointed toward the back room as the group came down the stairs. "Breakfast has been laid out for you already," she said. "Laurel and I are also preparing travel packs for your group."

"Thank you," Myrith said tossing the server a gold coin.

"Everything is being paid for by the council," the server said as she held the coin up to toss it back.

"Then consider that a tip for the work you and your friend have done so far," Myrith said.

The woman nodded and dropped the coin into a small pouch before heading back into the kitchen.

The group sat in silence as they ate. It was several minutes before Myrith spoke. "So are we all agreed to help Ravlian?"

Everyone at the table nodded except Hendandra. "I'm only going along with this," she said, "because this may actually help us in getting home."

"I think that's something we already know," Myrith said.

Kyrianna looked up. "We should visit Farrell's as the mayor suggested. I would like to get a few more arrows," she said.

"Some potions of healing and those that neutralize poison would also be a good idea," Bukon said. "I'll ask Sven to send a message to the mayor and Ravlian to meet us there."

"If we're finished here," Myrith said as she stood up, "we can try to find this Farrell's."

There were seven bundles sitting on the bar as they left. "Trail rations and some other foods," Sven said handing one of the bundles to Myrith. "Farrell's is a block south of here on the other side of the street."

"Thank you," the Myrith said. She put the bundle into one of the pockets on the side of her pack and waited as the rest of the group also collected theirs.

Kyrianna tried to stay in the middle of the group as Myrith led them down the street. Even with her hair covering her ears, several people still stopped and glared at her as they passed.

"Damned elf!" The comment came from a group of people standing near the door of one of the stores they passed.

Kyrianna's hand went to her sword as Bukon moved to stand next to her.

"Kyrianna," he said softly. "You're the one who didn't want to provoke any problems. Don't do anything rash."

She forced herself to relax and focused her attention on Myrith's red hair as it bounced in front of her. *Never be ashamed of who you are,* her father's voice echoed in her memory. *There are many who are foolish enough to judge you on the basis of your heritage. They will try to make you believe you are inferior to them because you are not a true human or they will want to blame you for some perceived crime or injustice. Both are wrong! You are neither inferior nor superior to anyone else simply because of your heritage. Everyone must earn their own place in the world, based in their individual abilities. And those who want to blame you for actions those of your heritage may have taken against their ancestors in the past are also wrong. While we should always strive to learn from the past, there is no place in the present for trying to punish the ghosts of the past. You are not responsible for the actions of those who came before you—only your own. Those that try to blame you for the past are only prolonging and deepening the hatred and prejudices that harm us all.*

Her father had given her that speech after the first time she had gone to the market with her mother and had wandered off to listen to a minstrel playing on one of the corners. He had been telling a tale about the Chaos War and the creation of Pyremar's Waste. Several of the other bystanders had spotted her in the crowd and had begun calling insults until her mother arrived. While the harassment had stopped, no one there apologized, although a couple of people had acknowledged the Lady Arielle.

That was the only time she had had to face the hatred humans had for those of elven blood that directly. At least it was the only time before this one. She shook her head slightly and took a deep breath as the group entered a large store.

Kyrianna found herself drawn to an elegant bow hanging on the wall. The black wood gleamed with bluish highlights, reminding her of the Rynial elves of her home.

"You have an excellent eye."

Kyrianna turned to see a middle-aged man standing behind her. "I'm Farrell," he said. He frowned slightly as he seemed to study her then nodded. "The bow is left over from those who once ruled this land and it takes a strong person to wield it properly."

"It does appear to be of outstanding workmanship, however I have a bow crafted by a master arms maker and do not wish to replace it at this time. I do need to restock my supply of arrows."

"Of course." The proprietor bowed slightly. "If you will follow me." He led her to an area filled with various quivers and arrows. "I assume you prefer the same quality of craftsmanship in your arrows as your bow?"

Kyrianna smiled and nodded. "Any archer wants the best they can afford. However, as this is on someone else's tab rather than my own, I prefer to keep the cost reasonable."

Farrell raised an eyebrow then grinned. "I have the perfect compromise then." He reached into the stack and pulled out a couple of small quivers.

Kyrianna drew one of the arrows and examined it carefully. The quality was comparable to the ones she had obtained from her uncle before she had left home. "These will do nicely," she said taking the quivers.

"Was there anything else?" Farrell glanced around the store.

Kyrianna followed his gaze to see several other workers also helping the rest of group with their purchases. "Potions of healing?"

"The council has authorized you to have five," he said placing the vials on the counter.

Kyrianna picked up the vials and dropped them into one of her belt pouches. "I believe that is all I have need for. Thank you." She moved to stand by the door as she waited for the rest to finish with their purchases. She frowned as she realized at least one of the store workers or Farrell was where she was under their observation constantly.

So, the personal attention from the owner was only so he could make sure I didn't cause any problems, Kyrianna thought. She made sure she stayed well away from anything easily pocketed as she waited for the others.

Kyrianna shook her head slightly as Myrith came over, a look of concern on her face as she glanced back at Farrell. "It's nothing," Kyrianna said.

Myrith didn't say anything; only glancing toward the door as the mayor and Ravlian entered the shop.

Farrell quickly tallied the group's purchases and handed a paper to the mayor. The elder gentleman glanced at it then smiled. "My thanks for your restraint," he said to Myrith.

Myrith nodded then looked around at the others. "Whenever you are ready," she said after a moment.

"Follow me." Ravlian turned and strode out the door; his powerful stride making a lie of the age in his voice.

Ravlian led them through the town, but not back in the direction they had originally arrived in. "Excuse me," Bukon said as they reached the edge of the town and started down a narrow path. "Isn't the dock in the other direction?"

Ravlian didn't pause his stride. "There are three main docks on this island," he said. "The one you arrived at, another on the southern end of the island; used primarily by the fishing boats, and a smaller dock opposite yours. As this one is closer to the island we wish to go to, we will use it." He gestured to a small dock at the base of a crumbling cliff.

Kyrianna stepped in front of Ravlian as she surveyed the path. It was steep and rocky—not the type of path she would have wanted to lead this group down. The pier appeared to be treading water in the calm of the sheltered cove.

"Excuse me." Ravlian pushed past Kyrianna and started down the path.

Kyrianna watched him for a few seconds. "I advise moving cautiously," she said as Myrith stood next to her. "The path doesn't seem to be very stable. Maybe we should wait and see how he does before we head down."

"I will not dignify that remark by commenting on it," Myrith said. She glanced down the path again. "You're the one with the appropriate training. What's your recommendation?"

Kyrianna watched Ravlian for a few more seconds. "As the one with the most equipment, you should go first. I would put Etewyn in the back as an anchor in case the path gives way. I want approximately ten feet between people and a rope tying us off. I'll go after you, with Falden next then, Bukon, Hendandra and finally Etewyn. If the path is going to give way, odds are it will do so with you. I'm fairly strong and can react quickly."

"I would prefer you have Bukon behind you rather than Falden. If the path does give way, I'll feel better with him assisting you than Falden," Myrith said.

"Uh," Kyrianna glanced back at Falden and Bukon. "You're correct. Bukon, then Falden and the others."

Myrith called the rest of the group over and explained the order they were to go in as Kyrianna checked the rope they would be using.

"Remember, you have to keep the rope taunt between you and the person in front of you. If you don't and the path gives way, the person falling will be able to pull you with them before you can react.

Despite a couple of slips and muttered curses as the rocks and dirt shifted under their feet, the group made it down the path without any incidents.

"Took you long enough," Ravlian said as Etewyn coiled the rope and put it back in his pack. "There was nothing to worry about, the path has an enchantment on it, it cannot give way, no matter how badly it has eroded and humans can't fall off it."

"And you're just now telling us about this!" Kyrianna took a step toward him.

"I didn't think about it. Of course your kind have fallen from the path many times. The enchantment was laid so this area could be used as a trap when we were enslaved. That also slipped my mind as well." Ravlian turned and stepped into one of the two waiting boats.

"You pathetic excuse...." Kyrianna took another step toward the mage then stopped as Myrith and Bukon grabbed her arms. "Let go of me!"

"No!" Myrith pulled her back several steps as Ravlian turned a bit paler than he already was. He never took his eyes off the trio as the rest of the group stepped between him and Kyrianna.

Myrith and Bukon guided Kyrianna to the second boat. "Get in and settle down." Myrith spoke harshly as she released her grip.

Kyrianna stepped down into the boat, her eyes locked on Ravlian as she took a seat. Myrith and Bukon followed her into the boat, sitting close on either side of her. The rest took seats in the first boat and the crews pushed off from the dock and began rowing toward one of the nearby islands.

Kyrianna continued to stare at Ravlian's back for several minutes before she finally dropped her gaze to the bow she held across her lap. Her knuckles were white as she held the weapon. It had been a long time since she had felt this kind of hatred. Her father's position had isolated her. Now, as she sat here fighting her anger, she wondered just how much the people she associated with in Nydith had hated her for her heritage but hid it because she was Lord Brygan's daughter.

Chapter Fourteen

"Are there any protective magics on this path you are aware of?" Kyrianna continued to stare at the narrow path leading up from where the boats had docked, instead of facing Ravlian.

"None," the mage said.

This path was in worse shape than the last one had appeared to be. Even though it looked like steps had been cut into the stone, time had taken its toll and most had crumbled away leaving only tiny hand and toe holds.

"This is not going to be an easy climb," Myrith said.

Kyrianna only nodded in acknowledgement.

"The same order as last time?" Myrith pulled a length of rope from her pack.

"No. I'll lead this time." She took the rope from Myrith. "Etewyn, your rope also." Kyrianna tied the two ropes together in a complicated knot then pulled on them to test where they were joined. "I want a little more distance between myself and the rest of you," she said as she tied the rope around her waist. "This would work a lot better if we had the appropriate equipment," she muttered.

"Myrith, you're next then Falden, Bukon, Ravlian, Hendandra and finally Etewyn. Going up is different than going down, leave a bit of slack in the rope between you, but be prepared to brace quickly. If you dislodge any debris or rocks call out so those below you are aware. If you slip, yell falling, so we can brace the rope. Keep an eye on the rope, it will telegraph what is going on with the person ahead on you. We are going to be moving very slowly. Make sure you listen to each other and pay attention."

Myrith took the rest of the rope from her. "How much distance?"

"Between you and me at least thirty feet; between everyone else—about ten feet. We're somewhat limited based on the amount of rope we have. I would honestly prefer to carry a rope to the top and have everyone come up separately, but we may not have enough to do it that way if there is nothing near the top to tie off on. I don't want to climb up then back down to climb up again. Get everyone tied off and I'll start up." Kyrianna turned her attention back to the narrow path.

Kyrianna moved cautiously as she tested each hand and foot hold before putting her weight on it. She wasn't concerned about her ability to make the climb, but needed to make sure the others would be able to follow her. She paused as the rock under her left hand shifted slightly. *No good*, she thought as she looked for a different handhold.

"So we're to trust *her* to pick the best route up this path." Ravlian's voice floated up.

"Rocks!" Kyrianna yelled the warning as the handhold she had been testing gave way and several pieces of rock fell.

"We're going to talk about this Rangerette," Myrith said.

Kyrianna didn't say anything. Myrith probably suspected she had dislodged the rocks on purpose, but she wouldn't be able to prove it.

Kyrianna paused as she reached the top of the path. There was a large boulder near the crest and she moved behind it and braced her feet as she wrapped the excess rope behind her and leaned back. She gritted her teeth as she felt the rope dig into the leathers she was wearing. Her hands stung where the rough hemp cut the palms. Her calves were burning as she kept her legs locked.

The pressure against her back and legs reduced slightly as Myrith finally reached the top of the path. The woman stood to the side and pulled the rope up to assist the others.

When Etewyn reached the top, Kyrianna fell back against the ground gasping as the weight on the rope vanished.

"Rangerette!" Myrith dropped the rope she was holding.

"Just need a few minutes," Kyrianna said between deep breaths. "That was a tougher climb than I expected it to be."

"You made it look easy," Bukon said.

"My mother and brother would have made it look even easier," she said.

"We need to get moving," Ravlian said. "The temple is just over there." He pointed toward the remains of a small building.

"How long has this place been abandoned?" Myrith asked. Piles of sand and rumble that might have once been tall columns framed the entrance.

"It has been over a millennium since the tyrant Lavial and his people left this plane for another," Ravlian said.

"Lavial?" Myrith stared at Ravlian.

"That was his name."

"Myrith, what's wrong?" Kyrianna forced herself to her feet.

"Are there any descriptions of this Lavial?" Myrith ignored Kyrianna.

"He was an elf; that is enough of a description." Ravlian glared at Kyrianna.

"That much we know," Myrith said. "What color were his hair and eyes?"

"Stories say they were both as black as the nadir of the darkest night, though there are some stories that claim his eyes were flecked with silver, like the stars in the night sky." Ravlian paused for several minutes. "You know of this Lavial," he said finally.

"He and those who follow him now rule the place I call home. Though Lord Lavial is the only one who is an elf."

Ravlian laughed. "Do the ranking members of his followers also have black hair and eyes as he does?"

"They do."

"Elves use magic like most humans breathe. For whatever reasons, he has chosen for those who carry out his whims to appear as human in your land. However, they apparently cannot hide their most distinctive identifying features." He glanced at Kyrianna. "Other than their ears, that is."

"Midnight Elves," Kyrianna whispered.

"What?" Myrith turned to look at the other two.

Kyrianna took a deep breath before she spoke. "On Rhysia there are three races of elves. Each one was given a name in the common tongue that reflected their distinctive appearances. Twilight Elves have silver eyes and silver hair; Dawn Elves have golden eyes and hair while the Midnight Elves have black hair and eyes. Ancient legends say Twilight Elves and Midnight Elves were once one and because of the blood tie, many of the Midnight Elves still have silver in their eyes." She refused to look at Ravlian who was staring at her.

"It is possible this Lavial is the same person, and that he originally came from Rhysia." Bukon spoke softly as he placed a hand on Kyrianna's shoulder.

"The description makes him sound like a Midnight Elf and elves can live for millennia, so it is possible."

Ravlian pushed past Myrith as he reached for her chin and

forced her to look into his eyes. "You have silver in your eyes, elf, even if you do not have the proper coloring."

"My mother was a Twilight Elf and my father was human," Kyrianna said drawing her dagger. "Do not touch me again."

"Abomination!" Ravlian raised his hands and began gesturing.

Myrith dropped one hand over his mouth and grabbed one of his hands with her other as Bukon stepped up and hit Ravlian in the stomach. Only Myrith's grip kept Ravlian from doubling over as he started coughing behind her hand.

"You will not threaten any member of this group, is that understood? We are all here to help you fight the demon you claim is here. We cannot afford to be fighting among ourselves."

Kyrianna nodded as Myrith glanced at her then slowly sheathed her dagger.

"Hendandra, you and Kyrianna should go and see if you can find a way into the temple," Bukon said. "From here it looks like the main entrance is completely collapsed."

Hendandra nodded then grabbed Kyrianna's arm and pulled her away from the group. Kyrianna stood at the edge of the rubble as Hendandra began her search. Her ears could just make out the conversation between the others as she watched the girl.

"If your people are living under the tyranny of Lavial, then you know what my people had to endure as slaves to her kind," Ravlian said.

"I do understand," Myrith said. "However, I also know your complaint is with Lord Lavial and his followers not with Kyrianna. You said yourself it had been over a millennia since they left this place. To carry your hatred for a particular group for so long, when you weren't even the ones hurt by that group is wrong. I have personal experience with the tactics of Lord Lavial and those who answer to him and I am still able to see Kyrianna is not one of their ilk."

There was silence and Kyrianna glanced back to see Ravlian spit on the ground and walk away.

"I think I found it," Hendandra called. She was kneeling next to a small, dark hole buried under the rumble of the crumbling stairs.

As the group approached, Kyrianna moved to take a guard position where she could watch several areas of the ruins while Myrith and Etewyn started moving the debris covering the entrance.

Etewyn took one of the torches and moved down the set of stairs that finally came into view. A few moments later, he came back up.

"They don't go down very far," Etewyn said. "And they appear to be clear."

"Rangerette, you take the rear position," Myrith called as Etewyn started back down the stairs, Hendandra slipping around to get in front of him.

Kyrianna nodded and watched as Ravlian glanced at her then pushed his way past Myrith. She shook her head when Hendandra started laughing.

As she followed the others, Kyrianna found herself shivering as she was surrounded by a deep cold. She watched a cloud of fog form in front of her as her breath condensed in the chill air.

Kyrianna watched Hendandra's hands shake as she checked the only door out of the chamber in which the stairs finally stopped. "It's locked," the girl said reaching for her picks.

She looked around at the others. Myrith's red hair was still wet and hung limp over her shoulders. The only ones not showing any sign of strain from the climb were Bukon and Etewyn. Both Ravlian and Falden were in a corner of the room leaning against the wall.

"Perhaps we should camp here and rest before moving on." Kyrianna glanced at Hendandra who was having problems with the door lock. "Two person watches. I'll take the middle watch as I had first watch during the last camp."

"It is still early," Ravlian said. "I think we should continue. Why give the demon time to realize we are here?"

"After your little shouting match with Kyrianna and your calling on your powers in an aborted attack, I'm sure this demon already knows we're here. I doubt one night of rest will make a difference," Bukon said. He removed his cloak and wrapped it around Hendandra.

Kyrianna spun around to glare at Ravlian, her hands resting on her swords. "I don't know and I really don't care about you, but that was a hard climb and we need time to rest. The last thing we need to do is face a minion of Thynitic while we are tired and affected by this sudden cold. We risk more by charging in before we are ready than by taking a break here." She glared at Ravlian, but didn't move to draw her weapons as he raised his hands as if preparing to cast a spell.

Myrith moved to stand next to Kyrianna. "I agree with Kyrianna. We need to rest before facing your demon."

"Time is growing short! With each day the demon is here, the power of chaos grows in this land," Ravlian said.

"That is something I believe we all understand at this point," Kyrianna said. "While I have no desire to face any god or goddess, in particular that one, I will not rush into certain battle unprepared. We need to take a break before going any further."

"Fine," Ravlian said dropping his pack on the floor. "I only hope we are not too late when we finally get there." He pulled a book out of his pack and ignored the rest of the group.

From behind them, a sudden rush of warm air filled the room along with the sound of a small explosion. Myrith spun around as Kyrianna drew her blades and turned also.

"Sorry, was just trying to help with the temperature," Falden said with a grin.

"A little warning next time," Myrith said as Kyrianna and Hendandra started laughing.

Chapter Fifteen

"To arms!" Myrith's voice echoed in the room.

Kyrianna was on her feet, an arrow nocked to her bow as she stared at the door that had been locked the night before. "Myrith," she said softly. The door was now ajar.

The others began stirring and slowly getting to their feet. Despite being up and armed as quickly as she was, Kyrianna still felt unsteady on her feet as she approached the door.

"Hold up, Kyrianna," Bukon called. "Let Hendandra check the door while you and Myrith stand ready."

Hendandra moved across the debris-strewn floor, her soft leather boots barely making any sound. She stood by the door for several heartbeats then shook her head. "I hear nothing on the other side." She grasped the handle then waited for Myrith and Kyrianna.

At Myrith's nod, she jerked the door open. Both bows seemed frozen in time as Kyrianna and Myrith scanned the darkness of the hallway beyond the door. Nothing moved.

"I would be willing to bet something knows we're here by now," Bukon said.

"How is it you don't seem to have been affected by whatever magic put us into such a deep slumber?" Myrith watched Bukon as he picked up his cloak and shook it out.

"I was affected. In case you forgot we were both on the last watch together. It is just that my training allows me to reach a state of full wakefulness quicker than most." He looked at Kyrianna who was still rubbing her eyes. "Although this was very powerful magic."

"How do you know that," Falden said. "I haven't even tried to read the lines of magic left from the spell yet."

"Any magic that can overcome an elf's natural immunity to sleep effects would have to be very powerful," Bukon said.

Kyrianna jerked her head up and stared at Bukon. "I was already asleep, perhaps the magic only deepened my slumber," she said.

"Or perhaps, it is an act on your part," Ravlian said.

"Rangerette," Myrith said before Kyrianna could react to the insult.

Kyrianna relaxed the arrow she held then turned back to her equipment and started getting her gear together. With a long glance at Ravlian, she brushed her hair out then pulled it back into its customary ponytail. She continued to stare at Ravlian as she reached up and made sure her ears were completely uncovered.

"A sleep spell that affects elves? It would have to have been created and cast by an elf. I doubt a *mere* human could overcome that natural immunity," Ravlian said. "That spell would have to have been cast before the door was opened as I doubt the watch would have been caught by surprise enough for someone to open the door then cast the spell." He let his eyes travel over the group for a moment before he finally focused on Myrith. "It may have been possible for someone here to activate a magic item that released the spell while you were on watch without alerting you, but I doubt anyone could come through the door with the same effect."

"It is also possible your demon has been scrying on this room and was able to cast the spell from a distance," Bukon said.

"We were all tired and didn't make a thorough check of the room before resting," Falden said stepping forward. "There may have been pre-set alarms as well as something that triggered a set spell in the room."

"And it was the elf who suggested we rest here," Ravlian muttered as he picked up his staff.

Bukon moved quickly and grabbed Ravlian's staff. "We all know how you feel about elves. By all the gods of Chaos and Order, I think most of us even understand the reasons for your feelings. However, that doesn't give you the right to keep badgering Kyrianna the way you are." He handed the staff back to Ravlian. "Leave her alone!"

"Myrith!" Kyrianna's voice was a harsh whisper as she read-ied an arrow. "Something just moved in the shadows at the end of the hall and vanished to our left. I believe the question of whether they know we're here or not has been answered." She lowered the bow slightly, still watching the corridor. "I didn't see it in time to get a shot at it."

"Any idea what it was?"

She shook her head.

"I warned you about waiting," Ravlian said. "Now, the de-mon will have time to prepare for us."

"Nothing we can do about it, so we might as well get moving," Myrith said.

"I agree," Kyrianna said.

"We're here to do a job," Hendandra said. "Let's get it done so we can go home." She moved to stand next to Etewyn, her own bow ready.

Myrith motioned Kyrianna to take the lead through the door. As soon as they passed through the doorway, a chill that felt like it was wrapping them in layers of ice surrounded them. Falden's magic had left the previous room warm, but that magic ended at the door. In the back of the group, Ravlian began chanting quietly and soon a blanket of warmth seemed to pass over them, dispelling the cold.

"My thanks," Myrith called.

"I don't want the elf to be able to use it as an excuse to rest when we don't have to," Ravlian said.

Kyrianna paused several feet from the end of the corridor. "The hallway continues to the left," she said. She let Hendandra pass her as she moved forward. "I'll check it," the girl said.

Hendandra waited at the corner, her head cocked to the side as she listened for the sounds of any movement around the corner. After several minutes, she grinned, held up her hand for them to wait then vanished around the corner.

Kyrianna glanced back at Myrith and shook her head slightly. Hendandra shouldn't be going off without the others.

"Chaos take it!" Kyrianna yelled as a small explosion echoed from the corridor Hendandra had gone down.

Hendandra was slumped against the wall, her leathers covered in soot. As Kyrianna dropped her bow and pulled one of the vials of healing potions out of her pack, Bukon helped her to sit up. Hendandra took several small sips of the liquid before she was finally able to swallow the potion.

"What happened?" Myrith asked.

"I found a trap." She pointed to a charred tile in the floor. "I was attempting to disarm it when it went off."

"You okay?" Etewyn knelt down next to Hendandra as Bukon moved away.

"I will be," Hendandra said.

"We need to find the demon." Ravlian started to move down the hallway.

Kyrianna stepped in front of the mage. "Where do you think

you're going?"

"Out of my way elf! I have had enough of your stalling. It was your people who first called the chaos to this place and I'm not convinced you aren't a part of what is going on now." He brought his staff up across his body in a guard position.

"For one who should be versed in these matters, you are seriously lacking in knowledge and common sense, Mage."

Kyrianna's hands went to her swords as she stood there. "You try to blame all elves for the actions of one group. Tell me are all humans responsible for the actions of every member of their race or is each individual responsible for their own?" She paused and took a step closer to Ravlian.

"Let me explain some things to you." Kyrianna spoke slowly, her words deliberate and well punctuated. "In my land there has always been some enmity between the three elven races. However, the hostility between the Midnight Elves and the Twilight Elves is very strong and bitter. The Midnight Elves were once part of the Twilight race, but were driven out millennia ago when their love of chaos began to take an evil turn. While they have very little contact with the Dawn Elves, they do not go out of their way to attack them as they do my mother's kin. For someone who should know better, to confuse me with one of the Midnight Elves is a grave insult and one I am not willing to let pass again." She started to slowly draw her swords.

"By Geladas," Myrith said as she grabbed Kyrianna's hand holding it tightly.

"You are an elf; just like the others." Ravlian took a hesitant step back from Kyrianna "You have even admitted the Midnight Elves were once part of your mother's race. That means their cruelty can show up in one of that race as well. It is a part of who you are."

"You dare to judge me without knowing who I am." Kyrianna twisted as she attempted to pull away from Myrith who tightened her grip and refused to release her hand.

"I don't have to. You are an elf; there is no difference to me. And, your behavior has been chaotic and ill-tempered—just like the elves who once ruled here."

"Kyrianna let it go. He doesn't know any better. He has reasons for his feelings. Not everyone has the wisdom to see past their own prejudices. Let it go." Myrith moved to stand between Kyrianna and Ravlian, her hand still holding Kyrianna's against her sword sheath.

Kyrianna looked up into Myrith's face then nodded slowly and relaxed slightly. She released her hand then moved to stand next to her as she faced Ravlian. His dark eyes seemed to burn with the fires of his rage as he glared first at Myrith then Kyrianna.

Kyrianna sighed then stepped to the side leaving the corridor passable. "If you wish to go after this demon by yourself—go ahead. However, the rest of us will wait until we are *all* ready to continue." She took a step closer to Ravlian.

Myrith put a hand on her shoulder, but didn't pull her back.

"Be advised if you insult me like that again, I will take it out of your hide." Kyrianna's voice was harsh and low as she spoke.

"You would not succeed," Ravlian said as he walked past her.

"Don't count on it," Myrith said softly. "You have been warned. The next time you start making threats and accusations, either directly or indirectly, I will not stop her."

"In that case I will not hold back in my defense either. You risk much if you attack a mage, elf. Are you willing to put these others in danger because of your hurt feelings? If they mean so little to you that you would risk their safety over a few insults then you are no different than the others." Ravlian smiled as he gestured at the rest of the group.

"I'm feeling better," Hendandra said as she forced herself up and leaned back against the wall. "Let's get going, before anyone else decides to draw steel against something other than the demons we will be facing."

Myrith pulled Kyrianna away from the group and stared at her. "I don't know why you're taking his comments so personally, but you need to let them go. We will need his power when we face this demon, just as we will need your skills."

Kyrianna didn't say anything; only pulled away and started to join the rest of the group.

Myrith grabbed her shoulder and turned her back to face her. "Kyrianna, I want you to stay away from Ravlian. I know you heard me tell him I won't stop you if he started again. However, while I might let you pay him for his comments, I will not let you hurt or kill him. Do not put me in a position where I have to stop you." She let go of Kyrianna's shoulder and moved to the front of the group.

Chapter Sixteen

Kyrianna watched Myrith for a moment, then sighed and moved to the back of the group.

"You should smile more, Kyrianna," Bukon said as he waited for her. "You have an open smile; one that speaks of a heart and soul that values freedom and chaffs at the paths we are often made to follow by others. If that means others see you as chaotic, so be it. Do not let the prejudice of others define you. You must follow the path your soul belongs on."

Kyrianna stared him. "Tell me Bukon, which of the many deities do you serve?"

"You would not know her. She is one that does not make a show of her power or position, yet she is opposed to the Lady of Chaos. Perhaps that is all the endorsement you should require." Bukon's gaze lingered for several seconds on Kyrianna then he turned his attention back to the corridor. "Looks like the little one found another trap," he said.

Kyrianna followed his eyes to where Hendandra was kneeling next to the wall. "That unidentified shadow I saw," she whispered. "That's who probably set the traps. I wonder how many more we'll find in this hallway."

"That's one of the triggers," Hendandra said. "Only looks like one more to go."

Kyrianna frowned at Hendandra's comments. Two triggers on a trap wasn't too unusual, but if whomever had set it was being this thorough this early it didn't bode well for the group as they got closer to where ever this demon was hiding.

"Excuse me; I'm going to go see if Hendandra needs any help with this device."

Kyrianna shouldered her bow and moved to where Hendandra was working. She stood quietly as she watched the girl manipulate a set of fine wires under one of the floor tiles. The girl was moving slowly as she slid the wires in a smooth, steady cutting motion.

There was a slight snap from under the tile and Hendandra

froze for a second then looked up and grinned. "This one is disabled. I just wonder how many more surprises we're going to find." She stared at the darkness that stretched from the shadows at the edge of the light from their torches.

"I don't care, as long we find them before they find us," Myrith said offering her hand to the smaller woman.

Hendandra nodded as she checked the area once more before moving down the hallway.

"I thought you had taken a position in the rear," Myrith said softly as Kyrianna started to follow Hendandra.

"I have two years of training with the thieves' guild in Nydith. I may be able to assist her if needed. Working on complicated traps can become very taxing—particularly those that require close concentration and delicate manipulation. And, despite her protestations, I doubt she is recovered of her injuries."

"Two years with the thieves' guild, then you left them," Myrith said.

"There were certain things about the guild that caused me to want to leave."

Myrith reached out and placed a hand on her elbow. "I'm sorry," she said. "That you are homesick like Hendandra is obvious to all of us, but there seems to be something deeper to it than just that. It is almost as if you lost something of great value in your life. I have also noticed that you spoke of your parents in the past tense."

Kyrianna dropped her eyes away from Myrith's and found herself chewing on her lower lip as she tried to find the right words. The last thing she wanted to do was tell Myrith she had been exiled because of her activities with the guild. However, she didn't want to lie to her either, she knew the woman would sense it if she tried. "I'm not ready to talk about it," she said softly.

~ * ~

Kyrianna stopped as Hendandra held up her hand then dropped to floor. She seemed to freeze as the leather strap she used to hold her hair back came undone and fell on the tile in front of her.

"Leikor's cursed luck," Hendandra muttered as she grabbed her hair and stuffed it under the collar of her shirt and leather jacket.

"Three triggers this time," Hendandra muttered. "Let's see what happens if I choose this one first." She spent almost an hour working on the trap before she finally stood and indicated it was safe for the group to move on. Kyrianna frowned at the paleness she saw in Hendandra's face.

They encountered two more traps before they finally came to the end of the corridor. Hendandra's hands were trembling as she checked the locked door that greeted them. She took several deep breaths before pulling a set of lock picks from her pack and started to work on the lock. After a few minutes there was a snap and the ringing of metal on the stone floor.

"Leikor's cursed luck," Hendandra said. "That was my last set of lock picks."

Etewyn placed a hand on Hendandra's shoulder and pulled her back from the door; he then drew his sword and began swinging. Three solid hits and door shattered to reveal a small chamber with a set of stairs leading down into the darkness.

"Myrith," Kyrianna said softly. "I think we should take a break here. Hendandra needs rest." She guided the smaller girl into the room and helped her sit in one of the corners. "Most people don't realize how draining the amount of concentration needed for complex traps can be. Plus it seems the cold is getting worse." She pulled a blanket from Hendandra's pack and wrapped it around her.

"No!" Ravlian stepped between Kyrianna and Myrith. "We cannot wait. We waited one night and look what it got us: An enemy who has been warned of our presence. If we wait any longer, we will not have a chance against him."

Bukon stepped up close behind Ravlian so he was between him and Kyrianna. "And, if we do not give Hendandra a chance to rest, we will stumble blindly into whatever traps he has set for us."

Ravlian ignored Bukon and continued to glare at Myrith. "Once again it is the elf advising us to wait and give the enemy time to prepare. How well do you know her? Do you believe her motives are based on concern for one member of your group? Or are you afraid to lead and thereby let her whims direct you?"

Kyrianna stepped up next to Bukon, her dagger in one hand as she placed her other hand on Ravlian's shoulder and pulled him around to face her. "When this is over, you and I will settle the matter of your insults," she said. "For now, you are safe because of a promise I made to Myrith." She wrapped her left hand around the blade of the dagger then pulled the dagger back slowly. She tightened her left hand into a fist and held it up as blood dripped from it onto the mage's boots. "By Ibacia, the patron of thieves and he who guards contacts and oaths, I swear I will repay you for your insults."

Ravlian started to raise his hands and Bukon stepped forward. "I wouldn't even think about casting a spell, if I were you," he said.

Ravlian spat on the floor at Kyrianna's feet then turned and stalked over to the far corner of the room.

"Looks like we will take the time to rest," Myrith said. She glared at Kyrianna as she walked over to stand in front of her. "You play a dangerous game with him, Rangerette. Do not jeopardize this group because of your pride." She turned and went to sit by the stairs, her sword held across her lap.

Kyrianna didn't say anything as she went to sit by Hendandra.

Chapter Seventeen

Hendandra glanced at Kyrianna and smiled softly. "You swore by Ibacia, whom you called the patron of thieves, yet you are not a thief or rogue," she said.

Kyrianna looked down. "I spent two years training with the thieves' guild in Nydith before I decided to walk the forest paths," she said.

"I was never a part of the guild, but I do know that is a lot of time and hard work to walk away from. Why did you do so?"

Kyrianna glanced toward Myrith, who met her gaze with raised eyebrows. The woman was also interested in hearing what she might tell Hendandra.

"Do not misunderstand me," Kyrianna said. "However, it is something I do not wish to discuss."

"But, it is the reason you do not trust thieves isn't it?"

Kyrianna nodded. "It is."

"I'm sorry," Hendandra said.

"So am I." Kyrianna turned her attention back to Ravlian. He and Falden were in the far corner talking together. Despite their discussion, Ravlian kept throwing angry glances in her direction.

Next to her, Hendandra seemed to relax a bit more and there was a slight change in her breathing that told her the girl had fallen asleep.

~ * ~

"Myrith," Kyrianna called softly as Hendandra moved. The older woman looked up as she nodded first toward the girl and then the stairs.

Myrith nodded then stood and looked around. "We should get moving."

Bukon was awake and stood up as did Etewyn. Falden and Ravlian finished their discussion before joining the rest of the group. Hendandra grabbed her pack, grinned as she drew her rapier and headed down the stairs into the darkness. The rest of the group followed her, their weapons ready.

"Okay, which way do we go?" Myrith glanced at the two doors they found in the small chamber at the base of the stairs then turned to look at Ravlian.

He seemed to study the doors for several minutes then shook his head. "If I remember the documents I've seen on this place correctly, the main sanctuary should be to the south of the main entrance."

Myrith glanced at Kyrianna who slowly shook her head and frowned. "We are too far turned around and underground for me to discern the direction," she said.

"Figures," Ravlian muttered.

Kyrianna curled her left hand into a fist as she glared at him. *We are not through this yet*, she thought. She closed her eyes as she forced herself to relax.

"I haven't got any ideas either," Myrith said.

Hendandra moved to one of the doors and stood with her ear against it for several minutes, before moving to the other door and doing the same thing. She moved back to the first and listened again. "Someone's on the other side of this door," she said as she stepped back. "With my picks broken, I doubt I can work the lock. Plus there is a chance who or whatever it is will hear me and open the door on their own."

"Agreed," Myrith said. "Hendandra, you and Kyrianna get your bows ready." She readied her sword. "Etewyn, if you would take care of the door please."

Etewyn drew his sword and with a smile started hacking. The door, which appeared to have been made of wood, proved to be some sort of mesh between natural wood and the mushroom stalks they had seen in the forest. Etewyn's blade cut through the material easily. A scream came from the other side, and the sword came back with black blood on it. Another cry came as the opening in the door widened enough for Etewyn to step through.

Etewyn was standing several feet away from the shattered door, his weapon at the ready as the rest came through the opening. "More come," he called.

Kyrianna looked past him to see a group of the demons approaching. There were approximately ten smaller demons, followed by three larger ones and one even larger than those in back of the group. "Arrows," she called as she and Hendandra released two and they streaked past Myrith to strike the largest of the demons.

The largest of the demons raised his hands and began chanting softly. Bolts of arcane power streaked from the demon's fingers and Ravlian yelled as he fell to the floor.

Falden also began chanting and a bolt of force struck the larger demon.

Both Myrith and Etewyn scored hits on their opponents as Bukon attacked the third. The larger demon began chanting again.

"He's healing them," Myrith yelled.

Myrith ducked a swing from the claws of the demon she was facing and went back to trying to hit it. The thing seemed to shimmer in the air as a kaleidoscope of colors danced around the creature.

"They are surrounded by a field of Chaos," Bukon yelled. "It is causing disruptions."

"Even in chaos there is a spark of order," Kyrianna yelled as she fired another arrow. "Keep pressing the attack and look for the patterns."

Myrith's blade cut deeply into one of the demons' necks. The creature's howls were filled with the bubbling of its own blood as it fell to the floor and she charged toward the larger demon.

He stepped back into a portal of swirling colors as her blade left a deep gash down his chest. The portal snapped shut and the demon was gone.

Bukon and Etewyn quickly took care of their opponents and Hendandra was silently cutting the throats of the ones that had fallen to the sleep spell cast by Falden and Ravlian.

Kyrianna glanced at Falden who was bandaging Ravlian's injuries, turned and walked over to where Hendandra was checking the bodies of the demons. They finished their check of the room and bodies and moved to stand next to Myrith.

"What did you find?" Myrith asked.

"Only a few gold pieces, a dagger, and three potion vials with what appears to be healing potions," Hendandra said.

"A shield made from the same material as my sword, a few nice short swords, and this." Kyrianna held out a large black medallion that had white crystals set around the edge. "No clue what it signifies, if anything."

Myrith took the medallion and looked at it. "I suggest you have Falden check it to see if it radiates magic and if so what kind."

Hendandra nodded then took the medallion and walked over

to Falden.

"What about the room?" Myrith shifted her weight slightly as she looked at Kyrianna.

"Nothing. This is a dead end. We will have to go back to the other door. By the way, I think I now have a way to determine the correct direction." She looked up at Myrith.

"How?"

"The amount of mushroom material in the door. I have a feeling that before Chaos swept across this land, that forest was probably true trees of some type and now they are a reflection of the changes wrought here."

"That would explain why the buildings in the village looked as old as they did. Built before the last of the trees were changed and now there is very little wood available for repairs."

"Actually, I think some of that is due to them removing wood that has been changing over the centuries. It would be interesting to know just what did happen here," Kyrianna said. "I doubt these changes were happening when the Midnight Elves were here. This seems more indicative of chaos being unleashed on the area."

"I doubt we will ever find out those answers. Ravlian and his people have their prejudices clouding how they remember their history. And the amount of time that has past would have also caused changes in memories."

Kyrianna looked down at the ground and shuffled her feet. "You're right, but it would still be interesting to know." She looked up. "Looks like Ravlian's back on his feet, we should probably get moving."

"What? No recommendation to rest and waste more time?" Myrith laughed softly.

"Not for him. He wouldn't appreciate it." She paused and glanced back at Ravlian. "Particularly if I was the one making the suggestion. I will not object if anyone else brings it up."

Myrith raised an eyebrow and nodded.

Chapter Eighteen

Kyrianna watched as Hendandra moved to the front of the group. The girl had found four traps in the last corridor, and Myrith didn't want to risk finding out they had been lucky and had bypassed any in this hall as they fought the demons.

Fortunately, there were no additional surprises waiting for them as they returned to the room. Kyrianna stood with Myrith and Hendandra as they readied their bows. Etewyn grinned as he raised his sword, but stopped as Ravlian stepped up and touched the door. The door swung open and Ravlian motioned him through.

Kyrianna took a step toward the mage and Myrith placed a hand on her elbow. "Let it go," she said.

"If he had the power to do that, he could have done it last time; and we may not have alerted the demons to our presence."

"Now, is not the time," Myrith whispered. "Let it go."

Kyrianna jerked away from Myrith but didn't say anything further.

The walls of the room were the same obsidian as the medallion Kyrianna had found. In the center of the room was a well, which opened into darkness and seemed to stretch down into the abyss itself.

"The air is moving further down," Hendandra whispered.

Etewyn dropped his torch into the well and waited for it to hit the bottom. There was a splash and the group could see the torch had landed in a shallow pool approximately one hundred feet down.

"Looks like we climb," Myrith said.

Kyrianna nodded as Etewyn handed her a rope out from his pack then began looking for a place to tie it off.

"Etewyn, can you test this for me?" She pointed to a hook on the side of the well.

Etewyn grabbed the hook and pulled on it. "It's secure," he said.

Kyrianna tied the rope off then pulled on it several times, testing the hook and the knot. She tossed the rest of the rope into the well. "We'll be about ten feet short of the water, be careful when you drop, the water doesn't appear to be very deep."

Etewyn only grunted as he climbed over the edge of the well and started climbing.

"I'll stay up here and watch," Kyrianna said checking the hook and knot again.

Myrith nodded as she sheathed her sword and waited for Etewyn to reach the bottom.

"There's a corridor leading out of this area," Etewyn called. "There's also a small ledge about five feet from the rope. The little one probably won't even get wet."

Hendandra looked around and grinned. "Sounds like a challenge. Anyone care to bet on it?"

"I doubt anyone will want to actually bet against you," Bukon said. "However, does anyone else think they can make it without getting wet?"

From the well a loud splash echoed and the group started laughing. "Not me," Etewyn called up. "By the way the water is cold."

Myrith shook her head. "I'm not taking that bet; not with all this gear," she said as she climbed over the edge.

"I'm going next," Ravlian put a hand on the rope.

"You will wait until she is off the rope," Bukon said.

"Well, anyone else think they can make the ledge without getting wet?" Hendandra focused her gaze on Kyrianna then Bukon.

"I'm willing to make the try," Kyrianna said. "And I am willing to bet Bukon makes it as well."

Another splash came from the well. "Great, the rope's getting wet," Hendandra said. "That's not going to help."

Ravlian climbed over the wall and started down the rope.

"You hoping to hear another splash," Hendandra asked looking at Kyrianna.

"And if I said I was?"

"Then I would say you were no different than most people," Bukon said. "Just be careful your anger doesn't lead you down the wrong path."

Kyrianna nodded.

"Looks like it's my turn," Bukon said as the rope went slack.

"Doesn't sound like your *friend* got wet," Hendandra said. "That makes two who have succeeded," she said as the rope went slack again. Are you going to make it three?" She asked as Falden started to climb over the edge of the well.

"Of course."

"He's already cast a spell on himself," Hendandra said after Falden slipped out of sight.

"We never specified you couldn't use magic, so it still counts," Kyrianna said. "That's probably how the other one did it also."

The two girls waited until the rope again went slack.

"Next," Falden called up.

Kyrianna nodded to Hendandra as the girl dropped over the edge. When the rope went slack Kyrianna shouldered her bow and checked the knot once again. She disliked the idea of leaving the rope hanging here where someone following the group could use it. But, unless she wanted to dive from around fifty feet, she saw no way to remove the rope.

Kyrianna climbed over the edge and started down the rope. The majority of the group was waiting on the ledge with Etewyn and Myrith standing guard on the corridor leading from the pool. As she got close to the end of the rope, she started the rope swinging and let the momentum carry her toward the ledge. Unfortunately, her hands lost their grip on the wet rope and she missed making a dry landing by only a few inches.

Hendandra was laughing as she offered Kyrianna a hand out of the water. "Now, what was the bet?" She looked around at the others.

"It was never agreed upon," Kyrianna said opening one of her belt pouches. "However, I offer one gold piece. Sound fair?"

Hendandra took the coin and slipped it into one of her pouches.

"A gold piece along with the laugh—agreed."

Kyrianna readied her bow, drew an arrow then took careful aim at the top of the well where the rope dropped into it.

"What are you doing?" Ravlian hit the bow just as Kyrianna fired causing the arrow to miss its target.

Kyrianna dropped her bow and drew her dagger as she spun around to face the mage. "Explain yourself!"

"I believe you are the one who needs to explain herself," Ravlian said. "That rope might be our only way out of here and you were going to sever it."

"He has a point," Myrith said standing next to Ravlian.

Kyrianna looked at Myrith then back at the mage. She scowled at the smug look on the man's face as he smiled at her, before she turned her attention back to Myrith. "And with all your gear, you would be able to reach a rope hanging five feet from you and ten feet above the ground? You dove into the water just to get cooled off when you came down then, I guess."

"Do you think I would ever do something I didn't intend?"

Kyrianna took a deep breath. She wasn't sure if Myrith was teasing or serious in her attitude. "Unless one of the mages has a spell to accomplish the task, there really is no way to reach the rope to climb back out. And, if we leave it there, it can be used by anyone who might be following us."

Ravlian stepped around Kyrianna and muttered several syllables under his breath then held out his hand as the rope seemed to grow. Within a few seconds, he was holding the rope and several extra feet lay coiled at his feet.

"Fine. Now it can be used as a way out of this place." Kyrianna moved to stand by Etewyn at the entrance. "Providing something doesn't use it to follow us and then sever it behind them," she said. "I would suggest finding a way to secure the rope to the ledge as it will still be useless if it ends up back in the middle of the pool. If the magic will last until we get back here, that is."

"Will it last?" Myrith asked.

"That will depend on how long it takes us to get back here; if we get back here." He smiled at Kyrianna. "The magic is not permanent, however I can recast the spell if need be."

"Good. Let's get moving," Myrith said.

~ * ~

Myrith motioned for quiet as the rest of the group entered a chamber. Kyrianna took a breath grateful to be out of the tight, twisting turns of the passage they had been traveling through. Hendandra moved to the entrance for several minutes then slipped back to the others.

"Another large open cavern like the one with the stairs that led to the mushroom forest," Hendandra whispered. "There is a stone bridge spanning a deep chasm. It appears to be about one hundred feet across; Kyrianna can probably give us a better estimate of the distance. There is another opening at the other end; however two of the large demons are standing guard there."

She glanced at Kyrianna. "It might be possible to get a shot from behind cover at the entrance. Care to test your skill?" She strung her bow and grinned.

Kyrianna raised an eyebrow as she glanced at Hendandra then at the entrance. "After you," she said.

Myrith motioned for the rest of the group to wait where they were as the two girls took their positions on either side of the opening. Kyrianna and Hendandra didn't say anything to each other, but communicated through a series of hand gestures. The two moved as one as they stood, took aim and released their arrows.

"Chaos take it!" Kyrianna said as she glanced through the opening. "We both missed and they've ducked into the opening on their side."

"Can you continue to fire as we move?" Myrith asked.

"You're kidding," Hendandra said.

"Not very accurately," Kyrianna said.

"I'm not kidding and it doesn't have to be very accurate, just enough to keep them from attacking us as we cross that bridge."

"There's a problem," Kyrianna said. "We won't be able to move very fast even without aiming and if we're not able to aim well, there really is no telling where the arrows will go. I think a quick sprint across the bridge and taking positions on either side of the opening is a better option."

"Sounds like it would be safer for us," Ravlian said. "I don't relish the idea of being in front of a *poorly* aimed arrow from the elf."

"How about being in front of a well aimed one?" Kyrianna reached for her quiver.

"Kyrianna!" Myrith stepped between her and Ravlian. "That was uncalled for."

Kyrianna bowed her head slightly and stared at the floor, not saying anything.

"We need to move quickly," Myrith said. "Those who reach the other side first should take up positions on either side of the opening as Kyrianna suggested. Be ready to fight anything stepping through that doorway."

Both Kyrianna and Hendandra shouldered their bows and drew their blades as they headed for the bridge. Falden began chanting softly.

"He's preparing a sleep spell," Ravlian said. "He can hold the last syllables of the incantation until we reach the other side then cast it just inside the opening to catch anyone waiting for us."

"Good." Myrith looked around at the others. "Let's go."

Kyrianna was the first to reach the other side, followed by Bukon and Hendandra. As Falden approached the doorway, he began chanting again. As he finished, he raised his hands toward the opening. Kyrianna waited a heartbeat then ducked into the opening for a moment then stepped back out quickly.

"Both of the ones by the door are asleep. Someone needs to take care of them before the spell wears off. The demon that vanished through the portal is here as well. He appears to still be suffering from the injuries we dealt him before."

"You two," Myrith pointed at Kyrianna and Hendandra, "bows. Etewyn, you and I will charge in first and engage the demon. Bukon, you know your skills best. Same for Falden and Ravlian." She looked around at the others. "We move quickly when we move. Let's not give him time to react."

Myrith nodded to Etewyn and they charged into the room, swords raised. Kyrianna nodded to Hendandra and they loosed their arrows together at the demon.

The creature roared in pain then began casting. Before either Myrith or Etewyn could hit it, the demon had completed the spell and several of his wounds began healing.

"Interesting," the demon said as he looked over the group. "Two of the daughters working together. I doubt that was anticipated." The demon took a step toward Myrith, his claws gleaming as he watched her eyes. "Too bad one of them has dedicated herself to order."

"Chaos!" Kyrianna yelled as a bolt of energy hit Hendandra. "There's a mage on the ledge over the door," she yelled.

"We've got him," Falden said. "You concentrate on the demon."

"Ah, there you are and you have it. Good." The demon grinned as he raised a small wand. "The first daughter awaits your arrival."

"Bukon!" Hendandra's voice echoed in the chamber.

Chapter Nineteen

"Bukon?" Etewyn said.

"No!" Myrith yelled.

Kyrianna dropped her bow as Etewyn started to turn and the demon's claws slashed across his chest. Blood spurted and Etewyn fell to the ground.

"Etewyn!" Hendandra's voice called as her arrow flew over his body to bounce off the demon's arm.

Kyrianna drew her swords and charged forward, past the demon. She slashed his arm with her short sword as her long sword came around to hit the back of his leg. The demon howled then spun around, his claws reaching for her.

His claws raked Kyrianna's arm and she dropped her short sword as she screamed. The demon roared as he swung his other hand and she avoided the attack. Myrith's blade cut a deep gash in the demon's side and he spun to face her as Kyrianna again slashed at the back of his leg.

The demon's leg gave out and he fell toward Myrith, his claws raking the air as she stepped to the side and brought her sword down, cutting into the back of his neck. She wrenched the blade back up, plunged it into his back and twisted. The creature flailed for several seconds then stopped moving.

Myrith jerked her blade out of the demon's back and glanced at Kyrianna. "Etewyn," Kyrianna said nodding toward the warrior and cradling her arm against her chest.

A pool of blood surrounded the large man. Hendandra was kneeling next to him, sobbing.

"I'm sorry," Myrith said kneeling next to the girl.

Falden chanted softly and a pillar of flame surrounded the body. There was nothing left when the flames died down. "I don't know if it was the appropriate custom for his people, but it is better than leaving him here for the scavengers."

Myrith and Hendandra nodded.

"Let me take a look at your arm," Myrith said turning to Kyrianna.

"It'll be fine," Kyrianna said turning it to hide where the blood was still flowing from the cuts.

Myrith reached out and gently pulled Kyrianna toward her as she straightened her arm and pushed the sleeve of her tunic up.

"Those claws made a mess," Myrith said looking at the gashes on Kyrianna's arm. "The potion may have slowed the bleeding some, but it isn't going to be enough. Hold your arm still." She removed several bandages from her pack and wrapped them around Kyrianna's arm. "You will need to have a healer look at that when we get back."

"Who else was hurt?" Myrith looked around the chamber. Falden and Ravlian were both sitting on the floor near the body of another man dressed in multi-colored robes. "The mage attacking from above?"

Falden only nodded as he examined a scroll.

Hendandra had cut the throats of the two demons guarding the entrance and was now moving to check the body of the large demon. Ravlian followed her to where the creature lay and pulled a large vial from his robes. He held the vial next to the cut Myrith had made in the demon's neck and the black blood flowed into it. As soon as the vial was full, Ravlian covered the top and placed it in a pocket of his robes.

"That's what you were after?" Kyrianna stared at Ravlian. "We lost two of our comrades so you could collect a spell component!" She took a step toward him.

"Yes, I wanted to collect the blood," Ravlian said. "However, the primary reason for this trip was to stop the demon from opening this place to the Lady of Chaos. How convenient you seem to have forgotten that particular point, elf."

"Kyrianna," Hendandra called. "Come take a look at these." She held up a long sword and short sword.

Both of the weapons gleamed with a green shimmer similar to the sword Bukon had given her. "May I?" Kyrianna held out her hand. Hendandra glanced at the blades again before passing them to her.

Kyrianna stepped back and swept the two swords through a slow series of sweeping swings and parries. "Lighter than normal blades of the same size," she said when she stopped. She took a couple of deep breaths fighting the stabbing pain in her arm. She glanced at the two scabbards Hendandra was pulling from the rest of the demon's equipment. "You can't use the long sword," she said kneeling down in front of Hendandra. "How about I give you the sword Bukon gave me in exchange for these. They appear to be a matched set—why break it up."

Hendandra turned one of the scabbards over in her hands, not looking up. "These swords seem to be of extremely high quality and workmanship. Even if I cannot use the long sword, I can still sell them for a nice price. I would get far more for a matched set of swords than for a single sword."

"That is true," Myrith said. "However, by making the trade, you may be getting a greater benefit."

Both Hendandra and Kyrianna jerked their heads up to look at Myrith. "This is between Hendandra and myself," Kyrianna said.

"I understand that, I only wanted to point out that those blades in the hands of one of the party may be of more benefit than gold she may or may not earn; providing we make it back to a place where she can sell them." Myrith stepped back.

"She has a point," Hendandra said. "I do want to make it back in one piece. I will trade this set for both of the blades you wear. I'm still losing several hundred gold pieces on the deal though."

Kyrianna's hand rested on the long sword she was wearing and she paused for several minutes before finally nodding her agreement. She unbuckled the sword belt and handed the weapons to Hendandra then took the two new weapons and carefully buckled them on, shifting the belt several times as she adjusted the weight and placement of the blades. "My thanks," Kyrianna said. "My blades will continue to defend you and the others."

"Just remember you owe me one," Hendandra said as she attached the other two swords to her pack. She looked over at Myrith. "These are the only other items of interest I found." She held out two gold collars. "The other two were wearing them."

Falden walked over and glanced at the collars. "I am detecting a strong aura of enchantment on the collars," he said. He turned and looked at Kyrianna. "There is no magic on your blades."

"Thank you," Kyrianna said.

"I can identify the magic on the collars if you wish," Ravlian said.

"Please," Hendandra said.

He muttered several words as his hands moved in a complicated pattern. "It is a spell of obedience," he said.

"So not all the creatures here were serving the Lady of Chaos or her minions by their own will," Myrith said. "This is interesting."

"Almost as interesting as what the demon said before," Falden said. He looked around at the others. "He made some sort of reference to there being two of the daughters here. Then when he opened the portal, he told Bukon the first daughter was waiting."

"Daughters of whom or what?" Myrith looked at the other women in the group.

"Daughters?" Kyrianna asked. "Daughters of Chaos?" She began trembling. "I will welcome you as one of my daughters."

"Rangerette?" Myrith asked.

Kyrianna took a step back.

"Are you okay?" Myrith grabbed Kyrianna's hands.

Kyrianna closed her eyes as a storm of color erupted between her and Myrith.

Myrith tightened her grip. "What is going on? You said something about the Daughter of Chaos. What do you know about this?"

"Nothing. I don't understand any of this." Kyrianna pulled away from Myrith and shook her head.

Myrith frowned and Kyrianna dropped her head to avoid the woman's judgmental gaze.

"So we're still left with the questions of what the demon meant by his reference to the first daughter and what Bukon had and where the demon sent him," Falden said. He looked toward Ravlian and raised an eyebrow. "You have obviously studied this demon and this temple. Can you tell us anything?"

"This was once a temple to the Lady of Chaos. The demon was a member of one the highest castes of her demons." Ravlian looked around. "As for the references to daughters, there were references in one of the texts I studied about the temple of a person called the Daughter of Chaos. One claimed she was a descendant of the Lady of Chaos whom the goddess elevated to divine status and gave control of the plane of limbo. Other references only stated she was the ranking priestess of the Lady."

"If he was one of the highest castes of the chaos demons, how did we defeat him so easily?" Myrith glanced toward the body of the demon. "Surely he had other powers at his command."

"It wasn't that easy," Hendandra muttered, glancing at the

spot where Etewyn's body had lain.

"Perhaps there was someone he didn't want to kill," Ravlian said glancing at Kyrianna, "or had been instructed not to kill, even if it cost him his own life. He did make that reference to two of the daughters working together." Ravlian turned his attention to Myrith. "Thinking about it, he seemed interested in you as well with his comment about one having dedicated herself to order."

"I am from a land that does not know this Lady of Chaos and to which elves are not native. I doubt there is any connection," Myrith said glaring at the mage.

"Myrith," Falden whispered. "There is another area of magic in this room," Falden said. "The back wall has an illusion cast over it. I can attempt to dispel it."

"Let's see what we can find," Myrith said.

Kyrianna watched as Falden reached out and touched the center of the wall. There was a rippling across the black surface and the outline of a door appeared in the wall. As the rippling faded the obsidian of the doors took on a reddish glow. In the center of the door was the impression of a rearing unicorn.

"Kyrianna, are you still wearing that unicorn medallion?" Myrith asked.

"I am." Kyrianna joined Myrith in front of the door.

Myrith pointed to the impression in the obsidian.

Kyrianna knelt down and removed the medallion from around her neck. She held the disk next to the impression in the door. "They appear to be a match," she said after a few minutes.

Myrith stepped back and drew her sword. "Stand ready," she said to the others.

Kyrianna took a breath then pressed the medallion against the etching. A crack appeared in the door and it slid open to reveal a large room. In the center was a pedestal with a long sword suspended above it. The walls and pedestal were all made from the same material as the door—an almost translucent obsidian, which held a red glow.

Kyrianna threw her arm across Myrith's chest as she started to enter the room. "Wait," she said pointing to a large fiery red rune on the floor just inside the door.

"Protection against chaos," Falden said looking at the rune. "The runes along the pedestal are the same. There is strong magic in those runes." He paused for a moment. "They are also warnings about touching the sword."

"I'll do it," Hendandra said stepping past Kyrianna and Myrith.

"Hendandra, don't be foolish." Myrith's voice was harsh.

"I'll be fine." Hendandra began a slow search of the pedestal and the area around it. After three trips around the sword, she finally stopped and reached for it. The weapon glowed for a second then faded as Hendandra held it.

"A powerful weapon," Ravlian said. "It has several different magics on it, including spells that make it most dangerous against undead and demons. The others, I can't seem to identify. It is almost as if the magic has been quieted in some way. While the residue is visible it is not active at this time."

"Looks like we need to start heading back," Myrith said.

"Here, you take this one," Hendandra said handing Myrith the sword.

Myrith stared at her. "You claimed it, it is yours."

"I know, but we have been facing demons here and may still face them before we get out of this place. The weapon would be better put to use in your hands than in my pack."

"I am in your debt," Myrith said taking the weapon.

"Don't forget it either," Hendandra said.

Myrith handed Hendandra her sword. "It has no magics on it, but it should be worth something. It is a small payment on what this blade is worth."

"I am done here," Ravlian said looking around. "We have defeated the demon and I have what I came for." He pulled a wand out of his robes and handed it to Falden. "Payment for your services; as agreed," he said. He turned to look at Kyrianna then smiled as he snapped his fingers and vanished.

"You coward!" Kyrianna drew her swords and swung at the place the mage had been standing. Her blade only met air.

"Let it go, Kyrianna," Myrith said. "We need to get back and check in with the Moon Swords."

Kyrianna sheathed her weapons. "He better not lose the invisibility spell until we do," she said as she headed out of the room and back along the path they had traveled.

Chapter Twenty

"Looks like the mage was right about the rope," Hendandra said as they entered the room with the shallow pool in it.

"At least the spell is still in place," Kyrianna said.

"Who's first?" Myrith asked.

"I'll go," Hendandra said reaching for the rope.

"I'll go last," Kyrianna said readying her bow and watching the opening they had come through.

Myrith anchored the rope as the others made their way back to the upper level. "Rangerette?"

Kyrianna paused and stared back down the tunnel, waiting for several breaths.

"Kyrianna, we need to get moving," Myrith said.

Kyrianna nodded then shouldered her bow as she joined Myrith. "Up you go," Kyrianna said as she took hold of the rope.

"Look on the bright side," Myrith said. "We should all be able to go home soon. Our defeat of the demon who was calling the others in should make things easier for those looking for this artifact."

"That only matters if you have someplace to actually go home to," Kyrianna whispered.

Myrith paused as she started to climb up the rope and glanced back at the girl anchoring her. "Get going," Kyrianna said. "They're waiting." She turned her attention back to the corridor and ignored Myrith as the woman climbed up the rope.

"Hey, Rangerette," she heard Myrith call from the top. "You going to join us or not?"

Kyrianna shook her head, glanced up and waved before she started up the rope.

Kyrianna tightened her grip as the rope swung out over the water. Unlike the others, she had no one to anchor and stabilize the rope for her and her right arm still hurt badly. She took a couple of deep breaths as she waited for the rope to calm its erratic swings.

"Chaos take it!" Kyrianna's voice echoed in the room as energy pulsed through the rope. Her hands seemed to react on their own, releasing their grip and she yelped as she hit the water.

Laughter echoed in the room. "You thought to threaten one who wields arcane power. Foolish elf, let's see how you do without your companions to protect you." Ravlian's voice came from above her and Kyrianna glanced up. There was nothing there; at least nothing she could see.

"Rangerette, watch the water," Myrith called.

Kyrianna drew one of her swords and held it just below the surface of the water. The green of the blade seemed to brighten for a moment then darkened. She shuddered as she pulled herself out the water and watched as a large shadow vanished under the ledge.

"Ravlian, you chaos spawned bastard," Kyrianna said as the lower part of the rope melted away in her hand.

"Falden, can you lengthen the rope like Ravlian did?" Myrith asked, her voice carrying to where Kyrianna stood.

Kyrianna stood watching the water as she held her short sword in her left hand.

She staggered back as several bolts of arcane energy hit her and found herself gasping as she fell to the ground.

"There!" Hendandra shouted and Kyrianna heard an arrow hit one of the walls above her.

"Rangerette," Myrith called. "We've extended the rope and are lowering it now. Be ready."

Kyrianna sheathed her sword and waved an acknowledgement. As soon as the rope reached the water, she dove in and grabbed it. She gritted her teeth and tried to ignore the pain in her arm as she pulled herself up the rope. Fortunately, she could also feel the others pulling the rope up while she climbed. As she reached the top, another group of energy bolts streaked down to strike her. Myrith released her grip on the rope, grabbed her just under her arms and wrapped her own arms around her to prevent her from dropping. Kyrianna nodded her thanks as she fought against the blackness trying to claim her.

Myrith helped Kyrianna down against the well. "I suggest you leave now!" she said looking up.

Kyrianna forced her eyes to follow Myrith's gaze. There, floating near the ceiling was Ravlian.

"I believe my point has been proven. She never should have threatened me," Ravlian said.

"Myrith!" Hendandra spun around to face Myrith. "He attacked her without provocation. You're not going to let him get away with that are you? You can't let him get away with attacking a member of our group!"

"Hendandra, they have both been at each other since we started this little trip. She had threatened him, and he got the first strike in. I am giving him a chance to leave now before it escalates any further. If he attacks her again; we will finish it." Myrith glanced up at Ravlian.

Hendandra frowned. "I don't like it. No one should be able to get away with attacking one of our friends."

Myrith glanced back up. "You need to leave now." Her hand went to her crossbow.

"I'm leaving," Ravlian said then vanished.

"How could you let him go?" Hendandra stood in front of Myrith, her hands on her hips.

"We don't need a potential fight with the guards or troops when we get back. The mayor has the same feelings about Kyrianna as Ravlian did. If he doesn't make it back, do you honestly think they aren't going to try and blame her?"

Hendandra took a step back. "I hadn't thought of that," she whispered.

"It is something I have to think about." Myrith glanced back at Kyrianna who was now standing, though still unsteady on her feet. "Whenever you're ready Rangerette," she said.

"Let's get out of here." Kyrianna drew her long sword and headed back down the hallway.

"Better hope Ravlian is out of the area," Hendandra said. "I doubt you'll be able to stop her going after him if she meets up with him."

"Why would I try?" Myrith said.

Kyrianna paused at Myrith's words. She understood why the woman hadn't allowed them to attack Ravlian. The prejudice of his people was strong enough they would never believe it had been in self-defense. And, even if they did, they wouldn't accept it had been because he had tried to kill her. Still it surprised her Myrith would let her go without interference if something else should happen.

~ * ~

"Do we need to tie off together again?" Myrith asked as Kyrianna secured the rope to a large tree and tested the knot.

"No," Kyrianna said tossing the rope over the edge. "We can use the rope for extra stability, but if everyone moves carefully we should be fine. Be glad this tree is close enough we can do it this way."

"Okay, this is your area of expertise." Myrith looked around. "Who's first?"

"I'll go," Kyrianna said. "I can anchor the rope at the bottom, making it more stable for the rest."

"Be careful," Myrith said.

Kyrianna just winked as she grabbed the rope, wrapped it around her back and stepped backward toward the edge.

"What are you doing?" Myrith's jaw dropped as Kyrianna leaned into the rope then jumped backward.

"Cool," Hendandra said looking over the edge.

Kyrianna walked backwards down the crumbling slope; occasionally taking little hops. Once she reached the bottom, she tightened the rope and moved so it was centered on the narrow steps. "Ready," she called.

"Bet I can go down the same way she did," Hendandra said.

Kyrianna kept the rope tight after Hendandra's first jump, keeping the girl to a walk as she came backwards down the slope. They weren't tied off properly for that type of maneuver and she didn't want her to fall.

The only one of the group who didn't attempt her method was Myrith. The older woman instead made her way down the stairs using the rope as a guide.

"Where's Ravlian?" one of the men waiting for them asked from behind Kyrianna.

"He left after we killed the demon," she said.

"You will swear to that under a truth spell," the man said staring at Kyrianna as she turned around.

"I will."

"Very well." He glanced at the others "We will return to Nanitial."

"Is that the name of your town or the island?" Myrith asked.

"Both." He gestured to the boats. "Let's go."

The trip back seemed to take longer as everyone sat in silence, staring out at the water. Myrith tried once to engage Kyrianna in conversation, but she ignored the woman's questions about her home.

The mayor was waiting for them with several other people, including Ravlian. "Your mission was successful," the mayor said. "For that we are grateful. I would invite you to stay with us this night; however, there is another here who claims to have business with you."

The mayor stepped to the side as another man came forward.

"I am Martin, Timber sent me," he said. "The artifact has been located and secured; therefore we can now risk sending you through one of the portals."

"Perhaps, they should be allowed to rest tonight," Ravlian said. "They fought a hard battle then came back without taking time to rest. And, I understand there was some trouble on the way back." He glanced at Kyrianna and grinned. "I also suggest the council offer the services of a healer."

"I have no objections to waiting," Martin said.

"It is getting late," the mayor said. "I can send a runner to the inn to see rooms are made ready, and a healer is there for you."

Myrith looked at the others. "Well, do we get a night's rest or do you want to leave now?"

"Let's get some rest," Hendandra said. "I know I'm tired and would welcome a good meal and a real bed."

"I agree," Falden said.

Myrith turn to Kyrianna. "Well," she said. "What do you think?"

She glanced at Ravlian then back at Myrith. "I won't argue with the others."

"That settles it," Myrith said. "We will accept your offer."

"Good," the mayor said. He nodded to one of the guards who took off for town. "Rooms and a meal should be prepared by the time we get back." He gestured to the trail as another of the guards led the way back to the town.

Chapter Twenty-One

Kyrianna stared out the window as another burst of color flashed in the sky. Despite the spells the healer had cast, her arm still hurt and she doubted the scars would ever go away. Her body still ached from Ravlian's attacks and she had been unable to sleep as a result.

She glanced over at Hendandra, who had curled up in a ball on her bed after her session with the healer and had fallen immediately asleep. She knew she should have been doing the same, but the lingering pain wouldn't let her.

Kyrianna knew the healer had treated her properly, but it had been the bare minimum needed. She wondered if even that would have been offered if Myrith hadn't been standing over him watching.

"We need to talk," Myrith whispered from behind her startling her out of her thoughts.

"What about?" Kyrianna didn't take her gaze from the gray sky.

"You."

She turned to look at Myrith. "Why? It's not like we're going to be together much longer," she said.

"I'm worried about you. I want to make sure you're going to be okay."

Kyrianna nodded then glanced over at the sleeping form of Hendandra.

"We can go down to the private room, if you prefer," Myrith said.

Kyrianna nodded and Myrith gestured to the door.

The two of them walked through the common room in silence. Kyrianna's back stiffened at some of the looks she was getting from the few patrons still there; however she managed to control her emotions.

Myrith waved off the serving girl then closed the doors to the private dining room. She leaned against the closed doors, effectively blocking them as Kyrianna started pacing the room.

Kyrianna took a deep breath when she heard Myrith clear her

throat then leaned back against the table. "What do you want to know?"

"Why you don't want to go home. It's obvious you're home-sick, yet you indicated you had nothing to go back to."

Kyrianna stared at her, not saying anything.

"Rangerette?" Myrith asked after several seconds.

"I was caught doing something incredibly stupid and my fa-ther disowned me. I do not have a home to return to."

"If I may ask, what did you do?" Myrith left her guard posi-tion in front of the door to stand next to her.

Kyrianna looked up at Myrith. "I was a member of the Thieves' Guild in Nydith and I got caught on my first assignment for them. The Magistrate turned me over to my father who is a respect-ed man in Nydith. He disowned me and had me exiled from my home."

Myrith reached out and placed a hand on Kyrianna's shoul-der. "At least you had a father and a family," she said. "I never knew my father and my mother abandoned me as soon as I was old enough to work in the tavern where I was raised. I spent many long years trapped in that place before I was able to escape that life. I found myself in a temple of Geladas where the senior cleric offered to have me trained to wield a sword. It was shortly before I was caught in the portal that Geladas called me to be one of his holy knights."

Kyrianna nodded slightly. "When I was exiled I was visited by an avatar of Frayrith who marked me with this." She pulled back the sleeve of her tunic to reveal the unicorn tattoo on her right wrist.

"So we do have something in common," Myrith said. "It took both of us leaving the places we grew up before we found our gods."

"There may be other things as well," Kyrianna said. "You said you were pulled to this place by a portal similar to the one I described. Did you also hear a woman's voice speaking in the chaos of the portal?"

Myrith took a step back. "How did you know?"

"Because she spoke to me as well. What reason would the Lady of Chaos have for bringing us here?"

"I do not know this Lady of Chaos, Thynitic I believe you called her, so I cannot even begin to guess what her reasons would be. However, it is possible there is no real reason, after all she is chaos, is she not?"

"That she is. Even with that possibility, I am still bothered by all this. There has been so much here that ties to her and it seems to be calling to some part of me."

"Silly elf," Myrith said. "You have a chaotic nature; anyone can see that. While you may not completely disdain the Order, you do not embrace it in any way. She is the Lady of Chaos—surely that is all it is. Her Chaos has touched that part of your nature."

"Perhaps," Kyrianna whispered. "I hope that's all it is."

"I'm a warrior of Geladas who is a deity of Order and justice, of course that's all it is," Myrith said with a laugh. "Come on Rangerette; let's get some rest, tomorrow we get to go home."

"Why are you so anxious to go home, Myrith? It sounds like you have even less to look forward to than I do."

Myrith froze; her hand on the door handle. She did not turn around as she spoke. "Because I want to fight to free my people from the tyrant who rules them. I want to bring justice to those who need it. I don't want anyone to be forced into the life I was forced into." She jerked the door open and headed for the stairs through the now empty common room.

"You want to earn what you've been given as do I," Kyrianna said.

Myrith paused then turned to face her. "Exactly. Geladas gave me his favor as one of his knights even though I wasn't interested in training as one and refused to attend the religious classes the clerics offered."

Kyrianna nodded. "And Frayrith marked me as one of Hers even though I was nothing more than a thief and an exile. Seems we both have much to prove to ourselves. May Geladas guide you."

Myrith brushed her hair back from her face. "And may Frayrith give you strength and purpose," she said. "Now, to bed with us both." She gestured to the stairs.

~ * ~

Martin was waiting for the group when they entered the private room the next morning.

"I would recommend not eating very much," Martin said. "We will be teleporting and that is never easy on the stomach."

"Perhaps we should just pack a breakfast to take with us," Falden said. "We can always eat once we get to where we're going."

There were several nods of agreement as the group started putting together food packs.

"As long as Ravlian isn't casting the magic to teleport us," Kyrianna muttered.

"Kyrianna!" Myrith turned to glare at her.

"No Lady Kyrianna," Martin said. "It will not be Ravlian casting the magic. I have an enchanted item designed specifically to teleport us." He held up a clear crystal rod. "If everyone is ready, I will ask you to join hands."

As soon as the group had joined hands, Martin snapped the rod and a bright light surrounded them.

Kyrianna was glad she had heeded Martin's warning about not eating very much as her stomach threatened to expel itself through her throat. Myrith didn't look like she was in any better shape and Hendandra was on her knees gagging. The only ones who seemed unaffected were Falden and Martin. Falden was a mage and was probably used to using magic to travel, as it appeared Martin was also.

"Welcome to the gateway," Martin said. "As the artifact has been secured and sent to where it needs to be, we can now start allowing this portal to be used."

"How does it work?" Myrith asked.

Kyrianna found herself staring at the portal. The swirling colors were the same as Thynitic's symbol. She tried to catch her breath as she took a step back.

"The person or persons stepping into the portal must be focused on their destination. The portal uses that focus to send you to that place." He paused and looked at the group. "Who will be first?"

"We will," Hendandra said as she and Falden stepped forward.

"Raspa?" Falden asked as he looked down at Hendandra.

"Raspa!" Hendandra placed a hand on Falden's arm as they both stepped into the portal together.

Martin glanced at Kyrianna then turned his attention to Myrith. "Lady?" he asked as he gestured toward the portal.

Kyrianna nodded and forced a weak smile when Myrith looked at her. "Good luck in your quest," Kyrianna said.

"And to you. Even if you have nothing to prove what happened here, perhaps they will take note of having your goddess' favor."

"Perhaps," Kyrianna whispered as Myrith stepped into the portal.

"May The Lady guide you on your journey," Martin said as Kyrianna stepped into the portal.

Kyrianna hesitated at his words, but the swirling colors of the portal surrounded and pulled her into the portal as a cacophony of noise added to her disorientation. She forced herself to concentrate on the clearing she had originally been taken from. Even as she fought the distractions of the portal, she found herself unable to hold onto the image of Smokemist's dapple-gray coat or his black eyes. Her memory tried to focus on Shadow Seeker as the wolf had stepped out of the trees and walked over to her that day, his cold nose touching her wrist and sending tiny daggers of ice up her arm.

As the colors finally faded and a gray haze surrounded them, Kyrianna inhaled deeply. She searched for the sharp scent of pine and the muskiness of wolf and horse. Though her senses brought her the smells of damp earth and the slight sting of pine, there was nothing that reminded her of Smoke or Shadow. This was not the same place she had left.

Chapter Twenty-Two

Kyrianna stepped out of the portal and onto a road overgrown with grass and weeds. There were lines in the dirt showing where wagons had once traveled along the road, but they were no longer ruts, only shallow depressions and scratches in the surface.

She glanced skyward, but the thick clouds blocked her from searching the stars for any of the familiar constellations of Rhysia. The air, though still chill with the lateness of the hour, was warmer than it should have been if they were in Kilenter.

Kyrianna took another deep breath. The scents of the forest were at their coolest; it was well past the nadir of night. The glow of torches flickered a short distance down the road and she turned toward them, hoping it might be a village where she could get her bearings and find out where she was.

As she approached the small town, the guard stood up and stepped in front of the gate. "We don't get many travelers these days," he said.

"I noticed the state of the road. A shame, as this appears to be a decent town," Kyrianna said.

The guard straightened a bit. "Thank you," he said. "Duvshire used to be the center for this region of Shokar. Since the disaster at the Duvall Estate, it has been in a steady decline."

"When did this disaster occur?"

"Thirty years ago." The guard paused as the slight breeze ruffled Kyrianna's hair. "You're an elf?"

"I am half elven," she said.

The guard's eyes widened, but she saw no fear or hatred on his face.

"May your fortunes soon turn," she said. "Perhaps you could recommend a tavern with rooms for rent."

"The best place in town is the Wailing Banshee." The guard forced a laugh as he waved her through the gate. "Of course, it's the only place in town."

"Guess that makes it the best," Kyrianna said.

The tavern, the guard had named, was only a few blocks

from the gate and was quiet as she entered. There were only a few patrons seated around the large common room; all of who looked up at her for a few seconds before returning to their previous conversations or meals. That is all but two of them. Kyrianna noticed two men who continued to watch her intently. In one corner sat a young human with light brown hair and intelligent blue eyes. His clothing was of fine make, though it had seen better days, much as the town had. However, it was enough to mark him as possibly being a noble of this area.

In the other corner was an elf, and Kyrianna could feel his eyes watching her as she glanced in his direction. His coloring was similar to that of the Alowien, but instead of the bright gold of her cousins, his eyes and hair were more golden brown. Darker and warmer as he smiled and lifted his cup slightly in her direction.

"Good evening," a slender, dark haired woman said as she approached. "You're new to this area." It was a statement not a question.

"I am," Kyrianna said. "What would you recommend for a late dinner?"

The woman smiled warmly. "It is late, as you have observed, however the venison was very good this night and I believe there is still a decent amount available."

"Sounds good," she said.

"Would you prefer wine or ale with the meal?"

"Actually water would be best," Kyrianna said.

"I'll be back shortly." The server headed over to the bar.

She sat quietly after the server brought the water then came back with her meal.

"Two silver," the server said coming back to the table, as Kyrianna was finishing.

She placed three silver coins on the table then laid a gold coin next to them. "As you've already guessed, I'm new to this region. What can you tell us about it?"

The server looked at the gold piece on the table then glanced around the room at the other patrons. Kyrianna followed her gaze and saw, other than the young nobleman and the elf, no one was paying any attention to them. She blushed as she realized the elf's full attention was still centered on her.

"I'm Marlene," the server said as she sat down. "This is Duvshire, a small insignificant place in the land of Shokar. There are only a few major cities: Gormanghast, Raspa, Tormasus, and Irrmar. Irrmar is the capitol of Dh'Mark and it is where you will find the majority of the nobles." She glanced at the gentleman in the corner. "With a few exceptions, that is. Gormanghast is where the wizards are found. It is a place of mystery and magic, Raspa is considered a place of learning and the closest political center to Duvshire. There are also several noble houses located there. Tormasus is an independent city with some of the best-trained armies in the world to defend her. There is also a large elven settlement to the north as well, but they do not travel much and do not welcome humans or strangers."

"And what about Duvshire?"

"Duvshire was once a much larger and more important city. Until about thirty years ago, that is." Her eyes darted to the young nobleman in his corner as she took a deep breath. "That's when something struck down the Duvall family. Tristan," she nodded her head toward the young man, "is the last of that line. He has been here trying to hire people to go with him to the estate west of town to cleanse it of the evil that has taken residence there. So far no one has been crazy enough to go with him."

Marlene turned her gaze toward the elf who was still staring at Kyrianna. "He's an odd one," she said. "As I said, elves don't travel much, however Legewyd has been here for about a week now. Claims he is traveling to study the various types of magic in Shokar. He has spent considerable time with Tyril. Tyril is also an elf, but I understand he was exiled from his home for something involving a magic experiment that went bad. He's not really much of a wizard either, just a hedge-mage."

Kyrianna let her gaze linger on Legewyd for a moment. *Studying magic? Why would anyone bother? As Tyril's own history proves, magic is not to be trusted. An experiment gone badly—that would be considered normal by most on Rhysia.*

Marlene spent several more minutes pointing out the rest of the people in the tavern, including the mayor and his son, both of whom seemed to be watching Tristan Duvall. "I need to get back to work," she finally said.

"Before you go, is it possible to arrange for a room and a hot bath?" Kyrianna asked as she held up a gold coin.

"Yes, we have a bathing room available. I will have a bath prepared. It will be a few minutes."

"Thank you." Kyrianna finished her meal ignoring the continuing stare from Legewyd. She glanced up at the young man Marlene had identified as Tristan Duvall and grinned as he quickly looked away.

"Please follow me," Marlene said when she returned to the table.

She showed Kyrianna to her room first. "If you want to drop off your packs and gear, I will show you to the bath chamber," she said opening the door to a small but clean room.

Kyrianna dropped her pack on the bed. She left her swords and bow, but pulled a dagger from the pack and stuck it in her boot.

"Been traveling for a while?" Marlene asked.

She ignored the question as she followed the woman down the hallway to the bath chamber. Towels and robes hung by the door as they entered the warm, steam filled room.

"If you wish, you can leave your clothes on the bench there and they will be cleaned for you by morning," Marlene said.

"Thank you," Kyrianna said. "It will be nice to get the dust and grime out of my clothes."

"I will pick them up after you finish." Marlene pointed out the lock on the inside then wished her a goodnight and left.

"A hot bath was definitely a great idea," Kyrianna said as she slipped out of her clothes and pulled the tie from around her hair. She closed her eyes as she leaned back in the tub and sighed deeply as the heat relaxed her sore muscles.

None of the names Marlene had given her meant anything, other than she had not returned to Rhysia. Now, the question was how to get back. Martin had promised the portal would allow them to return to their homes, but instead she was here.

She slid under the water for a moment then sat back up. "What was it Martin said? May The Lady guide you on your journey." She slammed her fist against the water. "Chaos take it! Why?"

Because you are the last of my Daughters and you will embrace me when it is time.

Kyrianna shook her head. "No! I serve Frayrith."

There was only silence in her mind.

Dressed in one of the warm robes from the bath chamber, Kyrianna hurried back to her room where a fire had been started in the small fireplace. A note had been left on the door and she opened it slowly.

"I would be honored if you would join me at breakfast." There was no name on the note, only a small elvish style rune.

Chapter Twenty-Three

A soft knock at the door woke Kyrianna the next morning. She opened the door to see a young girl standing in the hallway holding a bundle of clothes. "Marlene asked me to deliver these to you, my lady," the girl said bowing her head slightly.

"Thank you." She took the bundle and smiled. "Wait there a moment." She stepped back from the door and dropped the clothes on her bed. Kyrianna opened her coin purse, pulled out a silver coin and tossed it to the girl.

"Thank you." The girl curtsied then dashed down the hallway and down the stairs.

Kyrianna pulled her tunic over her head and took a deep breath. The blood, both hers and from some of the demons they had faced, was gone and the cloth smelled clean.

Even though her leather armor had been cleaned, none of the damage had been repaired. The tear one of the demons had made was still there across the front, and the right sleeve was shredded. It was useless. She would have to see about getting new.

She dumped the contents of her pack on the small bed and carefully sorted through what she still had and what might be able to be used for barter. The dress she had brought from home, might be worth a few coins, but it was something she was not willing to part with. She still had the short sword her uncle had made, the unusual shield she had found in the temple, less than two quivers of arrows, her bow, swords and a few other small items. She repacked her equipment then emptied her coin purse on the bed. Approximately twenty gold and thirty silver coins lay on the bed. *It should be enough*, she thought.

Kyrianna left the armor on the floor of the room as she buckled her swords on over her pants, secured the bow to her pack then headed down to the common room to meet Legewyd.

Kyrianna glanced around the room and saw the elf from the night before sitting at the same table watching the rest of the patrons. He glanced at her and nodded his head politely as he smiled and gestured to the chair across from his.

Kyrianna smiled and moved toward the offered place, she turned and glanced toward the door of the tavern as it opened.

The man who walked through the door was large, with shaggy black hair and piercing black eyes. Though he was shaven, there was still the shadow of a beard on his face. He didn't look around, instead going straight to a table near the bar and sitting with his back to the other patrons.

"Who is that?" Kyrianna said when Marlene came over with a pitcher of water and a cup for her.

"Boris. He is the only man to have ever entered the Duvall estate and survive the experience."

"Did Duvall ask him for help?" Legewyd asked.

"He did." Marlene paused as Tristan came down the stairs. "Boris only laughed at him."

"Sounds like an interesting fellow," Legewyd said.

"He stinks of death," Kyrianna said.

"He is a hunter," Marlene said as she left the table.

"Poacher is more likely what he is," Kyrianna muttered. "I doubt he has any respect for his prey."

She glanced around and saw Tristan still standing by the stairs. He didn't seem to be much different than many of the young noblemen she knew from her home. The ones who were born to their positions, and didn't have to earn them. The ones who thought society owed them respect simply because of the family they were born into. Dilettantes, most were; only interested in their position and personal power.

Still there was a confidence in his stance that didn't seem to be born from arrogance. For a moment, Tristan's eyes met hers and he smiled. It was a warm and sincere smile, one that was reflected in his eyes; not the façade she remembered on the faces of the prideful nobles she had once known.

"I do not see many elves away from home," Legewyd said. "It is pleasant to see a familiar face."

"I too have been away from my kin for some time as well," she said.

"I am called Legewyd."

"Kyrianna."

"I have done considerable traveling, studying the various magic disciplines. However, I believe you are from further away than I have ever been."

Kyrianna smiled. "You are correct in your belief. I am from another land, brought here by powers unknown." She went on to tell him how she was trapped in the portal and transported from Rhysia to the temple. She also found herself telling him about the Moon Swords, the artifact they had been searching for and the demons they had fought.

Legewyd sat quietly as he listened to her story. "Moon Swords," he said when she finished. "They are identified by the crescent moon daggers they carry are they not?"

"They are." Kyrianna leaned forward with interest.

"I have seen members of that group before," Legewyd said. He paused and took a long drink from his cup.

Kyrianna watched him closely as she waited for him to continue.

"They are usually seen in the company of one of the members of the Council of Mages in Gormanghast, Cassandra Shindar. There are rumors the Moon Swords serve some dark and chaotic power from another world and travel the planes searching for artifacts of power."

"Yet they are opposed to a dark, chaotic power from my home."

"That only speaks to their opposition to a particular power, it says nothing of their actual motives," Legewyd said softly.

"True." Kyrianna said glancing around again. She nodded politely as Tristan smiled at her and she felt her face flush.

"You are dressed like one who follows the paths of the forests," Legewyd said drawing her attention back. "Is this a symbol of your deity?" He gently touched the unicorn medallion.

Kyrianna smiled as her hand reached for the medallion and her fingers brushed Legewyd's hand. "Frayrith is her name," she said softly.

"Tell me about her." He shifted his hand so it was now on top of Kyrianna's as he smiled at her.

"She is also called the Lady of the Forests and Protector of the Balance. The unicorn is her chosen symbol and avatar."

"Here the one comparable to your Frayrith is called Dwycia and she is the protector of all animals. Her symbol is a wolf as she is also a huntress." He let his gaze slide to Boris for a brief moment. "It is said she has a special hatred for shape changers such as were-wolves and others like them."

"Frayrith has a particular hatred of abominations, those whose changed and twisted natures insult the natural balance."

Legewyd nodded slowly. "It has been said all of the gods are only reflections of each other; each one only another aspect of the whole. Perhaps, your Frayrith and our Dwycia are sister deities."

"Perhaps." She took a breath. "What else can you tell me about the mages of this land. I need to find a way to return to my own. Is it possible this Cassandra Shindar you mentioned can help?"

"Teleportation across planes and worlds is a risky business and it costs a lot. From what I have heard of this Cassandra Shindar, she is one of the youngest mages to be made a member of the council. She is considered ambitious and powerful; she never does anything without a reason and something to gain. Unless you have something she wants, she will not perform the spell."

"I still have a few gold pieces. But I doubt it would be enough." Her hand dropped to the swords she was wearing. They were very unusual and might have some value to a collector.

"There is another mage who might help, Tyril. He lives only a short distance to the north of Duvshire."

"Marlene mentioned him last night. She called him a hedge-mage and said he had been exiled from his people for a magic experiment gone wrong. I do not know that much about eldritch magic, but the term hedge-mage seems to indicate he does not have that much power. I doubt he can help."

"Do not judge him too hastily. He has more power than many realize. It is because he never attended the Academy in Gormanghast that his magic is often belittled. I would recommend you talk to him at least."

"I will," Kyrianna said. "I thank you for your time."

"It is always a pleasure to spend time with someone like you," Legewyd said as he stood and gave her a half-bow. "By the way if you need supplies and such, I recommend Mulbanith's a few stores south of here."

Kyrianna smiled. "Thank you again."

~ * ~

Kyrianna paused in front of a store window; above the door was a carved sign that read: "Mulbanith's". The place seemed to be crowded with all kinds of miscellaneous stuff; including weaponry, jewelry and other collectable items.

Kyrianna walked in and pulled the green shield she had picked up in the temple out of her pack and laid it on the counter. The man standing there slid his hand across the glowing metal and frowned. She cocked her head slightly and smiled. She had no idea what the item was worth, but she knew it was unusual and she hadn't missed the gleam in the shopkeeper's eyes.

"Mulbanith," the man said offering her his hand as he glanced at the shield.

"Kyrianna," she said grasping his hand for a second.

Mulbanith picked up the shield and spent several minutes examining the metal. His eyes darted from the shield to her and back a couple of times. "There are no magical properties, I take it?"

"None that I am aware of," Kyrianna said.

He shook his head and tsked several times. Kyrianna only smiled softly. While she didn't know what the shield was truly worth, she did recognize the potential value in the unusual lightweight material it was made from. The shield was easily half the weight of a comparably sized steel shield. And, if her blades were any indication, it was just as strong as any made of steel.

"I do know of a collector in Gormanghast who likes the unusual, I believe he'll be interested in this piece. Now, to the price," he said.

Kyrianna spread her hands out in front of her. "Make an offer," she said.

"I don't have the gold on hand to offer a fair price, however, I have an item, which, judging by your clothes and gear, might interest you," Mulbanith said after several seconds. "It is a valuable magic item, one that someone in your apparent profession would find useful. However, I am not sure I wish to make the trade."

"I personally don't care for magic. What else can you offer?"

Mulbanith stared at her for a moment. "Something that is not magical?" He started to push the shield back then paused. "You wear no armor. Perhaps I can offer you something appropriate—no magics on it." He looked up at her and waited.

Kyrianna waited as well. She knew the value of the shield—particularly if he was going to sell to a person who was a collector of the unusual was worth considerably more than a new set of leathers.

"Two hundred gold pieces in addition to the armor," he said.

After several seconds she nodded. "I have a short sword I am willing to throw into the bargain if you add a couple of quivers of the highest quality arrows you have." She pulled the sword out of her pack and placed it on the counter.

Mulbanith checked the weapon then nodded his agreement. "Done." He picked up the shield and vanished behind the counter. Kyrianna listened to the clicks that indicated several locks were being opened then closed.

He placed a money pouch on the counter when he stood back up. "I'll be back in a moment," he said when he finished. He left the sword on the counter as he moved to a back room of the shop.

"These should be to your satisfaction," Mulbanith said startling Kyrianna, who hadn't heard him approach. He held out three quivers of arrows as well as a set of leather armor.

Kyrianna took the quivers and leathers. "Thank you," she said. The leather was soft and very supple as she held it. She glanced at Mulbanith and frowned.

"The process of tanning is very advanced in the town of Raspa where that came from. The town also boasts some of the finest armorers in all of Shokar. It is very comfortable to wear, yet as sturdy as any leather armor. You will find the trade to be worthwhile."

"Agreed."

"A pleasure."

Kyrianna took a few minutes to attach the quivers to her pack then picked up the new armor and headed out of the shop.

She paused and glanced down the street. The gate she had come through was to the south. A few yards past the tavern to the north was a large square. Another path led north from the square into the woods. "Talk to a mage," she muttered as she shook her head and turned toward the path leading north. "Frayrith guide me through the Chaos."

~ * ~

Kyrianna wasn't sure what she was expecting to learn from this Tyril. He was a mage and therefore not to be trusted.

She was about a hundred yards into the forest, when a sudden silence fell over the area. The sound of her footfalls among the leaves and underbrush gone, she stopped and started scanning the area. She dropped the armor she was carrying, drew her long sword and spun around as a cloaked figure appeared next to her.

"Chaos!" Kyrianna backpedaled as the figure drove a dagger into her side. Her blade flashed and she felt a brief satisfaction as blood appeared on her attacker's shirt.

She continued to move back as her side started burning. *Poison*, she thought. *Oh Frayrith, the blade was poisoned.*

Another cloaked figure appeared on the other side of her attacker, several daggers flying as he hit him several times in rapid succession.

Kyrianna staggered as her blade dropped lower. She shook her head as a wave of dizziness hit her. "Be careful," she called. "He's using poison." She fell back against a nearby tree.

The two continued to dance around each other, moving with a grace Kyrianna envied as she fought to stay on her feet. She glanced down; her side was covered in blood; apparently, the dagger also had something that was preventing the blood from coagulating. Her sword fell from her hand as she found herself sitting on the ground, the tree still at her back. She cleared her head enough to see her attacker pull a vial from his pocket and swallow the contents. He dropped the empty glass on the ground, turned into a gaseous vapor and floated away from the area. The other person ran after the departing mist leaving her alone. She reached for her sword and laid it across her lap as she focused on fighting the poison in her system.

A twig snapped behind her and Kyrianna tightened the grip on her sword as she listened for any other sounds.

"I am Tyril," a soft voice said behind her. "I believe you were coming to see me."

Kyrianna nodded.

He knelt beside her and began checking the dagger wound. She gasped as he pulled the weapon from her side and a rush of fresh blood spurted from the cut. "Poison's are a nasty business," he said as he pressed his hand against her side.

Kyrianna felt warmth flow from the mage's hand to her side and smiled as he began bandaging the injury. He wrapped the dagger in a black silk cloth and handed it to her as he helped her to her feet. She placed the dagger in her pack then leaned against the mage as he helped her up.

They were within sight of a small cabin, when Kyrianna found everything going black. She felt Tyril tighten his hold on her as her knees buckled and she fell into darkness.

~ * ~

"How long?" Kyrianna pushed herself into a sitting position as the darkness finally faded. She was in a small room, a male elf with dark brown hair and gray eyes sat next to her.

"Welcome back," Tyril said. "It has been several hours. You will still be very weak from the poison the assassin used and should continue to rest." He turned toward the door. "Please excuse me for a moment."

"How is she?" Kyrianna heard someone ask as Tyril exited the room she was in. The mage left the door ajar and she slipped out of the bed to stand next to the opening so she could hear.

"She will be fine. She is strong and I had the proper antidote to the assassin's poison on hand. A precaution I have taken for myself," Tyril said.

"Here are the items she dropped when she was attacked. Please see they are returned."

A creak in the floorboards told her the person was leaving. Kyrianna pushed the door open and stepped out into the main room. "Wait, who are you?"

"You should be resting, my lady," the cloaked stranger said, offering her a slight bow.

"I still wish to know who you are. Please."

The cloaked figure pushed the cowl back to reveal an elven face with black eyes and surrounded by long black hair. Kyrianna took a step back, her hand reaching for the sword she was no longer wearing. She found her eyes drawn to the pendant he was wearing; an oval shaped pendant whose surface was a mass of swirling colors.

"I am called Elvioril," he said as he held out his hand.

Kyrianna ignored the outstretched hand and remained silent, not giving her name.

Tyril ignored the silence between the two and reached for a dagger laying on the table.

"Interesting." He raised an eyebrow and let his gaze focus on her again. "You are very lucky to have survived an encounter with this one." He turned the blade over. "See this." He pointed to the symbol on the blade. "This is the symbol for the Reverie—a group of elven purists. They hate humans and refuse to have any commerce with them unless they can use them for their purposes. They do hire out as assassins quite frequently and are single minded in their determination to fulfill their contracts. This man will not stop until he succeeds in killing his target. The fact he is here shows he has a target. From the whisperings I have heard, I believe Lord Duvall may be that target. Nor, will he think twice about killing anyone who may get in his way." He looked her and shook his head.

Kyrianna felt a chill wrap itself around her at the mention of Tristan Duvall being the target of an assassin. It made no sense to her; she had not even met the young nobleman, though he had been pointed out to her.

"You are in serious jeopardy," Tyril was saying as she forced her attention back to him. "As you are a half-elf, he will target you, even before his assigned target—if he is able. The members of the Reverie have been known to destroy the entire families of those with mixed blood. To consort with a non-elf is considered the lowest corruption there is and they do not tolerate it." He placed the blade on the desk. "He will do everything he can to kill you. Be on your guard."

"Thank you for the warning," Kyrianna whispered.

"If you are feeling strong enough, your equipment and property are in the chest at the foot of the bed. Place your right hand on the unicorn symbol and it will open. Elvioril has retrieved the items you dropped when you were attacked." He gestured to the bundle on a nearby chair. "Also, there is a long tunic in the chest you may have to replace the one you are wearing."

Kyrianna glanced down at the blood on the side on her tunic and nodded. She picked up the bundle with her armor and returned to the room. She left the door open enough to listen to the two of them talking as she changed.

"You are also in great danger," Tyril said. "You are from an alien world and therefore considered to have tainted blood as well."

"I have already shown I can handle myself. It is this assassin who should worry if our paths cross again," Elvioril said.

"Perhaps. However, as you have told me, you have been given a duty to protect the lady. Should you not be concerned about her safety above yours? If your being near her places her in greater jeopardy, have you truly fulfilled your duty?"

"If you are speaking of me, I do not welcome or desire your help, Rynial," Kyrianna said slamming the door open.

Elvioril shook his head. "Stubborn, which is to be expected," he said. "However, there are others involved that have given me this task and whether you welcome or desire it, I will not fail them." His hand went to the symbol of Thynitic he wore.

She continued to stare at the Rynial then glanced at Tyril as a light seemed to flicker around him. She found herself looking not at the elf who had been sitting with her when she had awakened, but instead at a half-elf whose features resembled those of the elf.

"An illusion I maintain to protect myself. The Reverie have been looking for me for some time. They killed my mother a few years back for having sunk so low as to marry a human."

Kyrianna could think of nothing to say to Tyril. The prejudice humans and elves had for each other on Rhysia was almost as bad as what this group of elves harbored here. She had seen the results of that prejudice in a city considered the most tolerant of all the human cities. She knew her mother's people were considered the most tolerant of the elves toward humans and even they tended to shun contact with them. She glanced at Elvioril again and lowered her eyes. Was she not also guilty of a similar prejudice?

"As another word of warning," Tyril said. "Other than those here, I only know of one other elf in the area."

Kyrianna felt her jaw drop as she stared at Tyril. Only one other elf in the area? Legewyd. The traveler at the inn who claimed to be making a study of magic. The same elf who had given her the information on Dwycia. The same elf who appeared interested in her when they had first arrived and had acted as a friend. Now she understood what his interest truly was—a chance to get close to her so he could kill her. He had been the one to direct her to Tyril and had known she would be speaking to him.

She paused as she realized this knowledge could give her an advantage the next time she met Legewyd. Of course, it might also be difficult to prove he had tried to kill her first if she killed him on sight.

Elvioril looked at her and frowned as he moved toward the door. He reached for the handle and Kyrianna snickered as he was thrown back several feet. He turned and glared at Tyril, who raised his hand then nodded. This time the door opened.

"Coward, show yourself!" Elvioril stood in the doorway, his sword in his hand as he scanned the area. The rustle of wings among the trees as several birds took the air was the only answer to his challenge.

Kyrianna stared at Elvioril as he stood there. With the light from the cabin illuminating behind him, there was no way Legewyd could not see him for what he was. He took a step away from the door. "Only cowards and weaklings attack from the shadows. Perhaps one of your forbearers was a human!"

Kyrianna held her breath waiting for the attack she knew had to be coming after that insult. Still only silence greeted the challenge. "I think he's left the area," she said.

Elvioril ignored her and took several more steps forward, still shouting his challenge.

Kyrianna shook her head then turned her attention back to Tyril. "I thank you for your time. Is there anything else you can tell me about this assassin?"

"You have already tasted his blade," he said gesturing to the dagger on the table. "You understand the skill you are facing. Be on your guard." Light shimmered around him and he was once again a full elf in appearance. "I offer my apologies that I do not have the means to return you to your own land. I would give you this." He held out a vial of a dull yellow liquid. "It is the antidote to the poison used on you. You may have need of it again."

"Thank you." Kyrianna took the vial then turned toward the door.

"I would suggest you seek the sponsorship of one of the nobility who might be able to help. Lord Duvall perhaps," Tyril said.

"Only those with no skills strike from the shadows, unable to defeat their opponents in honorable battle," Elvioril's voice echoed in the silence of the dark forest.

Tyril nodded toward the door. Kyrianna returned the nod and realized he was dismissing her. She doubted Legewyd was still in the area. He might be patient, but why stay here waiting for one potential target with no idea how long that wait would be when there was another target?

"Tristan!" Kyrianna sprinted out of the cabin, past Elvioril and up the path back toward Duvshire. For just a heartbeat she paused. *Why should I care?* The thought echoed in her mind, as she continued running. *I do not know him and owe nothing to him.* Still, there was something in her soul telling her she had to protect him.

The sound of Elvioril's armor was louder than the pounding of her own heart in her ears as Kyrianna began to outdistance him. She could still hear him yelling his challenges, but no longer cared about him. She had one goal now, to reach Tristan before Legewyd did. "Frayrith and Dwycia, please let me get there in time," she said between breaths.

There were three familiar people standing in the square as she came into it and she hesitated long enough to grab Myrith's arm. "Come with me," she said.

Kyrianna slowed her pace slightly as the woman joined her without asking any questions. As they reached the tavern, she looked up to see a figure standing in a window. Tristan's head moved up and down several times as if he was judging the distance to the ground. "No!" Kyrianna's voice broke as he jumped from the window.

"Are you okay?" Kyrianna asked she helped Tristan up.

Tristan shook his head, but didn't say anything as he held his hand to his side. Kyrianna gasped at the amount of blood.

"He was able to force his way into the room. He marked me with a dagger before I was able to force him back out," Tristan whispered.

Myrith looked around the area, her crossbow up and ready. "Who is this person who attacked you?"

"He was an elf. I believe he was hired to kill Lord Tristan here," Kyrianna said.

"I had the door well barricaded when smoke began entering from under the door."

"He started a fire?" Kyrianna jerked her head back toward the building behind them. Tyril had said Legewyd wouldn't care about the lives of others as long as he got to his target. But, for an elf to have that callous of an attitude toward life was hard to believe. Life was sacred; something to be nurtured and cherished—at least that was the belief of most of the elves Kyrianna had known. This kind of indifference was more common among humans.

"Where is that coward! Stand and face me!" Elvioril was still shouting as he came into the square. He held one of his blades in his hand and was running straight toward Kyrianna.

"Stand fast," Myrith ordered raising her crossbow. Elvioril ignored her and she fired. The bolt struck him in the chest and he staggered back a step.

Elvioril paused only long enough to draw one of the daggers at his belt then charged Myrith. She dropped the crossbow, drew her long sword and stood ready to meet him.

Kyrianna supported Tristan as they moved away from the

growing crowd. She wasn't happy with him being out in the open like this. With the number of people watching the fight between Myrith and Elvioril it wouldn't be hard for someone to slip a knife into Tristan's back then vanish. "Here," she said pushing the vial Tyril had given her into Tristan's hand. "An antidote to the poison."

"How?" Tristan took the vial, his hand shaking.

"Tyril gave it to me, saying I might have need of it," Kyrianna said turning her attention back to Myrith and Elvioril.

She looked up to see Elvioril stagger back from one of Myrith's blows. Blood was flowing from several places on the elf, while the knight didn't look to have been touched yet. Myrith landed another hit even as Elvioril's blade slid against her armor.

What are they doing here? Kyrianna thought as Hendandra slipped in behind Elvioril, her rapier ready. Falden was standing behind the girl, his hands raised as if he were preparing a spell.

"Chaos take you," Elvioril said as he fell to the ground.

"You three remain where you are and drop your weapons," Marvial ordered as he stepped up and pointed to Hendandra, Falden and Myrith.

Myrith immediately complied with the order and stood there, her hands held away from her body. Hendandra hesitated for several seconds until Marvial started to draw his own sword as he stared at her. She never took her eyes off the captain as she undid her belt and placed the weapons on the ground. Falden dropped his staff and copied Myrith's stance with his hands away from his body.

"Everyone else leave this area!" At the captain's order, three members of the watch started moving through the crowd encouraging them to leave.

Kyrianna stayed with Tristan as she watched the rest of the crowd leaving. She frowned slightly when she saw the mayor and his son standing nearby watching them.

"Captain Marvial! Over here!" One of the guardsmen yelled as he approached Tristan and Kyrianna.

Kyrianna looked at Tristan. He was still very pale, his breathing shallow as he stood next to her. She started to put an arm around him to steady him but was stopped by the guardsman who held his blade between her and Tristan. She took a step to the side and held her hands up so she did not appear to be reaching for her swords.

"An attack on a noble of this area along with the other three attacking the elf. This is not good," the mayor said.

His son stepped forward and turned to the large man who had come over at the guard's call. "I believe all four of these people are strangers to the area. The elf woman arrived at the inn last night and the others just appeared in the square moments before the fire at the Wailing Banshee. In fact, the elf woman," he pointed at Kyrianna, "came running through the square, grabbed the woman with the red hair and ran to the Banshee. There they encountered Lord Duvall. She stayed with Lord Duvall while her companion attacked the elf."

Kyrianna swallowed as she looked from the mayor's son to the guard captain. He was a large, red-face man who had seen better days. He had none of the dignity she remembered seeing in her father, standing slouched and a half step behind the mayor's son. He might be the Captain of the Guard, but he answered to the mayor and his family. She doubted it was a situation he had accepted willingly.

The mayor's son was a slender young man, whose pristine attire and smooth hands told as much about him as Tristan's warm smile said about him. She had no doubt, this person had a streak of cruelty in him that would rival some of the stories she had heard about the priestesses of Thynitic. However, she doubted he ever did anything himself, but instead enjoyed watching others carry out his orders.

She turned her attention to the mayor. "Lord Mayor, I was trying to help Lord Tristan escape the one who attacked him. The elf who called himself Legewyd forced himself into his room before the fire started. It was he who attacked and injured Lord Tristan," she offering the mayor a slight bow. "I believe you will also find it was he who started the fire. I believe this was also an attempt to kill Lord Tristan."

"And why would he destroy the entire inn if the only person he wanted to kill was Duvall. That makes no sense. Assassins do not go around blatantly destroying something that obvious and killing extra people for only one target. It draws too much attention," the mayor's son said. "Perhaps it was you who started the fire as a diversion then ran when it got out of control."

The mayor glanced at the cleric who was attending to Elvioril. "My Lord, he is dead," he said.

The mayor turned at Tristan. "Has she spoken truthfully?"

Tristan nodded. "She has."

"Very well. I will not hold you responsible for the attack on Lord Duvall or the fire at the Wailing Banshee. You may leave."

Kyrianna bowed her head. "With your permission, I wish to wait and find out the status of my friends."

The cleric who had declared Elvioril dead was now checking Tristan. "He was poisoned, My Lord," he said looking at the mayor. "It appears he has already been given the antidote and will be fine in a few hours. He just needs rest."

"See you do not interfere," the mayor said looking at Kyrianna before turning to Myrith.

The mayor turned to Myrith. "Who are you that you draw weapons against another in our town?"

"I am Myrith, a knight of Geladas. That person entered the square with his weapons drawn and was charging toward us shouting challenges. I ordered him to stand fast and he ignored me, so I defended myself and my companions."

"You admit you drew first blood by attacking him," Marvial said.

"I do not admit to attacking him as he was clearly attacking us. Do I have to wait to be injured before I defend myself?"

The mayor ignored her. "The name of your god means nothing to me. For all I know Geladas could be the Lord of lying, deceit and murder. You will stand before the council tomorrow on a charge of murder. You may choose anyone who is willing to speak for you at the hearing. You are not allowed to speak for yourself unless directly questioned by the council."

"Rangerette?" Myrith glanced at Kyrianna. "You seem to have knowledge in the ways of the nobility—would you speak for me?"

"Of course. Though what knowledge I have will be lacking as I am not from this place. However, I stand by you."

"Enough. The request has been noted," the mayor said. "Guards!"

Kyrianna watched as the guards escorted the other three to a small building. She was glad they hadn't resisted them in any way.

"I suggest the rest of you find someplace else to be before I jail you for loitering," Captain Marvial said reaching for Myrith's and Hendandra's weapons. One of the other guards picked up Falden's staff.

"If I may make a suggestion," a voice said from the shadows

of a nearby alleyway.

Kyrianna spun around, her hand on her sword, as she looked for the speaker.

A young man stepped out of the alley and bowed his head slightly. He was dressed in various shades of gray. His black hair hung to his shoulders and he had brilliant blue eyes that seemed to linger on Kyrianna for a moment before they began darting around the area, watching everything. "I am Laraf. I believe you would be safer seeking refuge with Tyril for the night than anywhere else in this place. I can show you where his cabin is if you like," Laraf said.

"Thank you, that will not be necessary," Kyrianna said.

Laraf dropped his eyes and Kyrianna bit her lip at the harshness in her voice. "I appreciate your suggestion," she said in a calmer tone. "Thank you."

The young man nodded again then stepped back into the shadows of the alleyway and vanished.

Kyrianna escorted Tristan to Tyril's cabin, her mind racing over the events of the evening. The mage opened the door before they reached the building and motioned them inside. A fire was already burning in the fireplace and several blankets had been laid out on the floor.

"Do not touch anything! Do not light any other fires!" With that warning, Tyril vanished into the back room.

Kyrianna shrugged. "Let's get some rest," she said. "Tomorrow is not going to be pleasant."

Chapter Twenty-Four

"We thank you for your hospitality, Tyril," Tristan said as the mage opened the door of his cabin. Tyril only nodded and stood silently beside the door as they left.

Kyrianna paused and took a deep breath. The canopy of leaves still created dark shadows on the path along with the illusion of early twilight. The scents of the forest told her it was still early; the sharp sting of the pine and the damp musk of the moss and earth, each one still distinct. By afternoon, the scents would be stronger but they would be blended.

She glanced back at the mage for a moment. She knew her mother had regrets about being separated from her kin. However, Arielle still had those she could call family as well as friends. She also still had elven friends within Kilenter Forest whom she visited on occasion. Tyril was completely separated from his kin. He had to maintain a constant illusion and could never be as he truly was for fear of attack. Even with the illusion, he still had to live apart from other elves because of the risk he might slip up one day and let the illusion slip. And, he could not really associate with humans either.

Despite having to deal with the prejudice of many of the humans of Nydith, Kyrianna had never had to hide who she was. In time, most of the people she dealt with on a daily basis learned to accept her for who she was. She doubted she would ever truly understand what someone like Tyril actually felt having to be so isolated.

She and Tristan walked in silence back to Duvshire and presented themselves at the building being used to hold her friends.

"Only those designated to represent the prisoners before the council are allowed to speak with them," the guard at the door said.

"The Lady is designated to represent those who stand before the council this morning," Tristan said. "As she is from another land I will be advising her."

The guard checked the papers in front of him. "I do not have a full name for the lady." He looked up at Kyrianna. "I will need your name, title *if any*, and city."

"I am Kyrianna Dalynne of House Dalynne of the city of Nydith," she said.

"Is that a noble house of that city?" Tristan asked.

"My father is considered a minor noble, yes. However…"

"You will list her as Lady Kyrianna Dalynne," Tristan said. He leaned over close to Kyrianna. "Whatever else you were going say is not relevant at this time," he whispered.

The guard glanced from Tristan to Kyrianna and back then nodded and made the annotation on his paperwork. "My Lord and Lady, if you will follow me." He gestured to a nearby door.

The guard escorted them to Myrith's cell. Hendandra and Falden were in the cell next to the knight's and stood up when they saw Kyrianna. Everyone waited in silence until the guard left.

"Well," Kyrianna said as she and Tristan sat on the small bench outside the cells.

"I honestly believed he was after you, Kyri," Myrith said.

Kyrianna stared at her friend for a second. This was the first time she had ever called her by a nickname other than Rangerette. *She's worried.*

"We didn't do anything other than stand ready to help Myrith," Hendandra said. "We didn't get into the fight at all."

"Unfortunately, you were obviously in a position to help your friend," Tristan said. "And, that is why the mayor ordered all three of you to be taken into custody. Even if you did not attack, you were all three together."

"What we have to do is find some way to convince the mayor you were acting in defense of another," Kyrianna said.

"The mayor? I understood I was to appear before the town council."

"The mayor controls this town. You were not in a position to observe what I did. The Captain of the Guard took a subservient position to the mayor's son and it was the mayor issuing the orders out there." She paused and took a deep breath. "This is only my third day in this town, but I can read the signs."

"Two days," the knight finally said. "How can that be? Hendandra and Falden stepped into the portal before you did as did I."

"I don't know, but it has been two days. If we can convince the Mayor Geladas is a god associated with the path of light and justice it might help us. But, this is not my land, nor is it yours. I don't know how we might be able to do that." Kyrianna stood up and paced back and forth in front of the cell several times.

"Perhaps I can give them another name," Myrith said. "I spent last night in vigil and as a result received a vision."

"Tell me about it."

Myrith's jaw dropped and her head snapped up. "That is a private matter."

"I'm sorry," Kyrianna said bowing her head. "However, it might make a difference."

Myrith took a deep breath and nodded. "You're correct. I saw a battlefield with a woman in armor leading the charges. She fell during an intense battle and her body was lifted up into the heavens. I heard a male voice say to her; 'For your courage and skill I make you my Lord Marshall and the Protector of these realms.' Then the vision faded to be replaced by a scene of the same woman, now in brightly polished armor standing beside a throne, her sword held point down as the one on the throne held audience. The man spoke again. 'Is this the one you call?' The woman replied, 'Yes, I have called her.' 'Very well,' the man said. 'Know this Myrith Lake; you have been called to service by the Goddess Mykaylene. She is the sworn protector of the weak and a battle tactician. You do her honor by aiding those seeking justice and by never running from battle.' It was then the vision faded."

"Mykaylene, perhaps that name will mean something to the Mayor. If she is counted as a deity of the light, then he may accept your explanation."

"I doubt it," Tristan said as he stood up from the bench. "I believe it is no coincidence Mykaylene called you. My family has a long history of service to Her. At least one person in each generation has served as one of Her warriors. That is until the disaster that befell thirty years ago. My grandfather was the last warrior of our line to serve the goddess." Tristan paused for a moment. "Lady Dalynne, allow me to represent your friend," Tristan said.

Kyrianna looked at Myrith who only shrugged then turned her attention back to Tristan. "As you are more familiar with the laws and customs of this area, I agree."

"Lord Duvall, the council is ready," the guardsman called from the door.

"Thank you Manis," Tristan said.

"Per protocol, My Lord, you and the Lady must wait outside

for the prisoners."

Tristan nodded. "I know the protocols Manis, however, I will not allow them to be restrained in any manner for this appearance before the council. I will be bond for their behavior."

The guardsman stepped into the holding area and nodded. "Very well."

"Lady Dalynne, if you will come with me," Tristan said.

"Please, no title," Kyrianna said as they left the jail. "My father has exiled me; I have no claims to anything belonging to House Dalynne."

"Very well, but in this situation there is no one else who knows this, I recommend you say nothing. You are from a noble house and as far as the Mayor and Council of Duvshire are concerned it must remain that way."

"Very well."

Kyrianna nodded toward the door as two guards escorted Myrith and the others out of the building. It was a short walk to the council hall and Kyrianna felt her heart skip several beats as she looked at the council table and those sitting there along with the Mayor who was scowling as they took their places. She had come close to facing a similar tribunal before her father had intervened and instead had her exiled for her actions. There it had been her father's rank, which had protected her and now Tristan, was insisting she use her rank and his to help protect her companions. She hated political games, but knew it was time to play them. After the others were in their positions, Kyrianna moved to stand before the table bowing deeply. She had been acknowledged as being from a noble house; she was showing her respect for the Mayor and Council by recognizing their authority in this matter. "Lord Mayor and honorable members of this council," she said raising her eyes to look at the men seated before her. "At the request of the accused, I ask to be released as counsel for the knight Myrith Lake. She has chosen to be represented by Lord Tristan Duvall in this matter." Her head remained bowed as she waited for the Mayor to agree to the request.

"Very well," the Mayor said after several minutes. "The records will show that Lord Tristan Duvall will be representing the ones before us today. You may take a seat Lady Dalynne."

Kyrianna nodded then turned and walked to the spectator's area. She smiled as Tristan winked at her as she passed him.

"In the matter of the fire at the Wailing Banshee, further investigation has shown there was indeed an attack on Lord Duvall in his room before the fire apparently started." The mayor said as he stood up. "Marlene has reported to the council that she distinctly remembers seeing the elf Legewyd go upstairs, though he did not have rooms at the Banshee and shortly thereafter followed the sounds of a fight. She had run to fetch the watch and upon returning discovered the fire." He paused and looked at Kyrianna. "The members of the watch who accompanied her back to the tavern also bear out that this is what she told them as well. Because of this evidence, we find it highly probable it was this Legewyd who set the fire. There will be no further discussion of this incident during these proceedings."

"Now, on to the matter of the murder of the elf Elvioril," the Mayor said.

Tristan stood and gave the mayor only a slight nod. "Mayor Ustedler, the testimony of the lady will not change in any way from the statement given yesterday when she was arrested. Lady Dalynne and I have reviewed the statements taken from the other witnesses and these also bear out that Elvioril did fail to acknowledge the lady when she called to him. All of the witness statements also show the elf was shouting challenges to parties unknown and charging into the square with his weapon drawn. It was also reported he was following the same path Lady Dalynne had been on in a manner that could easily be perceived as chasing her. Myrith Lake is a friend to Lady Dalynne, it is to be expected she would take action to defend her."

"The facts are not in dispute, Lord Duvall," the Mayor said. "What is in dispute is whether the accused acted precipitously and initiated a fight which resulted in the death of another. It is currently the belief of this council that the fight was avoidable and wholly the responsibility of the accused. She has offered only the name of a foreign god, whose motivations are not known to us as her proof she acted in a manner in keeping with the position she claims as hers. For all this council knows, those who follow this Geladas and claim the title of knight follow the opposite principles of those who follow the various gods of this land."

"As I also know nothing of Geladas, I cannot argue with your reasoning," Tristan said.

Kyrianna stared at Tristan. What was he doing? By agreeing with the Mayor, he was adding credibility to the accusation.

"Therefore, I would like to give you the name of a god with

whom you are familiar," Tristan said. "Mykaylene."

"Mykaylene? Surely you, of all people here, are not compar-ing the Battle Maiden with a god whose principles are unknown?"

"No, Lord Mayor, that is not what I am doing," Tristan said. "What I am saying is Mykaylene has called Lady Lake to be one of her warriors. If she were indeed guilty of attacking without provoca-tion, there is little chance the Battle Maiden would do this."

The Mayor leaned forward and frowned. "Lord Duvall, just how are we to know the accused's claim of having been called by Mykaylene is true. We have no one here who can cast the magics needed to verify her veracity. She could be playing to your family history to convince to you of this in order to save her own neck. And, before you bring up the point warriors of the Battle Maiden have the ability to detect evil, that does not excuse her actions. Just because she might have detected an aura of evil on the deceased, it might have been from something on his person. You have said nothing to dispute the fact the accused dealt the first blow in a fight that resulted in the death of another. It was she who initiated the battle between them."

Kyrianna took a deep breath. She didn't see how Tristan was going to win this. The mayor was fixated on a single fact in this case and that fact could not be disputed. She also noted the way Tristan had casually begun calling Myrith Lady Lake—giving her a title.

"As I have stated, that fact is not in dispute," Tristan said. "What is in dispute is whether it was indeed murder or self-defense. I believe Lady Lake was acting in defense or herself and others based on the information she had. As for her being called by Mykaylene being a ploy; the Lady Lake is not from our land and does not know the names of our gods. Being kept isolated in a cell last night, she would not have been able to make up a story that matched the story of Mykaylene's ascension as well as hers did when I heard it this morning. She related the story exactly as it is known to be presented to those called by Mykaylene as well as the vision of Thedrin and Mykaylene confirming her having been called to serve the Battle Maiden. I have no doubts she has been called." Tristan paused and took a deep breath. "Perhaps the best way to determine whether she truly follows the path of light and therefore the truth of her word as a warrior of the Battle Maiden is to test her."

"An interesting idea, particularly coming from you," the mayor said. He paused for several minutes then smiled. "Perhaps a test is in order. The accused will stand."

Myrith stood, along with Hendandra and Falden, her shoulders squared and her back rigid as she faced the mayor and the members of the council.

"Lord Duvall had proposed a test and I will agree. If the Battle Maiden has called you, She will protect you during this. Therefore, you will accompany Lord Duvall to the estate. If you return, your innocence will be proven. Mind you, that is only if you return with Lord Duvall. However, if you fail in protecting him or in your task of cleansing the estate of the evil residing there you will be considered guilty and under sentence of death. Do you understand?"

Myrith offered the mayor a shallow bow "I understand."

"Good. Captain Marvial, see their weapons are returned to them. You and your companions are required to set out, as soon as your weapons are returned." The mayor started to turn away.

"I protest!" A voice called from the back of the audience.

Kyrianna turned to see a human male striding forward. His dark blue clerical robes swirling around him.

"On what grounds?" The mayor looked at the cleric and frowned.

"You are sending this person, who has no real proof she was called by the Battle Maiden to do something in the name of Mykaylene. You do not have the authority to sanction that."

"Ah, but I do in this case. I am not doing this in the name of Mykaylene. I am allowing the accused the opportunity to show us she does speak the truth. If the Battle Maiden did indeed call her, She will guide her in the task I have set her. If She did not then...." He spread his hands out in front of him.

"That you send her with one who has all but renounced his faith is unconscionable. If this is to be a true test of the Battle Maiden's call, then I will go with them to verify its outcome."

"As you wish. I would not presume to interfere in your religious duty." The mayor paused, raised his head slightly and looked at the audience. "This proceeding is over." He turned and left the dais; the other members of the council followed him.

Marvial waited until the hall was empty except for Tristan and their group. "I will escort you to the road to the estate," he said as he handed Myrith her weapons.

"We still need a few supplies," Kyrianna said.

"You heard the mayor; you are to set out as soon as your

weapons are returned. They have been returned." Marvial paused and glanced around. "The escort is not mandated by the mayor, it is to make sure he has no other reason to accuse you of something before you can leave the area. Therefore, I suggest you make do with what you have."

"I guess we'll have to," Kyrianna said.

~ * ~

Laraf was waiting at the edge of town when the group arrived. "I wish you success," Marvial said before he left them.

"If you'll have me, I offer to join you in this endeavor," Laraf said. His attention was focused on Kyrianna.

Kyrianna glanced at Tristan who nodded. "Be welcome on the journey," she said as she extended her hand.

"Thank you." He grasped her hand firmly and smiled.

"I believe a few introductions are in order," Tristan said looking around.

Kyrianna nodded. "Myrith, Hendandra and Falden," she said indicating the group who had traveled through the temple together.

"I am Sarasnar. I serve the Battle Maiden in Irrmar," the human who had protested the task said.

"I am called Laraf," Laraf said.

Tristan nodded. "I am Tristan Duvall. While I do not like the way it was forced upon you, I appreciate your assistance in helping me to cleanse my ancestral home of the evil growing there. Unfortunately, I know nothing of the details of what happened, just that everyone who was on the estate that night, with the exception of my father was killed."

"Well, I didn't agree to this and as Raspa is only a few days from here, I think I'll be going home." Hendandra shifted her pack on her back.

"The mayor did not specifically name you or your other companion in the charge as he saw you as standing with Myrith. If you leave at this time, you ensure her guilt and thereby your own," Sarasnar said.

"I doubt he'll really care if we never meet each other again," Hendandra said.

"Perhaps," Sarasnar said.

"Despite the mayor having ordered you here I'm willing to pay a thousand gold pieces to each of those who go with me,"

Tristan said. "That was the price I was offering to hire a group and I will honor that price, even under these circumstances."

Hendandra seemed to be studying the young nobleman for several minutes, then her gaze moved over the others in the group. "Seven of us. I would imagine we have a good chance of surviving and collecting the payoff. I'll come with you," she said.

"And, I as well," Falden said.

"I will be joining you as well," a gruff voice called from the trees.

Kyrianna and Myrith both spun around, their weapons out of the scabbards and held ready.

"And, you can keep yer gold. Mulog, Lord of Storms has directed that I pledge myself to follow the Lady Lake for a time." A dwarf stepped out the trees and knelt in front of Myrith, his axe on the ground in front of him.

Myrith looked down at the dwarf and frowned. She looked at Kyrianna. "What do I do now?" she whispered.

"You can either accept his pledge or tell him to go away," Kyrianna whispered back. "I know nothing of this Lord of Storms he has named."

"Mulog is generally counted among the gods of light though he is considered very chaotic and temperamental," Tristan said. "His clerics and fighters enjoy battle and do make good allies."

Myrith nodded. "Very well, Sir Dwarf, I accept your pledge until such time as your Lord of Storms deems you are to move on to other battles."

The dwarf stood and picked up his axe. "I am called Nirev. I already know yer names," he said.

The dwarf shouldered his axe then headed off into the woods along the path the group was on.

"This will be interesting," Kyrianna said to Myrith. She smiled as her friend swallowed hard and nodded her agreement.

~ * ~

Kyrianna took a deep breath and inhaled the night air. The distinct odors of the woods had blended during the day and were now starting to separate as they settled to the ground with the cooler air. She had found a large clearing a decent ways off the road for them to set up a camp for the night. They had spotted the manor house of the estate, but no one had wanted to enter the grounds at night, particularly Tristan.

She looked out over the area, the trees seemed be twisted with the taint of evil that lay over this land. She could sense the chaos that had infused this place and it concerned her. They had just come from a place of chaos and evil that was linked to Thynitic and here she had encountered a Rynial elf; one who wore a symbol of the Lady Chaos. *Too many coincidences.*

She glanced up at the moon and stars. Her and Nirev's watch was over, Myrith and Sarasnar had the next.

After waking the other two, Kyrianna lay down on her bed-roll. She knew despite whatever sleep she managed to get, she would not get any true rest.

Chapter Twenty-Five

Kyrianna frowned as she awoke to Laraf shaking her shoulder. "What's going on?"

"There's something moving outside of the clearing. And, I know I heard goblin being spoken."

"Goblin?" She looked at him.

"Nasty little creatures, usually like to kill anything that isn't a goblin," he said.

Kyrianna nodded as she sat up. She held a finger to her lips as she listened to the sounds of the forest. A few insects chirped in the area, but that was all she heard. She shook her head. "Nothing there now," she said as she picked up her swords. "How long?"

"You've been asleep about four hours," Laraf said. "There's another hour left before we start out again."

"Fine, I'll finish the watch with you." Kyrianna glanced up at the faint glow of the approaching dawn and took a deep breath. The scents of the forest had settled during the night so the musty damp smell of the earth was the strongest. Still the sharp scent of the trees lingered and lightly pierced the others.

~ * ~

"Myrith," Kyrianna woke her as the others were starting to rise. "Laraf said he heard something moving during the night along with what he thought was goblin being spoken."

Myrith grabbed her sword. "And, he is just now reporting this?"

"No, he woke me and as there was nothing moving then, I decided not to wake anyone else, though I did finish the watch with them."

"Okay. We need to find out if we did have visitors during the night."

Kyrianna waited as Myrith finished getting her gear together then they moved to check the perimeter of the camp.

"There." Kyrianna pointed to some tracks on the soft ground. "Some type of wolf, possibly, though much larger than normal." She placed her hand next to the canine's prints. "There were two of them." She looked at the tracks again. "With riders, judging from the depth of the tracks left by the back paws. It appears they circled our camp a few times then left."

"Which direction?" Myrith asked.

"Away from the estate," Kyrianna said.

"Worgs," Laraf said. "About the size of a pony, but magically bred from wolves and corrupted. They are often used as mounts by goblins."

"So something or someone knows we're here," Myrith said. "We need to get moving."

Kyrianna paused and glanced down at the tracks again. The claws appeared to be long and sharp where they had dug into the ground. If worgs could fight with a rider directing their attacks, they would make dangerous opponents.

~ * ~

Myrith and Kyrianna stood at the gates of the Duvall estate. Despite the years that had passed since they had apparently last been opened, they swung open with only a light touch. There was no creaking or grinding only a light scraping on the ground where a small pile of brush had been caught against the bottom of the gate.

The immediate grounds were in proper condition, not over-grown as would be expected. The large manor house was also in pristine condition; with the windows clean and undamaged; the brick and wood the same.

Kyrianna scanned the area. To the left of the manor was a large l-shaped building with what appeared to be a grain silo attached to it, probably the stables. This building was showing its age as several of the upper shutters hung from their hinges and the paint was peeling from the wood. Just behind the stable was a large pile of ash. "One that burned?" Kyrianna nodded to the ash that appeared to have lain undisturbed for however long it had been there. There was nothing growing in the area and the ash was contained in a single area, a slight mound in the center; the edges clearly defined.

"I don't know if it occurred that night or not," Tristan said. "My father has spoken very little of what actually happened."

Behind the right corner of the house was another building. It was mostly hidden from their view. Again what could be seen appeared to be well kept and showed no signs of age or decay. Set forward of that building and more in a line with the house was a small building built with white brick that was unstained or marked by time. The large colored windows marked it as the family chapel.

Beyond the chapel was an area covered by shrubs and bushes. "A hedge maze?" Kyrianna pointed to the area.

"There was one on the grounds, that may have been it," Tristan said. "We should start with the main house."

"I don't think so," Kyrianna said. "I'm not comfortable with the idea of leaving areas that haven't been checked at our backs."

"I have to agree with the Rangerette," Myrith said. "There is a strong taint of evil here, we cannot risk leaving a potential enemy at our backs to attack us when we're engaged with something else."

"I agree with the lady knight," Nirev said hefting his axe.

"Where do you suggest we start?" Tristan glanced from Kyrianna to Myrith.

"The stables are the closest," Kyrianna said. "We can start there and work our way around."

"Sounds good," Myrith said as she headed for the building.

"Locked," Myrith said when the doors didn't open. There was the rattle of a chain on the inside of the door.

"If it's chained on the inside, I won't be able to open it," Hendandra said. "We should check for other ways in."

"There." Laraf pointed to a small door in the silo as they made their way around the building.

Kyrianna readied her bow as he opened the chute door. The door's hinges squeaked and echoed in the empty silo.

"No other reachable openings from here," Laraf said as he glanced into the silo.

"There's an opening in the loft area," Nirev called. "As well as an open door a few feet further down."

"Talon can check it," Falden said as the hawk launched itself in the air from his shoulder.

"Trapped!" Falden seemed frozen in place as his arms flailed at invisible bonds. "Trapped. Can't fly. Trapped!"

Myrith grabbed Falden's shoulders and held him still. "Break the link. Falden, break the link," she said. She repeated her statement several times before Falden finally focused on her.

"Talon," he whispered. "Talon is trapped in something. It is too dark to see what it is."

Kyrianna glanced up at the small window as the bird's cries

became louder. "Falden, we will get him out," she said. "You need to remain calm so he will stay calm also. He risks hurting himself if he keeps fighting. Can you calm him down?"

"I can try." Falden closed his eyes and tiny lines appeared in his brow for several seconds. Talon's cries quieted then stopped as he opened his eyes. "I have him calm for now, but we can't take too long getting to him."

Hendandra began climbing the silo to a narrow ledge just below the window; Nirev followed her.

Myrith headed to the door that was cracked open with the rest of the group.

Kyrianna crinkled her nose at the moldy smell coming from the bales of rotting hay sitting along the walls. Light was being filtered through the beams of the hayloft from the window the hawk flew through and Laraf pointed to a nearby ladder. He sheathed his sword as he began climbing.

"The loft is filled with a giant spider web," Laraf called. "No sign of the creature or creatures that spun it."

As Laraf made his way across the beams, several strands of the webbing floated to the ground.

"Laraf, to your right." Myrith pointed to a dark shape moving in the shadows.

Kyrianna glanced toward the window as she readied her bow. She could see Hendandra moving along the beams toward the trapped bird while Nirev waited in the open window.

Talon started trying to fight the webs again as Hendandra got closer to him. "Falden, get him to settle down," the girl yelled. "I can't get him out of the webbing if he is fighting me."

"I am having trouble getting through his emotions," Falden said. "But, I am trying."

The spider moved quickly along the webs and Laraf had to dodge the mandibles as he stabbed at the creature with a dagger. The spider came in close again and Laraf gasped and dropped his dagger.

"Damn," Myrith said pointing her crossbow at the spider. "Too many shadows. I don't want to risk missing the spider and hitting him."

Kyrianna didn't say anything as she loosed two arrows in rapid succession, hitting the spider in the abdomen. She nodded as Myrith copied her and managed a solid hit with her crossbow and Falden with a bolt of arcane power.

The spider backed away from Laraf as several more arrows and another bolt of arcane force hit it.

"Watch out," Myrith called as the large body fell from the loft.

Kyrianna jumped back away from a razor-like appendage as the spider's legs continued to flail for several seconds. Myrith backed away, her crossbow still held at the ready.

"I've got Talon free," Hendandra called down and a moment later the hawk swooped down to land on Falden's shoulder.

"Laraf?" Myrith called as the thief started toward the ladder.

"It got me with its stinger; I think I can make it down. I just hope someone has a way of taking care of the poison."

"I can take care of it," Sarasnar said.

"He'll make it," Myrith whispered.

Laraf was halfway down the ladder when he slipped and fell. Sarasnar knelt next to him and placed a hand on Laraf's chest and the other on his forehead as he whispered a prayer.

Kyrianna glanced around at the shadows created by the hay stacked in the room as Hendandra and Nirev came down the ladder. The dwarf nodded and pulled the girl with him. They began working their way around the room. Hendandra's rapier darted into the bales of decaying hay while Nirev's ax sliced through them.

"Any other surprises?" Myrith looked around as Hendandra and Nirev returned to the group.

"Nothing." Hendandra paused as she wiped her rapier with a clean cloth. "At least not yet."

"You will feel weak for a while as the poison finishes working its way out of your body," Sarasnar said as he helped Laraf to his feet. "However, you will be fine."

"Thank you," Laraf said as he drew his rapier. "We should get moving."

To the right was a set of double doors leading into the other part of the stable. "I think I can hear something moving on the other side," Hendandra whispered. "It sounds almost like the crackling of fire or of several somethings scurrying through loose leaves or hay."

Kyrianna glanced up at the area above the door that opened into the loft. "A spider nest?"

"Weapons at the ready," Myrith said.

"It's not latched," Hendandra said as she pushed the door open.

Kyrianna and Myrith stepped in the room together.

"This was the carriage house," Myrith said. In front of them were an old buckboard and two ornate carriages. Down the hallway were several more stalls on each side.

"There's the fire," Nirev said. On the back wall was a forge, numerous tools sat around it, along with one of the wheels from the carriages. The fire appeared to be well tended as it crackled. "Wonder who's been taking care of it."

Myrith glanced at Kyrianna then turned to study the rest of the room. She frowned as she pointed her sword down the hallway with the stalls. "The evil of this place seems to be strongest down there," she said.

Myrith and Kyrianna took the lead as the group moved past the carriages and toward the stalls. Two skeletal horses stepped from either side and turned to face the group. Behind them a man in robes, carrying a scythe appeared.

"Myrith," Laraf called. "The carriages."

Both of them glanced back to see the buckboard and one of the carriages had moved toward the group, blocking any chance of exit from this area of the stalls.

"I believe that fire needs stoking," Nirev said lifting his axe and turning toward the buckboard.

"Why are you here?" The hooded figure asked.

Kyrianna gestured to Tristan to step forward and speak to the figure.

"I am...," he said.

"I am Creed Lawton and you are a Duvall," the figure said interrupting the young nobleman. "Why are you here in my stables and not your father?"

Tristan drew himself up with an arrogant air and Kyrianna smiled as he managed to play the part of one who was not used to being questioned. "That does not concern you. I am here now," he said.

Creed Lawton only laughed. "Then you should not be here. You are not ready. Go to the house, your uncle is waiting for you there. If you do not follow his steps, you will be doomed." He reached behind him, opened the barred door and left as the skeletal horses stepped forward.

Chapter Twenty-Six

Myrith started after the departing stable master, but was stopped as the two skeletal horses blocked her path. Kyrianna and Tristan engaged the horse on the left while she took the one on the right.

Despite having to dodge the teeth and hooves of the horse in front of her, Kyrianna smiled at the sounds of splintering wood and dwarven singing she heard behind her. "Someone is enjoying himself," she said.

She brought both blades up as Tristan came in behind the horse. Their blades weren't doing that much damage as there wasn't any real flash for them to hit, only bones. Tristan's rapier was geared for point work, but at least they seemed to be providing a distraction.

The skeleton Myrith was facing fell and she darted for the door Creed had exited through. Kyrianna brought her long sword down on the other skeleton's neck as it turned to bite at Tristan. The spine cracked from the blow and the creature fell. She started to follow Myrith, then paused and glanced back at the others.

Hendandra was nowhere to be seen, although Nirev had chopped the buckboard to pieces and was now swinging at the carriage. Laraf was on top of the carriage and jumped off behind it. From what she could see, he was headed for the door they had come in through. Sarasnar was flat against the wall as the carriage rolled toward him. Nirev's axe cut through the wheel hub and it came off, disabling the vehicle. He continued singing in dwarven as he proceeded to chop the carriage into pieces like the buckboard.

Kyrianna turned toward the door Myrith had followed Creed through and stopped when she saw her and Tristan looking at the ground. She glanced at the tracks then pointed to the corner of the building. "He's headed for the other door," she said. "Running. Chaos! Laraf was headed out that direction."

Myrith, who had already moved to the corner of the building, took off at a run, Tristan and Kyrianna following her. Tristan reached the doors first. "Laraf is down," he called. "Ready your bows."

Kyrianna hesitated for a second then dropped both her swords, readied her bow and drew an arrow. Her breath caught in her throat when she saw the figure of Creed Lawton standing over the body of Laraf. Tristan was facing the stable master, his rapier small compared to the scythe the hooded figure was wielding. Kyrianna dropped to a knee as she tried to steady her aim. Next to her Myrith fired a bolt from her crossbow then dropped the weapon and drew her long sword.

"Frayrith guide my aim," Kyrianna whispered as she released the shot. The arrow flew true and struck the stable master in the neck.

The stable master paused for only a moment, then reached up and yanked the arrow from his neck. "That hurt," he said as he turned toward her and smiled.

She shivered at the malice she saw in his sunken eyes and gaunt face as he dropped the arrow and took a step toward the door. Myrith intercepted him, her blade blocking the scythe as the others came running in from the carriage house. Kyrianna dropped her bow, unable to take any more safe shots as the rest of the group surrounded the stable master, and sprinted back to where she had dropped her swords. The green metal gleamed in the morning sun and she grabbed them as she spun back around and sprinted for the door.

Myrith was pulling her blade from Lawton's chest when Kyrianna reached the stable door.

"I told you, you would still be weak from the poison," Sarasnar said as he helped Laraf into a sitting position.

"The creature never touched me," Laraf said with a grin. "He swung at me and I dodged, but got dizzy and passed out."

Myrith took a deep breath and stood there for several more seconds. "You got lucky," she said. "We need to check the rest of this building." She headed back to the carriage room.

The sound of splintering wood echoed through the building and Kyrianna swallowed a laugh at the sight of Nirev still chopping at the carriage and tossing the remains into the forge. The buckboard was already gone and the raging fire was threatening to spill out onto the floor. She wiped sweat from her eyes and watched as Laraf climbed into the remaining carriage and Myrith headed down the line of stalls, Hendandra and Falden close behind her.

The first stall door was locked and Hendandra knelt before

the door as she pulled the broken picks from her pack. "I doubt this will work," she muttered as she slipped them into the lock.

Myrith moved to the second stall and paused at the door. She turned and motioned for Kyrianna to join her. "Sounds like there may be something moving in there," she whispered.

Kyrianna nodded and drew her swords as Myrith opened the door. She lowered her weapons when the door opened to reveal a ghostly war horse standing in the stall. The ethereal creature only snorted and pawed at the hay on the floor. Her eyes scanned the horse's tack on a stand against the far wall. The cloth of the blue and silver barding showed no signs of rot; it was in perfect condition— just like the exterior of the house. Myrith moved the saddle then picked up the barding and approached the horse. The ghostly creature snorted then backed away, never taking his eyes off her.

Kyrianna frowned at the body of the horse that lay in the corner of the stall covered by its blanket. Like the house and the barding, even the body seemed untouched by the passage of time. She grinned as Myrith tried again to approach the ghostly horse again and he again moved away from her. "Let me try," she said.

Myrith backed away from the horse and draped the barding back over the tack stand. Kyrianna picked up a handful of grain from the nearby bucket and held her hand out as she approached the horse. "Easy," she whispered. She continued talking to the horse, and watched as his ears pricked forward and he took a hesitant step toward her. She found her thoughts focusing on her own horse, Smokemist and how she had been the one to break and train him. *Always stay calm, even when the horse is nervous and excited,* her father said the first time Smokemist had thrown her. *His emotions will reflect yours.*

The horse took another step forward and Kyrianna smiled as he pressed his muzzle into her hand and lipped at the grain she held. With her other hand, she patted his cheek, surprised that it felt solid to her touch. Myrith looked at her and shook her head then left the stall.

Kyrianna gave the ghostly horse a final pat then moved to check the body. He had been a large warhorse, dark chestnut in color with a black mane and tail. The blue blanket was covered with silver stitching including what appeared to be a holy symbol of some type and two names. "Rhinehart, Riker," Kyrianna whispered the names and smiled at the soft nicker she heard behind her.

"So your name is Riker." She stood up and turned to look at

the ghostly horse who bobbed his head in agreement.

"Then who was Rhinehart?"

Riker pointed his nose at the tack and gear then dropped his head.

"He was your friend, wasn't he?"

Again, an affirmative nod from the ghost.

Kyrianna gave the ghostly horse another pat on the muzzle then turned toward the door. Tristan was a member of House Duvall, descended from those who lived here, perhaps he could tell her more about Rhinehart.

"Excuse me," Kyrianna said stepping out of the stall. "I would like Tristan to look at something." She gestured to the open door to Riker's stall then followed Tristan in. Myrith followed close behind her.

Tristan nodded respectfully to the ghostly horse standing there as he approached the body.

"This was the mount of a warrior of Mykaylene," Sarasnar said as he walked over and pointed to the sword and shield stitched on the blanket.

"Rhinehart was my grandfather," Tristan said. "He was considered a powerful warrior of the Battle Maiden."

"That's what the mayor meant when he said Myrith might be playing on your family history," Kyrianna said.

"Yes."

Kyrianna pulled the blanket back a bit to reveal a cut across his neck. One that was clean—not ragged. "This horse was killed by someone he knew and accepted to be around him," she said.

"We need to move on," Myrith said looking at the horse as well. "I wish there was a way to put his spirit to rest."

"Perhaps when we have faced the evil in this place that will allow his spirit to go to a place of honor," Kyrianna said.

"Fire!" Laraf's voice called as they exited the stall.

Hendandra and Falden came charging out of the room they were checking and ran toward the open door. The rest of the group followed them.

For a moment, they stood and watched the flames as they rose up and engulfed the entire building. "What happened?" Myrith asked, looking down at Hendandra.

"A trap in the wall," she said. "We thought we had found something and I misjudged the mechanism. It caused the front of the forge to fall away and spill the fire out into the carriage house. The dry wood and hay only sped the spread of the flames." She glanced over at Tristan. "Sorry."

"I am not worried about it. And, as we all made it out in one piece you shouldn't be either." He paused and glanced toward the house. "Based on the statements made by Creed Lawton, I believe the manor should be next." He headed for the large building.

Kyrianna glanced at Myrith who only shrugged and followed Tristan.

Chapter Twenty-Seven

Even up close, the manor house was still in perfect condition. The windows were secure with no sign of dirt or damage to them. Kyrianna stood to the side as Myrith reached for the door handle; it didn't move.

"Hendandra," Myrith said as she stepped to the side.

"And, how do you propose I try and open it? I broke my last set of lock picks, remember? It was only the fact it was an extremely simple lock in the stable that let me open that stall door. This one won't be that simple."

"Falden do you know any magic to open a locked door?" Myrith turned to the mage.

"There are spells to do so, but they are not ones I have ever chosen to learn. However, there is another possibility." He turned to Tristan. "There are magics that can spell things to be specifically attuned to a certain bloodline. As you say this was your ancestral home, perhaps you should try the door."

Tristan stepped forward and reached for the door handle. The door swung open with the same ease the gates had. He stepped into the main hall of the manor as the others followed him. There was no true entry way as they were greeted by a wide set of stairs descending from the second story. The hall extended for at least fifty feet on either side of the doors. Brilliant blue and silver streamers hung from the ceiling, there were candles set around the room, their flames flickering.

"They were preparing for the wedding of their eldest daughter, Larissa, to Wilhelm Terissian," Tristan said.

Falden scanned the room. "There are several items that are magical in nature here," he said. "The armor on the stand there, the sword and lance."

Nirev stepped over to the set of full plate armor and placed a hand on the shining surface. "Sentryl," he said.

"The magical properties on the half-plate give it better protections than the armor you are currently wearing," Falden said to Myrith.

Kyrianna watched as the others moved through the room. Laraf seemed to be checking the various doors and walls as Falden looked up at the sword on the wall. Hendandra moved to inspect a group of musical instruments assembled in the near right corner of the room. Sarasnar looked around at the others as he reached up and pulled a silver sword from the wall.

"Kyrianna," Laraf called from under the stairs. "Can you take a look at this?"

She moved under the stairs to where Laraf was standing. She paused and looked out the large glass doors that led out into a well-groomed courtyard. The doors stood partially open and a cool breeze flowed through them into the hall. He was waiting at a door under the stairs. "Barred and locked," he whispered. "From the other side."

Kyrianna nodded as she checked another small door to the side. She opened it to find a small coat closet. The dust in the closet swirled as the breeze from the garden doors disturbed it. She frowned; this was the only evidence of dust to be found anywhere in the room.

A shadow appeared on the stairs and Kyrianna found her hand on her weapon as both she and Laraf stepped back and looked up. The ghostly figure of a woman descended the stairs into the hall.

"Nyssa?" Tristan whispered as the apparition glided past him. "Grandmother?"

The woman seemed to hesitate for only a breath then ignored him and stopped in front of Nirev who had removed part of the sentryl armor from its stand and was putting it on. She crossed her arms over her chest and stood there, her right foot tapping on the floor as she looked at the dwarf. Kyrianna smiled as she remembered the same look on her mother's face when she had been caught sparring in front of a mirror with her mother's unicorn horn sword when she was four years old.

Nirev bowed his head then began putting the armor back on the stand. The ghost stood there and watched him as he wiped the armor with a cloth before moving to the other parts of the room. As she passed Falden, the sword he had levitated down from the wall returned itself to its place above the large fireplace. Sarasnar replaced the silver sword in its brackets before the ghost could reach him and Hendandra put a violin back with the other instruments.

As she walked, the ghostly figure waved her hand over the

various pieces of furniture and other items in the room. Any dust that had settled in the room vanished as she passed. Her task done and the room once again clean and put to order, the apparition sat at the piano and began to play. Kyrianna found a knot forming in her throat at the emotion carried by the notes of music. As she glanced around the room, she saw the same emotions reflected in the eyes of her companions. As the music continued she found herself drawn to the piano. Even in the delicate notes of the music she could hear the same loneliness that undercut the howl of a wolf in the dark of night.

"My Lady, our apologies if we have intruded. We are here to set things right," Kyrianna said as she offered the woman a bow.

The woman looked up her, but didn't say anything as she continued to play. When she finished she stood up and moved back to the stairs. Tristan sat at the piano, his hands resting on the keys for a moment before he began playing. Note for note, he copied the song the ghost had just played. However, while it was technically the same song and perfectly played, the emotional impact the woman had conveyed was missing from his performance.

She stopped at the foot of the stairs and turned back toward the young man at the piano. Kyrianna saw Myrith and the others move forward, hands on weapons as the woman approached Tristan. She placed a hand on his face and seemed to study his features for several minutes.

"Nyssa?" Tristan asked.

The apparition nodded and a silver tear formed on her face as she began to speak. Though Kyrianna could see her lips moving, there was no sound coming from the ghost.

"She was killed by her eldest son, Mikyl," Tristan said as he watched the woman's face and lips.

When the woman pointed to the stairs and several steps as well, those places darkened as the blood spilled there thirty years ago appeared.

"Nyssa, my friends and I are here to try and cleanse the house of the evil that is here," Tristan said. "Can you help us?"

Nyssa pointed to Myrith, Tristan and Kyrianna. "You are allowed to take one weapon from the hall." She then turned and went back up the stairs.

"I suggest that one," Kyrianna said as she pointed to the silver sword. "It is made of silver and with the corruption in this place, it may prove useful."

Myrith glanced toward the sword Falden had identified as magical earlier and shook her head. "I think having another weapon with magical properties in the group would serve us better. I know yours are not magical in nature despite the metal they are made of or the edge on them. Nor, do I believe Nirev is carrying any magical weapons. If we are to potentially be fighting creatures with the taint of the grave, magically enhanced weapons would be the better choice."

"I agree," Tristan said. As he finished speaking, the sword floated off the wall and into Myrith's hands.

"It would appear that settles the discussion," Myrith said holding the sword out to Kyrianna.

Kyrianna shook her head. "No thanks, I prefer my two blades."

Myrith frowned, but nodded then turned toward the dwarf. "Nirev, are you willing to use the sword?"

"Does it have an edge on it?" He held the sword in his hand then stepped back and made a couple of swings with it. "Nice weight and balance. It'll do."

"There is a set of doors behind the stairs that lead into a courtyard of sorts as well as two sets of double doors on either side of those," Laraf said. "Also, there is a door that appears to be barred and locked from the other side under the stairs."

"Anything else?"

"I found no other passages from this room."

"Right or left?" Kyrianna asked.

"Right," Myrith said.

The doors opened into a long parlor with several chairs throughout the room as well as small tables and bookcases. On one side was a long counter. Dusty bottles sat on the shelves behind the bar.

Kyrianna slid her hand over the counter and coughed as the dust swirled around her. "Looks like no one has been in here since that night," she said.

Nirev stepped behind the bar and picked up one of the bottles. There was still a wax seal on the container and the dwarf grinned as he broke it and opened the bottle.

"Nothing like a good ale with an additional thirty years to age." He wiped his beard with his hand where some of the dark amber liquid had spilled. "Very nice vintage." He started rummaging through the rest of the bottles. He lifted a slender decanter with a shimmering silver liquid in it. "Now, this looks interesting."

"Actually, I'll take that one," Tristan said. He slipped the bottle into a sack at his belt. "If there are any other bottles of that particular wine back there, I would appreciate them also."

Nirev nodded as he handed three more bottles to Tristan. "What be that wine exactly?"

"A very rare wine. It is served only at weddings." Tristan looked at the rest of the bottles on display. "You can have whatever you want of the rest."

"This appears to be the kitchen," Hendandra called. The small woman was standing at another set of doors at the far end of the room. "In about the same shape as this one. And there is another door at the end. Probably opens into the area the other doors from the main hall open into. I would wager that's the dining hall."

"You coming Nirev?" Myrith called.

Kyrianna glanced back at the dwarf who was finishing another bottle of the ale.

"I'll be there if ye need me," Nirev said. The dwarf stuffed several bottles into his pack, picked up the sword and another bottle as he went to join the others.

Other than the layer of dust that covered everything, there was nothing in the kitchen apart from the normal utensils. "No smell of anything having rotted in here," Kyrianna said as she took a breath. "That doesn't make any sense. If they were preparing for a wedding, then a feast would have been being preparing as well."

"It's been thirty years," Myrith said. "After that much time, not only the smell, but the rotten food would probably be gone."

"There's no sign of vermin or scavengers, but I guess it's possible," Kyrianna said.

The dining hall was in the same state as the parlor and kitchen with a thick layer of dust covering everything. Kyrianna frowned as Hendandra picked up a small crystal statue from the table. She knew Tristan had told them they could claim anything they wanted from the estate, but felt they should show some restraint in what they took. Anything of significant value or anything that might have been in the family for any length of time should not be touched.

"No signs of any other doors or passages," Laraf said as the group exited back into the main hall.

Myrith stood in front of the partially opened doors to the

courtyard. The sun was almost directly overheard and the water splashing in the fountain in the center of the garden reflected the light in a shower of color. "I wonder who cares for this area?"

"Perhaps its guardian is not one of the family," Falden said. He nodded toward the statue of a woman holding a spear in the back corner of the courtyard. "Mykaylene."

Myrith entered the courtyard and made a slow circuit of the path. She paused and bowed her head before the statue before rejoining the others. She closed the glass doors, but they moved back to the open position they had been in before as she started to turn away.

Kyrianna nodded her head toward the stairs. "Ready to go up?"

"Yes," Myrith said.

Hands on their weapons, the group started up the stairs to the upper level of the house.

Chapter Twenty-Eight

The first room they came to was locked. However, as with the front door, the door opened to Tristan's touch. The bedroom smelled musty as they entered. A large canopied bed dominated the room, while a worn, blue, velvet covered chair sat next to a window overlooking the courtyard garden below. The preserved body of an elderly woman sat in the chair, her gray hair still held tight in a bun at the nape of her neck and a look of concentration on her face. There was no sign of obvious injury and her hands rested in her lap, as if she had died right there sitting in the chair.

"Alesandra," Tristan said. "She was my great grandmother."

A spectral face appeared in the window and smiled when Tristan mentioned the woman's name. He watched her lips carefully as they moved silently.

"She says she was only member of the family not killed by Mikyl." He paused for a moment then turned to face the group. "She says she took her own life to protect this place and to prevent the evil from spreading." He turned back to the window. "She is warning us that we must follow the trail in the proper order or we will face an evil we will not be prepared for. He has the book."

He shook his head. "She keeps repeating, 'He has the book.' I don't know what she means."

Falden stood next to Tristan and faced the window. "What book?"

"It was brought from another place. It is a powerful book with potential for great evil."

"Another place?" Kyrianna looked around. "Does she mean from another plane or world?"

"Yes," Tristan said. "The book was brought here by one not from this land though she now calls it home. She gave the book to Mikyl in exchange for his allegiance to a dark power, also not from this world."

Kyrianna glanced at Myrith. "Is it possible?"

"Perhaps you should ask, as you are the one who thought of it."

Kyrianna took a deep breath then turned to face the specter. "Lady Alesandra," she said with a slight bow. "Several of my companions and I were taken by magics unknown to us to another plane. One where it seems a dark goddess from my home, Thynitic also called the Lady of Chaos, once held power and where she was trying to assert her power once again. Do you know if this is the same dark power that seduced your grandson Mikyl?"

The image of the face seemed to cloud over for several seconds. When it cleared she spoke again.

"The knowledge is shrouded by chaos, but even that is a clue that perhaps verifies what you suspect is correct," Tristan repeated her words for the group.

Kyrianna turned to Myrith. "I was wondering why the portal brought me here instead of sending me home as it should have. And, it seems it did the same to you. I would also have suspected Falden and Hendandra of going back to their home cities, but they were brought here along with you. Perhaps there is a reason."

"Actually, Kyrianna," Falden said. "The portal would not have deposited Hendandra and I in either Raspa or Gormanghast as there are magical wards on those cities that restrict teleportation into or out of them. The same is true of all the major cities of Shokar."

Hendandra looked up at Kyrianna. "And why would Falden or I have been brought here. We have no knowledge of this Thynitic other than what we learned in that temple. The same is true of Myrith."

"Okay, maybe I'm being overly paranoid. Forget I mentioned it." As Kyrianna turned back to face the window she saw the specter give her a slight smile.

"She said we must follow the trail," Myrith said. "Then what is the next step along that trail?"

There was a pause as the others waited for Tristan to read what Alesandra was saying.

"The chapel," he said. "However, she also says there is information and history we will eventually need in the other wing of the house."

"Then we finish with the house first," Myrith said.

"Lady Alesandra, we thank you for your assistance," Tristan said offering the specter a slight bow. "Is there anything else you can provide to us?"

The face in the window smiled as she spoke a few more

words before fading.

"She said that what is here is for the living. I believe that means she has no problem if we take anything from her room."

"I doubt it's the one she was referring to, but I found a book under the bed." Kyrianna held a large, black, leather bound book in her arms. "Nothing on the outside," she said as she opened the cover.

"Chaos!" She threw the book on the bed and dove to the side as smoke swirled on the pages and something lunged out from the book at her face.

"A spirit snake," Falden said picking up the book. "It would appear to be a one-time spell." He began flipping through the pages.

"You are the one who almost got hurt retrieving this. Are you interested in keeping it?" Falden held the book out to Kyrianna still open.

Kyrianna looked at the book. The lines of text were moving and she felt a stabbing sensation in her temples. "No!" She stepped back from the offered book. "I have never had any desire to learn the arcane arts, you can keep the thing."

Falden grinned as he slipped the book into his pack.

There was a large sitting room opposite Alesandra's room, with only the dust of thirty years of neglect covering the sofa, chairs and tables. At the end of the hall a door opened into a large master suite. Again a thick layer or dust covered the furniture and floor of the room. Tristan closed the door before anyone could enter the room.

"This is interesting," Hendandra said as she pushed open a door into a small room. Inside was a woman's dressing chamber and on the wall hung two gowns. Both were blue, one darker than other. Both were of similar cut and design, though the darker of the two was stitched with fine silver thread and had tiny beads sewn onto the bodice.

Here the layer of dust was very thin with nothing on the dresses. Under the window was a dressing table where cosmetics and two sets of jewelry had been laid out. One set was comprised of a diamond pendant and earrings, while the other was sapphire and included a silver headband with sapphires.

"Leave them," Kyrianna whispered as Hendandra approached the table.

The girl frowned but moved away leaving the jewelry on the

table.

"This was where the bride and her mother would have prepared for the wedding," Kyrianna said. "I doubt there is anything here we need."

As the others left the room, Kyrianna looked back at the jewelry sitting on the table. Her mother's bridal set was made up of strands of woven gold set with tiny emeralds. With one last look at the gowns, Kyrianna closed the door and followed the others across the balcony to the other wing of the house.

Kyrianna paused as she moved in front of the staircase. There it was again, a slight creak. Something was moving downstairs. She cupped her hand to her ear then pointed down the stairs when Myrith turned to look at her. She nodded then moved to the corner of the staircase and took a guard position. She pointed to the corner where the rest of the group had entered the second wing of the house. Kyrianna nodded and stepped across the open hall where she could observe the group and watch Myrith as well.

Kyrianna watched as Tristan walked by and opened each of the doors for the others. She could see the two smaller rooms to the right of the hall appeared to belong to young children. Both had toys and clothes scattered across the floor. She smiled as Tristan picked up a carved figure from the floor of the second room. It was a horse and rider. The horse was the same color as the one in the stable and wearing similar barding and gear. The rider was probably Rhinehart, Tristan's grandfather. Tristan slipped the figure into a pouch on his belt. He moved further into the room and out of her view.

She watched as Hendandra entered one of the two far rooms. While she couldn't see very well, she did see her pick up something that sparkled and put it into a pocket. *She finally managed to claim some jewels*, she thought as the girl exited the room.

Laraf and Hendandra entered the other room and she saw the blonde-haired woman move to a chest sitting against the back wall as Laraf moved out of sight.

"Now these are interesting." Kyrianna heard Laraf say from wherever he was in the room. There was the sound of papers and books being shuffled and she saw Hendandra glance over her shoulder toward the place she assumed Laraf was.

Kyrianna glanced toward Myrith and saw her attention was focused on the lower level of the house. With her rigid stance, Kyrianna wondered if the older woman had seen something, but hadn't called it to her notice yet.

She turned her attention back to the group. She hadn't seen where Falden or Nirev had originally vanished to and was relieved to see them come out of the room on the left side of the hall. They both stepped back next to her and waited for the others. "Anything interesting?" she asked.

Falden shook his head. "The governess' room. Some history books, but nothing else of any value. I wonder what the little one has found." He and Nirev went to check on Hendandra.

Sarasnar stood waiting just outside the door of the room the others had entered.

"Tristan, I found a few items that may interest you," Laraf called.

The nobleman exited the child's room he had been in and went into the last room. Kyrianna could see Laraf was holding what appeared to be several journals and ledgers in his hand. Falden stood near the two of them as he pointed out several pages to Tristan.

Hendandra reached into the chest then seemed to fall backwards as a cloud of yellow vapor poured out. In addition to the fog, a pair of large rats attached themselves to the girl, their teeth and claws flashing. The other members of the group darted out of the room, most coughing and gasping for breath from the effects of the noxious gas. Laraf paused, turned around and ran back into the room.

Kyrianna moved forward and grabbed one of the rats off Hendandra as Laraf pulled her out of the cloud then grabbed the other one. They flung the rodents against the nearby wall. One lay on the floor unmoving and the other twitched several times before Kyrianna stepped on its neck.

"Zombies," Sarasnar said looking at the two rats. He frowned as he checked Hendandra's injuries. "Fortunately, I am finding no sign of disease in the bites or scratches." He helped her up.

Kyrianna moved back to where she could see Myrith. The woman moved away from the stairs. "Goblins are in the house," she said. "One just went through a doorway under the stairs. I clearly heard it open and close this time."

"The center door," Laraf and Kyrianna said together.

The cloud dissipated and the rest of the group was able to breathe properly as Kyrianna told them about the goblin Myrith had seen.

"There may only be the one," Myrith said. "However, Kyrianna thought she heard something as we were passing the stairs a few minutes ago."

"And there were the worg tracks we found around our camp outside the estate. There were two—with riders," Kyrianna said.

"The question then," Laraf said. "Is whether we go straight to the chapel and ignore the goblins, leaving them as a potential threat behind us? Or do we take care of them now?"

Kyrianna and Myrith looked around at the others. "I know we were told to follow the trail, but I don't like the idea of leaving a known enemy at my back," Kyrianna said.

The rest of the group nodded their agreement. "Looks like the chapel is going to wait a little longer," Laraf said as he drew his rapier and headed for the stairs.

Myrith waited for Kyrianna and the others then they headed down the stairs together.

Chapter Twenty-Nine

The door under the stairs was partially open and Kyrianna stood to the side as Myrith used her sword to open it all the way. The area was poorly lit, and shadows filled the room. She glanced to the left and saw an area of blackness even her elven senses couldn't penetrate. However, something moved at the edge of her vision.

"Myrith," she whispered. "Did you see?"

"Yes. Let's get off these stairs and behind some cover." She quickened her pace on the stairs and Kyrianna followed.

"Chaos!" Kyrianna tightened her grip on her swords as her feet went out from under her and she slid the rest of the way down the stairs.

She glanced at Myrith as they hit the boxes, knocking several over. "At least they were empty," she said.

"Watch out," Laraf called. He jumped over them and landed on one of the crates, his rapier striking a goblin standing on the other side.

Kyrianna and Myrith both climbed over the crates and found themselves facing a group of goblins.

"We've got more over here," Sarasnar called.

"This side also," Hendandra said.

Kyrianna risked a glance back at the others and saw they had split into two groups as more goblins had come out of the shadows.

"We have our own problem, Rangerette," Myrith said as her blade blocked the blade of a goblin that had been aimed at Kyrianna's head.

Kyrianna stepped forward, her green swords glowing in the subdued lighting of the basement. The goblins gathered behind the crates turned and tried to run into the darkness. The three of them managed to take down all but four of the creatures. Two vanished into the darkness to the right of the stairs and two vanished to the left.

Kyrianna paused and focused her attention on the areas where the goblins had vanished. The movements of her companions made it difficult, but she could discern shuffling and whispers coming from both areas. She tapped Laraf on the shoulder then touched her ear and pointed toward the area to the right of the stairs they had come down. He nodded and held his rapier ready as he moved to the end of the crates. Kyrianna readied her bow and took a position on the crates, centered where she could watch both areas.

She watched as Myrith joined the group to the left of the stairs and helped them finish off the goblins they were fighting.

"This side is clear," Nirev called from where he was.

Myrith, Tristan, Hendandra and Falden joined Kyrianna and Laraf while Nirev moved into the darkness. She followed the sound of his movements and realized he was moving toward them.

"Chaos, what is he doing?" Kyrianna nodded toward Sarasnar who was walking down a small corridor. "If there are any more goblins down here, he'll get cut off."

"It's on his head, not ours," Myrith said.

"Until we have to rescue him," Kyrianna said as several shouts and the sound of ringing metal came from the hallway.

"Can you maintain the guard position?" Laraf asked.

Kyrianna nodded then grinned when she saw Nirev sprinting toward the sounds of the battle. Myrith and Laraf both moved to assist Nirev and Sarasnar as Hendandra and Falden took cover with Tristan to the side behind another group of crates. She shouldered her bow and readied her swords as she backed toward the others. She wanted to reduce the amount of distance between herself and the rest of the group.

The area of darkness to the left of the stairs had dissipated and there was no sign of anything or anyone hiding in the remaining shadows. The sound of creaking hinges echoed in the room and Hendandra pointed to a door opening between the corridor and the stairs. Two large wolf-like creatures with riders charged out of the room.

Myrith intercepted the first while the second headed for Kyrianna. She held both swords ready and made a crisscrossing movement as the creature reached her. The worg yelped and stopped. His rider lurched forward on his back but regained his balance quickly.

Kyrianna held her blades in a defensive posture as she watched the worg and its rider. She could see the teeth of the canine protruding from its snarling mouth and hear its nails tapping on the floor as it moved. Despite its size, it didn't telegraph its movements and she stumbled back as it gathered itself on its hind legs then rose up and clawed at her.

"Chaos!" Kyrianna backpedaled as the creature's claws tore open her armor and dug into her right leg. She shifted her weight to her left leg and watched the worg. She almost forgot about the rider until she had to twist to the side to avoid his blade and the worg tried to circle her.

She almost fell, as she put her weight on her right leg, trying to move with the worg and its rider. *Frayrith, no,* she thought when she saw someone moving in the shadows behind the worg. She didn't need a second opponent joining this one. The shadows moved again and she could see Laraf trying to get behind the worg. He held a short bow in his hands and grinned as he released an arrow, striking the rider in the back.

The goblin fell forward on the worg's back as the creature lunged at Kyrianna again. Her blades flashed, cutting the worg across the face. It only paused for a moment then came in again, its teeth grabbing her right arm and pulling her down as its claws again tore at her armor.

Kyrianna heard herself scream followed by the ringing of her swords hitting the floor. The worg shook her several times before dropping and standing over her. Kyrianna shivered as she fought to remain conscious.

Laraf yelled something she couldn't understand over the pounding in her ears. The worg turned and took several steps toward where she suspected he was standing.

"Hang on, Rangerette," Myrith yelled over the sounds of the fighting.

Rangerette. One of these days I've got to tell her how much I hate that nickname.

The cold was growing worse but she didn't feel herself shivering anymore and it was becoming a struggle to keep her eyes open. Tristan knelt beside her, his rapier on the floor and she brought her hands up to push him away from her. He was defenseless with the worg still there. If it turned to attack him, he wouldn't be able to get the weapon ready in time.

Tristan placed a strong hand on her shoulder and shook his head. He wasn't going to leave her. He moved his hand to her head and helped her up slightly and held a potion vial to her lips. Kyrianna coughed as he tilted it up, but managed to swallow most of the liquid. Warmth fought back the chill that had embraced her and she felt some of her strength return. He handed her her swords, smiled as he squeezed her shoulder then picked up his blade and stood to face the worg.

Kyrianna shifted her swords then rolled away from where the two men were fighting the worg and its rider. She reached the relative safety of the nearby crates and used one of them to pull herself from the floor. She leaned on the crate as she watched Laraf and Tristan finish the goblin. Its rider off its back, the worg ran away from the fight.

Laraf glanced toward Kyrianna who nodded. He then went to check the door the worgs had come through.

"Rangerette?" Myrith looked toward Kyrianna as her own opponents fell to the ground.

Kyrianna forced herself to stand up straight and pointed to the corridor where Sarasnar and Nirev were still engaged in a fight from the sounds that were coming out of the area. "I'll be okay, check on the others!"

Myrith watched her for a couple of seconds then moved to the hallway. As soon as the woman turned, Kyrianna collapsed against the crates. Her strength was returning, but very slowly.

"This room is clear," Laraf called from the doorway, he then turned and vanished back into the room.

"Kyri!" Hendandra pointed to a large group of goblins moving out of the darkness on the far side of stairs. They stopped in front of the door Laraf had gone through, separating the thief from the rest of the party.

"Chaos!" Kyrianna sheathed her swords and readied her bow. Using the stack of crates for balance she aimed and released an arrow into the crowd. A cry came from the group followed by the thud of a body hitting the floor.

"Hold a moment," Hendandra said.

Kyrianna glanced over to see Falden chanting and moving his hands. The mage smiled as the spell was finished. All but only a few of the goblins were on the ground and appeared to be asleep.

Hendandra drew out her own bow and grinned at Kyrianna as she took aim at one of the ones still standing. Between the two of them they took out the ones not affected by Falden's spell.

Kyrianna leaned against the crates as a wave of dizziness hit her and her bow dropped onto the one she was using for support.

"You going to make it?" Hendandra asked.

"I hope so," Kyrianna said, her voice only a harsh whisper. "What was that?" She looked up.

"Leikor's luck," Hendandra said. "More worgs." She readied her bow. "Let's try and take them out before they get too close." She let an arrow fly, catching the first rider in the arm.

Kyrianna nodded as she lifted her bow and took aim at the second worg and its rider. From the side, several streaks of arcane energy flew at the first worg. The creature yelped and sat back on its haunches, dislodging the goblin from its back. Hendandra fired several more arrows—first at the goblin then changing her target to the worg when the goblin fell.

Falden fired his arcane bolts at the second worg, which fell to the ground with a strangled bark. The rider turned to flee, but fell as Kyrianna put two more arrows into his back.

"Thank you," Kyrianna said.

Falden only nodded in return.

"We better go check on the others and see about getting you healed," Hendandra said. "That potion may have stopped the bleeding and started your body healing, but it's going to take more."

Kyrianna turned and put a last arrow into one of the worgs lying on the ground.

"Feel better?" Tristan asked raising an eyebrow as he looked at her.

Kyrianna grinned. "Yeah, I feel better."

"Good."

Hendandra's rapier flashed as she moved among the goblins still asleep from Falden's spell. Kyrianna and Tristan picked their way through the bodies and entered the room Laraf had vanished into.

Laraf was sitting on a large chest with three goblins dead on the floor. The rest of the room was bare except for a pile of bedding in the far corner. "Find anything?" Kyrianna asked.

"Just this." Laraf stood up and opened the chest. "Nothing but copper."

Kyrianna started coughing and Tristan put an arm around her to steady her.

"You okay?" Laraf looked at the ground as he asked the question.

"I will be, once I get some rest," Kyrianna said after the

coughing stopped.

"We should join the others," Tristan said guiding Kyrianna to the door.

"Yeah." Laraf refused to look at either Tristan or Kyrianna as he passed them to exit the room, his rapier held at the ready.

"Sarasnar!" Laraf yelled for the cleric who was searching the bodies of the goblins they had killed.

The cleric looked up and frowned. "Yes."

"Your healing skills are needed."

The tall cleric walked over and looked at Kyrianna. "Unfortunately, I have expended most of my clerical power for the day. I can only offer a single weak spell."

Kyrianna nodded. "Your assistance is appreciated at whatever level you can spare."

Sarasnar remained silent as he placed a glowing hand on her shoulder.

"Tristan," Myrith called from another room off to the side. "Could you and Kyrianna step in here for a moment?"

The room Myrith was in was small and held an altar carved from what appeared to be obsidian. Several wooden benches sat in front of the altar and a large tapestry hung on the wall behind it. The background of the wall hanging was a deep black that created an illusion of depth in the cloth. Woven into the blackness was a swirling vortex filled with various colors. None of the colors repeated in any pattern and almost blended together at times.

Kyrianna swayed on her feet and leaned back against the wall. "It is a symbol of Thynitic," she said.

"Thynitic?" Tristan said looking from her to Myrith.

"You don't recognize the symbol or the name?" Myrith stared at the young man. "I knew it looked like the symbols we saw elsewhere that we associate with Thynitic, but she is a goddess from another land. I was wondering if this might belong to a deity from this world."

Tristan only shook his head as he looked at the altar and the tapestry. "I know of none of the gods who use this symbol," he said. "Why would there be an altar to a foreign goddess here. The goblins have their own deities; they would have no reason to serve this Thynitic."

"Perhaps she is trying to extend her power beyond Rhysia," Kyrianna whispered. "She is a primordial goddess; born from the chaos from which the worlds were created. She is very powerful." She blinked several times as she tried to look away from the tapestry, but it held her attention and she took a slow step toward the altar.

"Kyri?" Myrith's voice rose. "Kyrianna! Rangerette!"

Kyrianna felt her breath becoming short as she continued toward the altar. She could hear Myrith's voice as it became louder, more insistent, but there was another voice in her head. A woman's voice whispering something she couldn't quite understand.

"Get her out of here." Myrith's voice penetrated the haze Kyrianna was in and she paused. Someone grabbed her arm and she jerked away from the presence to take another step toward the altar. She was almost close enough to touch it and she felt herself reaching toward the smooth black surface.

"No. You. Don't."

Kyrianna felt herself being grabbed again as two people dragged her out of the room. She gasped for breath and shook her head several times to clear it as the voice in her head faded. She jumped at the sound of crashing and splintering coming from the small room.

"Are you okay?" Myrith asked when she exited the shrine.

"Yeah." Kyrianna wrapped her arms around herself and walked away.

She moved to a corner away from the others. She was shaking and her heart was pounding in her throat. *Why was I so strongly affected by Thynitic's symbol? First, back in the planar temple and now here. It makes no sense.* Kyrianna knew her mother had an intense hatred of The Lady of Chaos, but she had never known the reasons. *Is there something in Mother's past that would make the goddess want to target me?* She knew there was only one way to find out—find a way home.

She stood there for several more minutes letting her body relax. She started to join the others when a glint of light caught her eye. She ran her fingers along the thin beam of light and was rewarded by a soft click and the door opening. "Tristan," she called.

"Looks like there is at least one door in the manor that either was never spelled or the spell has deteriorated," she said when he and Myrith walked over.

"Is there a way to bar this door?" Myrith asked. "We need to get some rest and I don't think we will be able to maintain full watches this night."

Tristan glanced the piles of goblin bodies. "The door opens

inward," he said.

"Good enough. Let's get these bodies moved." Myrith grabbed the nearest one and set it against the door as the others started moving bodies.

"Where do we want to make camp?" Hendandra asked once the door was secured as best they could make it.

"We'll move to the room Laraf cleared earlier," Myrith said. "There are two potential entrances to this room. The taint of evil is still strong in the room where the altar was. At least there is only one entrance to the other room and we should be able to hear anyone trying to come through this door."

Chapter Thirty

Kyrianna watched as Tristan and Laraf sat in a corner of the room studying the ledgers and journals.

"I'm not sure what all these entries mean, but it appears to me several debts owed to your family by House Ustelder were marked off, but not actually paid," Laraf said. "I would also make the guess Mikyl was skimming money from the family accounts."

Tristan looked at Laraf and cocked his head to the side. "Interesting analysis."

"You're wondering how I got all that," Laraf said with a laugh. "In addition to helping him acquire certain items, I also maintain certain records and books for Mulbanith." He pulled a packet of letters out of one of the books. "These were hidden under one of the drawers of his desk. I doubt he was given them as they look like they may have been early drafts of letters that were sent."

The papers, though folded neatly were badly creased and wrinkled as Tristan opened them. He read through the various pages, rearranging them and glancing from one to another several times. "It would seem Mikyl's manipulation of the books and accounts had not gone unnoticed and as a result, an agreement was reached between House Duvall and House Terissian that would have made Larissa and Wilhelm the sole heirs to both houses. There were provisions made for Christian and Melissa but nothing for Mikyl. There is no mention of Wilhelm having any siblings."

Tristan paused as he looked at the papers again. "My father did not know about this as the bulk of House Terissian's assets have been held in trust by the Coliseum in Irrmar in the event an heir to House Terissian ever came forward." He tucked the papers into his belt.

"Looks like House Duvall may have more assets available to it than you originally realized," Laraf said. He placed the books and ledgers back into his pack. "Something to think on."

Kyrianna watched the exchange and shook her head. She had started to believe Laraf wasn't here for the reward, but for the challenge, as he hadn't tried to claim anything for himself yet.

However, she wondered just what he had meant by his statement about House Duval's assets and Tristan having something to think on. Was he trying to get more money or something else out of Tristan?

"You up to taking a watch?" Myrith whispered. "I think we have enough people if you care not to this night."

Kyrianna looked up at the red-haired woman and smiled. "Tristan gave me another potion and the cleric offered a little healing magic. I can take a watch, though I would prefer it be the first watch."

"I want someone else with you."

"Why? It's not like I'm going to be summoning a familiar during my watch." Kyrianna put her hands on her hips and glared at Myrith.

"I know that, but you were seriously hurt and even with the magic that was used, it takes time for the body to properly recover. A second person will stand watch with you and that's final."

Kyrianna sighed. "Fine. Who?"

"Laraf has already volunteered."

"Not my first choice, but very well," Kyrianna said. She felt herself sway on her feet and Myrith, putting a hand on her shoulder, guided her to sit on the floor.

"And, this is why I want a second person," Myrith whispered.

Kyrianna nodded her head. "It looks like it's going to be a bit before the others settle in. I need to spend some time in meditation. Let Laraf know to touch my right shoulder when our watch starts."

Myrith nodded then moved away to speak with Laraf.

Kyrianna sat there for several minutes as she tried to relax. Myrith was probably thinking she wanted this time because of the injuries she had taken, but in truth she was more worried about the effect Thynitic's symbol was having on her. She needed to get herself centered and focused. She had been away from the familiar sights and sounds of her home far too long. Her soul longed for the quiet whisper of Frayrith in the forest. She closed her eyes, the fingers of her left hand touching the silver unicorn tattoo on her right wrist.

She finally pushed the images of the swirling chaos out of her mind and was able to focus on the memory of the clearing where she had been visited by Frayrith's avatar. Soon the sounds of the group where replaced with the rustling of trees and grass. Instead of

Falden's murmuring as he read the book she had found, she could hear squirrels chattering and Smoke snorting. The musty scent of the horse mixed with the dusty smell of Shadow's coat and the warm perfume of the flowers and earth to cover the stench of the dead goblins permeating the area. Kyrianna sighed as she let the memories fill her senses so she was back in the clearing instead of a foreign land having just barely survived a fight with a creature she had never heard of before. The only thing missing was the presence of the goddess.

Frayrith, her mind called the name of the Lady of the Forests and a gentle breeze drifted through the clearing but nothing more. *Dwycia, that was the name Legewyd gave me as being the deity perhaps the most compatible with Frayrith.*

Despite having a name, Kyrianna was uncomfortable calling on a foreign goddess directly, a name she had had no time to properly research and which had been given to her by a person who tried to kill her. Instead of trying to call to Dwycia, she continued to focus on the scents and sounds of the forest and hoped a sympathetic heart would find her.

A warm breezed drifted over Kyrianna. Warmer and stronger than the last one, it seemed to swirl around her for a moment and she felt a presence in the air. A shadow moved in the trees as the breeze faded. A young woman stepped from the trees. She was carrying a long bow and was accompanied by a host of woodland creatures. Her long blonde hair was pulled back into a ponytail, yet was still untamed as wisps of it escaped from their confinement.

The woman smiled as she knelt down in front of Kyrianna and held out her hand. "My blessings on you, daughter of another land. I have felt your loss and I want you to know you are not alone. As you have been told, I am called Dwycia, and my sister from your land has asked me to accept you as one of my children while you are here."

Kyrianna bowed her head. "My thanks, My Lady," she whispered.

The goddess reached out and lifted her chin so they were looking at each other directly. She then leaned forward and kissed her forehead. As Dwycia stood, a gray wolf separated itself from the other animals and padded over to Kyrianna. He touched his nose to her left wrist and a silver tattoo of a wolf appeared. Warmth flowed from the tattoo, in contrast to the chill of the wolf's nose and filled the emptiness she had been feeling. The silver unicorn mark of Frayrith brightened for a moment and warmth flowed up that arm as well. The power of both goddesses embraced her and Kyrianna smiled as she realized she had never truly been alone.

Dwycia looked around and her gaze seemed to rest on something or someone that was not visible in the clearing. She smiled then turned back. "Kyrianna, I would offer you two pieces of advice. First, do not spurn the gifts given to you by those you follow. Second, do not let those who hurt you in the past cloud your perceptions of the present," she said before she stepped back into the shadows of the trees.

As the images of the clearing started to fade, a small girl appeared as she ran through the hedges of a maze. Suddenly, she vanished into darkness and all that was left was a scream that pierced Kyrianna's heart like a dagger.

The scream brought Kyrianna back to the world around her. Gone were the refreshing scents of the forest, to be replaced by the stench of dead goblins. She sighed and looked around. The rest were already asleep except Laraf who was watching her. "Are you okay?" he asked.

Kyrianna smiled then took a deep breath. She could still feel the warmth from where the power of both goddesses had embraced her. "Yes," she said. "Yes, I am."

Laraf smiled. "Good, I didn't want to have to interrupt your meditations, but it is time for our watch to start."

She nodded then drew her long sword and laid it across her lap as she leaned back against the wall. She watched as Laraf removed his armor and began inspecting it. "Interesting design," she said when she saw the tattoo on his arm.

Laraf looked down at his arm then jerked the sleeve of his tunic down to cover the mark. He refused to meet her gaze.

"What does it mean?" she asked after several seconds of silence.

"Are you certain you really want to know? It's not a pleasant story and we have had enough bad things to deal with today; at least you have." He continued to study the floor as he spoke.

Kyrianna only looked at him and smiled without saying anything.

Laraf looked up, returned the smile and nodded. "When I was six, I ran away from home. My father was very abusive and my mother had left him several years prior, but she didn't take me with her. I think she knew he would have hunted her down for taking his son away from him. Unfortunately, with her gone, I became the target of his drunken rages. When I was finally able to, I took off. I had the misfortune of running into a group of slavers. This is the brand that particular group uses to mark their property. Several years later, I was finally able to get away from them and found my way here. Only Mulbanith knows about the mark and he uses that knowledge to make sure I'm available for various jobs. If anyone else found out about the mark, they would turn me back over to the slavers."

Kyrianna smiled. "Your secret is safe with me," she said. She turned her attention to her own leather armor. The worg's teeth and claws had torn it in several locations. She ran her hands over the damaged areas and frowned. The armor would not be easily repaired, and she realized it would probably be better to try and obtain new armor. It was a shame as the armor had been as good as Mulbanith claimed it would be.

"I won't fail you again," Laraf whispered. "I had a clear shot at taking that rider down and I missed it. I'm sorry." He looked down at his clenched fists. "I swear I won't fail you again."

Kyrianna stood up and walked over to Laraf. "Thank you for the oath, but you don't owe me anything." She knelt down in front of him. "You have your own future to worry about, without trying to worry about me as well."

He looked up at her, and Kyrianna was startled by the intensity of emotion she saw in his blue-gray eyes. It was the same type of emotion she remembered seeing in her father's when he looked at her mother.

"My future," he said after a few seconds. "That's something I don't really think about—at least not beyond where my next meal or coin is coming from. I've been a thief and a smuggler for too long. Maybe I'll stick with you guys for a while and learn something else."

Kyrianna sat back and stared at Laraf for a minute. "Are you part of a guild?" She whispered the question.

He looked at her, his browed creased and his eyes sparkling with silent laughter. "Actually, I am the head of the guild in this area."

Kyrianna stood up and walked away.

"What's wrong?"

She ignored the question.

"What's wrong?" Laraf was more insistent.

"I don't have much use for thieves' guilds. Excuse me." She spoke through clenched teeth, not wanting to risk raising her voice and waking the others.

"Hold on a minute. I told you about my sordid past. Now, it's your turn."

Kyrianna felt her eyes starting to burn as she turned back to face Laraf.

"The local thieves' guild where I'm from is part of the reason I'm here. I'm from a minor noble family, my father was granted his title when he retired as commander of Nydith's guard. Growing up I was a bit rebellious and a couple of years ago I was recruited by the guild. Knowing my father would disapprove, I agreed to join. On my first *official* assignment I was set up by my mentor to get caught." She paused and swallowed the lump that had formed in her throat.

She took several rapid breaths before she continued. "Even though he is officially retired, my father still works closely with the guard. The entire point of recruiting me was to set me up so the guild could use that as leverage to blackmail my father into stopping an investigation he was conducting of several ranking members of the guild. However, instead of doing that, he had me exiled from my home and disowned me."

Laraf looked at her and nodded. "I understand, and I am sorry," he said before turning his attention back to his armor.

Kyrianna watched him for a few minutes as tears flowed silently down her cheeks and she remembered Dwycia's words about not letting the past cloud her perceptions of the present. "Thank you," she whispered. She realized the goddess was telling her to not reject Laraf's friendship out of hand and she wouldn't. She wasn't happy that he seemed interested in more than simple friendship, but that was all she was willing to offer at this time. She hoped it would be enough.

Chapter Thirty-One

Kyrianna barely glanced at the others still sleeping as she woke in the morning. The sound of crashing metal came from the larger room and she went to see what was going on. She jumped back as a broken sword flew past her to land in a pile of weapons and armor. "Blasted goblins, equipment not even good enough to be classified as slag," Nirev muttered as more stuff was flung into the growing pile.

There was another, much smaller pile, and she realized these were the items the dwarf had decided might be worth closer examination.

Nirev looked up and nodded before going back to his sorting, the clang of the weapons and armor echoing in the basement.

"Okay, who's making the racket?" Falden asked rubbing his eyes as he stood next to Kyrianna. "We only got to sleep a short time ago."

"Actually, I was getting ready to wake everyone," Myrith said. "Find anything worthwhile?"

"Not really. Average quality on these items here unless any of them carry magical enhancements," Nirev said looking at Falden.

The mage stared at the pile of equipment and raised his right hand, his fingers moving quickly. "Here." He pulled a partially buried sword from the bottom of the pile and handed it to the dwarf.

Nirev looked at the weapon then held it out to Kyrianna. "You carry no weapons with magical qualities. Take this one," he said.

Kyrianna raised her hand and shook her head. "I prefer the swords I carry and have no desire to replace either of them," she said.

"But, they carry no magic," Nirev said.

Kyrianna put her hands on her sword hilts and frowned. "These are lighter than normal weapons and are exceptionally sharp. They are adequate to the task."

"I suppose ye felt they were adequate to the task when yer life was pouring out of ye yesterday after that worg's claws tore into ye," Nirev said.

Kyrianna stared at Nirev, her hands tightening on her swords as she took several deep breaths.

"I have watched Kyrianna handle the swords she carries," Tristan said placing a hand on her arm. "She uses them like they are extensions of her body. It would not be wise for her to have to learn the balance and quirks of a new blade in our situation."

Kyrianna felt her cheeks flush at the unexpected praise.

Nirev only shrugged then tied the sword to his pack.

"We should get going," Myrith said.

~ * ~

"I believe this is most likely the wine cellar," Tristan said looking at the ornately carved wooden door.

Myrith looked at Kyrianna and nodded. She readied her bow and moved away from the door where she could still watch the main part of the basement as well as the door. Myrith stood closer to the door with her long sword drawn and ready.

Laraf opened the door and slipped into the room with the rest following him.

"Wine?" Nirev's voice echoed in the basement. "That be nothing more than flavored water. I don't care for water. I prefer a proper drink. But, I thank ye for the offer."

As Tristan entered the room behind the dwarf, the door slammed shut. Myrith charged the door, hitting it with her shoulder. It bowed slightly, but she was unable to force it open.

"Stay there," Myrith said as she stepped back, took a deep breath and hit the door again. It still didn't move. She paused then leaned into the door; this time she managed to force it to open a small amount.

Kyrianna could see the strain in the creases on Myrith's face and the sweat forming. She frowned as smoke billowed inside the room but didn't flow past the threshold of the door. Some force was containing the smoke completely within the room.

Myrith continued to force the door open inch by inch. Several members of the group ran past her, coughing as they collapsed on the ground and Kyrianna started to turn her attention back to the area she was watching. She hesitated when she saw Nirev carrying Tristan out of the room. The young man's face was ashen and his breathing was labored and shallow. His clothes were burned in several places. She forced her eyes away from Tristan and back to the area she was supposed to be watching.

The door slammed shut again and Kyrianna glanced back over at the group. Everyone was there except Myrith, Sarasnar and Laraf. Of those who had made it out of the room, only Nirev seemed to be functional. Both Hendandra and Falden were still coughing and gasping as they knelt on the floor. Tristan was on his side and seemed to be fighting to draw a solid breath. The dwarf glanced at her, picked up his axe and returned to the door.

Nirev paused as he lifted the heavy axe and seemed to study the door for a moment. He then swung the weapon, stepping toward the door as he did. Three more swings and the door splintered, sending pieces of wood flying. The dwarf drew his axe back for another swing and stopped the blade as someone staggered out of the room and collapsed.

Laraf's face was as gray as Tristan's and his breath was coming in sharp gasps.

Kyrianna said. "Hendandra, you better?"

The girl looked up and nodded.

"Good, you and Nirev keep a close watch." She dropped her bow and drew her swords as she ran into the room. Just before she crossed the threshold into the billowing smoke, she took a deep breath of the clean air.

The normal green glow from the blades of her swords did nothing to illuminate the gray of the room; instead they created a green aura around her as she moved deeper into the smoke.

She paused and listened to the sounds in the room. There, to her right—the sounding of armor creaking. With care she began moving toward the sound. The smoke obscured her vision, hiding not only the location of those left in the room, but also the racks of bottles. All she could see were dark shapes, their distances from her changing as the smokes shifted.

In the far corner of the room, in an alcove created by the placement of the racks in the area, she found Myrith and another figure. Through the veil of smoke, the apparition appeared to be female.

Kyrianna held her sword out so the green aura would be visible to Myrith as she approached. Myrith twitched her blade and tapped Kyrianna's. She lowered the weapon into a defensive position as she stood beside her friend.

The apparition in the corner of the alcove raised her hands and a globe of fire appeared. With a flick of her wrist, she flung the globe at Myrith and Kyrianna, missing them and striking the wine rack behind them.

"Chaos!" Kyrianna yelled as they jumped and the alcohol in the bottles exploded showering them in burning liquid and glass.

"What?" Myrith glanced at her.

"Nothing," Kyrianna said. "That glass hurt, is all."

The apparition tried to move past them and Kyrianna swung both of her swords. A slight hesitation in the apparition's movement showed she had managed to hit the ghostly figure.

"Hang on," Kyrianna whispered as she held her long sword in front of Myrith. "With the alcoves here, she could be hiding—waiting for us to expose our backs to her."

Myrith nodded then gestured for her to take the lead. Kyrianna sheathed her swords to hide their glow and stepped forward. She cocked her head to the side as she listened to the sounds in the room. She could make out coughing from the group outside the room, but nothing else. A few more steps and she paused again. The thick smoke in the room muffled and distorted the sounds. Her throat was burning as she tied to prevent the cough that was fighting to escape. She knew Myrith had been in this stuff longer than she had, and had to be having a harder time at this point than she was. They had to find their attacker and soon.

There, something was moving in the next alcove, the smoke was reacting to whatever was there causing it to be displaced. She drew her swords and felt Myrith tap her shoulder with her blade. Kyrianna gestured to the side, then pointed to herself and at the far corner of the alcove. Myrith nodded.

They moved closer, if she had been able to detect the disruption of the smoke caused by the apparition, Kyrianna knew their attacker had noted it also. Holding her swords in front of her, she darted across the opening of the alcove to the far side. Myrith should have darted into the area to confront the woman while her attention was, hopefully, directed at Kyrianna.

Kyrianna turned to see a flash of light from the area as a ball of flame hit Myrith in the shoulder. The woman only shrugged as she stepped forward, her sword gleaming even in the dark smoke. The blade cut through the spirit and it dissipated.

As soon as the ghost vanished, the smoke also cleared from

the room and both Kyrianna and Myrith drew in several long, deep breaths. The body of an older woman lay in the far corner of the alcove; the only mark on it was a blue tinge to her face and hands. "Asphyxiation," Myrith said. "She was probably trapped in here while the room filled with smoke." She sheathed her sword then picked up the body and carried it from the room.

Myrith paused as they exited the room and looked at the remains of the door and the splintered wood on the floor. "Kindling Maker," she said looking at the dwarf.

Nirev grinned and nodded.

Tristan was still pale as he came over to look at the body. "Not one of the family, probably the governess," he said reaching down and opening a gold locket the woman was wearing.

Kyrianna nodded as Hendandra gasped at the pictures in the locket. The tiny portraits were almost life-like in their representation of the four Duvall children.

Tristan pointed to one of the pictures, a young man in his late teens and the oldest of the group. "This would be Mikyl, the eldest," he said. He paused for a moment as everyone glanced down at the picture of the person who was apparently responsible for what had happened here thirty years ago. He continued to point out the remaining portraits. "Larissa, the eldest daughter and the one getting married. Christian, my father and Melissa, the youngest."

Kyrianna shuddered as she stared at the locket and the tiny image of Melissa. She could hear the girl's screams in her mind as she again saw her running through the maze.

"Kyrianna?" Myrith placed a hand on Kyrianna's shoulder.

"It's the same girl," she whispered.

"The same girl?" Tristan stared at her. "What do you mean?"

"Last night, I was meditating before I began my watch and I was visited by Dwycia. When the goddess left, I received a vision of a small child running into the hedge maze. This child, Melissa, she died in the maze. I could hear her screams as they lingered in the stillness of the air. I can hear them now." She paused and took a deep breath. "That is where we will have to go after the chapel."

"Perhaps, but we need to take a few minutes rest before heading to the chapel," Sarasnar said as his hands glowed with a silver light and he touched Laraf's chest. When he was breathing easier, the cleric turned his attention to Tristan.

"So what happened?" Kyrianna asked sitting next to Laraf.

"When we entered the wine cellar, I moved to the far corner of the wall with the door and began a search of the racks in that area. The others began moving to search other areas.

"As I was searching, a thick cloud of smoke began engulfing the area. Falden's hawk appeared out of the cloud and landed beside me. I also heard what I believed to be the door to the room closing. Straining my ears, I listened carefully, trying to distinguish where my companions were and what might be going on. I heard movement in various areas of the room. The thick smoke distorted the sounds and I could not pinpoint anyone in particular. A flash of light filled the room and I heard Tristan yell something like 'Where did that come from.' He said someone or something had moved past him before he began coughing. I drew my rapier and took up a guard position. I didn't want to move into the smoke and was uncomfortable with the idea of fighting in the dark when I could not clearly see my opponent or more importantly my allies." He paused and looked up at Myrith who only nodded.

"As I waited for the right opportunity, the smoked filled the area where I was and I could feel my lungs and throat constricting and burning as I fought its effects.

"I was finally able to locate our opponent, or at least what I hoped was our opponent, in the nook across the narrow hall from where I stood and I moved into a position where I could attack if it moved toward me. I saw the hawk moving out of the area and I hoped Falden would be able to protect him. Listening carefully, I thought I heard the others moving out of the room.

"I joined one of our companions at the entrance to the nook and noticed the creature as she called forth a ball of fire and hurled it at me. My neck and arms burned as the fire struck me. I retaliated and managed to deal a weak blow to the apparition. The person I was standing next too, Tristan I think, stumbled, still coughing as he retreated out of the area." He glanced over at the nobleman who was still being tending to by Sarasnar.

"As Tristan left, someone else stepped into the area, Sarasnar. He held something in his hand and raised it up as he chanted. The symbol seemed to glow for a moment then dulled and his hand dropped, slowly as if he was fighting an unseen force. His magic defeated, he turned and left the area, leaving me alone with the apparition.

"The smoke continued to fill my lungs as I tried to breathe. I again attacked the creature and she hurled another globe of fire. I finally realized I could not stay in the room any longer and moved toward the door, praying it was open. I reached the door, saw it was shut and collapsed against one of the wine racks.

"A crack finally appeared in the door and I again said a silent prayer I would be able to escape the smoke. Finally, the door splintered and I sprinted out of the room barely dodging the dwarf's axe and collapsed on the floor. The rest, you know."

Kyrianna placed a hand on his shoulder. "Get some rest," she said before standing to check on the others.

"Kyri, you're bleeding," Laraf said.

She placed a hand on her neck and flinched as the glass embedded there cut deeper.

"Hold still, this will probably hurt a bit," Myrith said as she pulled her hands away from the glass shards.

"A bit?" Kyrianna clenched her hands and fought to keep still as Myrith pulled the glass out of her neck.

"There last piece," Myrith said.

"Thanks," Kyrianna said as she felt Myrith place a hand on the back of her neck, followed by the tingle and warmth of healing magic.

Chapter Thirty-Two

Kyrianna paused on the steps of the house as the group exited the building. The rubble where the stable and carriage house had been was still smoldering. Standing near the rubble, was the ghostly figure of a horse. "Myrith," she said nodding toward the horse watching them.

"Come on, we need to get to the chapel," Myrith said. "We won't be able to do anything for him, until we know more about what's going on here."

Kyrianna nodded as she glanced again at the horse. "Please be with them," she whispered.

The chapel sat a short distance from the house and appeared to be in the same pristine shape. The colored glass of the windows sparkled with the early morning sun. A woman stood outside the chapel looking at the runes carved on the doors. At her side sat a large black wolf. The woman's brown hair was short and loose and she smiled and turned toward them as the wolf barked several times.

Kyrianna grinned as Hendandra and Laraf both hesitated in their steps and seemed to be watching the wolf. "That's a friendly bark," she said. "He's greeting us as if we were friends."

Myrith placed a hand on her shoulder. "Perhaps you would be the best to speak to her," she said.

"Okay." Kyrianna took a step away from the group, her hand held out so the wolf could sniff the back. "Well met on the journey," she said. The wolf's cold nose sent a chill up her arm as he touched her hand then gave it a gentle lick. She felt the two marks on her wrists tingle as the wolf looked at her, his brown eyes darting between her and the others.

"And to you. My friend and I were traveling through the wooded area when he decided to chase a rabbit. I followed him in here and stopped to admire the carvings and windows of this chapel," she said. "I am Mylena." She held her hand out.

Kyrianna took the hand and gasped at the electric surge of power that went up her arm.

"I apologize if we are trespassing," Mylena said. "We will be going."

"This place has been abandoned for many years," Kyrianna said. "I doubt anyone would be concerned about your *trespassing*." She glanced toward Tristan who shrugged.

"We have been hired by the family to cleanse this place of the evil that has taken root here. Perhaps you would care to join us in this undertaking, as the evil is spreading and twisting the land."

Mylena paused and glanced around, a distant look in her green eyes. "There is indeed great evil here. Evil that seeks to corrupt all that it touches. However," she paused and turned Kyrianna's arm so the unicorn mark was displayed, "It is not exactly what it seems to be either." She released Kyrianna's hand and smiled. "While I wish you success in your endeavors, I cannot stay here." She looked at the runes carved into the doors of the temple. "It is surprising this place could be so strongly afflicted in this manner. Surely the family who lived here was once blessed by the gods themselves."

"Why do you say that?" Tristan asked stepping forward. "If the family was indeed blessed by the gods, then this would never have happened."

"When other gods are involved, even patrons are sometimes unable to protect those they cherish." Mylena's gaze darted from Tristan to Kyrianna and Kyrianna saw a deep sadness in her eyes.

"These runes are ancient and they are written in the language of Velasar, the kingdom once ruled by Sira. It is a language reserved only to the descendants of Sira and the ranking members of his clergy. It hasn't been spoken by any—other than his high priest for centuries," she said. She ignored the look of confusion and mild irritation on Tristan's face as she continued to focus on the runes.

"And, *you* can read these ancient runes?"

Kyrianna placed a hand on Tristan's arm and shook her head at the sarcasm she had heard in his voice.

Mylena either didn't notice or chose to ignore the sarcasm. "Here is a temple to one of the houses that has served Mykaylene so well for so long," she said. "All hail its Lord. All hail its Goddess." She turned to look at Tristan, her head cocked to the left. "This temple was built in tribute to the family not the Battle Maiden. However, the gods themselves have blessed this ground. I would imagine this is one of those rare instances where the patron deity, Mykaylene in this case, was honoring the lord of the family for his service to her."

The wolf whined and looked up at his companion then stood and trotted toward the gate. Before he exited the grounds, he stopped, turned and looked back at the woman. "We must go," she said. "The Goddess' blessing on each of you."

Kyrianna watched as Mylena sprinted out the gate following the black wolf.

"Kyri?" Laraf asked as he placed a hand on her shoulder. "Are you okay?"

"Yeah," she said stepping away. "That was a bit unusual, wasn't it?" She looked at Tristan who was staring up at the chapel. He hadn't bothered to hide the sarcasm or disdain in his voice when he was talking to Mylena and she was worried his resentment toward Mykaylene would cause them all problems. However, it wasn't her place to say anything at this time.

Tristan ignored the comment and reached for the doors to the chapel. They opened into a small foyer with two sets of stairs leading up to a small balcony overlooking the sanctuary. In the center of the balcony stood a suit of armor.

"She is called the Battle Maiden," Falden said looking at the armor.

Kyrianna grinned at the comment and stepped over to the rail and looked down at the sanctuary. A woman's body was laid out on the altar.

"Nyssa," Tristan said. "Someone must have brought her body here after she was killed in the house."

"Goblins," Myrith said pointing to several bodies scattered between the pews.

"Myrith, take a look at those," Kyrianna said pointing to two depressions in the floor. She glanced back at the suit of armor then back at the floor. "You don't suppose…"

"Look out!" Nirev yelled the warning as he stepped between Tristan and the now moving suit of armor. His axe bounced off the armor and the sound resonated in the small building.

"Head's up," Laraf called. "We have another ghost here as well as the armor."

Kyrianna readied her bow as she looked out over the sanctuary. Moving toward them was a ghostly figure in robes. Its hands moved in a spell-casting pattern as it reached out and touched the suit of armor. The metal of the armor glowed for a brief moment then it swung the sword it was holding at Myrith.

Myrith ducked under the swing and brought her sword up and parried the next blow. Nirev swung his axe again, hitting the legs of the animated armor with no apparent effect.

The narrowness of the balcony allowed only Myrith and Nirev to get into position to fight the armor, while the rest of the group watched the hovering spirit. Falden held his hands up and muttered something as several streaks of arcane force flew toward the spirit. The ghostly figure seemed to recoil a bit, but otherwise appeared unhurt by the magic. It maintained its position near the ceiling; not approaching the group.

"Watch out!" Laraf called as several pieces of metal flew from where the dwarf was steadily chopping at the armor's legs.

"Sorry about that," Nirev said.

Kyrianna flinched as the armor fell forward, its blade catching Myrith's arm and causing her to drop her own weapon. Nirev brought his axe down and severed the armor's sword arm from its body before it could attack again. Even on the ground and in pieces the animated armor was still twitching, trying to reach Myrith. She kicked one of the gauntlets away from her as she headed for the stairs.

"Looks like the spirit has left," Laraf said.

"For now," Sarasnar said. "It will probably be back."

"Great." Hendandra ducked behind the cleric as they entered the sanctuary.

Tristan walked up to the altar and laid a hand on the woman's cheek. "Nyssa," he whispered.

The spirit reappeared on the other side of the altar, and seemed to focus his attention on Tristan. Myrith raised her sword, but did not advance. The ghostly figure appeared to be an older man, dressed in the robes of a cleric. Around his neck was a torque bearing the sword and shield symbol of Mykaylene. After a few seconds he nodded then spoke to Tristan.

"My apologies, Lord Duvall, for the automatic defenses that attacked you and your group," the spirit said. "When you failed to provide the appropriate password to the guardian, it triggered its command to defend this place."

The figure stepped forward and bowed its head. "I am Vantalle, a cleric of Mykaylene. We have waited many years for one of the Duvall line to return to the estate and cleanse the house of the evil that claimed Mikyl. I will assist as I can." He reached out and touched Myrith then Nirev.

Kyrianna watched as the cut Myrith had taken to her arm was healed at the spirit's touch. The cleric then turned and opened two rooms behind the altar and motioned the group over. In the first he pointed to a shield bearing the symbol of Mykaylene on it. "A warrior should have something to show her allegiance to her deity," he said looking at Myrith. "May this shield serve to protect you."

Myrith picked up the shield. "My thanks," she said.

The cleric nodded. "This is consecrated ground and as long as my body remains undisturbed, you may come here for rest and healing," he said. "Unfortunately, the defenses are no longer as strong as they should be." A slight smile appeared on his face.

"Vantalle, please tell us what happened," Tristan said.

"I believe I was the first to be killed by Mikyl," the spirit said. "He came out to give me the family's pledge gift to the church for my services in officiating the wedding. When I turned to secure the pledge in the altar, he thrust a dagger into my side." Vantalle pointed to the blade still embedded in his body where it lay behind the altar. "I do not understand why, but my spirit was trapped in this place after I died. I do not know how much time but eventually, I watched as Lord Rhinehart Duvall carried his wife's body into the chapel and laid her on the altar. I remember the tears flowing down his face as he knelt there for some time. When he finally rose it was with a heavy heart and deep sadness. I could feel his anger and his resignation that he was being forced to do something he did not want to do."

Tristan nodded. "Father told me once grandfather loved Mikyl dearly, to the point of forgiving him almost anything. Of course, he was that way with all the children. But, Mikyl was the eldest and the heir. He also told me the only time he had ever seen his father angry with Mikyl was when he refused to spend the traditional night in vigil seeking a vision of Mykaylene. Grandfather wasn't trying to force the issue of Mikyl serving the Battle Maiden, if he wasn't called, but Mikyl wouldn't even honor the tradition." Tristan turned away from the ghostly cleric.

"Father said he was still very young when that happened, but he remembered Mikyl laughing at the tradition calling it stupid then running off to hide in his room. Grandfather never yelled or said anything to Mikyl about the incident ever again, but Father said he remembered the pain in his eyes as he left the house to stand vigil in the chapel—alone."

"We should talk to Alesandra again," Falden whispered.

"A powerful woman, Alesandra," Vantalle said. "Listen well to her advice." He paused for several seconds then continued speaking. "You should know she was not killed by Mikyl, but instead took her own life as part of a complex spell to protect this place and prevent whatever Mikyl was hoping to achieve that night.

"We thank you for your information and we will return to this place," Tristan said as they left the chapel to return to the house.

Chapter Thirty-Three

While the air was warmer and the sky brighter, the scents of the early afternoon had changed little as the group exited the chapel. Kyrianna stopped in front of the chapel and looked out toward the gate. For some reason she had expected to see either the wolf or his companion standing there, instead there was only the empty road leading to the house. Mylena's words echoed in her mind again as she hurried to catch up with the others. *When other gods are involved, even patrons are sometimes unable to protect those they cherish.* The look she had given her appeared to have been one of sorrow.

Had that been both an admonition to Tristan regarding his statements about the gods not having protected his family as well as a warning to her? And if so—why? That Mylena was something other she appeared to be, Kyrianna had no doubts. There had been the tingle of power in the marks given her by Frayrith and Dwycia when the wolf had touched her hand. The surge of power she had felt at Mylena's touch had marked her as a messenger of some sort. What did she mean about the evil not being what it appeared to be? Why not give her message straight? Why the veiled words and looks? It made no sense.

Nyssa's spirit did not greet them as they entered the house and went to Alesandra's room. The ghost of Tristan's great-grand mother was already waiting when they entered the room.

Myrith stepped forward and quickly told Alesandra about their encounter with the stable master, Creed Lawton; something they had forgotten to relay last time they had spoken to her. From there she told her about finding the body of the governess then about the chapel.

"You told us that we must follow his steps, have we created a more serious problem by defeating the stable master and the governess out of sequence?" Myrith asked.

"Creed Lawton was not killed by my grandson, and therefore he is not part of the path you must follow," Tristan said relaying Alesandra's words. "It is even possible his spirit has been laid to rest by the destruction of the stable. The governess was only a minor spirit; you have not disrupted the path too much at this point. However, you must be very cautious as you proceed to not stray any further. If you carry her locket, it might provide some small protection against the spirits that linger here."

"Since we must follow the path, were do we go next?" Falden asked.

"You have already been given the information."

"Melissa," Kyrianna said. "The maze."

"What about Rhinehart?" Myrith asked.

"He was the last to die, in an area below the basement. The entrance can be found through the kitchen or library. You must not encounter him until you are ready. He was a powerful man and his spirit is stronger still. You must follow the path, building your strength and knowledge."

"We thank you for your advice." Tristan said motioning for the group to leave.

"What can you tell us about the shrine in the basement?" Kyrianna asked turning back to face the spirit.

The spirit waited until Tristan turned back around to face her before speaking. "I believe you already know the name of the goddess to whom it was dedicated." She paused as her eyes focused on Kyrianna. "I do not know when the Lady of Chaos began trying to seduce Mikyl to her service, but I do know she played on his lust for power and the fact he felt he didn't fit in here. He had no desire to be a warrior like his father. He was more interested in magic, though he was too rash for me to accept as a pupil." The spirit faded from the glass.

"It takes a lot for a spirit to manifest itself on the material plane if it is not trapped here by other magics," Sarasnar said. "Vantalle said she took her own life to protect this place and she is obviously bound here, the same magic trapping the others is not what is holding her. She must use her own energy to appear."

"Then we should let her rest," Myrith said. "I'm sure we will need to consult with her again at some time."

The group exited the room and gathered on the balcony looking down at the great hall.

"We did not take the locket from the governess," Hendandra said. "Should we go back for it if it will help us? Keep in mind, it was my opening the locket that triggered the smoke and called her spirit forth."

"We have already defeated her spirit. It should be safe to remove the locket," Falden said.

"I agree," Sarasnar said.

"We can't waste time debating the issue," Myrith said. "Let's check the cellar." She headed for the stairs.

"This can't be good," Kyrianna said as they approached the wine cellar. "We left the body there and it's gone."

"And the door is back to normal," Laraf said.

"Hendandra, when exactly did the smoke start?" Myrith said.

"When I tried to remove the locket."

"Did you touch the body prior to that?"

"Yes." The small woman looked up at the knight. "She was lying on her side and I rolled her onto her back."

"Then the locket is the key," Tristan said. "Perhaps, if we remove her from the wine cellar before attempting to remove it, we will be able to do so without triggering another attack."

"Do you know where the cemetery is on the estate?" Sarasnar asked.

Tristan raised an eyebrow as he looked at the cleric. "As they served Mykaylene, it would be somewhere to the northwest of the house," he said. "Why?"

"As it would appear the body can be handled safely, I suggest we take her there and perform the appropriate prayers. Then I believe we will be able to safely remove the locket. If we can put her spirit to rest, there will be no need for it to attack us."

"It's worth a try," Kyrianna said.

Myrith held the door as the others entered the cellar and followed Hendandra to where the body of the governess lay. Tristan picked her up and carried her as the group left the house.

The path was the only area they had found so far that was overgrown; Kyrianna used her sword to make it a little more passable.

The cemetery surrounded a large mausoleum with the Duvall crest carved over the black marble doors. The various markers outside the building did not contain the Duvall name on any of them. "These would have been the servants who died while with the family," Tristan said.

"I found a tool shed over here," Nirev said as he stepped out of a small building that was showing the effects of thirty years of negligent. "We have shovels." He held one and tossed the second one to Laraf. "Give me a hand boy, and we'll get an appropriate hole dug fer the lady."

Nirev dropped his pack and laid his axe on top of it as he looked around at the markers. "This be yer family's land, Lord Duvall, where should she be laid to rest?"

Tristan looked around the area then nodded toward a spot near the mausoleum. "There," he whispered.

Laraf and Nirev started digging the grave together. "If ye can't keep up, get out," Nirev said after a few minutes. "Yer just getting in my way."

Laraf grinned as he dropped the shovel and sat on a nearby rock. "If you insist," he said.

"There," Nirev said. "This be a decent hole." The shovel was tossed out of the grave followed by several dwarven phrases.

Myrith looked around at the rest of the group. "Did anyone understand that?"

"It be wouldn't appropriate for me to repeat that kind of language in front of a lady," Laraf said. "Suffice it to say, he would like some help getting out of the grave." He stood up and pulled a rope from his pack and tossed it to the dwarf.

Sarasnar removed a silver flask from his belt and poured a small amount of the water into his hand. "May Resare give this woman's spirit the rest she has been denied for thirty years and guide her to the Battle Maiden," he said sprinkling the water over the body as Tristan held her. "Mykaylene, accept the soul of this person who has been trapped by the evil of this place and welcome her into your embrace."

The cleric removed the locket then Tristan and Myrith placed the body into the grave. Nirev stood there for a moment, his head bowed before he picked up the shovel and started filling in the grave.

"My Lord." Sarasnar held the locket out to Tristan.

The nobleman looked at the locket and chain in his hand then opened it and stared at the pictures for several minutes. No one said anything as they waited for him to finish.

"Melissa and Christian were only children. What kind of madness or evil could have caused him to murder his family, particularly a child like Melissa? How could Mykaylene have allowed it to happen?"

Kyrianna placed a hand on Tristan's arm. "Perhaps we will find those answers by the time we are done," she said. "Remember what the messenger at the chapel said about 'when other deities are involved'."

Tristan looked down at her and she took a step back at the darkness she saw in his brown eyes. "You seem to know something about this Thynitic," he said. "Who is she that she would do this?"

Kyrianna took a deep breath and lowered her head as she spoke. "She is the Lady of Chaos and needs no reason other than the need to spread chaos. She delights in pain and torment, as these will also further chaos among order. If there was another agenda in this, I would not be able to tell you."

"She is not of this world, how can she be more powerful than those who are worshipped here?" Tristan reached out and lifted Kyrianna's chin so she had to look at him directly.

"It is said She was the first deity. Born from the primordial chaos from which all the worlds, planes and other gods later came. If that is true, then part of the power all the gods have comes from Her." She stepped back again and pulled her arms around her as she saw Sarasnar and Myrith staring at her. "I'm sorry, that's all I can tell you about Her."

"It is more than I already knew," Tristan said. He draped the gold chain with the locket over his head. "I believe we decided the maze was the next place we needed to go."

"It was," Myrith said.

~ * ~

"It would probably be best if you took the lead here, Rangerette," Myrith said as they looked at the entrance to the hedge maze.

Here was another place that was overgrown and showing signs of neglect. Kyrianna glanced up at the vines covering the path in a canopy of green that created an artificial twilight within the maze despite the approaching high sun. Remnants of blue ribbons were tied to the archway at the entrance and a weathered sign announced the game for the guests of the wedding. "If the prize you would claim, the center you must find. If in the twists and turns your way you should lose, just follow the eyes."

"I wonder what it means," Hendandra said.

"We'll soon find out," Falden said.

Kyrianna knelt down at the entrance, her hand brushing the leaves aside as she studied the ground. "No one has entered this area in some time." She drew her sword and stepped into the gloom.

Chapter Thirty-Four

The short entranceway to the maze intersected a cross path going right and left. Kyrianna paused as she glanced in both directions. The ground was undisturbed and there was nothing to give any clue regarding which direction the girl may have taken thirty years ago. Shrugging her shoulders she turned to the left.

"Chaos!" The ground gave out under her feet.

"Is that the way yer supposed to find traps?" Nirev asked offering her a hand out of the hole.

"Not normally," Hendandra said with a smirk.

Kyrianna threw a small clod of dirt at the girl. "As I recall a certain short, blonde-haired rogue has triggered at least one trap as well as breaking her last set of lock picks," she said. "Is that way you're supposed to do it?"

Hendandra muttered something about the arrogance of elves and Kyrianna smiled. Hendandra had spoken very softly probably assuming no one else would hear her well enough to understand what was said. Kyrianna wasn't about to respond to the insult and let her know she had clearly heard the comment. "What was that?" she asked.

"Nothing, just a prayer to Leikor for luck," Hendandra said.

"Luck is what you make it," Laraf said. "Myrith, you want Hendandra or I to take the lead?"

"That will not be necessary," Kyrianna said. She sheathed her sword as she raised her hands and spoke the words to a spell. "Something I should have done to begin with," she said as she drew her sword and turned to follow the path away from the pit. Dwycia had advised her not to spurn the gifts given to her, and that night she had been given knowledge of this spell by the goddess. Even though most on her world feared and hated those who practiced arcane magic, many still accepted divine magic as a gift from the gods, but one that should be used only when needed. As she had failed to see the damaged part of the path, this was a time it was needed.

The path turned to the left and Kyrianna paused as an area several feet in front of her began to glow. "Hold up," she said as she moved forward a couple of steps.

"We have another trap," Kyrianna said as she drew a line in the dirt. "It starts here and extends completely across the path for about ten feet in front of this line."

"We should be able to jump over," Myrith said.

"I agree." Kyrianna removed her pack and tossed it across before she stepped back and took a few running steps to clear the glowing area.

Kyrianna continued to lead the way through the maze watching for signs her spell detected any other traps or snares. Despite the various twists and turns, the path had not yet branched off into multiple directions.

She paused for a moment as a vine covered archway opened into a larger area. She dropped her swords and grabbed for her throat as she felt something wrap itself around her neck and begin lifting her up. *An assassin vine*, she thought as she fought the urge to flail. She grabbed the vine, trying to pull it away from her throat so she could continue to breathe, but the plant was too strong. She cursed herself for a fool, for relying on the spell to point out possible traps and not paying better attention to things the spell wouldn't find. *One more reason not to trust magic of any type.*

She found her breath coming in short gasps and she blinked several times trying to chase the black spots from her vision. It didn't help. Myrith was standing in front of her saying something, but the roaring and pounding in her ears covered the woman's voice. Something moved behind Myrith and Kyrianna tried to call out a warning, but only a choking sound emerged from her throat. She pointed and Myrith spun around in time to avoid the length of vine reaching for her.

The area erupted as the plants animated and began grabbing at the rest of the group. Kyrianna continued to claw at the vine around her throat as the others began slashing at the plants attacking them. She felt her eyelids dropping as her vision went black.

~ * ~

"Easy Rangerette," Myrith said. "You had a bit of a fall, when the vine finally dropped you."

Kyrianna nodded as Myrith pulled her hand back from her throat. "Thanks." Her voice sounded hoarse to her own ears and she saw Myrith's brow crease. "Don't worry about it, I'm fine," she said as she forced herself to her feet. "How long was I out?"

"I'm not sure," Myrith said. She grabbed Kyrianna's hand and seemed to study her fingernails for a moment. "Hendandra finally spotted the main *body* of the vine in the rest of the foliage over the path. She and Falden were the ones to kill it. It was apparently controlling the rest of the vegetation in the area, because when it died the rest stopped attacking. That's when it dropped you." She released Kyrianna's hand and nodded. "No lingering discoloration, you'll be fine."

Kyrianna brushed the grass and plants off her leathers. "You know, I'm getting a bit tired of assassins trying to kill me, no matter what form they decide to take," she said. "Let's get moving."

"You might want these," Tristan said as he handed her swords.

Kyrianna started to reach for the weapons then doubled-over as she began coughing. She waved off Myrith as she tried to touch her throat again. "I don't need any more healing," she said. "My lungs are still trying to recover is all it is." She took the swords from Tristan and headed down the path, away from where the assassin vine had been.

~ * ~

"This is getting frustrating," Myrith said as they stared at yet another dead end. "How long have we been wandering in this maze?"

"Seems like forever at the pace we're moving," Hendandra said.

Kyrianna turned to glare at Hendandra only to see the smaller woman peeking out from behind Tristan. She grinned at the smile on Hendandra's face then looked up at the overhang of vines and leaves. "No way to really tell how much time has passed, but I would estimate approximately three hours since we entered," she said.

"Maybe there be an easier way to do this," Nirev said raising his axe and walking over to the hedge.

The vegetation started quivering as he approached and Kyrianna dropped her swords as she covered her ears with her hands. "No!"

Myrith grabbed the dwarf's shoulder before he could strike the plant. "Wait." She turned toward Kyrianna. "What's wrong?"

"Can't you hear it? Screaming. Pain."

Nirev lowered his axe and took a step back. The plants stopped shaking and Kyrianna lowered her hands.

"I heard nothing. Ye nature types are too sensitive," he said.

"It wasn't just the plants; it was a child's scream. A young child," Kyrianna picked up her swords.

"Melissa?" Tristan whispered the name.

She nodded then turned and headed back the way they had come looking for another path.

"Another dead end, but at least there's something here," Myrith said looking up at the statue that stood in the alcove of the maze. The white marble was stained green and covered in twisting vines. Though the figure was female, it did not appear to be a representation of Mykaylene.

"Follow the eyes," Sarasnar said.

Kyrianna looked up at the face of the statue. The woman was gazing off into the distance behind and to the left of where they stood. She turned to face in the direction the eyes were focused and closed her own eyes as she tried to concentrate.

"You ready?" Myrith asked.

"Yeah, let's get going." Kyrianna opened her eyes and nodded.

"What was that?" Hendandra asked as a deep growl seemed to rumble through the maze.

"Something moved in the hedge," Sarasnar said.

"On this side, also," Falden said.

"Quiet," Myrith said looking around at the others.

Kyrianna touched the leaves of the hedge to her right and frowned as the growl grew louder. "Sounds canine," she said. "Stay on guard, in case there's a way for whatever it is to get out of the hedge and onto the path."

Kyrianna picked up the pace a bit trying to get out of the area with whatever it was stalking them but hopefully without missing anything else that would put the group at risk.

"Another alcove," she said pausing for a moment. "There's still something here, in addition to a large pile of rubble."

She stared at the winged statue, which had its face turned down preventing them from seeing which way the eyes were gazing. The rock was rough cut and speckled gray and black. Definitely of a lower quality than anything else they had seen in this place.

"Something don't seem right here," Nirev said as he and

Myrith stepped past her to examine the statue.

Myrith jumped back, her sword in front of her as the statue's wings stretched out and the creature reached out with its clawed hands at her.

"Gargoyle," Nirev said dropping the axe he had been carrying. He pulled a large hammer from his belt and slammed it down on one of the stone arms sending pieces of rock flying.

Kyrianna looked down at the swords in her hands and then back at Myrith and Nirev. The blades would have little effect on the creature. In addition, Myrith and Nirev had managed to stand where no one else could get into the fight. She started to sheath her blades as more pieces of stone flew out of the alcove but shouts from the rest of the group caught her attention.

"Kyri, those canines managed to find a way out of the hedges," Laraf called.

She sprinted to help the others; confident Myrith and Nirev had their battle well in hand as of stone flew past her head.

The barks and growls stopped and Kyrianna paused as she saw Falden's hands raised and two large dogs on the ground asleep. Both resembled large mastiffs, but there was something twisted and corrupted in their appearance. Their claws were long, sharp and seemed to gleam in the dim light. Their coats were rough, even more so than she would have expected for a pair of feral dogs. This was a symptom of the evil corrupting not just this place, but also the area outside the estate.

Laraf raised his rapier as he took a step toward the sleeping dogs. "Leave them to me," Kyrianna whispered as she stepped past him.

He nodded, sheathed his weapon and stepped back.

Kyrianna looked down at the misshapen creatures and felt her throat tighten and her eyes start to burn as she knelt down and drew her dagger. With two swift strokes she cut the throats of both dogs. "Frayrith guide them away from the corruption and evil of this place," she whispered. "Help me destroy that which has so perverted the natural order."

As she stood, she glanced back down at the pair of mastiffs, their features changed back to something closer to their normal appearance. Blood flowed from their necks, bright red, darkening as it spilled on the ground. Looking down at the dogs as they passed from this life to the next, she was reminded of her father and how he had had to stand over one of his favorite hunting dogs in this same manner. Grethor had bitten the youngest daughter of a member of the Nydith council when the family had been at her father's house for dinner one night. It hadn't mattered to the nobleman that his daughter had been teasing and tormenting the dog all night or that Grethor had tried to get away from the child by retreating to her father's office.

The girl had wandered off from her parents looking for Grethor and had found him in Brygan's office. The child's screams had disrupted the discussions her father was having with Brygan. They found Grethor sitting in a corner, his head down as if he knew he had done something wrong and the girl sitting in the floor holding her hand, which while not bleeding showed where the dog had bit her, and screaming. Without saying anything to anyone, Brygan had called Grethor over, taken hold of his collar and took him outside.

Kyrianna had watched him kneel down and hold the dog's head for several minutes, scratching his ears. Then very quickly, he had drawn a dagger and cut the dog's throat. Brygan had sat there with Grethor until the light completely faded from his eyes. One of the stable boys had been called out to take care of the body when her father came back into the house.

Brygan had firmly suggested the councilor and his family take their leave at that time then left the room. He had never invited that member of the council back to his house again. Nor, had he ever accepted any invitations from him.

~ * ~

"Finally," Myrith said as they looked at what had to be the center of the maze.

The path opened up into a large open area and widened enough for two people to walk together. Myrith and Kyrianna both stepped forward. "What happened?" Kyrianna stopped as a sudden chill wrapped itself around her.

"You okay?" Myrith looked at her.

"It's freezing in here. Don't you feel that?"

"No." Myrith shook her head. "Maybe it's only a small area affected."

Kyrianna nodded as she took another step into the area. Her shivering intensified as the cold still clung to her. In the far corner was the body of a young child. Melissa, the same girl she had seen in her vision; the girl she had heard screaming when Nirev had started to chop the hedges to clear a path. Next to the girl's body was the decaying body of a large dog.

"Here we go again," Hendandra said as the plants began reaching for the members of the group.

Kyrianna and Myrith both started slashing at the entangling grass and vines trying to cut a path to the body of the child.

"By all the gods of nature," Kyrianna said. "Myrith—the dog." The body of the long dead creature—now wrapped and filled by grass and vines stood up; it's size close to the size of a large pony.

"Falden!" Myrith fought against the vines holding her as the mage ran past her to stand in front of the creature, his hand moving in quick jerks.

"Falden no!" Kyrianna dropped one of her swords as she tried to grab for the mage.

Before Falden finished his casting the plant-dog dropped its head down and shuddered as three spikes flew from its back to strike the mage in the chest. Myrith ripped the last of the entangling vines from her body, grabbed Falden and ran out of the area carrying him.

"Warrior of the Battle Maiden." Kyrianna cringed at the disdain she heard in Tristan's voice as he managed to move past her to reach Melissa's body.

"No!" Kyrianna screamed as the plant-dog turned and started to lunge at Tristan. The creature appeared to be held by some unknown force as it stopped with its teeth only a few inches from Tristan's throat.

Laraf and Nirev both rushed in and began attacking the creature and Kyrianna continued to struggle against the vines holding her, the thorns cutting into her exposed skin.

"Melissa." Tristan whispered the name repeatedly as he cradled the small body in his arms.

The entangling spell faded and Kyrianna grabbed her sword as Nirev's axe cut the creature in two. The vines withered away from the hybrid of plant and canine leaving only the remains of a large mastiff. The collar it had been wearing was still around its neck and Kyrianna reached for the black leather. There was a slight tingle of magic as she removed it. As soon as the collar was off its neck, the dog crumbled into dust and was soon carried away from the area by a gentle breeze.

"Kyrianna," Tristan said as he looked up.

She followed his gaze to see the vines covering the maze wither away allowing the sun to finally cut through the gloom. Despite the warmth of the afternoon sun shining on her, she still felt a deep chill as she watched Tristan pick up Melissa's body.

"Here it is," Hendandra said as she pulled a small box from the ground. "The prize for those brave enough to enter the maze." She opened the box to reveal a handful of small sapphires and diamonds sparkling on the black velvet that lined the silver chest.

"A generous prize," Laraf said with a glance at Tristan.

Hendandra nodded and put the small chest in her pack. "Myrith, will Falden be okay?" she asked.

Myrith looked up as Sarasnar finished removing the last of the spikes and bandaging the mage's injuries. Falden was starting to stir and she laid a hand on his chest. "He should be fine," she said.

Tristan looked at Kyrianna. "Can you retrace the most direct path out of this place?"

"I believe so." She moved to lead the group back out of the maze as Myrith and Sarasnar helped the mage back to his feet. "Should we take a short rest for Falden?"

"I would rather get out of here first," Falden said.

"Very well. Let me know if you need to stop."

~ * ~

Tristan laid Melissa's body on the altar next to her mother's and stood there as Vantalle called on Mykaylene to give the child's spirit rest.

"We should go see Alesandra to find out where to go next," Myrith said after the cleric had vanished.

"Of course." Tristan placed a hand on the girl's cheek then reached up and closed her eyes before turning away from the altar. No one said anything as the group walked from the chapel back to the house.

Alesandra was again waiting for them as they entered her room. "Melissa was the first member of the family to be betrayed by Mikyl," she said.

"What kind of madness would cause him to attack a child?" Tristan asked.

Kyrianna and Myrith who were standing next to the young nobleman both took a step back and turned to stare at him. The pain in his voice was evident as he stared at the apparition of his great-grandmother.

"What madness would drive him to attack any of them?" Alesandra said. "It was a lust for power, power he could not control. As for Melissa, just like the others he needed to kill them to complete the ritual he was performing that night. I believe she was the first of the family because she was the closest to Mikyl at one time. She would follow him around and he spent a great deal of time with her. She probably saw him attack Vantalle and fled into the maze as he pursued her. Rolf, her mastiff, would have been unable to defend her from Mikyl's attack as the collar he wore, while it enhanced his eyesight and hearing also prevented him from harming any member of the Duvall family."

"Then the ritual wasn't completed," Tristan said.

"No. Christian was able to escape from the estate with the help of Mulbanith who got him to Raspa and found a family to foster him till he came of age." The image wavered several times. "My strength is failing," Alesandra said. "Before I lose my hold on this plane—you must go to the servants' quarters next. Mikyl went there after he killed his sister. He trapped those who were inside by barring the doors and magically sealing the windows. Once that was done, he set fire to the building; killing all inside." The spirit vanished.

"Let's get some rest. We can check out what's left of the servants' quarters in the morning," Myrith said.

Kyrianna paused on the balcony as a spirit appeared near her staring out one of the windows toward the hedge maze. "Tristan," she called softly.

"What are you looking for, Nyssa?" Tristan asked as he and Kyrianna stood on either side of the woman's ghost.

"I am waiting for my daughter, Melissa. She likes to play in the maze at night and hasn't come home yet."

Kyrianna placed a hand over the apparition's. A chill went up her arm as her hand passed into the ghost's, but she left it there with the hope the woman could sense her presence and warmth. "Lady Duvall," she said. "We have just come from the maze and Melissa has been killed."

"Where is she?" Nyssa turned to look at Kyrianna, her words just loud enough for her to hear.

"Tristan carried her body to the chapel. We are going back

there now if you wish to join us."

The spirit of Lady Nyssa Duvall nodded once then seemed to surround Kyrianna before she vanished.

"Rangerette?" Myrith looked at her, her brow creased in concern.

"I'm alright. I think she needed to be joined in some way to something so she could leave the house."

"Many spirits can possess different types of items," Sarasnar said. "I doubt this one means any harm to your companion."

"Let's get back to the chapel as quickly as possible though," Myrith said gesturing to the stairs.

Kyrianna sighed softly as Myrith stood next to her for the entire walk back to the chapel, her hand not far from her sword.

As the group approached the altar, Kyrianna gasped as the spirit she was carrying separated from her. "Kyri?" Myrith placed a hand on her shoulder.

"I'm fine." She nodded toward the altar where another spirit was floating above the body of the girl. "Melissa," she whispered. The two spirits seemed to join together then vanished.

"Let's get some rest," Kyrianna said dropping her pack and weapons on the nearest pew.

Chapter Thirty-Five

Kyrianna closed her eyes, whispering a prayer to both Frayrith and Dwycia for peace for this place and those who had been killed here. She was worried about Tristan's growing anger toward Mykaylene, the deity who was the patron of his family. She only hoped the goddess's love and respect for his ancestors was such She wouldn't let his attitude be cause for them to fail in their efforts. Still, it wasn't her place to get involved with his relationship with Mykaylene; she would leave that to Myrith and Sarasnar.

Kyrianna opened her eyes and took a deep breath. She wasn't in the chapel, but instead found herself in a wooded area. Her hands rested on the hilts of her swords as wolf howls echoed around her. She also heard the higher pitched yips of foxes and the calls of several large cats in the sounds that came from the shadows of the trees around her. The sharp crack of a twig breaking came from behind her as all other sounds in the area stopped. She spun around, her blades out of their scabbards and ready. Standing in front of her was an elven woman with long blonde hair. She lowered her blades and bowed her head. "Lady Dwycia," she whispered.

The goddess smiled as she lifted Kyrianna's chin. "You ponder questions best left to the clerics, daughter of another land," she said. "Still your heart is in the right place and you fight well. I felt your anger at the corruption in this place and your sorrow for the animals, which had been twisted into the abominations you were forced to kill. For your courage and honor, I give to you my Sacred Blessing." She leaned forward and kissed her on the forehead. "May your enemies never be able to hide from your eyes or your ears," she said.

Dwycia took a step back and frowned as she seemed to be listening to something Kyrianna couldn't hear. "You must be on your guard; She will be coming. Coming for you—just as she did Mikyl." With that the goddess vanished.

Kyrianna gasped as she sat up, her breathing coming in short gasps as she looked around at the others also waking from their sleep. Hendandra was staring at her with wide eyes. "You okay?"

"Just an interesting dream," Kyrianna said.

"You too," Laraf said from where he sat holding his rapier.

Kyrianna raised an eyebrow as she glanced around at the others. Hendandra and Falden both nodded their agreement that they had also had interesting dreams. Myrith only sat staring at the blade across her lap, with one hand resting on the shield at her side.

"Greetings Brother Jerietlan," Sarasnar called to a figure kneeling by the altar.

Kyrianna stared as the figure turned to face them. He was a half-elf, like her. He seemed to be older than she was with a slight build. Age was hard to determine, those with elven blood tended to age slower than true humans but faster than true elves and each one was different. She herself had seen twenty springs, though Myrith thought she was only fifteen or sixteen. His face was still unlined and his blue eyes seemed to have a hint of gray in them as he nodded to the human cleric. He was also wearing a holy symbol of Mykaylene.

"Brother Sarasnar, I was sent to deliver a message from Sir Balthas. He wishes you to return to the Coliseum in Irrmar to preside over his ordination as Head of the Order," the cleric said.

"Only the Shield can perform that task," Sarasnar said.

"Shield Frelia has been called by the Battle Maiden. The vote has been taken; you are to assume the position when you return."

Kyrianna glanced at Myrith and frowned. Myrith was watching the exchange closely and she wondered if she was thinking the same thing she was. If this cleric was of high enough rank within the church to be elected to a position of leadership within his order, why did he seem to have such limited access to the divine magic reserved to clerics? It also bothered her he had not noticed Tristan's attitude toward Mykaylene and spoken to the young nobleman about it. Something didn't add up properly. Was the cleric deliberately acting this way for a reason, or were the clergy in this town of Irrmar that weak?

Sarasnar glanced at Tristan then back at Jerietlan. "There is still work to be done here," he said. "I would not leave this group without divine guidance and assistance in their mission."

"Sir Balthas directed that I should take your place and aid this group in their efforts to remove the evil from this place."

Sarasnar nodded. "Very well. While you have only recently passed from a novice to an ordained priest, I believe you will do well by these people and grow as a cleric. My blessings on you, Jerietlan."

"Mykaylene's Blessings on you Shield Sarasnar," Jerietlan said with a bow.

Sarasnar turned to Tristan. "Lord Duvall, it would appear my duties to the Coliseum must take precedence. However, I have confidence Jerietlan will be able to serve your group as you deserve. Mykaylene's Blessings on each of you," he said.

Tristan glanced from Sarasnar to Jerietlan and back. "You must follow the dictates of your goddess and her church. We welcome whatever aid Jerietlan can provide. A safe journey back to Irrmar," he said.

Sarasnar bowed then raised his hands and muttered a few words. A glowing portal opened before him and he stepped through. There was a loud bang, like the slamming of a door as the portal closed.

"Excuse me," Kyrianna said when she realized Jerietlan was staring at her.

"My apologies. It is just so rare to see another half-elf, I forgot my manners," he said. "I am Jerietlan." He extended his hand.

"I am Kyrianna. Even on my world, it is rare to meet one who is half-elven. I should not have taken offense when I too was staring at you when I first realized what your heritage was." She took the hand and gripped it firmly.

"Your world?" Jerietlan looked around at the others. "Are you not from Shokar?"

"Oh, everyone but Kyrianna and Myrith are from Shokar," Hendandra said. "Hi, I'm Hendandra, the rest of this group calls themselves: Nirev—he's the dwarf over there; by the way if you ever want anything turned into kindling he's the person to call. Myrith—she's the one in the shiny armor; a warrior of your goddess I believe."

"You never mentioned that," Tristan said.

"I didn't think about it," Kyrianna said. She frowned as Tristan turned away. *Why would this bother him?* She thought.

Jerietlan bowed to the paladin. "Lady Myrith, I hope I am able to help guide you in your faith as it is my understanding you are a recently called warrior of the Battle Maiden. As one who is an outsider to our world, I doubt you have received the proper religious training regarding the church of Mykaylene. I will offer you whatever enlightenment I can."

"I thank you for the offer, but I have little patience with

words and prefer to see your actions exemplify the teachings of the Battle Maiden," Myrith said.

"As yours did yesterday," Tristan muttered.

Kyrianna turned to look at the nobleman, but he was staring at the floor. *What did Myrith do that was so wrong yesterday?* She wondered. *She left the field of battle, leaving her comrades behind,* she told herself. *But Falden might have died if she hadn't gotten him out of there and to Sarasnar. Chaos, what was it she said she was told during her vision when she was called? 'You do her honor by aiding those seeking justice and by never running from battle.' Never running from battle. Was that how Tristan saw her actions?* She shook her head slightly. She doubted Myrith was running from the battle, she was trying to save a fallen comrade; there was a difference. The question now was—how did Mykaylene perceive Myrith's actions. She remembered the way Myrith looked when she awoke and hoped that wasn't the answer to her question.

She turned her attention back to Myrith and Jerietlan. The paladin was standing even stiffer than she normally did. *Oh, Frayrith, she heard him,* she thought. Kyrianna knew she would have to pull Myrith aside and talk to her; just she had done for her before they had ended up in this place. She only hoped she could find the right words.

"As for the rest of our band," Hendandra said. "Laraf—who fancies himself a bit of a thief; though, in truth he is no match for me. Falden—practitioner of the arcane arts. And, you've already been introduced to our resident nature lover, Kyrianna. I suggest you refrain from trying to chop through any hedges around her, she seems to be a bit sensitive to such things."

"And who might you be, with such a glib tongue and wit about you?" Jerietlan asked looking down at Hendandra.

"Hendandra, and like Tristan there, I also hail from Raspa."

"I believe I heard something about several people here having interesting dreams. In a place as infested by evil as this it might be wise to examine those dreams for deeper meaning," Jerietlan said as he took a seat on the floor in front of the altar.

"I seriously doubt that will do any good," Myrith said. She turned and walked away from the group.

"Lady Myrith," Jerietlan called.

"Let me talk to her," Kyrianna said.

Kyrianna followed Myrith up the stairs to the balcony overlooking the sanctuary. The guardian armor was once again whole and standing in the center. "Myrith," she called. She kept her voice low, not wanting to be heard by the others below them.

"Myrith," she called again. "What did you dream last night?"

"I really don't want to discuss it," Myrith said.

"Like, I didn't want to discuss how I was feeling regarding Thynitic and what happened in that damned temple? I seem to recall someone not wanting to let that one go then, and I'm not going to let this go now."

Myrith took a deep breath then turned to face her. "You're right. Mykaylene appeared to me and told me She was disappointed in my actions in the maze. That a true warrior does not leave the field of battle as long as there is an enemy to fight."

"But, we might have lost Falden if you hadn't grabbed him," Kyrianna said.

"That wasn't the problem. I could have handed him to Sarasnar and returned to the fight instead of leaving others to face the creature. You were still trapped by the plants, I doubt Laraf's rapier was really of much use against the plant creature, Tristan was more concerned with the body of his kinswoman and Hendandra was occupied with trying to find whatever it was that had been left as the game prize. Only Nirev was able to really face the creature properly. She said my priority should have been for the entire group, not just one member. Tactically, it was a poor decision as we could have lost more than the one if the creature had not been spell trapped by its collar when it tried to attack Tristan. I had no way of knowing that was going to happen and should have returned to the battle as soon as Falden was out of immediate danger."

"And, you have been well enough versed in the tenets of Mykaylene to know that is what She would require in that situation? Were Her words to you really that strong of a chastisement or are you being harder on yourself than She was on you? Yes, you were told to do Her honor, you should never run from battle, but you were not running, you were protecting a comrade and trusting your other comrades to deal with the threat. Perhaps you should have handed Falden over to Sarasnar, as he would have been better to see to healing him of his injuries. However, did Mykaylene not give you the ability to heal also? Should you refrain from using that ability when it is needed? Perhaps She was only trying to remind you to think about the total situation and not focus on only one part of it."

"Perhaps." Myrith glanced down at the others.

"Then use this as a learning experience. Your heart was in the right place, you just don't have the religious training one of Her followers would normally have; She can't expect you to be a perfect example of all Her tenets."

Myrith looked at her and nodded. "Perhaps you're right."

"Good, I may not be a holy warrior dedicated to Order and Light, but I am usually right a higher than average percentage of the time," Kyrianna said with a grin.

Myrith returned the grin. "We better get back down there." She grabbed Kyrianna's arm. "I will not discuss this matter with any of the others, including this new cleric."

Kyrianna smiled and laid her hand over Myrith's. "I understand. Though I hope you are not making that judgment based on his apparent age. As a half-elf, it is possible he is approaching fifty years of age."

"No, it is because I do not know him and have no reason to trust him as I do you; other than he is a cleric of the same goddess I am trying to serve."

"Good enough. One other question," Kyrianna said. "About Sarasnar."

Myrith paused and looked down at the group, then back at Kyrianna. "Yes, I agree he was more than he led us to believe he was. The idea he might have been withholding his power when it was needed, is not one I care to think about."

"Particularly as he serves the same goddess as you and has been promoted to a position of leadership in one of her temples."

Myrith didn't respond as she headed down the stairs. Kyrianna glanced down at the group and frowned slightly at the look she saw on Jerietlan's face. The cleric turned his attention away her, but she knew he had heard the last part of their conversation.

They walked back down to join the rest of the group.

Myrith looked at Jerietlan. "I do not believe my dreams of last night are relevant to anyone else here, though there may be knowledge to be gained from those others are willing to share."

Jerietlan nodded and gestured for Myrith and Kyrianna to take a seat with the others. "Who will start?" he asked.

"I will," Kyrianna said. "I was visited by Dwycia who warned that she was coming. Though She did not say who this she was."

"What were her exact words to you?" Jerietlan asked.

"You must be on your guard; she will be coming. Coming

240

for you—just as she did Mikyl," Kyrianna said.

"Could She have been referring to Thynitic?" Falden asked.

Kyrianna stared at the mage and felt her breath catch in her throat. "I don't know." She turned to Myrith and shook her head. "I don't know," she whispered again.

"Who is Thynitic?" Jerietlan asked as he looked from Myrith to Kyrianna.

"She is a goddess from Kyrianna's land," Myrith said. "The place we were prior to this seemed to have strong connections to her. Then we found a small shrine dedicated to her in the basement of the house. One of the spirits here, Alesandra, told us Thynitic had seduced Mikyl by playing on his lust for power."

"Then I agree with Dwycia, you must be on your guard. Do you know why this particular goddess would be interested in you?"

Kyrianna stared at the floor, not looking at the others. "I have no idea why the Lady of Chaos would be interested in me." She paused and glanced at Myrith.

"I'm sure things will be made clear, let us hope it is in time to prepare." Jerietlan looked around at the others. "Did anyone else have dreams or visions that related to what Kyrianna told us?"

"No," Hendandra said. "As an acquirer of certain things, I usually offer the occasional tithe to Leikor. However, I am not a follower of any one of the deities. In my dreaming last night, I was approached by Leikor who asked that I pledge my loyalty either to Him or to another. I agreed."

"That's similar to what happened to me as well," Laraf said. "I've never followed or even given lip service to any of the gods and I was approached by Leikor, Rhyra and Resare. I pledged myself to Resare."

"I find it surprising one so full of life would pledge himself to He Who Waits," Jerietlan said.

"I have my reasons." Laraf glared at the cleric.

"While I was not given a choice as I have always been a follower of Rhyra, She also appeared to me and gave me Her blessing," Falden said.

"Bah, all this talk of the gods," Nirev said. "I had no dreams or visits at all last night. Are each of ye so weak in yer faiths that yer gods must cajole and guide ye every step of a journey. All Mulog did was talk to me once then send me here to aid the Lady Knight. I do what He directed and as she commands. As long as I do that, He need not visit me in dreams or visions." He stood up and hefted his axe. "When the rest of ye are ready to face the day, I will be waiting outside."

Jerietlan only shook his head as the dwarf stormed off. "Two of your group are from other lands and yet they have patrons here; one of which has warned about possible dangers coming. Each of you was asked to pledge yourselves to a particular deity. This is not something to take lightly. When the gods themselves are concerned you have a patron it can mean that your very souls are at risk." He paused and looked at Falden.

"That Rhyra offered you Her blessing tells me the Mistress of Illusion supports this quest of yours in some way. Though why she would, I do not understand. Rhyra and Mykaylene are not allies, so She would not care about the cleansing of the estate and the putting of these spirits to rest. Perhaps, Rhyra has reason to oppose this Thynitic."

"Lord Duvall," Jerietlan said turning toward the young nobleman. "The service these people are providing is at your behest. What were your dreams last night?"

Tristan frowned. "I was asked to pledge myself to Mykaylene as one of her warriors. I refused."

Kyrianna caught her breath and stared first at Myrith then Tristan. "Why?" she asked.

"For generations, those of House Duvall were devoted servants of Mykaylene. What did it get them? Damned to this cursed existence? Betrayed by their own blood and a goddess who would allow this to happen. Generations of devotion and she abandoned them when they needed her protection the most. From what I have seen here and from her servants," he glanced at Myrith then back at Jerietlan, "she holds no real power." He stood and left the chapel.

Chapter Thirty-Six

"We should get moving." Myrith said as she looked around at the others. "We are supposed to check out what remains of the servant's quarters next, followed by the guest house."

The group was quiet as they walked around the house to the pile of ash that had been the servant's quarters. Kyrianna shook her head as she walked around the perimeter of the remains. The edges were perfect, not smeared or distorted by the wind or rain. The smell of smoke, wood and burnt flesh still lingered in the air. As disturbing as the pristine appearance of the main house had been; this was worse. She knelt down and held her hand over the ash; there was heat simmering in the debris, even after thirty years.

"Myrith," she called as she looked up. "I really don't like this. After this long, with the changing seasons this should have been disturbed in some way. Nyssa's spirit keeping the house in the condition it was in when we entered seems almost normal compared to this."

Myrith prodded the ash with her sword. Embers glowed as she shifted through the debris to find what was left of the floor. "Wood?" She looked around at the others.

"How can that be?" Hendandra asked. "The heat and flame that would have destroyed a structure large enough to leave this much ash should have destroyed the floor as well." She prodded the floor with her rapier. "Interesting," she said as she knelt on the ground.

"Be careful," Falden said.

Hendandra used her blade to clear part of the floor. "Ah, here we go—a loose floorboard and a small storage area." She pried the board up and removed a blackened box. She used a dagger to open the lid and grinned as a few green gems twinkled in the morning light. "Very nice," she said dropping the gems into a pocket. "Falden, if you would, perhaps you can tell if these are magical and what properties they might have." She held up a pair of pale tan gloves.

"This is not about treasure, greedy ones," Nirev said from

the far side of the rubble. "We be here to see the evil consuming this place is destroyed and the spirits of those murdered are allowed their rest." He reached down and lifted a skull from the rumble and set it aside as he began pulling other bones from the ash.

Kyrianna, Myrith and Laraf also begin searching the debris for more remains. "Once we think we have all the bones," Myrith said as she placed another skull with the others. "We should carry them to the cemetery for proper burial."

"Agreed," Jerietlan said. "Lord Duvall do you have any objections?"

Tristan shook his head but didn't say any anything as he watched the group.

"Little one," Falden said. "Those gloves have an enchantment on them that will allow your hands to move quicker and surer while performing delicate tasks; such as opening a lock."

Hendandra slipped the gloves on and flexed her fingers several times. "You can't even see I'm wearing them," she said holding her hands up in front of her eyes. "Thank you, Falden."

"Lord Duvall, I wonder if there is any record of the silver going missing in those journals Laraf found," Hendandra said as she stood up and brushed the ash off her clothes.

Tristan grinned and shook his head.

"Ah, Myrith, I think we may have a problem," Hendandra said pointing toward the piles of bones. The bones were glowing with a red light and smoke was drifting around them.

"Fires of the Abyss," Jerietlan said as a pillar of flame surrounded one of the sets of bones.

A skeleton rose within the pillar; ash swirled around it and formed a crude body, just as the vines and plants had done for Melissa's dog. Smoke was drifting over the other three sets of bones and they were starting to move together into separate groups.

"Those two there," Myrith pointed to two of the sets. "They have much stronger auras of darkness around them."

"We'll worry about that when they actually attack us, Lady Knight," Mulog said. The dwarf dropped his axe and readied his hammer.

"Do ye think ye'll actually be able to do any good against a skeleton with those blades, girl?" the dwarf looked at Kyrianna and shook his head. "Sharp they may be, but edged weapons only slide against bone, unless ye can put a lot of power into the blow or they carry magic along with a sharp edge."

"Take this," Myrith handed Kyrianna her long sword. "There is magic on it that makes it more effective against those who are undead."

Kyrianna sheathed her blades and took the weapon as Myrith touched a small pin on her cloak. The pin grew into a bastard sword and Myrith grinned at Nirev. "Are you going to suggest my blade will be ineffective against these creatures?"

"No Lady Knight, I not be suggesting that at all."

Flames still danced around the body of the skeleton as it paused and glanced at the trio waiting for it then turned to look at the others. The skeleton turned away from Myrith and Kyrianna and headed toward Tristan, the flames surrounding it growing brighter as it moved.

Tristan drew his rapier and stepped in front of Hendandra and Falden as Jerietlan also stepped forward holding the holy symbol of Mykaylene high in the air in front of him.

"In the name of the Battle Maiden, I order you to leave this place," Jerietlan said. The symbol flashed with a bright silver light that leaped from it to surround the undead creature. The skeleton stopped and crumbled to the ground, a pile of white bones against the dark gray of the ash.

"That be one taken care of," Nirev said. "However, there be three more."

"One for each of us," Kyrianna said intercepting one of the skeletons before it could attack Tristan or Jerietlan. She found herself off balance as she swung the heavier blade Myrith had given her. She had grown used to the lightness of the ones she was carrying. It was also difficult to switch her normal attack patterns as she was use to wielding two weapons instead of one. To better control her movements, she found herself using a two handed grip on the sword. It was a bit awkward, but at least it was forcing her to concentrate on what she was doing. Still, despite the enchantments on the blade and the blows she was landing, she found herself having to dodge the reaching grasp of the skeleton several times.

"Need some assistance?" Myrith said as her sword hit the skeleton's arm, cutting through the bone.

"Thanks," Kyrianna said swinging the sword at the creature's neck. There was a loud snap and the skeleton's head fell to the ground, followed by the rest of the bones separating and falling also.

"Nirev?" Myrith turned toward where the third skeleton had been attacked by the dwarf.

Nirev was using his hammer to turn the pile of bones in front of him into a fine powder.

"That's enough," Myrith said as she caught the next swing of the dwarf's hammer with her sword. "There is no need to desecrate the remains."

"Ye want to risk them reanimating, Lady Knight?"

"They have been defeated. We will bury the bones here and hope that is enough to give their spirits rest."

"If that's what ye want." Nirev pulled one of the shovels from the cemetery out of his pack and set about digging a grave.

"Myrith, we should wait until the grave is ready before collecting the bones together," Kyrianna said. "If that was the trigger, we don't want to have them reanimate before the rituals are performed."

Myrith nodded. "Agreed."

When he was finished, Nirev climbed out of the grave he had dug and used the shovel to collect the bones and drop them into it. "Cleric," he said looking at Jerietlan. "I believe ye're up."

Jerietlan nodded and opened the silver flask he was carrying. He sprinkled the contents over the grave as he spoke words of benediction for the servants they were burying and any who were still lost. His prayers completed he turned to Myrith and nodded.

Nirev filled in the grave and the group headed to the guesthouse.

~ * ~

"I doubt this building would have had the same enchantment placed on it the others did," Myrith said stepping between Tristan and the door.

Tristan paused and looked at the paladin. "Perhaps, you're right." He gestured to the door as he took a step back.

Myrith opened the door and it swung open without a sound to reveal a short entrance hall into a large open area. She and Kyrianna stepped into the hallway, weapons ready.

"Myrith," Kyrianna whispered as she gestured to the far left corner of the open area. A shadow moved in the corner.

"I see it," Myrith whispered back. She frowned as she gestured to the open door to their right.

Kyrianna shifted her blades and moved to the corner of the hall as Myrith darted to the door. She watched as her friend looked into the room then vanished inside. A few moments later, her ears caught the sound of a door closing, followed by the paladin reappearing at the doorway. Myrith closed the door and rejoined her.

"The kitchen and dining hall," Myrith whispered. "Nothing in either, that I found."

"Good." Kyrianna gestured to the others waiting by the door and waited as they entered the building.

"Leikor's cursed luck," Hendandra said as the door shut behind them with a loud bang. She reached back and grabbed the handle. "Locked," she said.

"Not surprising," Myrith said. "Time to find out what's waiting for us."

Before either of them could take a step, a cacophony of noise assaulted them. Screams, the sound of running, someone pounding on the door, the door opening and closing all blended together in a storm.

"There's a fire," a voice cut through the din. "We need help."

Another voice joined the first. "The servant's quarters are on fire."

The noise faded to a softer level as a female figure appeared on the stairs. She looked down at the group. "Where is my son?"

"Who is your son, my lady?" Myrith asked as she took a step forward.

The figure frowned. "Why are you asking foolish questions?"

Kyrianna placed a hand on Myrith's arm as she stepped forward. "Lady Terissian," she said. "We are here to lay the evil that covers this place to rest. We will find your son for you."

The woman looked at Kyrianna then turned her gaze to Tristan. "That you keep company with this one proves you lie." She raised her hand and pointed at the nobleman.

Tristan stepped forward and bowed to the figure. "Lady, do not judge me by the actions of my uncle."

"You will be the first to die," the woman said as she began making complex gestures with her hands.

Clouds filled the room and the air turned frigid as sleet began whipping down on the group.

"Rangerette, can you see anything," Myrith called over the sound of the pounding water and ice.

"Nothing clearly, only a few blurred shadows. Hendandra?"

"Forget it. Not in this storm. By the way, the door still won't budge."

"Falden can you do anything?" Myrith called.

"I have already tried. I am unable to dispel her magic."

Kyrianna started as something bumped into her arm. "Easy Kyri," Laraf whispered as he passed.

"Lady Terissian," Myrith called. "I am a knight of a deity who follows the path of light. By my honor, we will do what we can to find your son."

The storm subsided, though the bitter chill remained. "We will see," the woman said.

"Lady, please let us help you," Kyrianna said.

"No!" Kyrianna's voice was harsh as a male apparition appeared in the center of the room. He stood in front of Tristan, his rapier aimed at the young man's throat as he lunged forward. Laraf stepped in front of Tristan, not moving as the point of the rapier rested against his own throat.

"Who speaks for your group," the woman asked as the last remnants of the storm dissipated.

"I will," Myrith said.

"You have one day to find my son and return him to me. "He," she pointed to Tristan, "will remain here."

Kyrianna glanced at Tristan and Laraf. The thief's hands were moving behind his back as he turned his head and caught her eye. She focused on the signs he was making and was thankful some signs were almost universal in their meaning.

"If you fail, he will die," Lady Terissian said.

Kyrianna looked up at Laraf's face. His eyes were hard and she saw the almost imperceptible nod he gave her. She touched Myrith's arm to get her attention. "Ask if one of our group can remain with Tristan," she whispered.

Myrith's eyes went wide as she looked down. "Laraf will remain behind as a guard," Kyrianna whispered.

Myrith turned to face Lady Terissian and made the request.

"They will share the same fate," the male figure holding the rapier said.

Kyrianna swallowed as she looked at Laraf again. He gave her another slight nod then turned his full attention back to the apparition with the blade at his throat.

"Agreed," Kyrianna said.

"Lady, where is the last place you knew your son to be?" Myrith asked.

"He and Larissa were to meet at the gazebo." As Lady Terissian finished speaking the door opened and she pointed toward it. "You have only one day."

Myrith bowed then turned and gestured for the rest of the group to leave. "Let's go," she said.

Kyrianna paused as she glanced back at Tristan and Laraf. Two more figures had appeared next to the one she assumed was Lord Terissian and were gesturing with their blades for them to move to the far wall. She nodded at the wink Laraf gave her as he placed his rapier on the floor with Tristan's and moved to sit next to wall.

"You're not helping them by staying here, Rangerette," Myrith said. "We have a time limit; let's not waste any of it."

Kyrianna stared at the ground as she followed Myrith out of the building.

"What in the names of all the gods of light was that about?" Jerietlan demanded when the door closed behind them.

"Excuse me?" Myrith stepped between Jerietlan and Kyrianna.

"You volunteered one of us to stay behind. So instead of risking one, you risk two lives. I never heard anyone even ask Laraf if he consented to this madness. From what you told me of the situation earlier, you have also left what could be valuable information in there as Laraf was the one carrying the journals, wasn't he."

"That's enough," Kyrianna said stepping forward. "We have been here for three days, trying to fight the evil and corruption of this place. You only got here this morning. Do not presume you know more about the situation than we do." She paused for a breath. "From what we have been able to determine, all that is in the books are records that show Mikyl was stealing from the family and letters showing he was to be disinherited with Wilhelm and Larissa to be named heirs to both houses instead."

"Seems a bit petty to be the cause of him murdering both families in this way," Jerietlan said.

"Alesandra told us he had been given a book of great power, and was driven by a lust for power. The need for money and power can lead many down the darkest paths." Kyrianna paused and took a deep breath.

"Based on what we have seen here," Falden said in his soft voice. "He was probably working with both ritualistic and blood magic to accomplish some goal."

"I apologize for any offense, however, I still do not understand how she could have so callously left Laraf there without consulting with him," Jerietlan said as he looked at Myrith.

"I told her to," Kyrianna said. "And I did have Laraf's consent to do so. Let's get going—we've wasted enough time arguing about this."

Chapter Thirty-Seven

The group paused as they took the time to study the gazebo sitting between the chapel and the maze approximately halfway between the house and the cliff. The muffled sounds of the surf could be heard in the distance.

"I am detecting a faint magical aura on the right post," Falden said.

"Hendandra," Myrith called as she looked at the post and a piece of parchment tacked to it.

"A preservation spell," Falden said as he looked at the parchment. "A minor enchantment. I detect no other magics on the item."

Hendandra moved around the post, her hands moving over the surface as she seemed to study the whitewashed wood and the parchment attached to it. "Nothing," she said after several minutes. She pulled the parchment down and looked at it. "It appears to be a poem or possibly three; each one written in a different language. I can only read the top one." She handed the parchment to Myrith.

"The second appears to be written in elven, but I have only a passing acquaintance with the language." She handed the paper to Kyrianna.

"Amazing," she said as she read the parchment. "A love poem written in three languages. It is the same poem in all three languages. The poet is a master as all three translations are written with the same rhyming scansion and beat." She handed the note back to Myrith.

"As Lady Terissian indicated this was where her son would meet with Larissa Duvall, it might be a safe assumption that he is the poet," Jerietlan said.

"What does that get us though," Nirev said. "I not be seeing the lad or his ghost hanging around and unless there is some clue in that pretty writing we have no idea of where to go from here. In case ye have forgotten, we are on a time limit. If we don't meet the lady's deadline, both Tristan and Laraf will end up skewered and probably turned into a couple of ice cubes."

"Perhaps someone should read the poem aloud," Jerietlan said. "Those who are killed in violent manners are usually bound to some object or place if they are trapped on this plane."

Myrith handed the parchment back to Kyrianna. "You appear to be the only person who can read all three of the languages."

Kyrianna nodded as she took the paper and began reading the first stanza.

"That is not for you!" The figure of a young man appeared in the center of the gazebo. He held his hand out toward Kyrianna.

"Wilhelm Terissian?" Kyrianna held onto the paper as she looked at the young man.

"We are here to destroy the evil that has covered this place for the past thirty years," Myrith said. She took the parchment from Kyrianna and held it out to the ghostly figure.

"And, yer mother be wanting to see ye," Nirev said.

"I will not leave this place until I find my fiancé," Wilhelm said.

"Let us help you," Myrith said. "Where did you see her last?"

"Mikyl Duvall," Wilhelm's voice broke as he spoke and his image seemed to waiver. "He...he stabbed me in the side with a dagger then chased her that way." He pointed toward the cliff.

"We will assist in your search," Myrith said bowing her head.

"You may follow me if you desire." Wilhelm headed to the cliff, vanishing from sight when he reached the edge.

"Now where do we go?" Myrith asked as she looked down at the cove below them.

"There's a path here," Hendandra called. "Though it looks less reliable than that enchanted one we came down on the island." She looked up at Kyrianna. "You remember that one. The one where..."

"I remember," Kyrianna interrupted.

"I think we should tie off together like we did on the other climb," Myrith said. "Do you agree, Rangerette?"

"I do. I suggest you take the back position, Myrith and I'll take the middle."

"I'll take the lead," Nirev said as he grabbed the end of the rope and tied it around his waist.

Kyrianna helped Hendandra tie off as the next in line then attached the rope to her own belt. Behind her she placed Falden then Jerietlan and finally Myrith.

The path was crumbling under their feet and Nirev moved slowly down the path. "Hendandra, stay further back," he called over his shoulder. "The rope should remain taut between us." He glanced back at the girl.

"Chaos!" Kyrianna fell back as the path crumbled and Nirev dropped from sight, followed by Hendandra. "Keep the rope tight," she yelled as she tried to brace herself to hold the weight of the other two. She felt herself sliding toward the break in the path. "Myrith, brace the rope. Falden, Jerietlan take up the slack and hold position!"

She knew she didn't have the strength to pull both Hendandra and Nirev back up and whispered a prayer that, together, she and the others could hold the rope while those two used it to climb back up.

"You're going to have to climb up the rope," she yelled after a few minutes.

"You don't expect me to pull this dwarf up behind me, do you?" Hendandra's voice called back.

"Chaos take it! No! I don't expect you to pull him up. However, if he's not unconscious, he can climb up past you and then pull you up."

Kyrianna waited for an answer from either of the two, but none came. "By the Lady of Chaos, what are you two doing?" She could feel herself starting to slide toward the hole in the path again. "Myrith, brace the rope, we're sliding again."

"And, just how am I supposed to brace the rope with nothing to grab onto?"

"Dig your heels into the ground and lean back." She felt the weight on the end of the rope change slightly and the rope started moving under her hands. "They're finally climbing up. As soon as they get back up, we'll be able to relax a bit." Her right foot came up against a rock and Kyrianna brought her other foot over to it as well, trying to brace the weight of the one climbing as the rope creaked and protested.

She let out the breath she had been holding when Nirev's head appeared over the rim and the dwarf finally climbed out of the hole. He moved only a short distance from the edge then tugged on the rope. Hendandra only took a few seconds to climb back up and the two of them moved back to where Kyrianna was still seated.

"Now what?" Hendandra looked back at the hole in their path and frowned.

"How far across do you estimate it to be?" Myrith asked as she joined them.

"Less than ten feet, Lady Knight," Nirev said.

"Most of us will need a running start to get over it," Hendandra said. "And, I don't relish the idea of the fall if anyone misses the other side."

"One at a time and we can tie the rope off to the person jumping as a safety line," Kyrianna said. "Who wants to go first?"

"I'll go," Nirev said. "Then I can anchor the rope on that side for the rest."

"Agreed." Myrith untied the rope from her waist then assisted Falden and Jerietlan in removing the rope from themselves.

"Rangerette?"

Kyrianna looked at Myrith as she gathered the length of rope together then began measuring out enough for the dwarf to get a running start and clear the hole.

"I want to talk to you later," Myrith said as she took the end of the rope.

Kyrianna nodded then turned her attention back to Nirev. "Ready when you are."

Nirev dropped his head a bit then charged straight at the break in the path. "Mulog!" He called out the name of his deity as he jumped. He cleared the hole by only a few inches and fell forward as he started to wobble on the edge.

The rest of the group followed one by one, with Myrith being the last. She cleared the hole by several feet and only smiled at the surprised look on Hendandra's face.

Kyrianna had the group tie off together again, but insisted on taking the lead herself this time, so she could watch for any more weak areas that might collapse under the weight of the others.

The group made it to the base of the cliff with no other mishaps and Kyrianna handed the rope back to Myrith after everyone was untied. "What did you want to talk about?"

"Later, when we have finished with this task," she said.

"Very well."

The cove was well sheltered and the water smooth as a polished mirror. A dock jutted out into the water near where the path had ended and another path led around the cove to a cave opposite where they now stood. Near the entrance to the cave a small weathered boat lay upside down.

"No sign of Wilhelm," Falden said as he looked around. "What do we do now?"

"The cave might be the best place to start," Jerietlan said.

"Let's check the area for anything that might give us any clues," Myrith said. "Nirev, you and Kyrianna follow the path to the cave. Hendandra check this area. Falden and Jerietlan, stay ready." She looked at the others then strode out onto the dock and seemed to be studying the cove.

Kyrianna looked down at the dwarf and shrugged as she headed for the cave. Nirev followed several steps behind her and she kept a close eye on the ground as she moved. Wooden slats had once covered the path; but, the sand and weather had taken their toil and the wood was almost completely rotted away.

"Head's up Kyri," Myrith called when they were about half-way to the cave. "There's something in the water; headed in your direction."

"Something is headed your way as well, Myrith," Jerietlan called.

Myrith turned back toward the water in time to block a clawed hand reaching for her legs.

Kyrianna drew her bow and fired a shot at the large creature that emerged from the water and climbed up onto the dock where Myrith was. The creature was tall, with long arms that hung just past its knees and gave it an unbalanced appearance. It appeared to have seaweed for hair and there were large slits in its neck, visible even at this distance.

"Chaos!" Kyrianna danced back a step as long claws raked her arm and she dropped the arrow she had been readying.

Nirev jumped into the water, his axe held over his shoulder as he waded out a bit to engage the creature.

"Scrags," Falden yelled as a burst of flame flowed from his hands to burn the one fighting Myrith. "They are a type of water troll and can regenerate their wounds. They are vulnerable to fire."

"Great, now all we need is a way to burn the things," Nirev said as he ducked under the creature's claws again.

Kyrianna shifted her aim to the scrag fighting the dwarf and took another step back hoping to remove herself from its reach. Her hand shook as she nocked the arrow and her shot went wide. "Nirev!" She fired two arrows in quick succession as the dwarf fell into the water and the scrag again focused on her.

Jerietlan dove into the water and Kyrianna saw him headed in their direction. She danced around several more sweeps of the scrag's claws and dropped her bow as she glanced at the place where Nirev had sunk into the water. It had been too long; she would have to risk an attack to get Nirev out of the water before he drowned.

"Chaos," she yelled as the scrag dove away from her and grabbed Nirev's unconscious body and began swimming out of the cove. She dropped most of her gear, except for her swords and leathers and dove into the water. As she scanned the water for the scrag and Nirev, Kyrianna saw Myrith also moving in the water toward the water troll.

Kyrianna surfaced for a moment and took a breath of air before diving down again. The dwarf was now thrashing in the troll's grip, the water disturbing the sand on the bottom of the cove and obstructing her view. However, she saw Myrith standing nearby and realized she must have been able to use her healing ability on the dwarf.

The troll appeared to lose its grip on the dwarf for a moment then grabbed him again as both Kyrianna and Myrith thrust at it with their weapons. The arm holding the dwarf was cut through by the Myrith's blow and the dwarf began struggling for the surface as the scrag began swimming out into the ocean.

Myrith and Kyrianna surfaced together and gasped for air as they looked around for Nirev. "Myrith," Kyrianna used her sword to point to something past the mouth of the cove. A large ship with tattered grey sails was anchored near the cove.

"Might not have anything to do with the reasons we're here. Let's not jump to any conclusions."

"Of course not. However, it is something to be aware of. I'll race you back to the dock."

"And, you'll win. I'm not that good of a swimmer."

"I'm not that good right now either," Kyrianna said glancing at her arm, where the blood was still flowing from the injury from the scrag's claws.

"Let's see if Jerietlan has any healing power to spare after tending to Nirev." Myrith headed toward the dock.

The water troll Myrith and Hendandra had fought was lying on the dock in multiple pieces, each one starting to twitch as the rogue cut them into even smaller pieces.

"Good, that's everyone," Falden said as Myrith and Kyrianna

climbed out of the water. "If you would clear the dock."

Hendandra shoed Myrith and Kyrianna off the dock as Falden backed toward the cliff his eyes never leaving the quivering mass of flesh that had been the water troll. As he stepped off the dock, he raised his hands over his head and clapped them together three times. A ball of flame erupted where the remains of the scrag lay, consuming the water troll and the wooden dock.

"I'm going to get my gear," Kyrianna said as she headed back to where she had dropped her bow and pack.

"You'll wait for a moment," Jerietlan said as he reached for her arm. "That injury needs to be treated first."

"I'll get your stuff," Hendandra said as she sprinted away.

"Make sure you check your pack when she brings it back," Falden said.

"Myrith!" Hendandra waved to the group from near the overturned boat.

"We better see what she found," Myrith said.

Jerietlan finished bandaging Kyrianna's arm and cast another healing spell on it. "Troll wounds will fester for days, even after they appear to be healed. I want to check your arm again tonight when we rest and in the morning." He paused and looked at the arm again. "That arm has been hurt recently."

"A chaos demon got his claws on it a few days ago." Kyrianna hurried to catch up with the others.

Hendandra knelt next to the body of a young woman, her blonde hair still matted with blood. "Larissa Duvall," she said as Myrith and Kyrianna approached.

"We found his fiancé, now we need to find Wilhelm—again," Kyrianna said.

The spirit of Wilhelm Terissian materialized next to the body and he knelt next to her for several minutes. Finally, he reached down and lifted Larissa's body, cradling her against his chest as he turned toward the path up the cliff.

The group followed him. Kyrianna paused as the path re-formed under the spirit's feet and the place where it had collapsed was replaced with solid ground. She glanced back at Myrith, who only shrugged then nodded. The path held as they crossed it and continued to follow the spectral figure back to the gazebo.

Wilhelm laid the body on the floor, arranging her hair to hide the place where her skull had been smashed and crossing her hands on her chest to hide the dagger wound. "I will not leave her body until I know where her spirit is," he said as he looked up at Jerietlan and Myrith.

"Perhaps, you have the means to call her to you," Falden said. "Your poem; I suggest you read it aloud."

Wilhelm pulled the parchment from his pocket and nodded. His voice quavered and broke several times as he read the words of the poem. He completed the first two stanzas and frowned as there was no sign of his fiancé's spirit. As he completed the final stanza, she appeared and they embraced as best they could. Larissa's spirit sank into her body and Wilhelm picked her up again. The group escorted him to the chapel where he placed her body with the ones of her mother and little sister.

"Where is your body?" Myrith asked as they left the chapel.

"The guesthouse," the spirit said. "I managed to make it back, trying to warn my family of Mikyl's treachery, however I was too late.

"My spirit was trapped at the gazebo; the only other place I could go was the cove, but I never saw where her body lay until today. Thank you."

"Your mother is anxious to see you," Jerietlan said.

Wilhelm nodded and they followed him to the guesthouse.

~ * ~

"You have returned my son as you promised," Lady Terissian said as she materialized. "However, someone must still answer for his death and the other deaths that occurred that night."

Lord Terissian materialized in front of Tristan and Laraf, both of whom were sitting against the far wall, their weapons separated from them. The rapier carried by the spirit of Lord Terissian was drawn and pointed at Tristan.

"My Lady," Kyrianna said stepping forward. "You set us a task to prove what we said and we have accomplished that task. Have we not shown you our honor? Have we not demonstrated our intentions are to remove the evil that has overcome this place?"

"You are not the one who said she speaks for this group. I do not recognize your words," Lady Terissian said.

"Then recognize mine, Mother," Wilhelm said. "These people released me from the place where my spirit was trapped and helped me to find the body and spirit of Larissa. They have shown me their intentions are true." He glanced at Tristan and Laraf. "He may be of Duvall blood, but this was the work of only one Duvall; Mikyl who also murdered his own sister Larissa. Do not hold this person to blame for the actions of another."

"My Lady," Myrith said as she stepped forward. "Mikyl is not only responsible for the murders of your family and servants, he also murdered everyone who was on the estate that night with the exception of Alesandra, who took her own life to prevent the completion of whatever evil he was planning, and Christian Duvall, Tristan's father."

The Lady's spirit turned toward Tristan. "You are the son of Christian Duvall?"

"I am," Tristan said.

"Have you any siblings?"

"No, My Lady. My mother died when I was born and my father never remarried."

"Then you are sole heir to House Duvall," Lord Terissian said as he lowered his rapier.

"I am."

"Follow me."

Tristan followed the specter as he led him up the stairs. Both Kyrianna and Myrith followed.

"When you are finished here, you will need these papers to claim that which is now rightfully yours as I doubt your father even knew about this arrangement." He handed a packet to Tristan. "Those papers show the houses were officially joined with Wilhelm and Larissa as the heirs to both. They also stipulate that everything should go to Christian and Melissa or their heirs if Wilhelm and Larissa leave no heirs. They have been properly witnessed by the council in Raspa and the church of Mykaylene in Raspa and Irrmar." The spirit faded.

Only the spirit of Wilhelm was waiting in the main room when they came down. He looked at Tristan and inclined his head. "I charge you with making sure our bodies are returned to Irrmar."

"If I am able, it will be done," Tristan said.

"These are for you." Wilhelm dropped a dagger, his rapier and a ring on the floor then vanished.

"Falden?" Myrith glanced at the mage.

"It will take some time to properly identify the magics, but they are each enchanted."

Tristan picked up the items and looked around. He frowned at the bandage he saw on Kyrianna's arm and the numerous bandages on Nirev. "I believe it would be best if you took time to tend to your wounds and rest. We can return to the chapel and Falden can cast his spells over these items," he said.

"Very well," Myrith said then gestured to the doorway.

Chapter Thirty-Eight

"I believe that is everyone with the exception of Rhinehart and Mikyl," Myrith said as the rest of the group dropped their gear.

Kyrianna looked at the paladin and nodded. "We've interacted with the spirits of Riker, Nyssa, Melissa, Larissa, the Terissian's as well as Creed Lawton, Alesandra and Vantalle."

"You forget the spirits of the governess and the four skeletons that seemed to be all that was left of the servants," Hendandra said.

"So unless there is someone else we don't know about, that leaves Rhinehart and Mikyl," Myrith said as she looked at Tristan.

Kyrianna followed Myrith's gaze. The young nobleman was sitting with Falden as the mage studied the items given to them by Wilhelm Terissian. Tristan looked up and met Myrith's gaze. "There is no one else I am aware of. However, as I have stated, my father has passed on very little of what actually happened that night. If there were other guests here, I do not know about them."

"Alesandra said we would find Rhinehart in the area below the basement," Kyrianna said. "And, she warned us Rhinehart was a powerful warrior in life and an even stronger spirit. We need to rest and prepare for this encounter." She glanced at Tristan and lowered her head. She was worried about what would happen when they met his grandfather the next day.

"Myrith," she whispered. "You said earlier you wanted to talk to me. Perhaps, now would be a good time."

"Let's go outside," Myrith said with a nod toward the door.

"What did you want to talk about?" Kyrianna turned to face Myrith as the woman shut the doors to the chapel.

"What were you doing calling on the Lady of Chaos earlier today?"

"What?" Kyrianna took a step back from her friend.

"Kyri, we both realize that for some unknown reason this Thynitic of your world has taken an interest in you. I can tell you have no interest in serving her, as you seem to faithfully follow your Lady of the Forests. Why did you say 'By the Lady of Chaos' earlier?"

Kyrianna frowned. "Chaos take it is a common curse on my world, particularly among the humans I grew up with. It is a carry-over from the wars with the elves, which are often called the chaos wars. As for the other, I didn't even realize I had said those words." She felt herself shaking and she wrapped her arms under her chest and stared at the ground.

"Kyrianna," Myrith said as she lifted her chin forcing Kyrianna to look up. "I don't know what is going on, but I can tell it is scaring you. I will be here to help you if I am able. Promise me something."

"What?" Kyrianna took a step back and found herself unable to look away from Myrith's bright green eyes.

"That you will tell me what's going on. I can't protect you if I don't know what is happening to you."

Kyrianna smiled and nodded. "I will. Though I'm not sure you can protect me from Thynitic."

"Listen, Rangerette, I don't care if she is a goddess or even if she is the most powerful deity in all the planes. No one hurts one of my...," Myrith hesitated for a moment as if she was searching for the right words, "one of my friends without facing me as well," she finally said.

Kyrianna smiled again. "Thank you." She doubted there were very many people this woman called friend, particularly when she thought about how little Myrith had said about her past. She also doubted there were many people she would have told even that small amount to. "I appreciate your concern and your friendship, Myrith. I promise to tell you what I can."

"Good. Have you heard her speaking to you any more since we left that last plane?"

"No. Maybe." Kyrianna paused and took a deep breath. "In the shrine, I could hear something that sounded like a woman's voice chanting, but I couldn't understand what was being said."

"But, you don't know if it was her or not."

Kyrianna shook her head. "No, I don't know for sure." She turned away from Myrith and glanced up at the sky. "There was one other time. It was shortly after I arrived here." She took several deep breaths before turned back to face her friend. "She called me the last of her daughters and said I would embrace her when it was time."

Myrith placed a hand on her shoulder. "I will not let that

262

happen. You need to remain on guard and don't neglect your prayers and meditation."

"Thank you. Speaking of prayers and meditations, there is something concerning me about tomorrow—Tristan."

"Tristan?" Myrith glanced at the closed doors of the chapel.

"If Rhinehart Duvall was a powerful warrior in service to Mykaylene, he might be able to sense Tristan's anger at the goddess and will probably react to it. In many ways, Tristan has renounced Mykaylene; I only hope this will not affect our efforts here."

"Perhaps you should mention this to Jerietlan as I am too newly called to Her faith to speak to Tristan on this matter," Myrith said.

"I doubt talking to him will make any difference at this point. I believe it would be better if you and Jerietlan both were to set an example by your own faith and actions."

Kyrianna laughed as the door to the chapel opened and Myrith spun around, her hand on her sword.

"Okay, you two. People in here are starting to make bets on which of you has killed the other one. I believe Tristan was the only one to bet on Kyrianna," Hendandra said as she looked up at Kyrianna and Myrith.

"A foolish bet on his part, if we had indeed been fighting," Myrith said.

"Oh really? We may have to face off in a practice match someday to test that belief of yours, Myrith. You would find me more of a challenge than you're currently estimating me to be."

"Perhaps one day we will, but it won't be until we are done here. For now, we need rest and Jerietlan needs to check your arm." She gestured to the door.

Myrith placed a hand on Kyrianna's shoulder as she turned toward the door. "Don't forget what we discussed, Rangerette."

"I won't. And, thank you."

~ * ~

"I'm going to leave the bandage off for tonight and check it again in the morning," Jerietlan said when he finished with Kyrianna's arm. "I don't think there will be any lingering effects from the troll's claws although it may scar slightly."

Kyrianna nodded. "Thank you," she said as she moved to her bedroll. She watched as Jerietlan checked Nirev's injuries. He seemed a bit more concerned about the cuts across the dwarf's face, but Nirev only laughed at him.

"Scars are nothing more than trophies earned against a worthy opponent. I wear these with honor."

"Then you do honor to Mulog as well," Jerietlan said. "As I told Kyrianna, I will not be bandaging these this night, but will want to check them again in the morning."

"Fine." Nirev stalked away from the cleric.

Kyrianna grinned as Myrith shook her head at the dwarf's behavior.

"Watches tonight," Myrith said. "Myself, Laraf, Jerietlan and Kyrianna."

"Ye trust the thief to take a watch and do not assign me to one," Nirev said picking up his axe.

"None of us were as seriously injured as you were. I am giving you some extra rest before we go into battle tomorrow."

"Bah, I am not a weakling elf that I need extra rest before a battle, yet ye let this one take a watch." He pointed at Kyrianna. "She too was injured by the troll's claws. Do ye think she be a better fighter to defend this group than I be?"

"As you are insisting on taking a watch, you can take the first watch. You will wake me in two hours."

"Lady Myrith," Vantalle said as he appeared near the altar. "You are forgetting what I told you the other day. This is consecrated ground; there is no need to post watches, you will be safe here. If you are concerned, know I will be watching over you as will the chapel's guardian." He glanced up at the suit of armor standing in the loft.

Myrith bowed her head. "My apologies, I did forget what you had told us and as this is your place, I will defer to your guardianship." She looked at the dwarf and grinned. "Do you wish to complain about those now standing the watch?"

Nirev only grumbled to himself and dropped his axe onto his bedroll.

"He said something about first trusting elves and now specters," Laraf whispered to Kyrianna. "Apparently he doesn't think either is a good idea."

"What does he have against elves?" Kyrianna glanced at the dwarf who was now snoring.

"Various traditions and legends hold that dwarves and elves

don't get along very well. While not true racial enemies, they seem to snip and argue with each other when they are together. Don't worry I'm sure it's nothing personal." Laraf laid a hand on her shoulder and gave it a soft squeeze. "Get some rest," he said as he moved away.

Kyrianna glanced around at the others. Tristan was sitting watching Laraf as he walked away. The nobleman shifted his eyes toward her for a moment then turned away and opened his bedroll. Falden was sleeping to her right, also snoring, but in a softer tone than the dwarf. Hendandra looked at her then glanced at Laraf and Tristan and grinned before she curled up under her own blankets. Myrith had laid her own bedding out near the door and was currently cleaning and sharpening her blade. Jerietlan was kneeling near the altar, apparently in quiet meditation. She curled up under her own blankets and closed her eyes. Trying to focus on the remembered scents and sounds of Kilenter Forest, she drifted off into sleep.

~ * ~

"Something's coming this way," Vantalle said as a bell began ringing in the temple. Kyrianna sat up and looked around; Myrith was standing with her sword at the ready. Hendandra had sat up and had her rapier in her hand, as did Laraf.

"What do ye see?" Nirev asked looking toward Jerietlan who was backing away one of the windows.

"I think they're skeletons, but they're shrouded in flames." He paused. "The skeletons from the guest quarters! They're calling forth balls of flame."

Jerietlan dropped to the floor as flames struck the window he had been standing in front of. The glass shattered and one of the balls landed on the center pew igniting the wood. He stood and raised his hands over his head as a shower of water fell on the burning bench extinguishing the flames.

"All four of them are on this side of the chapel," Jerietlan called as Myrith and Kyrianna ran out the main doors.

Behind them, they heard glass shattering again followed by the crack of steel on bone. "Guess he didn't want to risk us taking them all out ourselves," Myrith said.

Nirev was swinging at one of the skeletons with his axe as two of the others continued advancing toward the door.

"Take this." Myrith held her sword out to Kyrianna. "I'll use my other one." She touched the pin on her surcoat and shifted her hands as it grew into the bastard sword.

Kyrianna shifted her grip on the enchanted sword and followed Myrith as she intercepted one of the skeletons. She took the next one then frowned as a sudden burst of light appeared near the two skeletons facing Nirev.

"What manner of summoning might this be?" the dwarf yelled.

"It is some sort of devil," Jerietlan said as he climbed through the broken window to join the dwarf.

Kyrianna grinned as the sword she was wielding managed to take the head off the skeleton she was facing. She dropped the blade and grabbed her bow from the quiver, quickly stringing it and readying an arrow. The arrow struck the devil in the neck and it turned to glare at her.

"I summoned it," Falden called. "It is fighting for us."

Kyrianna lowered her bow and turned toward the mage standing at the corner of the chapel. "You summoned a devil here? You brought in something from the darkness of the abyss?"

Falden stared at her and Kyrianna shook her head. She turned her attention back to see the skeleton Myrith had been fighting was lying in a heap on the ground and she was now fighting the devil.

The second of Nirev's skeletons fell to the ground and he spun around, burying his axe in the devil's back as Myrith's sword opened its throat and it fell.

Myrith turned and glared at Falden, but didn't say anything as she held her hand out to Kyrianna for her sword then stalked back into the chapel.

Nirev began gathering the bones of the skeletons and Kyrianna watched as he carried them in small groups over to the cliff and dropped them over the edge.

"Perhaps now they'll be having a harder time coming back to attack us again," the dwarf said when his task was finished.

Falden looked at Kyrianna and frowned. "What was wrong with my summoning the devil? It was fighting for us."

"Falden, you walk the narrow path between those who follow the darkness and those who follow the light, do you not?"

He nodded. "It is only in balance that true power can be achieved."

Kyrianna paused. Falden's words were intriguing. "The same

can be said about the even narrower path between order and chaos," she whispered.

"Correct. However, you still do not answer my question. When a battle is on us, should we not use every means at our disposal to win that battle?"

Kyrianna took a deep breath. "There are some who believe the ends always justify the means. However, for most who follow the rigid path of a holy warrior, particularly one who follows a deity dedicated to both order and the light; that is almost never true. Be careful which forces you call on as she may come to see you as allied with that side and deal with you as her personal code demands."

"You're saying Myrith may come to view me as following the path of darkness because I occasionally call on creatures of darkness. That is ridiculous. I call on those who are best suited to assist us when we need that assistance."

"Yes. The ends do not justify the means to most who walk her path." Kyrianna placed a hand on his shoulder and gave him a smile before she entered the chapel leaving him alone with his thoughts.

"Who is she, who knows nothing of the arcane to judge the actions I take in defense or support of her and this group?"

Kyrianna paused in her steps. "She is the one who leads this group. It is on her shoulders if we lose the battle or any of our number. She is the one who risked the displeasure of the one she serves by leaving her comrades while they fought a powerful opponent to rescue you when your own foolishness could have cost you your life in the maze." Kyrianna let the door slam shut as she entered the chapel.

"Everything okay?" Myrith looked at Kyrianna.

"Falden and I were just having a discussion regarding the choice of creature he summoned. It is nothing." Kyrianna unstrung her bow and placed it back in the quiver as she returned to her bedroll. "We still need to get some rest this night," she said.

Falden entered the chapel and refused to meet Myrith's gaze as he returned to his own blankets near Kyrianna. After a few minutes, he got up and walked over to Tristan. "Despite the interruption, I can now cast the spell to identify those items, if you wish. I will have the information for you in the morning."

Tristan handed the mage the rapier, dagger and ring and returned to his own rest as Falden walked back to his area. The mage placed the items in front of him on the blankets and began chanting in a quiet voice.

Kyrianna found herself drifting back to sleep as Falden continued his spell and hoped there would be no further interruptions that night.

Chapter Thirty-Nine

"The rapier you have been given has an enchantment of speed on it allowing the one wielding it to gain an extra attack in the time it normally take for one," Falden was saying when Kyrianna awoke the next morning. "The ring allows the one wearing it to activate it once a day and act as if under the spider climb spell and the dagger carries a spell that will cloak the one wielding it in shadows twice a day."

"Sounds like a weapon for an assassin," Myrith said.

"Not all who skulk in shadows are assassins," Laraf said. "However, if no one else is interested in the dagger I would like to have it." He glanced at Tristan who nodded.

"Can you tell me how the magic works?" Laraf turned the weapon over in his hand then looked back up at Falden.

"You just will it to activate. If you are already in a shadowed place the concealment will work even better. Keep in mind if you are in a brightly lit area being surrounded by shadows may actually bring you more attention than if you had not activated the dagger's special properties."

Tristan took the rapier and the ring then turned to Hendandra. "I believe these would be of greater benefit in your hands," he said handing the items to the rogue.

"Thank you," Hendandra said. She replaced the blade she was wearing with the one Tristan handed her then slipped the old one into her pack.

"If everyone is ready, we should get going," Myrith said. She waited at the door as the rest of the group exited. "Keep an eye on the mage," she whispered as Kyrianna waited with her. "I don't like the idea of him summoning in creatures like that devil. Those who follow darkness and the path of evil only serve when it suits their purposes, he could be putting all of us in danger."

"He is only trying to best help with what he knows. I doubt he will summon in something he cannot control. I know even less about magic than you probably do, but I believe I do know Falden well enough to trust his judgment of his skill with his art. Just as I trust your judgment regarding your skill with a blade."

"Still, it is disturbing to have something like that devil pop into the battle without warning."

"I agree and I will keep an eye on him as you have asked. But perhaps it would be better if you talked to him about your concerns."

"Hey, are you two coming or not?" Hendandra called. "If we're going to give up at this point, I can head out for Raspa, it's only a few days walk from Duvshire. Personally, I really don't feel the need to face two more undead in this place and would be happier back in my own bed." She stood in the door and looked up at the two of them, her hands on her hips. "However, I have never reneged on a job and I don't intend to this time either."

"Very well." Myrith sighed as she glanced down at the smaller woman then stepped past her to exit the chapel.

~ * ~

"Myrith," Kyrianna said as she paused and looked at the figure standing on the porch of the house. "His name is Boris," Kyrianna said. "According to the waitress at what used to be the Wailing Banshee, he's the only person to ever enter the estate and survive. Tristan supposedly tried to recruit him to help him with this and Boris laughed at him."

"Then, we should see why he's here." Myrith stepped in front of the group. "Well met," she called as they approached the house.

"Your group seems to have changed a bit, however, the majority are still alive, that is good," Boris said looking them over.

"Why are you here? And, is there something you need?"

"I came out here, as I am the only one who would. I carry a message for Tristan Duvall." Boris turned to the group, his black eyes looking for the young man.

"And, what is this message?" Tristan stepped forward.

"Your father has died."

Tristan paused for a second. "I thank you for delivering the message," he said in a flat voice.

Kyrianna placed a hand on Tristan's shoulder, but he didn't seem to notice.

"That be a holy symbol of Mulog, ye be wearing," Nirev said pointing to a grime-encrusted ring on Boris' right hand.

"So." Boris looked down at the dwarf.

"I too follow the Storm Lord and believe he be calling me to follow the path of a priest, however I do not have one of his symbols at this time. If ye be a follower of the Storm Lord, can ye obtain a symbol for me? I will collect it from ye when this business is over."

Boris removed the ring and handed it to Nirev. "I will pass this on to you. It belonged to my brother who was killed by a werewolf many years ago. He too had been called as a priest of Mulog. Hated to wear anything around his neck, so he had this specially made and blessed." He glanced at Kyrianna for a moment then turned his attention back to Nirev. "However, for one who follows the Storm Lord, I am surprised to not see a war hammer on your belt. I can return with one that is suited to one of your calling, if you desire."

"I thank ye for the offer," Nirev said.

"I will leave the hammer in the chapel. You will find it there tomorrow, providing you survive long enough to claim it." Boris laughed as he looked over the group again before heading toward the gates. He stopped and turned back to the group. "You would probably also be interested in knowing a decent amount of gold has been wagered on whether you will make it back or not. I will be letting the interested parties know about your current status." He turned and left.

"I wonder how he bet?" Laraf asked as he watched the large man walk away.

"Is there any doubt?" Kyrianna asked. "He bet against us."

~ * ~

The group made their way back to the library and began examining the walls and bookcases for some sign of the way down to the area below the basement.

"Here," Hendandra called as one of the bookcases moved back into the wall revealing a narrow opening with a ladder that descended into the darkness.

"Wait here," Myrith said as she climbed down the ladder.

"Anything?" Jerietlan called down after several moments had passed.

"Nothing yet. Found the bottom. Wait, I've got a couple of skeletons down here and might need some assistance." Myrith's voice faded to be replaced by the sound of ringing metal and splinting bone.

"Never mind," she called before anyone could head down the ladder. There was another pause. "Looks like this is the only passage and it appears clear for the moment. The rest of you get down here."

Kyrianna waited as the rest of the group climbed down the ladder then made her descent into the darkness. As she stepped off the ladder, a floating globe of light appeared over her head.

"This will work better and prevent you having to worry about a torch if we encounter any more problems," Falden said.

Kyrianna saw that Myrith, Jerietlan and Nirev also had light globes over their heads as well.

"I told ye to get rid of this light," Nirev said. "I can see perfectly fine without it and prefer to not have my position pinpointed for anyone down here who fancies himself an archer or mage."

Falden waved his hand and the light over the dwarf's head vanished.

"Myrith," Hendandra whispered. "There's a door here." She touched a small depression in the wall to their left. The soft click echoed in the corridor as the door opened.

"The back wall of the wine cellar." Hendandra said pushing the door closed.

"Anything change since the last time we were in there?" Myrith asked.

"No."

"Then let's move on."

The narrow corridor they were in continued with no other doors or openings for several yards before they finally found another door. Hendandra spent several minutes checking the door then reached out and opened it.

Hendandra stood at the door and studied the room. "Some coins and weapons in the pool," she said. "I'll see if I can retrieve them."

"We don't have time for this," Myrith said looking down at the smaller woman.

"We really haven't retrieved that much from this place and this will only take a few minutes," Hendandra said.

"Fine, be careful, the sides look slick," Myrith said.

"Could be a mold or algae growth," Kyrianna said. "Who has a rope? We can tie it to Hendandra so she can get back out without too much trouble."

Myrith pulled a rope from her pack. "This is the only one I have left," she said.

Kyrianna tied the rope around Hendandra's waist and Hendandra headed down the slight slope to the pool. Kyrianna braced herself in the doorway, just off the slippery part of the floor. "Nirev, would you anchor the rope behind me?"

"Of course," the dwarf said.

"Pull her up," Myrith said. "The water, or whatever it is, moved toward her."

Kyrianna jerked on the rope and frowned as it refused to move. "Hendandra!"

"That is not water, you idiots," Falden said. "It is a gel that absorbs almost anything except metal. Most larger estates have them as a way of disposing of waste and trash."

"Myrith," Kyrianna called. "Nirev and I could use a little extra help here." She pulled on the rope managing to gain a couple of inches.

"Hendandra, work on pulling yourself up as they try to pull the rope up," Laraf said.

"This stuff is starting to burn my legs. Get me out of here," Hendandra called.

"The rope is slipping," Kyrianna said as she twisted her hands and wrapped the rope around them. She took several steps back, pulling the rope. "Myrith, move to the front and pull. If we do this in a relay, we might be able to prevent the gel from pulling her any deeper. Nirev, you continue to anchor and keep the rope tight."

Myrith stepped in front of her and grabbed the rope, wrapping her hands as Kyrianna had.

"Nirev, you ready? I'm releasing what I'm holding so I can move in front of Myrith," Kyrianna said.

"I have the rope," the dwarf said.

"How are we doing?" Kyrianna looked at Laraf who was standing inside the room, perched on the edge where he could see Hendandra.

"Not too much further. The gel has encased her feet and ankles, but you've pulled her clear of the main body. Only need to get her free of what's holding her."

"Have your water spell ready, priest of Mykaylene, when they pull her out. You will need to get as much of that substance off her as quickly as you can," Falden said.

There was a sucking pop and the rope leapt in her hands as Kyrianna pulled it up. She grabbed Hendandra's right arm and dragged her out of the room as water began washing over her legs.

The initial spell finished, Jerietlan began chanting again and another stream of water flowed from his hands and over Hendandra's legs washing more of the gel from her clothing and leather armor.

"You will have to replace that armor eventually," Falden said. "I doubt the priest was able to get all of the gel off and it will continue to deteriorate." He passed his hand over her boots. "I don't believe there is any more risk to you from the gel."

"Thanks." Hendandra stood up and untied the rope still around her waist.

"I think that settles the matter of whether we have time for treasure hunting or not," Myrith said as she picked up the rope and put it back in her pack. "No more going out of our way for something we don't need."

"Fine." Hendandra turned and headed down the corridor.

Chapter Forty

"You really shouldn't be so hard on her," Kyrianna said as she and Myrith watched Hendandra walk away. "Her heart is in the right place."

"She is still a thief."

"Has she tried to take anything from any member of this group? Has she taken anything from you? I believe she was the one who retrieved that sword of yours. And, she did that despite the magical wards and protections we knew were in place around it, never mind the ones we might not have known about."

Myrith looked down, a frown on her face.

"I still do not trust her. I can't trust someone who will argue with me and disregard my instructions as she just did; particularly when it was over nothing more than a few trinkets." Myrith dropped her voice to a harsh whisper. "After what you told me, I am surprised to hear you defending her."

Kyrianna took a step back and blinked several times before speaking. "I have had to recently deal first hand with the type of blind prejudice that doesn't let someone be judged as an individual. Perhaps, I have learned something from that experience."

"Are you two going to join us or not," Laraf called from several feet down the corridor. "We have another room up here."

Kyrianna looked at Myrith and saw the disappointment on her companion's face as she turned to join the others.

Why is she disappointed in me? Kyrianna thought. *Does she think I should support her one hundred percent and never disagree with her at all? Accepting someone as a leader or friend does not require that kind of blind devotion. Even my father and brother will listen to differing opinions. And, they have better training and leadership skills than she has at this time.*

Kyrianna paused for a moment as the group studied the open room in front of them. Perhaps it was the lack of training causing Myrith's concern regarding how others saw her authority. Because she hadn't been properly trained to lead others, she saw every little disagreement as a challenge. She would have to talk to her again, but not until this was over.

Kyrianna touched Myrith's elbow and cocked her head to the side when she glanced at her. She nodded toward where the corridor turned to the left. "I saw something move down there," she whispered.

The group waited as Hendandra moved to the corner and checked the area before coming back.

"Another corridor," she said. "Though it is wider than this one and appears to have several doors on either side. I saw nothing in the corridor and all the doors looked to be closed."

Myrith drew her sword and held it ready as she took the lead. Kyrianna followed the paladin, her hands on her own swords.

"Holding cells," Myrith said as they entered the corridor. She paused and glanced through the small grated window in the wooden door.

"What's wrong?" Kyrianna asked when she saw Myrith's back stiffen.

"I'm sensing something dark and evil behind this door," she said.

"Do you see anything?" Jerietlan asked.

"No. The room is large and I cannot see the right side corner very well."

"Excuse me," Hendandra said. "But, if you want the door opened, I believe I would be best suited to take care of that for you." She pulled a set of lock picks out of her pack and moved to stand in front of the lock.

"I thought you broke your last set of lock picks," Myrith said.

"I did," Hendandra said. She didn't take her attention off the door as she slipped two of two the picks into it. "I borrowed these from Laraf."

"I normally carry two sets, I thought it best if we both had one," Laraf said. "However, if you break them, you will replace them.

"Rangerette," Myrith said placing a hand on Kyrianna's arrow quiver.

Kyrianna nodded and readied her bow as she took a couple of steps back from the door and positioned herself so she was in line with where the door would open, an arrow nocked and ready.

She frowned as Jerietlan moved away from the group and took several steps down the hallway.

"Got it," Hendandra said as a soft click echoed in the corridor.

The door swung open and Hendandra dove to the side as a pair of long arms reached out to claw out her. Kyrianna released the arrow she was holding and jumped back as the creature ignored the arrow in its chest and swung its long arms at her.

The creature was stooped and had long, stringy grey hair that was matted in places and missing in others. Drool dripped from its mouth as it darted forward and snapped at Hendandra.

"A ghoul!" Falden yelled as a bolt of arcane energy hit the creature. "Don't let it touch you. Priest, get back here and call on your goddess to destroy this undead thing."

"A little busy," Jerietlan called. "Whatever Hendandra did, also seems to have opened the other doors as well."

"Finally, a challenge," Nirev said as he darted forward to assist Jerietlan who was facing two more ghouls as well as a couple of skeletons.

Kyrianna dropped her bow and drew her swords while the ghoul was trying to claw at Hendandra again. She nodded as Laraf and Tristan both stepped beside her, their rapiers ready. "Myrith, go help Nirev and Jerietlan. I think we can handle this one," she said.

Myrith nodded as she pulled Hendandra away from the ghoul just before Kyrianna's short sword slid across the side of its neck.

The ghoul howled as it spun around, its claws blocking her second attack. Laraf and Tristan moved to either side of the undead creature, their rapiers dancing as they distracted it.

Kyrianna brought both of her swords up in a crisscross pattern across the ghoul's neck. The creature's head rolled back and she swung her long sword again, cutting deeper. A third slash across the ghoul's throat and the body fell to the floor as the head separated and bounced several feet away.

She turned her attention to the others as a burst of golden light surrounded the two skeletons and they collapsed to the floor as piles of dust. Jerietlan staggered as he lowered his holy symbol. Falden was releasing several more bolts of arcane energy as Nirev's axe bit deeply into the chest of one of the ghouls. The creature fell to their combined attack.

Kyrianna smiled as Myrith's sword cut through the neck of the ghoul she was facing in one stroke and the undead creature hit the ground with a wet thump.

Myrith turned and looked at a man in ragged clothes who was standing next to Jerietlan. She lifted her sword into a guard position and took several steps toward the man. "Your soul is covered in darkness. Who are you and why did you bring these foul creatures here?"

"I am a prisoner here."

Jerietlan stepped in front of her, his hands raised. "What are you doing? This man has done nothing to you or any of those here. On what, other than your sense of darkness around him, do you base your actions?"

Kyrianna darted forward and grabbed Myrith's shoulder. "Wait a moment."

Kyrianna released Myrith's shoulder and took a step back at the anger she saw in those eyes, normally a bright green, now almost black.

"Something had to bring those creatures here. He follows the darkness as much as those ghouls did. I will not turn my back on one who serves the dark powers!"

"I have information you will need," the man called. "But, only if you grant me safe passage." He glared defiantly at Myrith.

"Myrith." Kyrianna whispered as she gestured for the woman to step back. "Let's talk about this."

"If he has information regarding what else we might be facing or regarding Mikyl, we should let him go in exchange for that information," Laraf said.

"He follows the path of darkness, I cannot just turn a blind eye to that," Myrith said.

"However, it may serve the greater good in this case if you do," Tristan said. "The information he has may help us to be better prepared to face Mikyl and that may help to save one of your companions from falling. He will eventually answer for the crimes he has committed whether in this life or the next. Mercy is also a trait of a true warrior. While he has not formally asked for it, will you not demonstrate mercy?"

Myrith nodded slowly. "So be it. But, I still stand ready in case he tries something."

"I would expect nothing less," Kyrianna said.

The group moved back to where Jerietlan was standing with the man.

"Very well, we will grant you safe passage," Myrith said. "However, in this instance, safe passage only means that none of this group will harm you; unless you attack us. It does not guarantee you will be able to leave the house. There are other forces here and once you leave this area, you are on your own."

"I understand and I accept your terms." He held out his hand then grinned as Myrith ignored the gesture. "I serve on a privateer ship, which had been dealing for several months with two undead who control this place. We bring them supplies: food, various creatures, magic equipment and other goods they request."

"Who are these undead?" Myrith asked.

"One is known as Carver, an alchemist who also practices the art of necromancy." The man smiled. "Some of his experiments are very interesting. The other, I have never dealt with, however, I believe he is a lich. One who has not finished all of the rituals to complete his transformation." The man's gaze went to Tristan for a moment. "Rituals that require him to kill all members of the Duvall line."

Kyrianna gasped as she turned toward Tristan. Her heart fluttered for a moment and she swallowed hard as she tried to calm herself. She shook her head to clear it. There was something there, something dancing at the edge of her emotions and soul. She just couldn't figure out what. Something that had been there since the first moment she had seen him. Something that was growing stronger.

Tristan met her eyes for a moment then looked away. *Stop, overreacting,* she told herself. The young nobleman had saved her life when she fell to the claws and teeth of the worg. What she was feeling was nothing more than an overreaction to that. Once they were out of this area and she had time to center her emotions the feelings would go away.

"One other thing," the man said as he started to walk away. "Beware that which walks on four legs, but has more."

Kyrianna stood next to Myrith as the man walked past them, her long sword in her hand, but held in a low guard position. Myrith had given her word and while she trusted that, she still knew it was better to not take any chances.

Chapter Forty-One

"Myrith," Hendandra called from one of the open cells. "You need to step over here."

Kyrianna followed her to the open cell and turned so she could continue to watch the corridor in the direction the former prisoner had left. Like Myrith, she didn't trust the man.

"How did you come to be here?" Myrith asked a man huddled in the corner of the cell. He was dressed in tattered clothes and appeared to have been there for some time.

Kyrianna smiled politely as the man looked her. He had eyes that appeared to be colorless and long gray hair and a beard. He stood and faced Myrith, his body shaking as he placed a hand on the wall to steady himself. "I do not remember how I came to be trapped here." He looked at Falden who was stepping into the cell next to Myrith.

"Do not come into this room, my brother," he said holding up his other hand. "There are spells in place that will drain your power."

Myrith gestured to the door. "Then you should leave this place also," she said.

The older man nodded as she guided him out of the cell. "Thank you for finding me. I am Zanif and I am in your debt. When I have recovered my strength and powers, I will remember you. For now, I am afraid I have nothing I can offer you."

"Can you remember why you were being held here?" Myrith asked.

"Ah, that is an interesting question, Warrior of Mykaylene." Zanif looked around at the group.

Tristan stepped forward. "You have given us your name and we have not returned the courtesy. I am Tristan Duvall my companions are Myrith, Kyrianna, Jerietlan, Hendandra, Laraf, Nirev and Falden." He motioned to each of them as he introduced them.

"Duvall." Zanif paused for a moment as he studied the young man. "Tristan Duvall. You are part of the reason I am here," he said.

Kyrianna felt her grip on her sword tighten as she moved closer to Tristan.

Zanif shook his head slightly. "If only I could remember. I came here because Ferdinand wanted me to do something. Something involving the last of the Duvall line and another person, I just can't remember." Zanif shook his head.

"Who is Ferdinand?" Myrith asked.

"Ferdinand Vernas. He is a cleric of Mykaylene who lives in the Dragon Spine Mountains. Because of some bad judgment in his early years as a cleric, he has been outcast from Irrmar. He also must remain apart from others as he has been given the responsibility of guarding the Hammer of Forging."

"The Hammer of Forging," Nirev said as he pushed past Kyrianna to look up at the mage. "It truly exists?"

"It does. And a dangerous artifact it has become. There are few who could safely possess it. It is slowly destroying Ferdinand, but there are none whom he trusts to see it destroyed."

"Perhaps we could help," Jerietlan said.

Zanif laughed then shook his head. "At this time, the Hammer would destroy each of you." He paused and looked at Myrith. "However, perhaps in time you might be able to carry it to the only place where it can be destroyed."

"Before you accept any new commissions, we have a job to finish here," Kyrianna said as she placed a hand on Myrith's arm.

"Yes, we do," Myrith said. "You are welcome to stay with us or depart."

Zanif smiled and shook his head. "I believe it would be safer if I were to stay with you for now. As I warned Falden, there were magics in that cell that drained my powers. It will be a while before I am able to call on my magic to serve me."

"If we have more work to do here, we should get on with it," Nirev said. "Enough of this standing around when we have an enemy left to face."

"Do not be in a hurry to rush into this fight," Zanif said. "You go to face a lich who has gained access to various powers of chaos as well as another whose creations are foul crosses of alchemy and necromancy."

Silence followed Zanif's words for several seconds before Myrith spoke. "Let's get going."

At the end of the corridor a set of large iron-bound double

doors faced the group. A second steel door was ajar in the left wall. Myrith used her sword to push the door open to reveal a narrow hallway leading into darkness. "Which way?"

"I don't like that this door was left open, stinks of a trap," Nirev said.

"There are also several traps on this door," Hendandra said. "At least two of them are beyond my ability to disarm. Kyri do you want to take a look?"

Kyrianna shook her head. "My skills in that area were not as good as you have demonstrated yours to be and I have let mine grow rusty. What about you, Laraf?"

Laraf moved to the door and examined the areas Hendandra pointed out to him. "Beyond my skills as well," he said.

"I guess that means we go this way," Myrith said stepping into the hall. The light Falden had cast earlier flickered for a moment before lighting the area.

Just inside the door was a table with a small bundle of clothes and a leather belt dropped on it. "Ah, my robes," Zanif said as he reached for the bundle. He shook out the dark red material then slipped the robes on, smoothing them with his hands. "That's better," he muttered as he picked up the belt and put it on. He reached into one of his pockets and removed a red metal ring and handed it to Falden. "This will increase the amount of arcane energy you can call on each day. As I cannot use any of my power at this time, I believe it would be best if you wore it."

Falden took the ring and slipped it on his right hand. "My thanks," he said.

"Now, this is interesting," Myrith said.

Kyrianna moved down the hall to where Myrith was standing in front of a large mirror that covered the end of the corridor. "What was that?" She raised her sword as a bright light flashed behind the mirror and a shadow moved.

"Something's on the other side," Myrith said as she swung her sword against the glass.

"Let me in there, ye blasted elf," Nirev said as he shouldered his way past Kyrianna. "Those swords of yours won't be near as effective as me axe."

Kyrianna bowed her head as she stepped back away from the dwarf. As she watched Myrith and Nirev smash through the thick layers of glass, Kyrianna sheathed her sword and readied her bow.

The room or whatever was the other side had grown dark again and there was no way to know if something was waiting for them.

The last layer of glass smashed, the hall opened into what looked to be a laboratory of some sort. "Looks like this might be where the necromancer does his work," Myrith said as she stepped through the opening.

Kyrianna followed Myrith and Nirev as they stepped through the broken window and found herself staring at the table in the middle of the room and the creature that lay on it. "Chaos," she said dropping her bow and drawing both of her swords. "What kind of abomination is this?"

The creature on the table appeared to have been constructed from various other creatures, most notably a worg and a tiger. It had the basic body of a tiger, but with the head of a worg and two extra legs attached to its side as well as several tentacles coming from its back.

Kyrianna swung her sword down where the worg head was attached to the body. As her blade connected with the neck of the creature, a vial flew from somewhere to her right to strike the body of the creature. She jumped as both heads growled and snapped at her and the abomination stood up ready to attack.

"Someone just left through another door over here," Laraf called.

"Make sure they don't come back," Myrith called. "We have another problem to deal with at the moment." Her sword glanced off the creature's side as she twisted to avoid the grasping tentacles. "What is this thing?"

"An abomination," Kyrianna said as she blocked an attack from the tiger head.

"Damned thing's got bone plates providing it with additional protection under that hide," Nirev said as his axe hit the creature.

A loud metallic boom echoed through the room. "What was that?" Myrith yelled.

"The door we came through slammed shut," Laraf called.

"With Hendandra and Falden on the other side," Jerietlan said.

"There was a second door in here as well that shut and locked," Tristan said.

"Get one of those doors open," Kyrianna yelled as she danced back trying to avoid the claws and teeth of the creature. She brought both of her blades in under the tiger head and stabbed upward, hoping the bone armor wasn't protecting the normally soft area under the jaw. The creature jerked his head back tearing her swords from her hands as the worg head darted in and grabbed her arm. She found herself being thrown against the wall as the worg's teeth tore her arm open.

"Looks like it be up to the two of us to take care of this creature, Lady Knight," Nirev said as his axe cut through one of the creature's legs.

"Stay down," Myrith said as her sword came down behind the worg head.

Kyrianna nodded then frowned at the dull clang that sounded as the sword hit one of the bone plates. Unfortunately, she had dropped her bow on the other side of the table and both of her swords were now trapped in the tiger head. The one good thing she saw; the tiger head seemed to be dead as it drooped. She whispered the words of a prayer for healing and placed her hand over the gashes in her arm. Warmth flowed from her hand and she watched as the blood slowed. Her meager abilities were not enough to stop the bleeding, or to start the ripped flesh healing.

The worg head roared and the creature fell to the side. Kyrianna slid back against the wall as Myrith stepped in front of her and her sword thrust into the creature's mouth. She jerked the sword back as the worg's teeth grazed her hand and the head dropped. She sheathed her sword then pulled Kyrianna's swords from where they were still embedded in the tiger head. "I believe I told you once before that you need to hang onto to these better," she said.

Kyrianna took the swords as she stood up and sheathed them slowly, her right arm shaking as she moved it.

"Jerietlan!" Myrith motioned for the cleric to check Kyrianna's arm.

Kyrianna waited as Jerietlan cast his healing spells then nodded as she watched the skin close around the gashes. The injuries she had suffered from the claws of the water troll were still tender and now these added to the damage. "Thank you," she said as she flexed her fingers.

She moved to pick up her bow and winched at the tightness in her arm as she drew the bowstring and held it for a moment before returning it to her shoulder.

"Give it a few days," Jerietlan said. "Just be careful during that time. I really don't want to have to keep healing you on a routine basis."

"Kyri, can you give me a hand with this," Laraf called from the first door. "I'm having problems with the lock."

"The mechanism on this one is jammed," Tristan said.

"If the lock be jammed, then you be needing a strong arm to open it," Nirev said. The dwarf raised his axe and brought it down against the door. The sound of metal striking metal echoed in the room though door didn't seem affected by the impact.

"That room was designed to keep things in," a voice called from the other side of the door followed by laughter.

"Uh, guys," Hendandra's voice called from the other side of the door. "Those double doors we didn't try to open are opening now."

Kyrianna knelt next to Laraf as they both tried to manipulate the complicated lock. There was a click and the door started to open then slammed shut again. "A little luck here, Lord Ibacia," Kyrianna whispered.

One of the picks snapped and Laraf slammed his fist into the door. "Take it easy," Kyrianna said. "Hendandra, you and Falden need to find a place to hide until we can get this door open or whatever is on the other side of the double doors leaves."

"Got it."

Kyrianna put her ear against the door and heard movement on the other side as well as Falden chanting. "Come on let's try again," she said. She shook her head as the ringing of metal hitting metal continued from the other door.

"Falden!" Laraf yelled as a cry of pain came from the other side of the door. The mage's voice began chanting again. Laraf leaned against the door and shook his head. "They're moving out of the area," he said. "I didn't hear anything that sounded like a body hitting the floor, so I hope that means everyone is still in one piece."

"Let's try this door again," Kyrianna said. She reached into her pack, removed a rolled cloth and opened it. Inside was a set of lock picks.

"Guys, there's a lever on the other side of the double doors," Hendandra's voice says through the door. "I'm going to try that and see if it opens the doors."

"Let the others know," Kyrianna said with a glance at Laraf as she put her picks away and drew her sword.

Laraf hurried to the other door and she could hear him relaying the information. She glanced back to see Tristan and Laraf coming back down the hallway, their rapiers held ready. There was a click and the door swung free of the latch as Kyrianna pushed it open and darted into the hallway. She paused at the second door and saw it had been warped by the dwarf's attack on it and wasn't opening. However, the sound of running told her Myrith and the others had already come through the same door she had.

"Where's Falden?" Myrith asked.

Kyrianna glanced at the ground and saw several drops of blood. She pointed to the blood and began following it. They found Falden slumped against the far wall where another corridor turned to the right. A door at the end of the corridor appeared to have been bashed open and a dragon-like creature lay on the floor. Two other men were fighting next to the dead creature. One, wielding a large hammer, was large with stringy black hair and dirty robes. The other was gaunt and skeletal in appearance and holding two small knives.

Nirev lifted his axe and charged into the fray swinging at the man with the knives. The creature turned and Kyrianna gasped at the sunken face and glowing red eyes of the undead creature. The man wielding the hammer and Nirev swung their weapons together. There was a cracking sound as the man with the knives hit the floor.

"Zanif, there you are. I was sure something had happened to you," the large man said stepping forward.

"Ferdinand, you shouldn't have left your home. It is too risky, particularly when you are carrying that thing."

Nirev looked up at the large man and reached out to touch the hammer he was holding. Ferdinand looked down and laughed. "Not even on your best and on my worst." He stepped over and placed a hand on Zanif's shoulder then took a crystal rod out of his pocket and broke it. The two of them vanished in a burst of golden light.

"Falden, are you okay?" Hendandra asked as Jerietlan helped the mage up.

"He found me despite the invisibility spell. I was able to keep the spell on me and move away but he was able to follow me. I was hiding in this corridor, when something began hitting the door. The big guy, who just vanished, I think was in there fighting that thing." He pointed to the dragon-like creature on the ground. "He shoved its head through the door then stepped through and smashed it with that hammer of his." Falden paused for several seconds as he caught his breath. "The one who attacked me said something about destroying his creation and turned to attack the guy with the hammer. That was just before you showed up."

"I wonder what that thing was guarding?" Hendandra said as she headed for the door. The rest of the group followed her as Kyrianna stopped to check the body of the undead creature. She removed the leather armor he was wearing as well as a plain silver ring and the two knives he had been using.

"I am sensing magic on all those items, Kyrianna," Falden said as she picked them up and followed the others into the other room.

In the room, a body had been nailed to the far wall. "Rhinehart?" Kyrianna asked.

Tristan only nodded.

Myrith and Jerietlan carefully removed the body and laid it out on the floor as the cleric called on Mykaylene to give Rhinehart's spirit rest. A ghostly figure appeared next to the body and looked around at the group. His eyes stopped on Tristan and seemed to be measuring the young man before turning back to Myrith. The specter reached out and a sword appeared in his hand. He held it out to Myrith and nodded.

"It is called Mykaylene's Blade and it will bond with one who is faithful to the Battle Maiden. I present it to you as I have no heir to carry it," the figure said. "May Mykaylene guide your hand, my sister." The ghost faded.

"We need rest," Myrith said holding the sword. "We'll take the body to the chapel and return tomorrow to find Mikyl."

There were several nods of agreement as Myrith belted on the sword then picked up the body of Rhinehart. Tristan walked behind Myrith, his head bowed slightly, not saying anything until they reached the chapel.

Chapter Forty-Two

"Lady Lake," Tristan said as Myrith laid the body of Rhinehart next to his wife. "I would suggest you ask Falden to check the armor for magical properties. If it is stronger than what you are currently wearing, I will allow you to claim it."

The young man also removed the rings Rhinehart and Nyssa were wearing and held them out to Kyrianna. "Not only were these their wedding rings, they are enchanted and will allow a person to share an injury with another to help protect them. I believe you and your friends will be able to put them to good use."

"Are you sure?" Kyrianna looked at the gold rings in her hand then back up at Tristan. "These are your grandparents' wedding rings. Shouldn't you keep them?"

Tristan only shook his head and turned away. "He said he had no heir," she heard him whisper.

Kyrianna stared at the young man but didn't say anything. This was something he would have to work out for himself. "Falden," she called to the mage. "If you will be casting identification magics can you also check the items I found?"

The mage nodded and pointed to where Rhinehart's armor lay on the floor.

Kyrianna placed the leather armor on the floor along with the silver ring. The knives she wasn't planning on using, only selling and therefore didn't need to have Falden expending his power on them. "One other thing," she said holding out one of the rings Tristan had given her. "You seem to get into more trouble than the rest of us; perhaps you should wear one of these." She explained what Tristan had said about the rings being able to be used to shield one of those wearing them.

"Thank you," Falden said placing the ring on his left hand.

"I'll take the other one," Myrith said. "No offense, Rangerette, however I believe I am stronger than you and I can heal myself. Besides, the welfare of this group is my responsibility."

Kyrianna nodded and handed the ring to Myrith. "That it is."

"If you will leave me alone for a while, so I can study these items," Falden said.

"Of course," Myrith said. She placed a hand on Kyrianna's arm and guided her away from Falden as he sat on the floor and began casting his spell.

"Kyri," Myrith whispered. "I've been hearing a whispering in my head since Rhinehart gave me this blade."

She looked up at Myrith and frowned. "Perhaps you should ask Tristan what he knows of his grandfather's sword."

"Normally, I would agree, but he doesn't seem to want to talk about any of this." She glanced at the young man who was seated on one of the front benches, his head bowed.

"Myrith, he has been blaming Mykaylene for what happened here thirty years ago. I told you I was worried about how his grandfather's spirit would react to his abandonment of the goddess his family has served for generations. When he appeared, Rhinehart seemed to be studying Tristan for several minutes before presenting you with his sword. Tristan told us before that at least one person in every generation has served Mykaylene. Instead of just giving the sword to you because you were a warrior of his god, Rhinehart gave you the sword because, as he put it, he had no heir to carry it. He basically disowned Tristan and it was probably because of Tristan's lack of faith in Mykaylene." Kyrianna paused and closed her eyes. "I know what that feels like," she whispered as she opened her eyes.

Myrith glanced again at the young man. "This could cause a serious problem tomorrow. If he is feeling completely abandoned he will make an easier target for Mikyl."

Kyrianna nodded. "Boris told us, Tristan's father had died. He is the last of the Duvall line. To prevent this evil from fully entering this world he must be protected at all costs."

"But, what if he is not willing to protect himself?"

Kyrianna felt her eyes go wide as she looked at Myrith then at Tristan. "In that case we have a problem."

"Maybe you should talk to him. As you just said, you have an idea of how he feels."

Kyrianna nodded then reached out and placed a hand on the hilt of the paladin's sword. "I have heard rumors of intelligent weapons that are able to communicate with those who carry them and possess powers of their own. If you don't want to talk to Tristan regarding this, perhaps you should try talking to the blade."

"And how would I try to talk to a blade?"

"You said you were hearing whispering in your head. Listening to the whispers and answering them in your mind would be the best guess I can give you. Think of it as meditation." Kyrianna released the hilt of the sword and smiled. "You talk to Mykaylene's Blade and I'll talk to Tristan."

Myrith nodded and turned away. Kyrianna watched her climb the stairs to the guardian's loft. It was probably the most private area in the chapel and would serve as a good place for the woman to try speaking to the sword. She only wished, she had thought of it as the place to speak with Tristan.

Kyrianna dropped her gear on one of the benches, unbuckling her swords and leaving them with rest of her equipment then moved to the bench where Tristan was sitting. Most the rest of the group was checking equipment and didn't seem to be interested in her or the young nobleman.

"Are you okay?" she asked as she sat down.

Tristan didn't answer or look at her and she took a deep breath as she slid her hand over his. "Don't do this to yourself. Believe me this isn't going to help."

Tristan turned his head to look at her. "What do you know about it," he whispered.

"I know you've been blaming Mykaylene for letting what happened here thirty years ago happen. I can see because of that you have renounced your faith in the goddess your family has followed for generations. I know what I heard Rhinehart tell Myrith before giving her the sword about not having an heir and how you might have felt he was disowning you as a result of those words and your loss of faith." She paused as she squeezed his hand slightly. "I know because I know how I felt when I heard my father say to me, 'I have no daughter.'"

Tristan looked up and placed his hand on Kyrianna's cheek. "Why would he say that? What could you have done to deserve being disowned?" His eyes seemed to be searching her face.

Kyrianna didn't pull away from his touch but dropped her eyes away from his gaze. Like her father, his eyes seemed to be able to see past the façades people wore and find a way into their hearts.

"I was part of the Thieves' Guild in Nydith and was caught burglarizing the home of one the Council members. I would have been facing a death sentence if I had been required to stand before the Council for the crime. Instead my father managed to convince

290

the magistrate to release me to him and he issued the order of banishment not only from his house but from Nydith as well."

Kyrianna blinked several times to clear her eyes and she felt Tristan wipe at the tears with his hand. "That was the most he would do to protect me."

"That was protecting you?" Tristan sat up straighter and stared at her.

"Yes, it was. The noble whose house I was stealing some documents from was also my mentor in the guild. He set me up hoping my father would use his influence to protect me so the guild would have something they could use to blackmail him with. My brother is one of the District Commanders for the City Guard and it was his patrol that caught me—after they had been tipped off about the burglary. I believe the guild was hoping that having my brother be the one to catch me, my father would be able to make sure the magistrate or the council never heard of the incident. Unfortunately, they didn't really know anything about my father or my brother's ethics."

"Why would they do that? Was your father on the Council?"

Kyrianna shook her head. "No, he was retired as the Commander of the City Troops and Guard, that's where he gained his title. They did it because, even though he was retired, he was helping with an investigation of the guild and certain activities they were involved in. If he had tried to hide the fact I had been arrested they would have been able to blackmail him by threatening to report the incident and his behavior to the council unless he found a way to block the investigation. By issuing the order of banishment, with the approval of the magistrate and council, they really had nothing to use."

Tristan reached out and took both of her hands in his and held them. "He explained all this to you before you left?"

"No, but I've had time to think about it. Something you haven't really had these past few days." She pulled her hands away from his. "You came here to reclaim your heritage as your father wanted you to do, you do dishonor to his memory with your current attitude. While I understand part of what you may be feeling because of your grandfather's words, I will not pretend to understand your feelings toward Mykaylene—that is a matter between you and Her. However, think on what the woman with the wolf said the other day, 'When other gods are involved, even patrons are sometimes unable to protect those they cherish.'

"I have reason to believe one of the dark deities from my world has taken an interest in me and even Dwycia has seen fit to issue a warning that may relate to that interest. From some of the things we have learned here, I also believe it was Thynitic who caused Mikyl to choose the path he did. She is a primordial goddess, the first born from the chaos that gave birth to the worlds. That makes her very powerful. Mykaylene may not have been able to intervene if Thynitic's hand was indeed behind the events of thirty years ago."

Kyrianna stood up and smiled as she looked down at Tristan. "You need time to sort through the things that have happened today and you need to get some rest before tomorrow. Let me know if you need anything." She squeezed his shoulder as he nodded. "My heart feels your loss," she whispered before turning away.

"Thank you," she heard Tristan whisper behind her.

"Kyrianna," Falden called. "I have the information on these items for you and Myrith."

"And?" she prompted.

"The ring will allow you to modify your appearance slightly so you look like someone other than who you are, the leather has protection magics woven into it as does the plate-mail. In both cases the protection they offer is stronger than what you and Myrith are currently wearing."

"Thank you. You should get some rest," she said gathering up the items. She slipped the ring on her right hand then headed for the back of the chapel. She left the leather armor with her other equipment and carried the plate-mail up the stairs.

"The sword wants me to give it to Tristan," Myrith said when Kyrianna stepped out onto the balcony. "Either that, or it insists I vow to use it exclusively. I won't make that vow."

"Interesting. It seems it has a strong personality," Kyrianna said sitting down. "Falden said the armor has protection magics woven into it and it will be better than that which you are currently wearing."

"Thank you, but if the sword wants to go to Tristan, then perhaps his grandfather's armor should as well." Myrith's hand caressed the polished steel of the armor.

"He has already offered it to you. While he may accept the sword, he is an aristocrat, not a knight. I doubt he will ask for the armor." She stood up and looked down at the young nobleman still sitting on the bench where she had left him. "Myrith," she said as she turned back to the paladin. "Did you tell the sword how Tristan was acting toward Mykaylene?"

Myrith looked up and nodded. "He seems to believe he can help guide Tristan back to his family's patron."

"Then perhaps giving the sword to Tristan is a good idea," she said. "I would wait till morning though. Give him time to come to grips with the events of today before dropping that on him."

"I agree." Myrith stood up and looked out the large stained glass windows. "We all need to get some rest before tomorrow, but it is still early in the day. There is one other thing we should do before retiring for the evening." She moved to the railing and looked down at the bodies they had brought into the chapel.

"We should also collect Alesandra's body as well as those of the Terissian family," Kyrianna said.

Myrith nodded.

~ * ~

"May Mykaylene protect and guide their spirits," Myrith said as Tristan closed the door to the crypt. They had brought all of the bodies they had found there: Alesandra, Nyssa, Melissa, Larissa and Rhinehart now rested with their ancestors. The bodies of the Terissians as well as the cleric had also been placed in the crypt.

"I still think we should have waited till this was over before removing Vantalle's body from the chapel," Hendandra said. "He was part of the reason the chapel was considered a safe area for us."

"He has done his duty," Myrith said. "There is still the guardian and I believe tomorrow will see an end to this."

"Ye will be fine through the night," Nirev said. "I be taking the watch and will be protecting ye."

"We will all be taking part of the watch," Myrith said.

Kyrianna placed a hand on Tristan's shoulder. "Will you be okay?"

He turned to look at her and smiled. "I think so. Perhaps by the time this is over, I will be able to redeem myself in the eyes of my grandfather."

"Tristan, the only person you should be concerned about redeeming yourself to is yourself," she said they followed the others out of the cemetery and back to the chapel.

He paused and looked down at her. "And, do you no longer care what your father thinks of you?"

Kyrianna swallowed and closed her eyes for a moment. "It doesn't matter if I care or not as I will no longer have the opportunity to redeem myself to him," she finally said. "I only have to answer to myself now." She started to walk away.

"Then perhaps you would consider staying here instead of returning to a land where there is apparently nothing for you," he whispered.

Kyrianna hesitated but didn't respond to the nobleman's comment. She wasn't even sure he had even meant for her to hear it.

Chapter Forty-Three

"This be getting damned annoying," Nirev called.

Kyrianna sat up and saw the dwarf standing in the doorway of the chapel. Outside she could see the faint glow of fire.

"The skeletons?" Myrith called as she grabbed her sword.

"That it be, Lady Knight."

Myrith reached for her armor then paused as Kyrianna slapped the breastplate with her sword. "What?"

"You don't have time to put that on and you know it," Kyrianna said.

"Tristan," Myrith called as she tossed the sword Rhinehart had given her to the nobleman. "Use this; it will be more effective than your rapier."

Tristan caught the sword and drew it from the sheath. Kyrianna nodded as she saw his eyes widen. She only prayed the sword would accept him, without making the kind of demands it had been making of Myrith. *Of course*, she thought. *Those demands could have been designed to make sure Myrith would pass the sword to Tristan.*

"We'll see where it leads," Myrith said.

"When we were returning from the cemetery, he said he was hoping completing this would help to redeem him in his grandfather's eyes."

"But, to do that he must first redeem himself in his own eyes. Not an easy thing to do is it?"

"No, it's not," Kyrianna whispered as Myrith ran out the door of the chapel, her sword held ready.

She glanced back at Tristan who was still holding the sword, but not moving toward the door. She could hear the others shouting to each other as well as the sounds of bones breaking and the dwarf singing in his native language. A quick look around showed only she and Tristan were in the chapel. "We should probably go see if they need any help," she said. "Though from the sounds of it, I doubt it."

They walked out of the chapel together and Myrith turned to face them. "Late again, Rangerette," she said gesturing to the smoldering piles of bones."

"There has to be a way to put these spirits to rest," Jerietlan said.

"We dare not try to carry them to the cemetery as they will probably reanimate yet again," Nirev said.

"We tried burying them at the remains of the servant's quarters and Jerietlan blessed them and spoke the rituals," Laraf said. "The next time we dealt with them, you dumped the bones over the cliff. What else can we do? I honestly doubt smashing the bones into dust will prove any more effective."

"This is consecrated ground, we can try burying them here," Myrith said. She looked at Tristan who nodded.

"I have another idea," Kyrianna said drawing her dagger. "I suggest Tristan prick a finger or cut himself in some way and then sprinkle blood over the remains when we bury them."

"What?" Hendandra and Laraf said together.

"Where did this idea come from?" Myrith stared at her.

"The spirits animating these skeletons were not members of the Duvall family."

"So?"

"They were murdered by a member of the Duvall family; perhaps what is needed for them to find their rest is the spilling of Duvall blood."

"The Terissians were not members of the family either," Hendandra said.

"And both Lord and Lady Terissian were ready to kill Tristan simply for being a Duvall. However, we were able to speak to those spirits and convince them not to hold him accountable for the crimes of his uncle as we were going to seek out Mikyl ourselves. If we do not succeed in dealing with Mikyl, it is possible all of the spirits will once again be trapped here." Kyrianna turned to Tristan and handed him her dagger.

"I know your faith has wavered of late, however that blade was blessed by the avatar of the goddess I follow. She is generally counted among those deities associated with the path of light."

Tristan took the blade and looked at it for a second then nodded. "I have no problem with trying this idea," he said. "However, while I appreciate the offer," he handed the dagger back, "I will use my grandfather's blade for this task."

Kyrianna sheathed the dagger and smiled as she winked at Myrith.

They waited as Nirev and Laraf dug a single grave for the bones. Once they were done, Nirev began tossing the bones in as Jerietlan spoke the words of the burial ritual then sprinkled a flask of holy water over the remains. When he finished he turned to Tristan and nodded.

The nobleman gripped the sword with his left hand and slid it up the blade, leaving a trail of red on the gleaming metal. He then held his hand out over the grave letting the blood drip onto the bones. "Duvall blood has been spilled for you, in partial payment for the crimes that were committed. I give you my vow that I intend to see the one who did this pays also. May you find the peace you have been denied all this time," he said.

Jerietlan reached for Tristan's hand and the young man pulled away from the cleric. "No magical healing of this wound," he said. "Just bind it and let heal it naturally."

Jerietlan nodded and gestured to the door of the chapel. "My bandages and salves are in my pack," he said.

Tristan nodded and followed Jerietlan back into the building.

"Okay, if that's everything, some of us would still like to get some sleep before tomorrow," Hendandra said as she and Falden also headed for the door into the chapel.

Myrith glanced up at the dark sky. "How long till sunrise, do you estimate?"

Kyrianna took a deep breath as she also scanned the sky. "About five hours, I would estimate. I'll take the remainder of the watch. You and the others get some sleep."

"You sure?"

Kyrianna nodded as she gestured to the door. "By the way, have you ever had to put on full plate armor?"

"No. Why?" Myrith stopped and looked down at her.

Kyrianna grinned as she looked up at the taller woman. "You've been wearing a chain shirt all this time, something that is relatively easy to get in and out of. Wearing plate mail is more complicated and takes about ten minutes with proper assistance—longer if you try to do it yourself."

"Perhaps I would be better off with what I am currently wearing, if the plate is going to be that much hassle."

"That is for you to decide, however it offers better protection. Something else you should keep in mind though, Tristan specifically gave to you. Until he did that, he had not allowed anything to be taken from the bodies."

Myrith nodded. "I guess I'll find a way to deal with the armor."

"Get some more sleep," Kyrianna said as they entered the chapel. She paused and took a deep breath. "I'll wake you if something else happens."

As Myrith and the others returned to their beds, Kyrianna slipped on the armor she had picked up earlier. The leather shifted a couple of times as it molded itself to her body as if it had been sized for her. "Nice," she whispered as she glanced down at herself.

"Indeed," she heard another voice whisper.

She looked up to see Tristan watching her, his sword in his hand. "I'll stand the watch with you," he said.

"There is no need."

"Perhaps not. However, I wish to do so."

Kyrianna shrugged. "Suit yourself," she said. "I will not refuse a second set of eyes and ears." She turned away and went to check the doors.

"I do have one question," Tristan said when she finished her check of the sanctuary. "You have shown a disdain for magic yet you accept the ring and the armor knowing they have magical properties."

Kyrianna looked at the ring on her hand and nodded. "It is a puzzle isn't it? However, I grew up in a land where arcane magic is feared because of its chaotic nature. In traveling with Falden and knowing others carry items that have been enchanted, I have begun to reevaluate my position on magic. These are items for which I have a purpose. I will not carry something just because it is magic, for the sake of carrying magic. It must be something for which I have a use."

"Understandable," Tristan said.

She took a position where she could watch the doors and they passed the rest of the night in silence.

~ * ~

Kyrianna woke the others shortly after sunrise that morning.

"There," Nirev said as he helped Myrith with the plate armor. "Now, ye be looking like a knight of yer goddess."

"You need some type of tabard or surcoat to complete the knightly appearance," Kyrianna said.

"Appearance is not what makes a knight, instead it takes a desire to destroy evil and serve the deity to which one gave their oath," Myrith said.

Kyrianna grinned as Myrith grabbed her sword and left the building. "I guess breakfast is out of the question this morning," she said. "We should join her."

"Wonderful," Hendandra said as she buckled on her rapier. "No breakfast and we're going hunting for a lich. This is not going to be a good day." She headed for the door.

Kyrianna grinned at the smaller woman and waited as the rest of the group gathered their gear and left the chapel to return to the house.

They retraced the path they had followed yesterday through the area below the basement, passing through the corridor and rooms they had found the previous day without incident.

"Rangerette," Myrith paused and looked down at the creature Ferdinand had killed the previous day. "Any ideas what this thing was?"

Kyrianna reached out and touched the gleaming black scales and frowned. "It is draconic in nature, but it has been twisted into something else. What else was used to create this abomination I cannot tell." She walked around the creature, while the head was still that of a dragon, the body appeared to be bipedal and the scales were fused together into something resembling plate mail armor.

"Dragons are harbingers of great evil and are considered to be evil incarnate, why change one into something else?" Hendandra said. "Surely that would weaken it."

"Just like any other intelligent creature, dragons can follow the path of darkness or the path of the light," Kyrianna said.

"The path of light," Nirev said with a snort. "Yer thinking be off, elf. Dragons be evil, they only be seen during dark times."

Kyrianna glanced at Tristan then at Myrith. "If that is true in this land, then perhaps the death of this abomination is a sign the darkness covering this place will also die. Let's move on."

"I found the passage," Laraf said from where he stood next to the far wall. He pressed a spot on the wall and a panel slid to the side revealing a narrow hallway.

Kyrianna waited as the rest of the group entered the hallway then followed several feet behind. She nodded her head to the creature. The dragons of Rhysia were considered to be honorable

and noble creatures, even the ones who followed the path of darkness.

Chapter Forty-Four

"I don't like the looks of this," Hendandra said nodding toward the closed door in front of them. "I find no evidence of any traps on the door and it's not locked."

Kyrianna looked at the door and frowned. It was a standard, ironbound wooden door; however, mud appeared to have been forced between the sections of wood as well as around the door. "If there was a trap, it looks like it might have already been set off," she said.

"Does that mean there's a room filled with mud on the other side?" Myrith looked at them.

"Great," Hendandra said. "I'm positive there weren't any other doors between the room with that dragon thing and here."

"Hendandra said she found nothing on this side of the door. And, we have no way of knowing what's on the other side," Kyrianna said.

"Fine," Myrith said. "As we appear to have no other direction to go, I want each member of this group secured to each other before this door is opened." She pulled what was left of her rope out of her pack. "If mud or water floods out of that room, I want to make sure we don't lose anyone."

Kyrianna took the rope and tied it around Myrith's waist then passed it to the others as they found ways to tie the rope to themselves.

"What about you?" Myrith glanced at the ranger.

I need to be free to provide cover in case there are any other surprises behind that door." She raised her bow. "Besides, I'm pretty quick on my feet, I'll be fine."

Myrith shrugged and reached for the door.

A white billowing smoke poured out of the room as the door opened. "At least there's no mud," Myrith said.

"No heat," Kyrianna said as she waved the bow in an attempt to clear some of the smoke.

"Can we get rid of the rope since it would appear there was no mudslide?" Hendandra asked.

"Yes," Kyrianna said.

"The mud could have been packed in and around the door to trap the smoke," Falden said.

"Is it magical in nature?" Myrith asked.

"I am not detecting any magic within the smoke," Falden said.

"I'm sensing several areas of evil within the smoke," Myrith said. Her blade gleamed as she held it up.

"Show me," Kyrianna said as she moved next to Myrith.

Myrith held her sword out and pointed with it. "I can't determine the distance in this smoke."

Kyrianna didn't reply as she aimed the arrow along the path Myrith was indicating. The arrow flew straight and she smiled at the sound of it hitting something.

The smoke began to clear in the room and a line of creatures appeared near the far end. Their features decayed and their limbs twisted as they approached. One of the undead had an arrow stuck in its shoulder.

"Ghouls," Jerietlan said stepping forward, his holy symbol held before him. "In the name of Mykaylene, I command you to leave this place and return to your rests." His voice echoed as the shield-shaped medallion flashed. Three of the ghouls crumbled to dust, only to have three more move up from behind the front line.

Nirev pushed his way past Kyrianna and Myrith, charging into the ghouls, his hammer swinging in an arc around him as he starting singing. Myrith followed the dwarf, her blade held before her. Kyrianna dropped her bow, drew both of her blades and joined them. There was no room for any of the others to engage the creatures and Kyrianna found her right arm hampered by the wall to her side as she brought her blades up to block the slashing claws of the ghoul.

"Kyri, arrow, on your left," Hendandra's voice called.

She ducked to her right as an arrow flew past her head. The ghoul screamed as the arrow pierced its throat. Kyrianna jumped back from the creature's claws as it fell.

"By the power of the Battle Maiden, be gone," Jerietlan's voice called over the sounds of the battle. Several more of the ghouls turned to dust as a bright light flashed in the room.

"Fire!" Laraf yelled. "The support beams are burning."

Kyrianna's blades slashed across her opponent's throat in a

crisscross pattern and the creature fell to the ground. She paused to look back toward the door they had entered through. Smoke was pouring from the support pillars, though no flames seemed to be visible.

A loud crack resounded in the room and both of the beams buckled slightly. "They're going to collapse!" Kyrianna yelled.

"Nirev!" Tristan yelled.

Kyrianna turned to glance at the dwarf and saw he was frozen in place. Myrith had turned her attention to the creature that had attacked Nirev, leaving two of the ghouls. Arrows flew from Hendandra and Laraf at one of the two as several bolts of arcane energy struck the other. Behind them the support beams buckled again and the earthen ceiling collapsed sending dust and smoke throughout the room.

"Chaos take it, this set is burning now as well," Kyrianna said as smoke poured from the pillar next to her.

The last of the undead on the floor, Myrith sheathed her sword and grabbed the still frozen Nirev. "We need a way out of here," she said.

Hendandra darted past the paladin. "There's a door up here. Laraf give me a hand with the lock."

The two of them worked on the door as another section of the roof collapsed, the last set of pillars started smoking and the group moved forward. "Back off a little," Hendandra said as she slapped Kyrianna's leg.

"Sorry, but it's going to get a lot tighter in here real soon." Kyrianna shuffled back a bit and stopped as she bumped someone. A jolt of electricity seemed to jump to her arm and she turned slightly to see Tristan looking at her. His brown eyes were unreadable as they darted up to look over her shoulder.

"Where's your bow?" he asked.

Kyrianna reached for where the weapon normally hung over her shoulder then drew in a sharp breath as she started to push past him. "Chaos take it, I dropped it when I drew my swords."

Tristan put an arm around her. "Then it is lost. You're not going to be able to dig through that to find it."

"My uncle made that bow. He gave it to me on my last birthday."

"I'm sorry, Kyri."

She turned away from him and took a deep breath. The only

other weapon she had left of her uncle's making was the dagger that Frayrith had touched, and even that wasn't originally of his making. He had only worked it to change the symbol on it from the one belonging to the thieves' guild to Frayrith's. She had traded one of her swords to Hendandra along with the other green one for the matched set she now carried. The other she had added to the trade with Mulbanith for the armor and the extra arrows. While her uncle would have been the first to tell her the trades were good ones, he would also berate her for losing any weapon through carelessness. She shook her head slowly; she only hoped she would be able to return home someday and listen to his lecture regarding the loss of the bow.

"Got it," Hendandra said.

"Move," Myrith said as she carried Nirev through the door.

Tristan managed to shut the door behind them as the last section of roof collapsed in the other room.

"This was a great idea," Hendandra said.

The room was small and they were almost standing on each other's feet as they shifted around.

"Would you rather be crushed under the dirt and debris out there?" Myrith glared at Hendandra.

Hendandra didn't say anything as she ignored Myrith and began studying the next door. "Leikor's cursed luck," Hendandra said after a few seconds.

"What is it?" Myrith asked.

"The door is bolted from the other side. There is no way we can open it from this side." Hendandra hit the door with her fist.

"We might be able to break it," Tristan said. "Jerietlan, there are spells which will enhance a person's strength are there not?"

Jerietlan nodded. "There are, however, they are not ones I normally prepare."

"Let me try," Myrith said.

It took the group a moment to shift around in the confining space so Myrith would have enough room to get a partial run at the door. The door bounced in the doorframe, but didn't open. She continued to push against the door, sweat forming on her face. Laraf stepped next to her and added his weight to hers.

Myrith stepped back. "Let me hit it again," she said.

Laraf moved to the side as Myrith threw herself against the door again. A sharp crack sounded in the room as she stepped back to hit the door again. The door opened and a large, human figure stood there. He reached down and grabbed Laraf in his hand, pulling him out of the room.

Laraf wasn't fighting as the creature took a step back, still holding him. With his free hand the large creature reached for the door. Laraf drove his dagger into the hand holding him and the creature flung him down the narrow hallway.

The door slammed shut as Myrith charged forward again. "We need this door opened, now!" She rubbed her shoulder as she took several steps back.

"What was that thing?" Hendandra asked.

"A golem," Falden said. "They are similar to statues that have been animated by magical means. This one appeared to have been made from flesh." He paused for a moment. "Little rogue are you willing to let me cast a spell of invisibility on you when the others get the door opened?"

Hendandra grinned then nodded. "Yes."

"Laraf?" Kyrianna stepped toward the door as something hit the door from the other side, followed by the ring of metal as something hit the floor.

"Resare's eyes." Laraf's voice was muffled as it came through the door.

There was silence for several seconds followed by a loud clang of metal that seemed distant. Jerietlan muttered something then reached out and touched Kyrianna on the shoulder. She turned to stare at the cleric. "What did you just do?"

He ignored her as he reached out and touched Myrith's shoulder.

"The Battle Maiden gave me the spell Lord Duvall spoke of. Perhaps together, the two of you can get the door open."

The door opened as Myrith and Kyrianna stepped back to hit it together. Myrith drew her sword and moved to stand in front of the golem.

"The would-be knight of Mykaylene with the interesting sword," a voice said as the golem tried to grab Myrith.

"Mikyl has been watching us," Tristan said.

Kyrianna drew her swords and stepped up next to Myrith as she heard Falden chanting behind them. He had asked the rogue about casting an invisibility spell and she didn't want the creature to see Hendandra vanishing. "Myrith, leave some room to the side and between you and the door," she whispered when she heard the chanting stop.

Myrith didn't reply as she shifted her position, her sword held in a defensive posture as she continued to watch the golem.

The golem took a half step back and brought his club down striking at the floor between his feet. Kyrianna darted forward, her blades flashing as she slashed at the creature's arms and moved behind it. Her eyes studied the floor where the club had struck; there was no blood or other signs Hendandra had been hit by the huge weapon.

From her spot she saw Myrith step forward as the golem again raised his club. Kyrianna swung her long sword catching the back of the creature's leg and cutting deeply as it took a step toward Myrith. There was no impairment of its movements or blood from the wound.

"That sword has to go," a voice said as the golem brought his club down. Even with from behind the golem, Kyrianna could see it was targeting the sword and not Myrith. There was a loud snap followed by the sound of metal shards hitting the stone floor as the golem's club shattered the weapon.

Myrith stepped back as several bolts of arcane energy struck the golem in the chest. She touched the sword-shaped pin on her surcoat then raised the bastard sword that appeared in her hands as she again stepped forward.

The golem howled and turned around as Hendandra appeared behind it, her rapier buried in the lower part of its back. Kyrianna brought her swords up to intercept the huge club but found herself being swept to the side by one of the golem's hands.

There was a scream as the club hit Hendandra and she was crushed under it. A dagger flashed through the air to strike the golem in the eye. Kyrianna slowly turned her head to follow the dagger's path back to see Laraf standing there gesturing to the golem.

"By the Lady," Kyrianna muttered as she forced herself back to her feet.

The golem moved toward Laraf, the dagger still lodged in its eye. Kyrianna saw no other weapons in Laraf's hands as he stood his ground and waited. She waited as Myrith and Tristan both charged down the hallway. As they attempted to engage the golem from the rear, she tried to get around it to join Laraf. The golem turned around as Myrith's sword slashed deeply across its back. Kyrianna was hit in the shoulder by the creature's club and dropped to the floor, her long sword useless in her limp hand.

Kyrianna slid her short sword to Laraf, who grabbed it then danced away from the creature. Kyrianna placed her left hand over her right shoulder and whispered a prayer to Frayrith as a slight green glow flowed from her hand and down into the shattered bone.

Above her several streaks of arcane energy caught her attention and she glanced up to see the bolts strike the golem, leaving black holes in its chest as they passed through the flesh.

Tristan and Myrith were still dodging the creature's club, but it was definitely slowing in its attacks against the pair. Laraf moved in behind the golem and used Kyrianna's sword to cut a deep gash across the back of the creature's knee. As the golem shifted its weight, the leg buckled and the golem crashed to the floor. Dust and bits of stone fell from the walls as the hallway shook from the golem's fall. Myrith's sword flashed several times as she removed the golem's head from its body and it finally lay still.

"Kyrianna!" Tristan sheathed his sword and dropped to the floor next to her.

"I'm fine," she said waving off the vial of healing potion he held out. "What about Hendandra?" She leaned her back against the wall as she stood up.

"I'm okay." Hendandra was being supported by Jerietlan as they joined the rest of the group. "Thanks for trying," she said.

"We need to take a break and find a way to restore Nirev," Myrith said. The dwarf was still frozen as Falden guided the floating body out of the tiny room they had been trapped in and down the hallway.

"If we rest here he should be back to normal within a few hours," Jerietlan said. "The claws of the ghast cause a temporary paralysis usually lasting a few minutes to a few hours."

"Do we dare risk the time though," Tristan said. "Mikyl is obviously watching us now. He had the golem target your sword, probably because of its effectiveness against undead creatures. Do we give him extra time to prepare for us?"

"I don't think we have a choice," Myrith said. "Nirev is still paralyzed, Hendandra was seriously hurt by the golem and Kyrianna and Laraf were also hurt. We need to take a break." She stepped past the dead golem and studied the larger room. "Only one way out of this room other than this route and the previous hallway has been buried." She stepped into the room and out of sight of the others for a few seconds before returning. "There are several pits in the room, with gates over them, but there does not appear to be anything in them…"

"Not anymore," Laraf interrupted.

"Or any way into or out of the pits except through the top," Myrith said. "Tristan, you, Jerietlan and I can stand the watch while the others rest. Falden can you cast a warning spell of some kind over the other door, so we will know if something starts to come through it?"

"Of course." The mage started to move into the other room then paused and turned back. "I suggest you recover the pieces of your sword. There are magics that may allow it to be restored when we are out of this cursed place."

"What did you find?" Hendandra asked as Laraf removed several items from the body of the golem.

"I suspect his armor is magical in nature as it shrunk to a size to fit me when I removed it. And he was wearing these." He held up a pair of gloves.

Falden muttered several words then nodded. "Yes, the armor is magical as are the gloves and the club." He paused then muttered several more phrases as he studied each of the items. "The armor has magic woven into it that grants increased protection to the wearer, the club is slightly stronger than similar weapons of that type and the gloves grant increased dexterity to their wearer."

"Nirev will probably be interested in the club, if only because he doesn't have one," Kyrianna said. "And, I doubt any of us want it. I do not need to replace my armor, so have no interest in the armor. However, I would be interested in the gloves, as they will aid in my use of the bow."

"You lost your bow, so those gloves will be of little use to you while we are here," Hendandra said. "On the other hand, they will also aid in my ability to open locks and disable traps."

"As they would mine," Laraf said.

"Odds are we will be going our separate ways when this is over," Myrith said as she picked up the gloves. "I believe the gloves would be better off on the hands of Hendandra or Laraf. As Laraf is getting the armor, I believe they should go to Hendandra, but she already has the gloves we found earlier." She looked down at the smaller woman. "Are you willing to trade?"

"I found those other gloves, why should I give them up?"

"And Laraf found these," Tristan said. "Perhaps the two of you can just draw lots for them. If you do that, then Kyrianna should also participate."

"Fine," Hendandra drew three dice from her pack. "High roll gets the gloves." She handed the dice to Tristan. "Let them pick their dice first so no one can think I rigged the roll."

"I doubt any of us would think that," Kyrianna said as she took one of the dice then dropped it on the floor. "A three. Oh well, better luck next time."

Laraf smiled as his die came up with a five. "You have only one number that can beat me, care to concede?"

Hendandra ignored the remark as she dropped her die. It came to rest with two pips showing on it. "You win," she said.

Laraf nodded then glanced at the armor and back at Hendandra. "Your armor is still deteriorating. You take this, mine can be repaired, yours cannot."

"Good." Myrith handed the gloves to Laraf. "You three get some rest. Falden, if you'll take care of the door please."

Falden raised his hands and spoke quietly for several seconds. A faint glow covered the door then faded. "You'll have warning if something tries to come through," he said.

"All of you get some rest," Myrith said as she readied her sword and moved to stand in the center of the room.

Chapter Forty-Five

Kyrianna held her dagger in her hands and stared at the unicorn inlaid in the hilt. Her gaze went to the unicorn mark on her wrist and she frowned—they were different. The one on the dagger had a small green star positioned so it seemed to balance on the horn, while the one on her wrist was only the unicorn. She found herself staring at the green star for several minutes. "The green star is Frayrith's symbol; not the unicorn," she said.

"What?" Myrith looked at her.

Kyrianna jerked her head up. "I always thought the unicorn was Frayrith's symbol, as it is used by those who follow her. The unicorn is her sacred animal and is often seen as her avatar." She pulled the green star pendant out of her pack and laid it on the dagger—the two stars matched.

"You told me the unicorn is often used as a symbol by elves when I mentioned the Overlord uses one."

"What else comprises this Overlord's symbol?"

Myrith glanced around at the others then knelt down in front of Kyrianna, her voice pitched low as she spoke. "His symbol is a rearing unicorn; one that is gray in coat with a bloodstained horn. Above the horn, almost as if it is balanced on it, is a multi-colored oval."

"Like the star is shown here?" Kyrianna handed Myrith her dagger.

"Yes, but the unicorn is different in coloring."

"Myrith, the symbol you are describing includes Thynitic's symbol." She pulled the rest of the chains out of her pack and held up the one with Thynitic's symbol on it.

Myrith grabbed the pendant and stuffed it back into Kyrianna's pack. "Leave that thing alone. If I see you handling it again, I will destroy it. The only reason I didn't say anything about you taking it was that you took all of the symbols and they apparently belong to deities from your land. However, you have been affected several times by this symbol and I will not risk it controlling you."

"I'm just trying to understand what is going on. None of this makes any sense to me." She put the rest of the symbols back in her pack. "Myrith, I thought Frayrith was marking me with her symbol when her avatar gave me this." She held out her wrist. "Now, I don't know what to think. The mark that identifies this as hers is on the dagger, also made by her avatar, but not on my wrist."

"Perhaps she was not binding you to her alone, but to all the elven gods of your land," Myrith said.

"Then she was binding me to Thynitic also." Kyrianna looked back down at the mark on her wrist. "No, I don't accept that. I can't accept that."

"When you get home, you will need to have a long talk with someone properly trained in the theologies of your gods. I never received even the basic indoctrination in either Geladas or Mykaylene's teachings. I'm not the person to guide you here."

Kyrianna nodded.

"Besides, you just said that most accept the unicorn as the symbol of Frayrith. That mark is for others to see; perhaps she didn't want to confuse them by using a symbol no longer properly recognized."

"I need time to meditate and ask Frayrith these questions," Kyrianna said. "However, that will have to wait until we are done here." She sheathed her dagger. "I'm ready whenever the others are."

"Nirev was ready as soon as the paralysis wore off; however, Hendandra and Laraf are still sleeping. I don't think he wanted to admit how badly he was actually hurt by the golem. I'm going to give them a little more time before waking them." Myrith placed a hand on Kyrianna's shoulder. "Have Jerietlan look at that shoulder again. I want everyone ready for whatever happens next."

"I will." Kyrianna watched as Myrith stood and moved around the room to check on the others. She was worried about facing Mikyl and about them. Kyrianna looked around the room, she wasn't sure they were ready to face Mikyl either. She had had little exposure to actual magic growing up in a place that feared and hated the arcane. There were even some that refused to have any contact with clerics and the divine magics they had access to. Still, even without the exposure to magic, she knew what it was and what a lich was. An undead creature made that way through the use of magic; one that had willingly given itself to that state in order to gain greater power as well as prevent its final death. Many clerics taught arcane magic was a perversion of the power of the gods and this was seen as the greatest corruption of that power there was.

If Mikyl was a lich, as the pirate had said, he was a powerful mage and his power had likely grown over the years. They knew he was watching them now, at least enough to have taken note of Myrith's sword—what else did he know about their group?

She took a deep breath. There was too much going on here and there didn't appear to be any answers coming to the questions she had. Why Mikyl would have turned to a foreign goddess for power didn't make any sense as there had to be deities of this world who would have been willing to see a family devoted to Mykaylene destroyed. Then there was her vision and warning from Dwycia telling her She was coming. Who? Did the goddess mean Thynitic? And, if so, why? None of it was making any sense and it was scaring her. She had no doubt Thynitic had opened the portal that brought her from Rhysia to the place she had met Myrith and the others. She suspected the Lady of Chaos had even had a hand in bringing her and Myrith here. Again, why?

"Hey, Rangerette," Myrith's voice interrupted her thoughts. "You ready?"

Kyrianna only nodded as she stood and readied her swords. Jerietlan came over and placed a hand on her shoulder. Warmth flowed into her shoulder. "My thanks," she said.

She waited until the others had reached the door before moving herself. "Chaos," she whispered. "No wonder none of this makes any sense as it seems everything is surrounded by or has been touched by chaos."

Kyrianna smiled as she joined the others. The Lady of Chaos couldn't deny her own nature, so even if she had something planned for her and Myrith, chaos would interfere. As long as they didn't give in to the chaos themselves they could thwart those plans.

The corridor from the room was long and had several turns as the group moved cautiously through it. "Myrith," Kyrianna called after several hours of walking. "There is no way all of the places we have been in this sub-basement are in the same area as the house. We have been walking for what seems like miles."

The paladin stared at her for several seconds. "Just where are we then?"

"If I haven't gotten too confused with all these turns, we are past the sea cliff. However, we have not descended enough to be under the water." Kyrianna placed a hand on the nearest wall.

"There is no vibration like I would expect if we were near the cliff."

"There are spells that can create a maze in a person's mind so they wander in circles in a small area—forever lost," Falden said. "It would have to be a powerful spell to affect all of us in the same way. I doubt I will be able to dispel it. However, I will try." He raised his arms over his head and began chanting, his voice echoing off the walls of the corridor.

Kyrianna grabbed for the nearest wall as the floor began to shift under her feet. The rest of the group had vanished and she found herself surrounded by hedges. She looked down to see her dagger in her hand as she followed the only open path. Through the twists and turns of the maze, she continued—a prisoner in her own body. As she stepped into the open area at the center of the maze, she fought with herself to take a step back. She succeeded only in stopping. She was frozen in place staring at a girl of no more than eight years. "Melissa," she whispered. The great mastiff with the girl growled, but also seemed frozen as it watched her.

She found herself moving toward Melissa. The girl pressed back against the hedges, her eyes wide, and her cheeks glistening. Kyrianna tried to throw the dagger to the ground, but instead raised it up, level with the girl's chest.

"Chaos take it!" Kyrianna screamed the curse as she grabbed the hand holding the dagger with her other hand. "No!" The blade plunged into Melissa's chest.

"There will be order in the chaos!" Myrith's voice called as the hedges vanished to be replaced by the walls of the corridor.

Kyrianna dropped her dagger and fell to the floor. "By the Lady," she whispered. She drew several ragged breaths before she looked up to see the others standing around her. The only one who didn't look confused was Myrith, who was holding the hilt of her broken sword in her hand. Behind her, Kyrianna saw the ghostly figure of a horse shimmer then fade from sight.

"Who was it?" Tristan asked offering Kyrianna a hand.

"Melissa," she said. "Did everyone?" She looked around at the group.

"Nyssa," Tristan said.

"Lady Terissian," Falden said.

"Lord Terissian," Laraf said.

"Larissa," Hendandra said.

"Vantalle," Jerietlan said.

"Wilhelm Terissian," Nirev said.

"Rhinehart," Myrith said putting the hilt back into the bag holding the other pieces of the shattered blade.

"How did you break through the chaos?" Kyrianna asked.

"I was able to stop myself from attacking Rhinehart, then something told me to draw the blade and hold it up while calling for order in the chaos," Myrith said. "I didn't recognize the voice, it was masculine, but it didn't appear to be Rhinehart and it wasn't Geladas."

"Perhaps it was some magic in the blade itself that allowed it to challenge what was happening," Hendandra said. "Remember the runes that were inscribed in the room where we found the sword. Protection from chaos and other similar magics."

"Ravlian said there appeared to be other magics about the sword, quiet at the time; not truly discernible, but there nonetheless," Falden said. "Perhaps it was one of those magics which helped you banish the chaos."

"Perhaps." Myrith frowned as she put the bag back into her pack. "It may have assisted in dispelling the magical maze we were trapped in also."

The previously narrow corridor they were in, had opened into a wide hallway with a single door only a few yards from where they stood. Hendandra moved to the front of the group and glanced up at Myrith.

"Let's get this over with," Myrith said as she readied her sword.

"Leikor's cursed luck," Hendandra said as an alarm began ringing in the hallway.

"It doesn't matter," Myrith said moving to stand in front of the door. "He already knew we were coming." She touched the door with the tip of her sword and it swung open, away from her as the others came up behind her.

"Welcome and my thanks for bringing my nephew with you," a voice said as darkness surrounded the group.

"You will not have him, foul creature of magic and chaos," Kyrianna called.

"How interesting. It would seem you have a champion. But, for how long?"

Kyrianna slid her feet forward, keeping her blades low as even her elven senses couldn't penetrate the darkness surrounding them. Something whirled past her head and she ducked as she heard the sound of glass breaking on the floor behind her.

"Hold your breath," Falden yelled between coughs as a noxious smell filled the area. The odors of death, decay and sickness assailed her nose as Kyrianna tried to reach the place she thought the door to be.

"Be wary," Laraf yelled from somewhere in the room in front of her. "There's a wide trench across the room. The darkness extends to its edge."

"Where's Tristan?" Myrith whispered next to her ear. "Someone has to stay close to him."

"I'll find him," Kyrianna said. In the magical darkness she couldn't see Myrith, but she felt the woman place a hand on her shoulder and squeeze lightly then move past her. She paused for a moment listening to the various coughs around her. The noxious odor had dissipated quickly, but several of the others were still affected. She moved slowly to the nearest one, counting her steps. Laraf was apparently already in the room and she suspected Myrith was as well; that left Hendandra, Nirev, Falden, Jerietlan and Tristan unaccounted for. She jerked her head up as something buzzed past her and the smell of brimstone and sulfur wafted down over her.

"Chaos," she said. "There's an imp or a demon in the area with us, be cautious."

"We need to be getting to the door," Nirev said from in front of her.

"Nirev face toward me," she said. She held her hand in front of her and tapped the dwarf on the head. "I'm going to step to my right; you take five large steps forward. That should bring you to the door."

"Agreed."

Kyrianna could hear the dwarf counting his steps as he moved past her.

"Nicely done," Nirev called. "Too bad the darkness extends into the room as well."

"Kyri?" Hendandra's voice said next to her.

"Wait there," Kyrianna said. "Nirev, start one of your battle songs, but try to keep it from echoing. Everyone follow Nirev's voice, we need to get back together."

To his credit, Nirev kept his voice pitched low making it easier to follow the sound. Kyrianna concentrated on listening to the footsteps passing her. She recognized Hendandra's light step first as the girl moved past her, then she heard two heavier steps moving together. "Jerietlan, Falden?" she asked.

"Yes," the mage replied.

"Good." She paused as she waited for the last person. There was only silence in the darkness. "Tristan?" she called softly.

There was no answer.

The buzzing of the imp's wings circled over her and Kyrianna froze. Nirev was still singing in his native language, and she was sure she picked up a tone of impatience in his voice. From a short distance in front of her she heard a loud thud, almost like a door slamming shut. She knew that sound, it was the sound of a portal closing. She could no longer hear the imp flying either. "Tristan!"

"Kyri," Hendandra called. "The door is closing."

Kyrianna turned and sprinted toward the dwarf and the others. The darkness lifted as the door closed behind them. The sound of the lock clicking echoed in the large room.

At the far end of the room, standing on a large dais was a man of average height. His brown hair was neatly combed and hung to his shoulders. His robes shimmered as colors shifted in the fabric. In one hand he held a simple oak staff while the other held a ball of flame. The man's face was gaunt and almost skeletal in appearance as were his hands.

"Mikyl Duvall," Kyrianna whispered.

Her eyes darted around the room. Laraf and Myrith were both standing at the edge of the trench Laraf had warned them about. Myrith's hands were up, pressing on something that wasn't visible. The rest of the group was standing together at the door. She grinned as she saw Hendandra step behind Jerietlan and Falden and begin working on the lock. There was still one person missing— Tristan.

"Looks like the champion lost her protectee," Mikyl said. The lich threw the ball of flame into the shadows on Kyrianna's right. The flames landed on the floor and illuminated Tristan where he stood behind a wall of energy. He appeared to be frozen as he stood there with one arm raised as if he was warding off something and his rapier in his other hand.

"He's safe for now," Mikyl said. "The poison the imp injected him with only causes a temporary paralysis. In the meantime, he will get to watch as I destroy each of you." He raised his staff then brought it down hard on the floor. The vibration traveled through the floor shaking it for several seconds.

"Jerietlan, Falden stay here with Hendandra," Kyrianna said as she sprinted toward the trench, Nirev beside her.

"A show of courage from the fools as they charge in." Mikyl raised his staff again and waved his other hand.

As she started to jump over the trench, Kyrianna felt a chill go through her and she stumbled falling to the bottom. For several heartbeats she huddled there on the floor shaking. They couldn't face this powerful of a creature. He was right, they were fools. She had to get away from this place. But, there was no way out. She glanced around and saw Laraf toss a small grappling hook over the edge and start to climb out; she followed him.

Kyrianna found herself huddled on the floor by the door. Something was wrong, she knew she shouldn't be trying to run away, but she had no choice. She looked back to see Nirev and Myrith standing next to Mikyl, their weapons flashing. Falden stood next to her and raised his hands as streaks of arcane energy leapt toward the lich. Mikyl staggered back as the energy struck him and Nirev caught his staff with his hammer, shattering the wood. A multi-colored glow surrounded the dwarf for a moment then faded. Myrith's blade flashed as she brought it down across the lich's chest. The creature's robes opened to reveal the sunken flesh underneath. Myrith brought the blade back up and across Mikyl's neck. The lich stepped back and raised his hands to cast.

Falden released several more bolts of arcane energy striking Mikyl and interrupting his spell casting as both Myrith and Nirev scored hits. Mikyl grabbed a wand from his belt and pointed it at Falden. The mage fell to the floor as a bolt of lightning hit him in the chest.

Jerietlan knelt down next to Falden, his hands starting to glow as he placed them on the mage's chest. "He'll be fine," he said.

Kyrianna took a deep breath; the crippling fear was fading as she stood up. "Hendandra?"

"That damned lich must have put a magical lock on the door."

"Keep trying." Kyrianna moved to where Tristan was still trapped behind the energy field.

"Kyri! Behind you!" Tristan yelled as he raised his sword.

Kyrianna spun around, her swords raised as the imp dove at her. The creature vanished before she could hit it. "Chaos take it!" She turned back to face Tristan. "Your sword belonged to one who served a deity of order. This barrier is chaos created; perhaps your sword can destroy it just as Myrith's was able to dispel the chaos of the maze."

Tristan nodded then raised the sword and placed the tip against the barrier. The energy sparked into a kaleidoscope of colors then vanished. "How did you know?" He looked at Kyrianna.

"I didn't," she said with a grin.

"Kyri! Something big is coming down the hall," Hendandra said.

"Get away from the door," a deep voice said as something hit the door from outside the room.

"Move!" Kyrianna grabbed Falden and pulled the still unconscious mage from in front of the door. "Myrith and the others?" Kyrianna turned to see the lich fall as Myrith's sword pierced its chest. The knight raised her sword again and severed the creature's head from its body before she joined Nirev at the trench.

"Ah, this should make it easier to get across," Nirev said pulling on a lever in the ground. A narrow bridge extended across the trench and the two of them hurried across.

"Wait," Jerietlan called. "A lich is not destroyed unless you find and destroy the talisman that holds the essence of its soul. This evil will only return if we don't find that."

Myrith paused and started to turn around. The door shattered as it was hit again and Boris charged into the room. Kyrianna reached for her swords as she stared at the large man. He was now covered in fur, his fingers had developed long claws and his face looked like a cross between a human and a wolf. "A werewolf! He's a werewolf!"

"Get out, I can't control it anymore," Boris said looking down at her. He charged at the pillar in the center of the room, hitting the stone with his full weight and causing cracks to appear and spread over its surface.

Kyrianna raised her swords and took several steps toward Boris as the others headed for the door.

"Kyri! Rangerette!" Myrith yelled as the ceiling began collapsing around them. "Let it go."

"No! That thing is a werewolf. An abomination of nature."

She dodged the falling debris as she moved closer to Boris.

"Mykaylene give me strength." Myrith grabbed Kyrianna and pulled her toward the door.

Kyrianna tried to free herself from Myrith's grasp, but the older woman only wrapped her arms around her and continued to drag her out of the room. She relaxed as the ceiling collapsed and she lost sight of the werewolf.

"Jerietlan, you said something about that thing coming back," Myrith said as they started back down the hallway.

The cleric paused and nodded. "Part of the rituals that transform a person into a lich also allows them to contain a portion of their soul in a separate container. Until that is destroyed and that portion of their soul released, they can never truly be killed."

"No!" Kyrianna said looking at Jerietlan. "Mikyl may come back after…." She stopped and took a deep breath. "If we didn't destroy it then have we succeeded?"

"I don't know," Jerietlan said. "Perhaps we will learn the answer to that when we get out of this part of the house."

Kyrianna refused to meet Myrith's or Tristan's gaze as the group made its way out of the sub-basement and back to the main level of the house.

Chapter Forty-Six

"What?" Kyrianna asked as Myrith stopped suddenly, staring out the glass doors into the garden.

"I believe we have one last appointment to keep," Myrith said as she opened the glass doors. "One that may answer your question about whether we succeeded or not."

In the garden stood a group of spirits. The statue of Mykaylene had a golden aura around it as she looked down on those before her.

"Well it looks like you survived after all," a booming voice said as Ferdinand stepped into the garden from behind the group. "Knight of Mykaylene, if you will give me the remains of your sword, I will repair it for you. The magics it held will remain intact."

Myrith handed Ferdinand the bag containing the shards of the sword Hendandra had given her. He emptied the pieces onto the ground then swung his hammer into the pile several times. Sparks erupted from the pile of metal. When Ferdinand stopped, the sword lay on the ground—whole.

"You have an interesting weapon there," Ferdinand said handing the sword to Myrith. "Treat it with respect; it has been touched by a great power. But, be warned, that power may one day want to reclaim the weapon." He turned and looked down at the dwarf.

"I believe this hammer was meant for you." He held a large war hammer with the symbol of Mulog etched on it. "Let me see your axe. You will be pleased with the results."

Nirev handed him the axe and stepped back as Ferdinand placed it and the hammer on the floor then raised his own hammer. When he was done all that was left was a single maul.

Ferdinand handed the weapon to Nirev. "May you cleave through your enemies with ease." He looked at the rest of the group. "I have nothing for the rest of you at this time," he said then vanished.

"You have removed the curse that was on this place, now the spirits of those trapped here can finally find peace," a female voice said. "Your service has been noted."

Kyrianna smiled as both Myrith and Tristan knelt before the statue of Mykaylene. Perhaps the nobleman had found his faith after all.

"Myrith you have proven true in your faith and your resolve," the voice continued. "I now charge you with learning about my church and the things I require of those who serve me." The voice paused. "Tristan Duvall, I understand your confusion. All I can offer you is the knowledge that even deities are bound by our natures and laws we must follow. There are times when we can do nothing more than watch and weep."

Kyrianna felt a tingle in both her wrists as Mykaylene finished speaking and she again wondered if there was some sort of warning being given to her as well.

"Both of you rise, there are those here who wish to thank you and your companions for your deeds these past days," Mykaylene said. The aura around the statue seemed to fade slightly, but the presence of the goddess could still be felt.

From out of the group of spirits a man dressed in full plate mail stepped leading the ghostly horse, Riker, whom they had first met in the stables. Riker now wore all of his tack and stood before them his head raised proudly. "Myrith, Knight of Mykaylene, you have proven to me that you have the heart and soul of a true warrior and as every warrior needs a faithful mount, I present to you Riker. May he serve you for as long as you serve the Battle Maiden." He handed the reins to Myrith and stepped back with the other spirits.

Myrith bowed her head as she accepted the reins.

"Riker can only appear on the material plane for a short time each day," Mykaylene's voice said. "Only call him when you have need."

"My thanks to both Rhinehart and you My Lady for the trust you have placed in my hands."

The next to step forward was the Lady Terissian. "You returned my son's fiancé to him and him to us. My thanks," she said as she handed Falden a set of bracers. "Most armor interferes with a mage's ability to cast their spells. These will not and they have been spelled to provide you with the same protection chain mail would offer. Use this gift to protect yourself and those you travel with." She stepped back.

"You showed trust, honor and bravery when you were willing to stand with Tristan as hostage against your friends finding Wilhelm. You were also prepared to defend Tristan in the event something went wrong. Unusual traits for one in your line of work most would say. However, your motives were known to us even then. I offer you this ring; its magics will help to shield your thoughts and motives from those who would try to pry into them." Lord Terissian handed Laraf a plain gray ring then stepped back.

Laraf placed the ring on his left hand and nodded his thanks.

From the group of spirits, Melissa Duvall stepped forward, tears falling from her eyes as she looked up at Kyrianna. She smiled as she knelt down in front of the child. "I can sense your loneliness. You have friends whom you trust, but even with them you feel alone. Don't pull away from them, you are not yet trapped as I was, you will need them," she whispered. As she spoke her tears fell on the short sword in Kyrianna's hand and the blade shimmered for a moment then also began weeping.

Melissa took a couple of steps back as the spirit of her great mastiff appeared beside her. "Thank you for rescuing me," she said.

"I'm glad I was able to assist you and the others," Kyrianna said standing and bowing to the girl.

Melissa smiled then faded from sight.

The next spirit to step forward was Larissa. The elder Duvall daughter approached Hendandra and leaned forward to give her a light kiss on the cheek. "May your words be more persuasive and your charm more alluring to those around you," she said before stepping back into the group.

Nyssa approached Tristan and gathered him into a hug as she spoke. "You will sit on the council of Raspa as the head of House Duvall," she said. "May your words and diplomacy always speak and act in the best interests of this House, Raspa and her citizens."

Tristan bowed his head. "May I always prove worthy of the trust you have placed in me," he said.

Wilhelm Terissian looked down at Nirev and grinned as he touched the dwarf's arm. "You serve the Lord of Storms as well as the knight of Mykaylene. Chaos and Order joined together. May your weapons always strike true against your enemies," he said before stepping back.

Vantalle approached Jerietlan and bowed his head respectfully. "You only recently passed from a novice to a priest, yet you have guided those in this group with wisdom and compassion. May you always do so." He held up his holy symbol and touched Jerietlan on the forehead.

Rhinehart stepped forward again and faced Tristan. "You have proven yourself a worthy heir and I am proud to see you carrying my sword," he said.

Before Tristan could say anything, the spirits of the Duvalls, Terissians and their servants all faded from the garden.

As the group entered the great hall from the garden, Tristan paused. "I believe there were some items here, a few of you were interested in," he said. "Hendandra, you may have the violin, Kyrianna the silver sword, Nirev and Myrith the armor if you desire."

"I have the armor we found with your grandfather, it is more than sufficient for my needs," Myrith said.

"I accept your offer," Kyrianna said as she lifted the sword from the wall. "And I believe Hendandra does also." She jerked her head over to where the girl was carefully casing the violin and placing it into her pack.

"I thank you also," Nirev said as he removed the sentryl armor from the stand.

"My thanks to all of you for your assistance in freeing this place from the evil that was growing here," Tristan said softly as he bowed to the group. "We will need to return to town so I can pay you what was promised as well as to clear up the matter involving Myrith."

"There is one other thing I need to do before we leave," Kyrianna said moving to the door under the stairs.

"Rangerette?" Myrith stepped between her and the door.

"I need to face this," her voice was only a whisper. "And I need to do it alone."

"You have ten minutes, after that Tristan and I will come down and get you."

"No one else," Kyrianna said.

"Agreed."

Kyrianna stared at the door for a moment then reached past Myrith, opened it and descended into the basement. The stairs were still slippery where the goblins had greased them, but this time she managed to keep her feet under her as she walked down the stairs.

She reached the door to the shrine and felt her chest tighten as she stared at the damage done to the room. Myrith had left very little of the altar untouched, and the tapestry had been ripped from the wall and lay in pieces on the rubble. Kyrianna took another breath and stepped into the small room.

"You do not have any claim on me," she said as she walked up to what was left of the altar. She reached into her pack and removed the pendant with the chaos portal. She held it in front of her watching it for several seconds then dropped it on top of the rubble. "I reject you and what you represent." She turned and left the shrine.

Kyrianna smiled as she thought about returning home; away from the chaos that had followed her. She knew if she could find a way to go back, she would probably be able to even return to Nydith. She had received Frayrith's Blessing and that had to count for something. Only now, she wasn't sure she wanted to return home. She remembered Tristan's whispered words in the cemetery. Perhaps there was a reason to stay here. Either way the choice would be hers and she would have time to decide and not rush blindly into something because someone was pushing her in one direction or the other; and that was what was important.

Her thoughts stayed on Tristan for a moment. Tristan, yes, there was a reason for staying here, but she knew she should also go home and see her family at least once before making that decision. She needed to apologize and make amends with her father. Even if she couldn't or choose not to remain, she was still a part of them and they a part of her. A part that needed healing; a part she had the power to heal and would.